"Brilliant!" —*Kirkus Reviews*

CHILDREN OF THE WICKED

They were supposed to be a gift to humanity—shape-shifting beings who would save mankind from its own worst elements and leave behind a virtual paradise.

CHILDREN OF THE DAMNED

But they developed unplanned intelligence and a mission of their own—to conquer the world for themselves. And when the very man who had created them was powerless to destroy them, the bloodshed wrought under the guise of salvation threatened to exterminate the human race.

CHILDREN OF THE END
Mark A. Clements

Nominated for the Horror Writers of America's Bram Stoker Award

CHILDREN OF THE END

MARK A. CLEMENTS

LEISURE BOOKS NEW YORK CITY

A LEISURE BOOK®

April 1994

Published by special arrangement with Donald I. Fine, Inc.

Dorchester Publishing Co., Inc.
276 Fifth Avenue
New York, NY 10001

For further information, contact: Donald I. Fine, Inc., 19 West 21st Street, New York, NY 10010

The name "Leisure Books" and the stylized "L" with design are trademarks of Dorchester Publishing Co., Inc.

Printed in the United States of America.

To John and Eileen Clements.
If only all parents were like you.

CHILDREN OF THE END

PROLOGUE

Once upon a time there was no snake,
  no scorpion.
There was no hyena, no lion,
There was no wild dog, no wolf.
There was no fear, no terror.
Man had no rival . . .

> —ENMERKAR AND THE
> LORD OF ARATA

ARCADIO KNEW HE WAS IN TROUBLE the moment he opened his eyes. The last thing he remembered, he had been following the trail down which the Blond Man had always taken the women. Dense chaparral pressing close in the starlight . . . Now he was sprawled on his back in a small, bare room. His head throbbed. Moving only his eyes, he looked around. Overhead was a concrete ceiling studded with lights behind heavy metal grilles. On each side was a concrete-block wall. No windows—instead, in the center of each wall was a cluster of four blank television screens. The only sound was a gentle hiss of air.

Arcadio turned his head stiffly. The floor was also concrete, a smooth expanse dipping slightly toward a rank-smelling hole in one corner. Across the room was a closed door. Arcadio stared at it. There was no knob, no handle, not even a keyhole.

This was a cell.

As he tried to sit up, his reflection slid across the lenses of the TV screens, sixteen captured Arcadios, and he thought of the multiple eyes of a tarantula locked on its prey. Braced on one hand, he touched his

1

head. Winced. Above his left ear was a bump as large and soft as a rotten egg.

He tried to think back. The trail. In the darkness it had seemed to lead toward nothing but ridge after ridge of bush-tangled rock. But he had known there was *something* back there; why else would the Blond Man have always escorted the women in that direction? So Arcadio had kept going, marching deeper and deeper into the hills. Gradually he began to get worried. Was he lost? There was *nothing*—

Then there was something. A brilliant flash, spiraling into blackness. The Blond Man . . .

Moving very slowly, Arcadio sat all the way up. The headache was marginally better. He patted his clothes. His shoulder holster was still there under his jacket, but the *pistola* was gone. So was the knife he kept in his boot.

On the TV screens, his reflections tried to stand. Failed.

Suddenly he noticed something: the walls were covered with scratches, hundreds of them, especially around the television screens and the door. Parallel stripes that looked as if they had been made by fingernails. Fingernails digging desperately at the solid concrete . . .

Suddenly Mama's voice arose in his head: *Greed will be the end of you, Arcadio*. He remembered when she had said that: He was thirteen, and she had discovered the wallet he had lifted from some *gringo* tourist on Ave. Revolución in downtown Tijuana. He had taken a long look around the family's one-room shack with its dirt floor and walls of scrap wood and corrugated steel, and said firmly, "No, Mama. *This* will kill me."

Now, two decades later, he owned two homes, each of which could contain a dozen of those Tijuana hovels. One he had bought especially for his mother and three unmarried sisters; it was on the beach in Rosarito. The other stood on the American side of the river among the glittering lights that had haunted his youthful dreams. Had Mama questioned where all her son's wealth had come from? Only this: "Arcadio, you aren't involved with drugs, are you?"

"No, Mama," he had replied.

And it was true. His merchandise was hope. For almost twenty years, Arcadio Sarabia Hernandez had been *Coyote Rey*—King Coyote—the man responsible for the transport of thousands of human beings from Mexico into the United States.

Twenty years ago he had been a simple *coyote*, or guide, leading groups of *pollos*, "chickens," through the canyons between the Tijuana River and the American border communities. It had been treacherous, dangerous work. The canyons were a half-mile strip of lawless wasteland where *banditos* from the Mexican side of the border preyed on the *pollos*, stealing their scant possessions, raping the women, often killing on a whim. After three assaults by such bandits, Arcadio had organized a gang of his own, tough armed men happy to run interference for his people—for a price, of course. This worked so well he began to arrange protection for other *coyotes*, and before long he was able to retire from field work entirely.

Now he controlled half the flow of aliens across the border. Noble work, he considered it. These were hard-working people looking for a better life, that was all, and a trip north under the guidance of *Coyote Rey* benefitted everyone except the bandits and, of course, the American Immigration and Naturalization Service. It especially benefitted *Coyote Rey*, but that was as it should be. He was, after all, an entrepreneur.

Then came the *real* benefit.

The Blond Man had first appeared almost ten years ago, standing at the front door of Arcadio's San Diego house. "Mr. Sarabia," he had said, "I would like to use your services."

Arcadio had been shaken. The American house was not in his real name. "*Perdón?*" he said, using the Spanish pronunciation.

The Blond Man smiled. "I know who you are. I know what you do. And I want you to perform a service for me."

Arcadio took a closer look. The man appeared to be about twenty-five years old, lean and relaxed. He had long flaxen hair like one of the local surfer-boys, wore no uniform or insignia, showed no identification. Not *La Migra*, then. Not a new Border Patrol agent, either; Arcadio's sources would have warned him.

Then he noticed the Blond Man's eyes: dark blue and unwavering, like pools of indigo ink. He felt a sudden chill. Besides *La Migra* and the Border Patrol, there were certain other people who wanted him out of business: Free-lance *coyotes*. Bandits. Jealous competitors in Tijuana. Behind the door, his left hand reached for the baseball bat he kept there. He might be a cultured man now, patron of the arts and supporter of community services on both sides of the border, but he had never forgotten the old days. "Sorry," he said again, affecting a thick accent. "Don' speak English."

The stranger raised his hand. Arcadio looked at it, and his throat seized hard. The man's palm had somehow grown a pistol. Arcadio released the bat.

"May I come in?" the Blond Man asked. "Thank you."

After that, everything had gone fine. It really *was* a business transaction. The Blond Man merely wanted Arcadio to furnish him with an ongoing supply of illegal Mexican immigrants. Women only. And not old ladies or children but strong, healthy young ladies sound of body, free of disease, and—the Blond Man was very specific about this—not sought by the police of either country. Arcadio had no problem with any of that but, pistol or no, he felt bound to make one stipulation clear: "These women are not to be used for prostitution. I will not be a pimp."

The Blond Man, gun now resting in his lap, smiled slightly. "Don't worry. We just need them for . . . demanding domestic work."

So Arcadio had concluded the deal. His responsibilities were simple: select appropriate women, arrange their transfer into the U.S., then deliver them to a specific spot at a specific time. Deliver them personally, and without escort. If Arcadio did exactly as he was told and never discussed his activities with anyone—ever—he stood to make a great deal of money. Did he understand?

At this point the Blond Man had bent forward and slipped the pistol into a holster fitted to the small of his back. Arcadio, remembering the magical way the gun had appeared in the first place, understood quite clearly.

The system had fallen into place. Over the past decade, the Blond Man had come to Arcadio's door every three months or so, requesting a half-dozen women each time. He always paid on the spot, in American dollars. Two days later, late at night, Arcadio would deliver the *pollos* to a location in the remote hills between San Diego and the Laguna Mountains. This was a wild land of steep ridges encrusted with manzanita bushes and great boulders that thrust up like the skulls of giants.

Parking the van on a crude fire road, Arcadio would lead the women along a narrow path through the chaparral, with the maple-syrupy scent of manzanita heavy in the air and nothing visible anywhere but the stars and a few feet of trail. He had been instructed to never carry a light of any kind. No one made any noise; the women understood how this worked.

After an interval, but never in exactly the same place, the Blond Man would suddenly appear. Arcadio always jumped. In the starlight, the Blond Man didn't seem to age. Always the same blond hair, always the same smile, his teeth even brighter than his hair as he smiled and waited for Arcadio to hand the women over. Then he would just stand silently with the *pollos* until Arcadio was gone.

Ten years of this.

It had always been Arcadio's policy not to concern himself with what happened to the *pollos* he helped across the border. Of course, he knew that most of them returned over and over again like the tide to trace the weary circuit between deportation and reentry to the promised land. But eventually he heard that the families of several of the Blond Man's women had been searching desperately along the border for their loved ones. After a little discreet checking, Arcadio came to realize that not one of the Blond Man's *pollos* had ever returned from her "unusually demanding domestic work." Not one in ten years.

Arcadio had given it a lot of thought. It was none of his business, really . . . and yet . . . in a week or two the Blond Man would be approaching him for more women. Perhaps it would be wise if Arcadio already knew, at that time, where the *pollos* would end up. For their own good, of course. Oh, *possibly* he would also discover something he could use to improve his economic leverage with the Blond Man, but only if the women were all right. *Coyote Rey* was in the business of helping people, not taking advantage of them.

He prodded his scalp again, gently. The knot was still the same size, but the throbbing had eased considerably. It occurred to him that the Blond Man had known exactly how hard to hit him, to knock him out without maiming. A chip of ice crystallized in his stomach. How easily he had been caught.

Struggling to his feet, he moved to the door and placed a hand against it. Metal. Thick and unyielding. Like the walls it was heavily scratched, especially where the door and frame fit together. Up close, it was clear that the scratches were much too deep—gouges, really—to have been made by fingernails. A knife? Whatever the tool, it still hadn't created a gap around the door. The fit was too tight, almost seamless, like that of the entrance to a vault.

Or a tomb.

He loosened his collar, swallowed. The air suddenly tasted awfully flat, like it came out of a barrel. Or was getting . . . *old*.

A tomb.

He whirled, panic flooding in on him, then realized he could still hear the gentle rush of air. He relaxed slightly. There were two vents, each about eight inches square, set into the ceiling.

For the first time, he noticed the small video camera mounted on a swivel high in one corner. It was pointing straight at him. He stared at it for a moment, then turned away with an ostentatious twitch of his shoulders.

Once, during his career as a *coyote*, he had shot and killed a border bandit. He hadn't enjoyed it, but he hadn't had nightmares about it afterward, either. It had been *necessary*. The memory did him a service now, filling him with steel. He was *Coyote Rey*—a man capable of anything, certainly of finding a way out of this situation. If anyone was watching via that camera, let them see that Arcadio Sarabia was not afraid.

He turned his attention to the television screens. What was to prevent him from smashing one of them out and pushing through to whatever lay beyond?

He learned as soon as he tried: the screens were protected by slabs of glass or plastic, inches thick. Even these were dimly scratched, as if someone else had also thought of using the TVs as avenues of escape. Cold fear sparked in Arcadio's stomach again. How many other people had been imprisoned in this—

Without warning, the surrounding television screens all came on in a staticky flare of light. Arcadio jumped back into the center of the cell, one hand darting automatically for his nonexistent *pistola*. On each screen appeared an identical scene: a man, not the Blond Man, sitting behind a sleek wooden table. On top of the table was nothing but the man's folded hands and two panels of buttons. Behind him was a huge glowing map of the world, divided into irregular pools of color: green, blue, yellow, orange, red. Mostly red.

The man had pale blue eyes glinting behind rimless glasses, and a high, deeply lined forehead. His hair was a waterfall of graying curls, contrasting strangely with the surgically neat beard that outlined his face. His skin was very pale for Southern California. Arcadio thought he looked like an aging hippie who had lived in a cave since the 1960s.

But he wasn't the Blond Man, and that was what mattered. This could all be a mistake . . .

"My name is Dr. George Irving Pendergast," the aging hippie said. "Welcome to Ginnunga Gap."

Resisting the urge to address the TV screens, Arcadio turned and stared into the lens of the security camera. "Can you hear me?" he demanded.

"Of course, Mr. Sarabia."

Arcadio's heart crashed. The hippie knew his name; this was no mistake. He gathered himself. "Why am I locked in this room?" he demanded.

"You were trespassing on my property, so naturally I assumed you wanted to visit me."

His property? "I was lost," Arcadio said. "Trying to find my way to . . . to my car. And I was *attacked*."

"Attacked? I'd say Mr. Mitford treated you quite gently, under the circumstances."

"Mr. Mitford?"

"The man who's been paying you to deliver subjects to me for the last few years."

Arcadio fought back a shiver of dismay. Now it was final; his imprisonment *was* due to the Blond Man, at least indirectly. Then something else occurred to him: What did this old hippie mean by *subjects*?

Sixteen televised Pendergasts leaned forward. "Tonight is May the first, Mr. Sarabia; you know we wouldn't have been in contact with you for at least another week. So what brings you here?"

Arcadio sensed that the man was genuinely curious, and dug quickly into the soft spot. "I . . . was asked by the family of one of the women to discover what happened to her. That's all."

Thirty-two blue eyes shifted toward something off-screen. "Mr. Sarabia," Pendergast sighed, "I have instruments in that room that can detect changes in your vocal patterns and localized body temperatures— an effective lie detector, under these circumstances. And they tell me you're lying." Suddenly, like a pistol shot: "*Who have you told about us?*"

"No one."

"No one knows you ever brought women here?"

"No. That was the agreement I made with the Bl . . . with *señor* Mitford. And I always keep my agreements."

"The road to Hell is paved with good intentions," Pendergast noted cheerily. "Now, you're saying no one knows you're here?"

Arcadio briefly considered lying about that one, but Pendergast was still staring off-screen. "No."

Pendergast smiled, his face crinkling with good cheer. "That's better.

Honesty is, of course, the best policy. All right, Mr. Sarabia, you may leave."

"What?"

"When the door opens, you'll find your gun and knife in the hallway. They haven't been tampered with in any way. Take them and leave."

Instead of relief, Arcadio felt a chill tracking down his spine. He reminded himself that none of the women he'd brought here had ever been seen again. Not one. What had happened to them? "Where is *señor* Mitford?" he asked, not moving.

"Oh," Pendergast said vaguely, "I'm sure you'll find him around here somewhere." He pushed a button on his desk, and the TV screens began to flash in rapid syncopation. Arcadio tried to follow the racing scenes: narrow hallways, rooms stacked with boxes and cans, views of manzanita bushes and starlit boulders. Suddenly he glimpsed what appeared to be children in white smocks, each standing or sitting in a cell like this one. Children? *Here*? But he saw no *pollos*. And no Blond Man.

Then he caught a flash of a lone adult, also wearing a white smock, just darting through an open doorway. Mitford? Too quick to tell.

The show ended. Sixteen Pendergasts stared at him again. "Well," they said, "maybe Mr. Mitford is busy somewhere after all. But don't worry about it. If you find your way out of this building, you may go home." There was a buzz, a click, and the door to the cell swung open a few inches. Beyond, Arcadio could see his gun and knife lying in a strip of hallway.

But he still didn't move. Sweat crawled down his spine. *If you find your way out of this building, you may go home*. That wasn't exactly the same thing as *Please follow exit signs to the parking lot*.

"I mean it, you know," Pendergast said. "If you get outside, you're a free man."

Another trickle of sweat. "And if I don't?"

The blue eyes were disarmingly cheerful—or were they just eager? "You'll have sacrificed yourself for the greatest cause in the world."

"I won't play this game," Arcadio said, his voice suddenly thin.

"It's not a game, Mr. Sarabia. It's a test." Pendergast leaned forward, eyes bright. "This is history we're making here."

The TV screens went blank.

Arcadio stood motionless. Once again the only sound was the faint hiss of the air conditioner.

Knife and gun. They looked all right, as promised. Inviting. He took a step toward them. Froze.

Maybe Mr. Mitford is busy somewhere. Like right outside this door, pressed against the wall and waiting for Arcadio to poke his head into the hallway like a clay pigeon? On the other hand, if he waited too long, the Blond Man could simply walk in and slaughter him like a calf in a pen.

Taking a deep breath, he crept to within a pace of the door, then lowered himself onto his hands and knees. An old *coyote* trick—ambushers always expect victims to appear at their own eye level. He thrust his head through the doorway and turned it quickly from side to side. No one was there. The hallway was long, with closed doors on both sides. It turned out of sight at either end, and from each corner peered a security camera. Arcadio thought of rats and mazes. *It's a test.*

Letting out his breath, he retrieved his weapons from the floor. The knife was still sharp; he slipped it into his boot and examined the gun. Full clip. Had Pendergast told the truth, then, or were these dummy shells? He considered firing one at a security camera, but decided that would be foolish. If the Blond Man was indeed playing the part of the cat somewhere in this complex, why draw his attention more quickly than necessary?

He took a closer look at the doors. They were identical to the one on his own cell, smooth surfaces with no doorknobs or handles. But each was decorated with an engraved metal plate. He glanced at the one on his own door; it read: VULCAN.

Vulcan? Like in "Star Trek"? What was that supposed to mean?

From the door across the hall came a soft scraping, scrabbling noise, and Arcadio spun toward it. The plate on this door was inscribed LOKI. The scraping noise sounded frantic, but very faint. Was there a prisoner behind that door, too? Arcadio thought about the scratches on the walls of his own cell. He hesitated, then turned away. Maybe it was a prisoner. But maybe it was the Blond Man, armed and smiling. This was no time to be a good Samaritan.

The hallway was slightly shorter to the right, so he moved in that direction, treading softly. As he passed the doors, he glanced at their engraved plates: SEKHMET. CHARON. ANUBIS. He frowned. Were those names, or what? MEDB. KHO DUMO-DUMO . . .

The security camera watched him from the corner. Perhaps Pendergast was using it to guide Mitford toward him. Fingers tight on the pistol, he crept close and peered around the corner. Ahead lay a hallway identical to the one he had just transited—except that this one ended not at another corner, but at a pair of closed doors. Doors with handles.

After a moment's debate he walked briskly toward the doors, passing the rooms on either side without a glance.

Somewhat to his surprise, the double doors were unlocked. He thrust them open and found himself facing a steep concrete ramp leading upward. At the top was another pair of doors, these equipped with wire-reinforced windows. Beyond the windows was darkness. The night sky? Could it be?

Heart pounding, Arcadio ran up the ramp and pressed a wary eye to one of the windows. Nothing but blackness. He glanced behind him, then took a deep breath, shoved the doors open and darted through. He knew immediately he was not outside. Beneath his feet was the ubiquitous concrete, and the stale air was redolent of oil and gasoline.

Behind him, the doors wheezed shut with an ominously heavy *click*, as if they had locked. Echoes rippled out and back. This was a large chamber.

As his eyes adjusted, he spotted a faint, purple gray rectangle hovering overhead in the distance. He stared at it, saw stars gleaming. A skylight—but it was hopelessly high.

Then he noticed another patch of light, farther away but much lower. It was yellowish, triangular in shape, and brightest at the apex—a lightbulb shining down a wall. He strained his eyes. Maybe not a wall. The light seemed to reveal a couple of horizontal seams . . . like the kind on sliding garage doors. His heartbeat picked up, but still he hesitated. He didn't trust the fact that the only light in the room shone on a possible way *out*. Perhaps it was a lure. Come, little mousie, here's freedom . . .

His eyes were adjusting. Now he could discern several hulking, angular shapes in the gloom beneath the skylight—machinery of some kind. But he couldn't tell exactly how large the room was, or what occupied the blackness around the edges. Or *who*.

He had three courses of action: search blindly through the dark, go back to the madman's maze—or head across the room toward the distant light. Taking a deep breath, he moved toward the light.

As he approached the center of the room, carefully avoiding the hulking objects in the pool of starlight, he glimpsed a tall, lean shape racing toward him from one side. He spun and aimed his gun at it, but there was no one there. Panicky fool.

He moved on again. One step. Two. Three. And a voice growled in his ear, "How do you sssssspell rrrrrrrelief?"

He whirled, gun swinging up, heart slamming, and thought he glimpsed a pale flash again, vanishing into the darkness. He listened so hard his head was filled with the static of his own nerve endings, but he heard no running footsteps, certainly no voice. Besides . . . "How do you spell relief?" Wasn't that from some old TV commercial? Idiotic. His imagination had to be playing games with him.

Or perhaps the Blond Man was . . .

Of course. Of course. No fear. Show no fear.

He moved on again, more slowly now. His palm was slick on the grips of the pistol.

The voice whispered in his other ear, "Luuuucyyyyyyyyyyyy, I'm home . . ."

Arcadio spun again, gasping, finger tensing on the trigger. But there was no one there. No one!

Easy. Easy. It was just a voice, possibly even coming from a speaker somewhere. Now that he thought about it, it had a strange crackling undertone, as if it were being filtered through the whirling blades of a fan. An electronic trick.

Suddenly, directly behind him, the voice said, "Don't get mad, get Glad!"

Arcadio whirled again, and this time definitely spotted a lean shape dodging away through the surrounding machinery. But it was gone too fast for him to even take aim. His skin tightened. Whoever that was—the Blond Man, no doubt—he must be able to see through the gloom. Infrared glasses? A Starlight scope, like Border Patrol officers sometimes used in the canyons?

Arcadio gathered himself again. He could still go back, back into the maze with all the cameras. He wondered if that was what his captors wanted.

I will not play your game.

The strange voice did not return, and after a minute he began to relax. Perhaps he had passed this particular test.

Suddenly he was running toward the triangle of light, and in a moment it loomed before him. It *was* a shaded bulb shining down a big garage door, and the handle was right there, waiting to be turned. He skidded to a halt, reached out—

—and a chuckle puffed against the back of his neck.

Spinning with an involuntary scream, bringing the gun around fast, he saw a tall, diaphanous shape looming over him and he pulled the trigger three times in rapid succession. In the first blast of light he glimpsed a long, watermelon-shaped head, its hairless scalp puckered with craters, its face a mosaic of features joined by a network of livid scars. It hovered above him, close enough to touch.

The second and third shots, which almost overlapped one another, revealed nothing at all. *Got you! Got*—

Arcadio's finger locked open. Afterimages floated around him like *piñatas*. His heart kicked savagely in his chest.

Whom had he shot? It hadn't been the Blond Man at all. Such awful scars . . . and what had he been wearing? A white, flapping gown, like a hospital gown. Arcadio suddenly remembered the running figure he'd glimpsed earlier on the TV monitor, and gasped. Oh, *Dios*, he'd shot another prisoner, some other poor rat in the maze. Suddenly he wondered if *this* was why he'd been given his weapons and set free—so he would panic and commit murder, all on videotape. Blackmail. . .

Extending a foot, he prodded for the corpse. Found nothing but smooth cement. His relief lasted only a moment. There *must* be a body. He could not have missed from such close range. He probed further. Nothing. Impossible!

Suddenly, here in the gloom, superstitious terror flooded his mind with all the compelling clarity of childhood: *Brujos*. Witches. Demons. Vampires. Something undead was in this room with him . . .

Then the fear was, in turn, buried under an avalanche of fury so intense it surprised even him. Blank cartridges. Of course. Pendergast had meddled with his ammunition after all . . .

Now his hands were steady again. Taking a deep breath, he turned back toward the garage door. The smocked man stood directly before him, a vulpine silhouette. "Boo," he said.

Arcadio stumbled back, barely stopping himself from shooting again. "No!" he cried, and added in English, "I'm a prisoner, too! Don't be afraid!"

The man didn't move. He was a narrow slice of darkness against the light.

Arcadio repeated his statement in Spanish. There was no reply, but . . . was the man *smiling*? No, that couldn't be a smile. The dim crescent hovering at the top of the silhouette was almost as wide as the man's entire head.

Suddenly, with a fluid step, the man slipped directly in front of him again. This close, the scarred face was a writhing oval—now long and thin, now stretched hideously wide. Arcadio instinctively raised the pistol again, and the barrel snagged on something. He quickly tugged it free, crying, "Please! Please, we must . . ."

From nowhere, a wave of dizziness swept over him. He started to lower the gun, but his arm felt so light, floating upward by itself . . . He looked at it and blinked. The gun was gone. So was his hand. From the glistening stump of his wrist spewed streamers of blood.

"Tassssstessss grrrrrrrrreat," the smocked man said, and chuckled.

Screaming in pain and fear, Arcadio lunged forward, but struck only a swirl of disturbed air. No one could move that fast. *Ghost!* he thought again, wildly. *Demonico!* He crashed into the garage door and groped madly for the handle, the bleeding stump of his other arm pressed tightly against his hip. His whole mind was focused desperately on one thought: *All you have to do is find your way out of this building* . . .

His fingers discovered the handle, slipped off, found it again. Tightened.

And suddenly a hot breath brushed the back of his head. "Lesssssssssssss filling," hissed the voice, and Arcadio screamed again as he whirled and—

The echoes of the scream faded in the darkness. A moment later, in the triangle of light, there was movement. A wet glistening. Inky puddle spreading. Cracking sounds rose up, then a juicy tearing noise like orange segments being pulled apart.

A pause. "Thissssssss izzzzz living," murmured the harsh, rippling voice. Then it was just the rending sounds again.

Near the ceiling, high in the darkness, cameras whirred.

PART I

In this House of Dust which I entered,
there lives the funereal priest who brings
together gods and men . . .
                    —THE EPIC OF GILGAMESH

PART One

CHAPTER ONE

As ALWAYS, THE FIRST THING Deborah Kosarek did when she arrived at the office was sit at her computer terminal and call up her LIST OF THINGS TO DO.

1. Finish NIMROD text reconstruction.
2. Study for Amer. Lit. test on September 15!

She sighed. Item One had been on the list, unchanged, for nine weeks now. That was when she had run out of data to recreate the text that had gotten lost in the computer last December. And the remainder of the information she needed was available only through Dr. Pendergast, who had been gone on sabbatical since May second, nearly six months ago.

She still had a copy of the memo that had arrived from him: "Last night, I conducted a test that proved I'm far ahead of schedule on a crucial ongoing project. If the next stage works as expected, you'll all know by mid-September."

Deborah had been shocked. What "ongoing project" could be important enough to justify delaying NIMROD for so long? She hadn't known, but might any day now. It was September thirteenth. Soon Deborah would be able to get to work on NIMROD again. Maybe she'd have the text finished by Christmas, and wouldn't *that* be a load off her mind.

Item Two was a personal problem. Yesterday, her son, Virgil, had gotten sick, and she'd had to sit up with him all night—which had shot down her plans to study for her American Literature test.

She frowned, and a pair of commas appeared between her brows. She wasn't aware that those lines had grown deeper, lately, than the laugh-wrinkles at the corners of her eyes. It wasn't her habit to moon

17

over herself in the mirror—her hair was short and easy to care for; her makeup was simple; her clothing well fitting but functional. She owned exactly six office outfits, which she kept impeccably clean and mended and which she wore in sequence.

She hated disorder, having leftover items on her list. If you let things get out of control in your life, what then?

"Did you hear about the plane crash in Miramar last night?" a voice said in her ear. She jumped, then turned and glared at the youth standing over her. At age twenty-four, Ted Scully was one of the youngest geneticists at Carlton Biomedical Research Center. Also one of the brightest. Also, she thought, the most annoying. He was wearing his typical uniform: old T-shirt, jeans, sneakers, grin. The T-shirt had a legend smeared on it in blood-red letters: FEARLESS VAMPIRE KILLER.

"No," she said wearily, "I didn't hear about it."

"Don't you read the newspaper?"

"Not in the morning. Ted, I have a lot of work to do."

He plopped onto the corner of her desk. His contact lenses gave his eyes an unlikely emerald tint, and his hair was brush-cut. He wore a silver stud in his left earlobe. To Deborah, he looked more like a janitor than a scientist; a kid who had dropped out of high school to empty trash cans. Except that here at the Carlton Center, only the geniuses got to dress like this. The janitors wore mauve jumpsuits. Absently picking up a framed photo from her desk, Ted said, "Well, you should be interested in this crash, since you live near Miramar."

Deborah took the picture away from him. It was a recent shot of Virgil, who was now fourteen months old. *And will never know his father.* The thought sprang up like a dark, cancerous weed, stinging her. Deborah put the picture back where it belonged and said in a careful voice, "We live ten miles from Miramar, you know that."

Ted smiled modestly. Only days after starting his job at the center, he'd used the computer terminal in the lab to access her personnel records. Which wasn't supposed to be possible, and was in any case against company policy—but then, the entire computer system was at the mercy of members of the Carlton Center Brat-Pack. Deborah added, "Now, I really have to get busy."

"An F–14 landed on the freeway instead of the runway," Ted said. "Hit a semi head-on."

"Ted, you're sick."

"It's true," Ted said, although it wasn't clear if he was referring to her comment or his story. Around them, the other cubicles were silent. Deborah always got to work earlier than the secretaries who shared this area with her, so she could keep her supervisor, Mr. Andrews, aware of her dedication.

"Decapitated the semi driver," Ted went on with relish. "Plane's wing went right through his—are you all right?"

"This isn't funny, especially at seven-thirty in the morning," she said stonily. "I don't care if your hero *is* Freddy Krueger."

"I'm just keeping you posted on the decline of modern civilization," he said. "This Miramar thing, for example, illustrates how our military keeps us safe."

Deborah stared at him, but as usual she couldn't read his expression. Was he always joking? Or was he *ever* joking? "Why don't you ever talk about anything *good*?" she said.

"This *is* good. The plane wasn't carrying nuclear missiles."

There was a thump from the adjacent cubicle as Winnifred Powell settled in. Winnie was the personal secretary for both Dr. Pendergast and Robert Andrews, the two men who held Deborah's job in their hands. Winnie was a nice woman, but why did she have to be early *today*?

"Ted," Deborah said, "I have to get busy."

"Come on, where's your appreciation of the tragic? You're a literature major, haven't you read your Shakespeare or your Jacqueline Susann? Speaking of which, how's the degree hunt going?"

"Fine," she said, thinking woefully about Item Two on her list.

"You won't leave the Center when you graduate, will you?" Ted asked. "We can't afford to lose our best tech writer."

She was the Carlton Center's only technical writer, and of course Ted knew that, too. "I'm not going anywhere for a while," she said. Maybe never, she thought. Teaching school simply didn't pay on this scale—and she was, after all, a single parent.

The silence from the next cubicle was beginning to make her nervous. "Speaking of tech writing," she said, "I have to get back to it."

Ted leaned over and squinted at her monitor. "NIMROD? No hurry there."

"What?" The commas suddenly reappeared between her brows. NIMROD was the most important project the Center had ever undertaken.

Code-named after an Old Testament king renowned for his hunting prowess, NIMROD was a genetically altered antigen—a mutant "killer" cell designed to attack specific tissues in a body. In effect, programmable cancer. The exciting thing was that the antigen could, in theory, be programmed to consume *existing* cancer. MedSpec was almost slavering to get the preliminary text, which Pendergast had put on hold to take his surprise sabbatical.

Ted *had* to be joking this time. Deborah said, "Of course there's a hurry. Dr. Pendergast should be back any day, and I'll have to work like a dog to catch up with—"

"He's not coming back any day, Deb. In fact, he just extended his sabbatical."

Her chest grew terribly heavy. "What?"

Ted shrugged, although she caught a vindictive gleam in his eyes. "He left a message on the modem this morning. He says things are progressing faster than he'd hoped, and he's not ready to come back yet."

"But . . . he's already been gone for almost *half the year*."

"Hey. When you're the company figurehead, you do whatever you want."

Deborah closed her mouth, dumbfounded. Although it was true that Pendergast's status at MedSpec was unique, he was hardly a figurehead. His work had, in fact, transformed MedSpec from a mere producer of prescription drugs into a world leader in biomedical technology.

It had started twenty years ago, when two scientists pooled their divergent talents and created a laboratory called BioEdge. George Irving Pendergast, M.D., Ph.D., was a biologist, neurologist and microsurgeon, while Dr. Charles Carlton was a molecular biologist and an early computer expert. Although their work on recombinant DNA earned them a joint Nobel Prize in 1965, it was the practical applications for genetic engineering that made BioEdge one of the most successful biotech companies in the world.

After the tragic automobile accident that took Carlton's life, Pendergast sold BioEdge to MedSpec Corporation—under two provisions: that he remain in control of research, and that the new division be named the Carlton Biomedical Research Center.

Ted's jealous scorn notwithstanding, Dr. Pendergast was still the heart of the Carlton Center. In the past fifteen years he had made dramatic breakthroughs in a startling range of areas—disease prevention, learning disabilities, birth defects, aging. No wonder some of the darker rumors at the center implied that he must be stealing other people's work.

Sour grapes, Deborah had always thought.

But now, for the first time, she was being slapped in the face by Dr. Pendergast's idiosyncratic behavior. And finding she didn't like it much. "This project he's working on," she said, trying to keep her voice level. "Does it have anything to do with NIMROD?"

Ted shrugged. "Who knows? Pendergast never has to explain himself to anyone."

She rubbed her eyes. "Oh, God. Andrews promised the home office they'd start getting new NIMROD text by the end of the month. I'm in for it now."

"Andrews refuses to understand you can't dictate scientific progress," Ted said. "Especially with Pendergast running the show."

It was the same old story. Andrews was Dr. Pendergast's opposite number on the administrative side of the Carlton Center and, according to company wags, had been placed there so his hardheaded business skills could compensate for Dr. Pendergast's unpredictability. Deborah remembered that the first thing he had done after taking over four years ago was to post productivity schedules all over the plant. The scientists had made paper airplanes out of them.

But Deborah wasn't a scientist. Officially, she was part of the administrative staff. And Andrews already had his laser eye on her. He was not a man who enjoyed having his authority undermined, as she had inadvertently done last December. Or rather, as Dr. Pendergast had, on her behalf. "You can't write her up for a computer crash, Andrews," he had said. "I don't care if we *do* have to reconstruct lost data. We'll only be set back by a few months."

And millions of dollars, Andrews' rigid face had said.

Pendergast had tipped Deborah a wink.

Which only made his current behavior more baffling.

Deborah said, "Surely somebody could contact him to find out if he has the information I need."

Ted laughed. "Good luck. He modems us, but nobody modems him. That's the rule."

"What about a telephone?"

"If he has one, the number isn't in the company records. He probably wants to keep his lone-wolf image intact."

"I can't believe this."

Ted patted her shoulder. "Look on the bright side. Maybe he's being held prisoner by terrorists until he reveals the secret of life."

"Ted?" Winnifred suddenly called from the next cubicle. "I've got you down for an eight-thirty meeting with Mr. Andrews. Are you ready for it?"

Ted winced. "Yeah, thanks, Winnie." He smiled at Deborah. "Later."

When he was gone, Winnie's face popped over the cubicle wall. "Didn't think you wanted him around anymore."

"Thanks, Winnie."

"Boy watches too many horror movies for his own good."

"Is Dr. Pendergast really extending his sabbatical?" Deborah asked.

"Yeah. Sorry. Just got a memo on it myself."

Deborah bit at a cuticle. "God, Andrews is going to kill me. NIMROD would probably already be finished if . . ."

"Honey," Winnie said, "now you know why they'll never get me to touch one of those damned computers. Did you know some people think one of the lab guys might have put a *virus* into that program you were working on?"

Deborah's eyes widened. "You're kidding."

"Nope. Not to get *you*, you understand—to get Dr. Pendergast. The whole thing's just a game to them."

Deborah leaned back slowly and closed her eyes. She could feel a headache building in her skull like a thunderstorm over the desert.

Winnie said, "Just remember, honey, it's not a game to Dr. Pendergast. If he's staying on sabbatical, he's got to have a reason. In fact, Ted might be right for once. Maybe Dr. Pendergast *is* figuring out how to save the world."

"I caught a couple of kids riding their bikes up toward the Hermit's place this afternoon," Tony Garwood said, leaning his lanky frame against the barricade that separated Rancho Vista del Oro from the adjacent undeveloped land. "I stopped them, but they're bound to try again. You know how kids are."

"Do I ever." Bill Chatherton plumped down on the hood of the Protector Security Systems cruiser and adjusted his uniform. He was a head shorter than Tony, but pumped a lot of iron and groused about his ill-fitting Protector uniform. "Hell, what's the Hermit going to do if some kid *does* get up there—shoot him?"

"More likely call management and complain about RVO's security," Tony said carefully.

Chatherton sighed. "Right. And then somebody's going to ask where Bill Chatherton was at five P.M., and I'll have to say 'Stuck in traffic, as usual . . .' I appreciate you covering for me, Tony."

Tony shrugged. "You can't help your schedule." Chatherton was a San Diego police officer, working the eight-to-five shift. He called this security guard work "my childcare payment job." He'd been married twice and divorced twice, and had a total of four kids. Or was it five?

Tony glanced across the valley to where I–5 stretched north and south like a glittering diamond necklace—but the points of light weren't gems, they were the windshields of cars locked in rush-hour stasis under the afternoon sun. It was like this every weekday, so Tony worked late until Chatherton could get here. He didn't mind.

"You don't need to worry anyway," Tony said. "Management would never fire you; they like having a real cop on the payroll. It makes them feel like they're getting more for their money."

"*You're* a cop."

"Was," Tony said shortly.

"Well, I've got to warn you—the minute the department moves me to the night shift, I'm dumping this job."

Tony had heard it before. Chatherton hated working in the Traffic Division and had dreams of a detective's badge. According to him, his career was stalled only because he was kept on the relatively uneventful daytime shifts.

"Do you think you might get switched soon?" Tony asked, surprised at how much he hoped the answer was no. Listening to Chatherton's cop stories was always the high point of his day. Tony had worked for Protector for two years, the last eight months here at Rancho Vista del Oro. And so far, apprehending the infamous Sprinkler Head Bandit—a twelve-year-old kid—had been the high point of his new career.

Chatherton shook his head. "I'm beginning to suspect I'll be on the day shift until I'm reincarnated into a minority group."

Chatherton was always blaming hiring quotas for his sluggish career;

Tony suspected the problem might have more to do with the man's sleep-deprived surliness. "So nothing exciting happened on the streets today?" he asked.

"Oh, just the usual shit." But then, as always, Chatherton became animated. "Around nine this morning, I pulled a DWO over for doing fifty in a school zone, and she goes, 'Hey, cop, I late for work—you let me go, okay . . . ?'"

Tony listened with his gaze on the curb and a half-smile on his lips. "DWO" was unofficial police code, a takeoff on "Driving While Under the Influence." It stood for "Driving While Oriental."

Chatherton went on, "When I give her the ticket to sign, she refuses. So I start taking the handcuffs off my belt and she goes, 'Hey, cop, what those for?' And I say, 'If you won't sign the ticket, I have to take you in.' She goes, 'Okay, cop, okay,' and signs faster than anybody you ever saw."

Tony laughed, although he had noticed that more and more of Chatherton's stories dealt with foreigners or tourists. Chatherton even had a bumper sticker on the back of his car that read: WELCOME TO SAN DIEGO. NOW GO HOME. A common enough attitude among native San Diegans, but probably not a great one for a cop. Not that Tony didn't understand the sentiment.

He gazed into the valley again. They were standing at the best vantage point in Rancho Vista del Oro. On a clear day a triangle of the ocean was visible between two distant ridges—the view for which the entire housing development was named, even though it was denied to the bulk of the homeowners here on Tortoise Mountain.

Once upon a time, the floor of the valley had been as rumpled as an old blanket, a maze of rocky hills and gulches broken only occasionally by tomato fields or stands of live oaks and wild artichoke. It had been a place where you could ride a dirt bike all day, startling jackrabbits and birds, throwing up a plume of yellow dust.

But a lot of things had changed in the last couple of years. Bulldozers had smoothed the valley, filling the canyons with the ridges, gouging up the rough chaparral and leaving room for sod. Within a few months, the land below Tortoise Mountain had filled with rooftops like a reservoir of tile.

Rancho Vista del Oro itself was typical of these "planned communities." Its design motif featuring Neo-Spanish stucco Single Family Residences (Four Distinctive Floor Plans to Choose From), with red tile roofs and a single stunted palm tree per lot. Wooden "privacy fences" separated yards the approximate size and color of pool tables. Swimming pools glinted like polished turquoise.

Beyond the barricade Tony was sitting on sprawled the land that would soon become RVO Phase Two. It was still wild at the moment, but in a few days bulldozers would start molding it into a wedding cake of terraces. Then, almost overnight, the houses would appear—lawns a shocking green, sprinklers running swish-swish-swish all night long.

Everything changed, of course. But nothing, as far as Tony could see, ever seemed to get better. Just as Ed Winston, who had been his partner on the police force, used to say. *The world's going to hell, Tony; a cop's job is to piss into the wind without getting wet. That's why we have to back each other up no matter what . . .*

Ed Winston, who had eaten the barrel of his own .38 last February. Tony had read about it in the paper.

Turning abruptly, he looked up the rocky, brush-choked slopes rising above Vista del Oro. The crown of Tortoise Mountain was still wild, too. It was the Hermit's property.

The kids living in RVO swapped rumors about the Hermit as if they were trading cards—he lived with a swarm of cats in a stone hut; he crept down into RVO after dark to eat the slugs that crawled on the sidewalks; during nights of the full moon, eerie cries came from the mountaintop . . .

Harmless nonsense, of course. All Tony knew was that the Hermit's house was not visible from RVO, and could only be reached by a dirt road that wound around the back of the mountain. Personally, Tony was rather fond of the Hermit and his individualistic ways. Christ, developers must have offered the man enough money to upholster the entire mountaintop, yet the Hermit held firm. Still, Tony suspected he would sell out eventually. Everybody seemed to, sooner or later, for one reason or another.

Chatherton had followed his gaze up the hill. "Did you know management asked me to check the Hermit out?"

"They did? How come?"

"I think the developers are hoping to get some dirt on the guy. Maybe they want to force him to sell."

"Did you do it?"

Chatherton shrugged. "Why not? Not that I have access to much. Turns out he's got a couple of parking tickets, that's about it."

"Who is he, anyway?"

"His name's Pendergast, *Dr*. George Pendergast. He doesn't much like to feed the meters in La Jolla."

"A doctor, huh? Must be a good one—that's a valuable piece of property up there."

Chatterton sighed. "He's probably a pediatrician."

CHAPTER TWO

PENDERGAST MUST STILL BE IN MOURNING.

Mitford sat in the control room and watched the rows of monitors as he switched from one security camera to another, searching for the doc. Most of the screens showed angles on corridors and rooms here in the complex, while others offered mouse-eye views through the sagebrush up above. Unfortunately, many areas, such as the private living quarters and storerooms, weren't monitored at all. So it was impossible to keep track of Pendergast all the time.

But Mitford was certain the doc was on his way to the surface, to visit Vulcan's grave. He did it a lot.

Toying with the controls on the panel before him, Mitford watched the views on the monitors shift. Besides the videos, he could also observe the readouts of motion detectors, microphones, trip-wires. All these devices had been installed at his urging. Ten years ago, when Pendergast had first moved *Project Enkidu* here from his old place on Tortoise Mountain, the doc had questioned the necessity of the system. "We've got a thousand acres of wasteland overhead," he'd said. "What do we need with all this nonsense?"

But eventually Mitford had prevailed—and Arcadio's attempted invasion last May had, of course, justified "all this nonsense."

Adjusting the gain on one of the surface microphones, he managed to separate a muttering voice from the soughing of the wind. There. Almost outside the security perimeter. He couldn't catch the words, but the voice was Pendergast's. Mitford shook his head. The doc was something else. A grown man, standing in a wasteland in the middle of the night, talking to an experiment he had killed and buried last May.

"I'll take care of Vulcan myself," he had told Mitford at the time.

"You? Why?" Mitford had been surprised. In the past, it had always been *his* job to get rid of obsolete prototypes.

"Because Vulcan deserves special treatment," Pendergast had said. "He might not be perfect, but he's still the first true Loner."

So the doc had pumped poison gas into Vulcan's cell, then hauled the limp body to the surface and carted it off into the sagebrush. Curious, Mitford had kept track as best he could via the sensors and mikes. Finally he had heard the crunch of a spade in stony earth, and then, to his amazement, Pendergast's emotion-filled voice: "Ashes to ashes, dust to dust . . ."

Mitford had smiled. So that was it, a funeral. For a scientist, Pendergast was strangely obsessed with religion. His private quarters were full of sacred books of all kinds, ancient scrolls in climate-controlled boxes, volumes on philosophy and theology, weird old icons, statuettes in wall niches. This obsession permeated everything. For example, the underground complex's name came from Nordic mythology: Ginnunga Gap, which according to Pendergast meant "the chaos from which all creation sprang." And the code name of the project, *Enkidu*, was after a Mesopotamian hero who represented the freedom of nature. Or something like that.

"Religion and philosophy were the science of their day," Pendergast had once said. "Whether they were based on reality or not, they had genuine power, and they molded the world we live in. Science has forgotten that. It's a mistake."

Personally, Mitford couldn't give a shit. He had other interests.

The security wall was dominated by a double row of monitors depicting eighteen small concrete rooms. Each was occupied by a solitary smocked figure. Except for a few who were sleeping, they moved around their enclosures in an oddly stylized way. It wasn't until you had watched them for a while that you realized they were imitating some character or other on TV. Mitford had seen them dance like Fred Astaire, leap into the air like Michael Jordan going for a slam-dunk, box like Mike Tyson. And they had plenty of practice: every half-hour, the TVs changed channels automatically—scanning sitcoms, commercials, documentaries, movies. "It's how they learn about people," Pendergast had told Mitford. "The TVs are giving them a crash course in the outside world. Of course, later generations will get their knowledge directly."

The behavior in the cells changed radically as feeding time approached, though. That was when the occupants stopped imitating the TV images and started attacking them. According to Pendergast, although the occupants knew the people on television were unreal and inedible, "Hunger is by far their major motivator."

Mitford looked at them more closely. Five and a half months ago, back when Arcadio had visited, they had been the size of five-year-old children. Now they appeared to be adults, a cross-section of people off the street: men and women, Caucasian, Black, Hispanic, Asian. But seen together like this, there was a similarity between them too: rather large heads, lean bodies, a curious fluidity of movement as they paced their cells.

And of course, they weren't people at all. Pendergast called them Loners; specifically, the "Alpha generation" of Loners. He also called them "Vulcan's children."

Mitford knew that wasn't strictly true. For all of Vulcan's advancements over his freakish predecessors, he'd still been sterile. The Alphas had been engineered directly from his DNA—"Like Athena springing whole from the forehead of Zeus," as Pendergast put it.

Up on the surface, Pendergast was still mumbling over Vulcan's grave. Bored, Mitford slid a videotape into a player and turned it on. The master monitor lit up and there was Arcadio Sarabia, lying unconscious on his back in a holding cell. Suddenly his eyes opened. He tried to sit up.

Mitford had edited this tape himself; he called it *Adiós, Arcadio*.

It had been Pendergast's idea to place Arcadio in what amounted to a test maze. Typically, the doc had had to rationalize the decision: Arcadio had brought it on himself by breaking their pact; Arcadio was a money-grubbing procurer; Arcadio was, in other words, a representative of the amorphous group the doc called the "Great Evil."

"We'll let Vulcan hunt him," Pendergast had said that night. "Vulcan deserves one real kill before I eliminate him."

"But if he kills Arcadio, who'll get the breeder women for us?"

"With any luck," Pendergast had said, "we won't need breeders anymore. This test will let us know."

On the videotape, Arcadio crept to the door and tested it, then jumped back in fright as the TV screens came on. Mitford fast-forwarded past the argument with Pendergast to the scenes in the underground garage. These had been taped with light-amplifying equipment. The images were silvery, as if molded out of mercury. Arcadio slinked across the garage with his pistol in his hand, not realizing that Vulcan was right behind him, matching him step for step like a stretched-out shadow.

Next, Vulcan playing games with Arcadio. Mumble in his ear, dance away, sidle back again. And finally, the encounter at the garage door. Even slowed to frame-by-frame motion, the actual attack was a blur. The blood looked black in the amplified light.

Mitford shifted his eyes toward a flicker on one of the security monitors. Ah! There was movement in the desert, forty feet over his head. Pendergast returning.

On the main monitor, Vulcan bent low over Arcadio's body. Turning up the audio, Mitford listened to the damp, tearing sounds. They didn't bother him. Once, during demolition training in the SEAL program, one of the squids had blown himself into handkerchief-sized chunks. Mitford had kept working as grim rain fell.

He touched buttons on the console, magnifying the image of Vulcan's head. The Loner's bald pate was as cratered as the moon from where various monitoring electrodes had once been implanted, and a web of scars mapped the route Pendergast had taken to patch his face into a relatively human shape. Producing a passable countenance had been a big problem at first, because the structure of a Loner's real head wasn't remotely human. The doc had searched for solutions on Vulcan, then translated the results into genetic blueprints for the Alphas.

A red light flashed on the panel, indicating that Pendergast had just entered Ginnunga Gap. Mitford switched from camera to camera, watching the doc move through the complex. Even Pendergast hadn't argued with the necessity of keeping constant surveillance on key underground areas. Everything was recorded on continuous twelve-hour video loops, so there would be a record if a disaster occurred.

At last Pendergast entered the control room, wiping sweat off his lined forehead. He glanced at what was playing on the main monitor, then at Mitford, then took his usual seat.

"Well," he said. "It's time."

"Time for what?"

"To start the field tests."

Mitford blinked slowly. "I thought you wanted to wait until December."

Swiveling in his chair, Pendergast stared up at the world map on the back wall. It was actually an enormous plasma video screen which, like virtually everything else in Ginnunga Gap, was linked to the central computer. From month to month and year to year, the colored areas on the map changed size and shape. Red predominated. "There's only one way to know if the Loners are good enough to set free," Pendergast said. He touched a button. "And every second we delay, the Great Evil just grows larger."

On the map, the red smears expanded fast, leaking like blood from continent to continent.

Mitford felt his heart accelerate. "So . . . when do we start?" He realized he'd never really expected this moment to come. Not *really*.

"Tonight," Pendergast said, staring at the screen. "Here's the simulation of what will happen if we release the Loners by Christmas." The pools of red slowed, stopped. "That's seven to eight years from now." Suddenly the red withdrew, leaving yellow behind at an accelerating rate. "Ten years after that," Pendergast said almost reverently as the yellow turned to green, "the world will be healthy again. Forever."

Mitford watched the screen as the map returned to its previous condition. According to Pendergast, the red represented the Great Evil, a group which evidently encompassed everything from polluters to small-time crooks like Arcadio. Actually, Mitford tended to tune Pendergast out when the doc got on the subject of the Great Evil; it was even more senseless than religion. Evil was, after all, a relative term.

Mitford's interest was pragmatic. SEAL training had stressed preparation, knowing the strengths, weaknesses, and motivations of everyone around you. Mitford hadn't exactly finished the SEAL program, but he had absorbed the vital parts, including this rule. And it had worked well for him over the years. Although he had never gone to war—he had been too young during the Vietnam fiasco and out of the service well before the Persian Gulf War—he had nevertheless killed two hundred and eighteen people so far during his lifetime. Some for Pendergast, others for himself. They had all been easy. But Loners might be different. Challenging. If the doc released them into the world and they really did spread, then such an encounter was not out of the question.

Pendergast turned toward the primary monitor again. "Everything for *Enkidu* is in place," he said, watching Vulcan feed. "It's interesting, don't you think, that Arcadio got himself eliminated at the same moment we no longer needed his . . . services. It's almost enough to make you believe in miracles after all."

"Too bad Vulcan's not around to see this," Mitford said.

Pendergast shrugged without looking away from the screen. "He wouldn't be aware of its importance; Loners aren't designed to think in abstractions. Besides, you know I had to get rid of him—he was obsolete."

Mitford smiled. It was amusing to watch the doc pretend to not be sentimental, especially about "The Father of Loners."

"Do you know what's ironic?" Pendergast asked. "Tonight marks a huge step forward in human history . . . yet if people found out I was responsible for it, I doubt anyone would thank me."

"A man's never appreciated in his own time," Mitford said.

CHAPTER THREE

"I'M SORRY, BETTY," Deborah said into the phone. "I won't be able to come over tonight—Virgil's cold isn't getting any better. He's pretty out of sorts."

"Oh, dear," her mother-in-law said, then her voice receded as she held the receiver away and cried, "Deborah can't come over tonight, Del! Virgil's still sick!"

The booming response carried clearly: "Hope it's not that flu! Ask her if she needs anything!"

She smiled. Del and Betty Kosarek had been good friends from the moment Brad introduced her to them, and much more than friends since his death. Her own parents were gone; Dad had died when she was twelve, and for the last seven years Mom had lived in a nursing home in St. Petersburg, Florida, near Deborah's brother.

But the Kosareks were always there for her. They watched Virgil while she was at school, and picked him up from day-care when she had to work late. In return she figured their taxes for them every year, and balanced Del's checkbook. They had once suggested that she move into their extra bedroom, to save her money and trouble. But when she had turned them down with gratitude, they had understood and never pressed her about it.

"Honey," Betty said now, "is there anything we can do?"

"No, thanks. He's got a bit of a fever and a cough, but I don't think it's the flu. He's sleeping right now."

"The poor honey. If you need anything, you know where we are. We'll miss you. Friday nights aren't the same without the two of you here."

"Thanks, Mom."

Mumbling in the background, then Betty again. "Del says to tell you there's a Human Powered Vehicle race on ESPN."

Deborah smiled. Del, frequently laid off from his job as a welder at the NAAVCO shipyards, liked to watch all the esoteric sports he could find on TV. No Padres or Chargers for him. Brad had had similar tastes, although he'd preferred to participate—rugby, lacrosse, scuba diving. On more than one occasion, she'd caught him eyeing the hang gliders soaring over Torrey Pines when he'd come to pick her up at work.

Work . . . She didn't want to think about that. Andrews had strolled past her cubicle several times today, staring at her but saying nothing . . .

"I'd better go," she said, keeping her voice cheerful. "I'll let you know if Virgil's well enough to come over Wednesday night, okay?" Wednesday was one of her school nights.

"Sure thing, honey. Take care."

As Deborah hung up, she heard a whimper in the recesses of the apartment, and hurried back to peek into what she called the nursery—actually a curtained-off portion of her bedroom. Virgil, nineteen months old, lay sprawled in his crib with his thin blond hair smeared over his forehead. One of his arms was thrown to the side, while the other was crooked possessively around a much-chewed plush toy called Brooke Worm, his favorite. Only recently had she been able to get him to survive at day-care without it.

He must have cried out in a dream.

Deborah gazed at his upturned nose and defiant chin, then turned toward the framed photo of Brad on the dresser. Same nose, same chin. Brad had died two months before Virgil was born. An end and a beginning. Even now, grief and joy were so confused inside Deborah, she wasn't sure where one ended and the other began. How long did psychologists say it took a person to get completely over a bereavement? Five years? No problem. Only three and a half to go . . .

It came on her like an ice storm. Hurrying out of the bedroom, she slumped onto the sofa in the fading blue glow of twilight, buried her face in a pillow and let the sobs pour out.

Well after sundown, a large panel van pushed between two manzanita bushes at the end of a paved street. It turned west and accelerated with a powerful rumble. There were no houses, no other vehicles in the vicinity.

Behind the wheel of the van, Mitford relaxed a bit. Although the tortuous route to Ginnunga Gap was virtually impassable even to this four-wheel-drive vehicle, there was always the chance that some dirt-bike rider or airplane pilot would spot the van and puzzle about its presence clear out here. There was no telling what might happen then. After all, the existence of Ginnunga Gap, if not its current function, was a matter of public record.

He glanced into the rear-view mirror. Directly behind him, a panel of reinforced one-way glass divided the cabin from the rear compartment, where Anubis lay unmoving in a disjointed sprawl. The anesthetic gas Mitford had pumped into his holding cell was powerful stuff.

In the passenger seat, Pendergast was turned sideways to watch the sleeping Loner. He was taking notes on a notebook computer. Mitford wasn't pleased with the doc's presence; he had argued strenuously against it, citing security factors. Actually, he just didn't like being watched. But Pendergast had said, "Would a rocket scientist miss his first space launch?"

Mitford looked back into the rear-view mirror. Anubis. What a name. Personally, Mitford would have called this Loner "Fred," because of all the TV programs fed into his cell, he seemed most excited by the antics of the cartoon Flintstones family. "What did you say 'Anubis' means, again?" he asked.

Pendergast never even glanced up. "Anubis was the Egyptian god of cemeteries."

Tony's heart still leaped whenever he heard a police siren. No matter where he was or what he was doing, he would stop and listen, quickly sorting possibilities in his head. High-speed chase? Domestic dispute? Drive-by shooting?

Murder?

The sound of sirens was part of the ambiance of North Park, where he lived. This was a section of the city that decayed with shocking rapidity from tidy estates bordering Balboa Park to an endless clot of adult bookstores, crumbling houses and cheap apartment buildings.

Tony's flat was located on the second floor of a two-story, eight-unit stucco building on the wrong side of the neighborhood. His living room window overlooked a concrete courtyard, while the bedroom window offered a view of an alley, assorted sun-faded rooftops and, in the distance, a glimpse of the trees in the park.

Tonight he was standing in his kitchen, peering without enthusiasm into his refrigerator, when his ear caught the cry of the siren. He listened for a moment, judged it was heading toward Hillcrest. Now came the bull-moose *whonk*ing of the cruiser's air horn as the cop warned traffic out of his way. Unaware of the cold air sweeping out of the fridge, Tony concentrated. Yes, definitely Hillcrest, maybe even the northwest corner of Balboa Park. Goosebumps chased each other down his back. He and Ed Winston had been briefly famous in the department because of the busts they had made in Balboa Park. The park had also been where he and Ed had been that last night.

Even though Tony had continued to work for the PD for another three months afterward, he still thought of it as *that last night*. The night he had stopped being a cop.

His gaze flicked toward two framed photographs hanging side by side in the living room. One showed a middle-aged man wearing a dark blue uniform; the other, a young man in khaki. The former was Milton Garwood, NYPD; the picture had been taken about a year before a mild stroke forced him into retirement at the age of forty-five. In the khaki, looking fierce and dedicated, was San Diego Police Academy graduate Tony Garwood, aged twenty-two. Milton had never seen that photo. He had died of an aneurysm three months before Tony finished the academy.

The siren suddenly fell silent. Tony decided it had quit too far north to be in the park, and wondered what had called the officer to Hillcrest. Hillcrest had a significant gay population; it could be some kind of hate crime. But whatever it was, the work of the police officer was underway out there now; pencil scratching on report forms, questions being asked, radio chattering with the secret dialogue of the initiate.

Tony sighed. He could never participate again, stand in the gloom with his peers, leather utility belt squeaking while red and blue lights flashed around and around like sunrises and sunsets on tiny planets. He missed it, though. Even the simple traffic stops Chatherton always complained about. He missed it so much.

Stop whimpering, you big baby. It's not like you had *to quit.*

Suddenly the inside of his refrigerator reminded him too much of his life—almost empty, not particularly clean, a little smelly. Shutting the door hard, he stalked back to his bedroom, changed into good clothes and checked his wallet for condoms. It was Friday night, and there were always places where you could find someone to help you lose the blues. He hadn't been with a woman for almost two weeks. Slowing down. Maybe it was age, maybe the hassle of sexual maneuvering in the age of AIDS. But tonight he'd lose himself in uncaring flesh. *You made your bed, buddy—now get someone to lie in it with you.*

Maybe tonight he'd drive downtown and check out the action in the Gaslamp District. Since the urban renovation began in the early eighties, some good bars and restaurants had opened down there.

As he drove south and began descending the long hill into downtown San Diego, he had to take it easy on the accelerator. A heavy fog was rising from the bay; he couldn't even see the skyscrapers that awaited him.

"Honey . . . do you know where we are?" Miranda Jeffers asked.

"Of course I know where we are." Bill Jeffers unfolded the map of downtown San Diego for the fifth time that night and braced it against the side of a building to keep his hands from shaking. A half-hour ago, he'd been certain of the route between the shopping mall and their car. But now here they were in this sleazy part of the city where everything smelled of oil and rancid seawater, and it was too quiet. The buildings were decaying brick and concrete, with barred windows and graffiti decor. The weird thing was, the transformation from good to terrible had come so quickly. One moment he, his wife and daughter were surrounded by the Historic Gaslamp Quarter (as the guidebooks called it); the next, by *this*.

Damned guidebooks. *America's Finest City*, that was San Diego's slogan. Supposedly the Gaslamp Quarter was living proof of how the downtown area had been cleaned up and restored in the last decade. Well, it had been pretty all right, but Bill had still seen a lot of bums hanging around among the yuppies, their dirty eyes casting dirty looks at his daughter, Amy. Gaslamp, Schmasslamp. Bill had wanted to go to Sea World again today, see Shamu. But Amy and Miranda, they'd insisted on shopping at Horton Plaza *one more time*.

But this time, Bill had decided he'd be damned if he'd park in the mall's cavernous garage. The floors were named after vegetables, the elevators went nowhere in particular and you could spend a week looking for your car. So he'd parked the rented sedan on the street and trailed grumpily after the ladies while they went shopping. Then they had insisted on seeing a movie there at the mall, some schmaltzy thing with Meryl Streep. As if there weren't movie theaters in Bozeman, Montana.

When they had finally gotten out of the theater, it was dark.

And foggy.

The guidebooks hadn't warned him about the fog, which was so thick it blotted even nearby buildings right out of view.

If they'd gone to Sea World, goddamn it, this wouldn't have happened.

He glanced up from the map. Gray everywhere. There weren't any street signs visible from here, and the only working streetlight on the block jittered and fizzed like the stump of a Fourth of July sparkler. Jesus, you had to go *searching* for places like this in Bozeman. You didn't just stumble into them.

He turned back to the map. "We take a right at the next corner," he said at last, striving for confidence, as he hastily folded the map and put it out of sight. If there was one thing he'd learned about being a tourist, it was that you tried not to look the part. No Bermuda shorts. No bus tours. And pawing around with a map . . . that was like putting blood in the water.

"I'm scared, Daddy," Amy suddenly said. Always helpful, his daughter. At Sea World it was "My feet hurt." At Mission Beach it was "The water's too cold." When she turned eighteen next year, she was on her own, like it or not. Let her try "I can't find a job" for a while.

"Don't be scared," he said sharply. "We're—"

Miranda's fingers dug into his arm. "Bill."

He took a deep breath, ready to wheel on her angrily, then saw what she'd seen, and froze. A man stood under the dying streetlight. He was tall and thin, wearing what looked like a long raincoat and high-topped basketball shoes. Just standing there without moving, eyes socketed with shadow. But unquestionably staring at *them*.

"Cross the street," Bill said softly, and, grasping each of his women by the hand, started off. They followed with stony steps; he felt as if he were dragging them.

The man in the raincoat watched them for a moment, then stepped casually into the street and strolled toward them. His calm demeanor made Bill's blood run cold. Maybe they should turn around and go back the other way. Or just run. Do something . . .

He heard a soft scuffing sound, and a quick glance over his shoulder revealed another figure approaching from the opposite corner. This man was bundled in rags, his long hair spraying out from under an oversized beret.

Bill's throat clenched. Jesus, it was really going to happen. Here. To the William H. Jeffers family. *I got mugged in America's Finest City.* Jesus. Jesus. He could feel both women tensing in his grip; they'd heard the second set of footsteps, too. But he kept dragging them toward the far curb. He couldn't think what else to do.

The man in the raincoat reached the sidewalk a second before Bill did and stood motionless about ten feet away, his hands hidden in his coat pockets. The darkness here was so complete that his head was nothing but a silhouette.

Bill stopped, too, and Miranda and Amy almost crushed his fingers in their grips. "Don't," he heard himself say to Raincoat, and then, absurdly, "We're from Montana."

The second set of footsteps came closer, then circled around as the man in the beret joined Raincoat. Beneath the beret was a dark, unsmiling face.

The two men said nothing.

"You want money?" Bill blurted in a pleading voice he knew would shame him for the rest of his life. "We've got money . . ."

The two muggers glanced at one another. Bill thought he saw twin gleams of teeth. Then the men turned back again. They were staring at Amy.

Miranda noticed it too. "Please . . ." she whined, leaning on Bill so hard he almost fell over. He knew he'd have to do something fast, before either of these scumbags made a move on his daughter. Oh, God . . . Maybe money would satisfy them, if he hurried.

"Here," he said, pawing for his wallet. "Here, I've got—"

Suddenly a head appeared around the corner of an alley twenty feet away. Bill saw a nondescript face, with small, bright eyes blinking at him. The newcomer smiled. No, please, not another one. Not *another* one.

Stepping out of the alley, the newcomer revealed a body even longer and thinner than Raincoat's. He wore a dirty bathrobe, baggy pants and open-toed sandals, and his forehead gleamed like a beetle's carapace in the uneven flicker of the light across the street.

Raincoat and Beret, apparently unaware of the new arrival, were still staring admiringly at Amy. Amy in her flattering new Nordstroms blouse, which she'd just *had* to wear out of Horton Plaza. "Nice," Beret said. "Real nice."

Bill finally freed his wallet, although he had to look at his hand to be sure he was holding anything. He felt numb all over. "Please," he said. "Please just—"

As he held the wallet out, the new arrival slipped up behind the other two in two long strides.

Bill waved his wallet wildly, the way a rodeo clown might draw a bull's attention by flapping a bandanna. "Please!" he cried again. "Please, just—"

"YABBA-DABBA-DOOOOO!" the newcomer shouted, and the first two muggers leaped into the air with caws of shock.

Suddenly everything moved very fast, jerkily, like a movie with missing frames. The newcomer's arms swept out, catching and embracing the muggers in midair—and, amazingly, holding them off the ground as if they were no heavier than blow-up dolls. They thrashed wildly; Raincoat managed to wrench an arm free. A knife appeared in his hand. He raised it high, then swung it blindly backward, toward the newcomer's vitals.

"Wiiiiiilma!" cried the newcomer, and his torso bent like a kneaded eraser, twisting out of the path of the blade. At the same moment, he jerked Beret into the gap. The knife pumped into Beret's lower stomach and out again; Beret's sudden, shrill scream dashed brittle echoes from surrounding buildings.

Amy screamed, too.

The newcomer leaned close to Beret, as if to kiss his neck. There was a flicker of motion, and Beret screamed again—a shrill whinny this time, like nothing Bill had ever heard before, not even in the movies. He began thrashing wildly, shrieks shredding the muffling fog. The beret flew away, and a rain of dark droplets spattered onto the sidewalk. Raincoat saw this and joined in the screaming, simultaneously slashing the knife wildly over his shoulder at the newcomer's face.

The newcomer rocked back onto one foot and, still holding both men off the ground, swept his free foot up in front of Raincoat. Somehow, it coiled all the way up to Raincoat's knife-hand, and two long toes clutched his wrist in midair. Bill stared. Nobody's leg could bend that way. And nobody's toes were that long and flexible. And those thorny growths curving over the front of the sandal—they looked like *claws*.

I went crazy in America's Finest City.

The lower part of the newcomer's face suddenly moved again, a blur speeding in and out. There was a loud *crack*, like two blocks of wood smacking together, and Raincoat's eyes grew so huge they seemed to flash in the gloom. His mouth fell open in a silent scream. The newcomer set him on his feet, and Raincoat stood there staring at his hand. Or rather at what was left of it: a single finger writhing like a worm in a scarlet volcano.

"Uck," said the newcomer, and spat. The knife, bent into a crooked W, clattered to the pavement. At the same moment the newcomer flung out an arm and slammed Raincoat into the wall; when the man's head struck the bricks, it sounded like Hank Aaron connecting on a homer. He collapsed bonelessly.

Miranda fainted then, and Bill suddenly felt as if the *Lusitania* was moored to his arm. Stumbling sideways, dragging Amy with him, he toppled over his wife's prostrate body and crashed heavily into the street. Amy fell onto his ribcage, slamming the air out of his lungs.

Bill never told the police what he saw, or seemed to see, then. After all, he was dazed, not thinking clearly. Now that Raincoat was out of the way, the newcomer's face was visible again . . . except he didn't look *human*. The bones of his face and skull were vastly elongated, tapered, the skin pulled so taut over them it was translucent. His eyes had sunk into dark slits. He grimaced, his lips stretching back into a huge, manic grin from which protruded a mass of gums and teeth the shape of icicles.

Beret, blood pouring down his neck, glanced over at that face and shrieked again. Instantly, the long jaws blurred. *CRAAAAAAACK!* The screaming stopped. Beret's legs gave one massive kick and hung limp.

The newcomer held him out by the shoulders, as if he were a suit of clothes on a hanger. The top of Beret's head was gone, and the brain as well. The inside of his skull looked as smooth and red as a plum. Then the bowl filled with blood, which overflowed and drizzled onto the pavement.

"Mmmmmmm-mmmmm good," Forehead said, and turned slowly toward Bill. Hot urine spilled down the back of Bill's pants. Miranda wasn't moving; Amy was trying to crawl beneath them both.

But now the newcomer didn't look like a monster at all. Of course not; he never had. No way. Still, there *was* blood all over him, and smooth menace in his stance as he took a long step forward.

Then he hesitated, halted. Raising his head, he peered distractedly into the fog as if someone had called his name. He sighed, glanced back at Bill. "Night, Barrrrrney," he purred, and strode back toward the alley, dragging Beret's body behind him. But instead of entering the alley, he grabbed hold of the brick wall and began to climb. Later, Bill told the police there must have been a rope or cable winching him up. But what it *looked* like was that he scaled the damp bricks like a giant insect, hauling Beret's corpse after him. And his limbs moved all wrong, bending in strange directions, as if they had come unhinged at every joint.

But Bill knew he would never mention these details to the police or anybody else. They would think he was nuts.

A moment later, the newcomer vanished into the ceiling of the fog, Beret's body sliding after him. A bright red ribbon on the side of the building was the only sign of their passage.

Laying his head back on the pavement, Bill listened to the streetlight on the far curb fizzing toward death. *I passed out in America's Finest City,* he thought, and did so.

CHAPTER FOUR

ALTHOUGH THE VAN was so heavily armored it could have served as a Brink's truck, Mitford did not believe in relying exclusively on passive defenses. There was a high-powered rifle in a compartment behind the seat, to be used in case Anubis tried to ignore his conditioning and run *away* from the hypersonic beacon. There was also a pistol in a holster between the seats, for special emergencies. It was this weapon Mitford instinctively touched when Anubis appeared at the end of the block.

The Loner stood still for a moment, then moved toward the van as smoothly as a shadow on oil.

"Look," Pendergast said excitedly, "he's *fed*." Ever since Mitford had opened the back door of the van and released the Loner fifteen minutes ago, the doc had been squirming like a kid waiting for his birthday party. He'd almost jumped out of his skin when the screams had risen hollowly through the fog.

As Anubis strode under one of the few operating streetlights, his grubby derelict-style bathrobe threw off a dark, wet gleam.

"Oh, yes," Pendergast said almost reverently. "Oh, yes. Come on, Anubis."

"How do you know who he killed?" Mitford asked.

"I *don't* know who. *Who* is irrelevant. If you're interested, we'll find out later on the news."

"As long as the victim was part of the Great Evil, right?"

"Loners have no taste for anything else. They only eat the monkeys we feed them because they *have* to. Okay, get ready to open the door."

As Anubis passed in front of the van, he seemed to stare in at Mitford briefly, even though the glass was mirrorized on the outside. Mitford automatically flicked off the pistol's safety switch. Anubis smiled slightly, only inches away. The expression was similar to a human's, but of course that was an illusion. There was blood on his teeth.

Mitford smiled right back.

A moment later, the vehicle shifted slightly on its beefed-up suspension as Anubis leaped into the rear compartment. "He's in," Pendergast said. Mitford hit the button, and the rear doors slammed shut, cutting off the homing signal.

"Okay," Pendergast said. "Let's get back to the lab."

Mitford started the engine and guided the van up the street, not too fast. Emergency pistol or no, now was not the time to get pulled over by a cop for any reason.

As they cruised through the Gaslamp Quarter, the number of people on the street increased rapidly. Even at this late hour, the crowd was a curious mix of the well-to-do and the down-and-out.

"Seven out of ten," Pendergast said suddenly.

"What?"

"Seven out of ten. When all this is over, seven out of ten of these people will be gone. Same in New York, Tokyo, Paris, Bangkok . . . the whole world."

Mitford smiled wryly. He had to agree that at least seven out of ten human beings deserved to die, but it was ironic to hear Pendergast say it. Despite the number of people the doc had ordered him to kill over the years—"obstacles," he called them—and the obviously homicidal intent of *Enkidu*, Pendergast had always struck Mitford as an over-the-hill flower child. Once, Pendergast had actually forbidden him to kill a mouse he'd caught in Ginnunga Gap. "Set it free," Pendergast had said. "What did it ever do to you?"

"What did these people ever do to you?" Mitford asked now.

Pendergast was silent for a moment, and Mitford glanced at him. The excited glow emanating from the doc's face had nothing to do with flowers or love. "Nothing personal," Pendergast said. "But that's entirely beside the point."

When the girl stumbled against Tony on the way out of the bar, he was pretty sure it wasn't just a ploy to get closer. She was drunk. Really drunk. He hoped not *too* drunk. Her minidress left no room for doubt about the authenticity of her body.

"Where do you live?" he asked.

"La *Mesa*," she cried, too loudly. Her eyes were squinty with booze.

La Mesa. Now came the logistical problems. She shouldn't drive—she was so far over the blood alcohol limit she'd be lucky to get her key in the ignition— but leaving either car in the Gaslamp overnight was asking for tr—

The whooping of a siren made him jump back. He stepped on the girl's foot; she cried out and stumbled, and they both almost fell. Another siren arose, then another. A cruiser roared past, lights strobing luridly in the fog. Everyone on the streets turned to watch. A second cruiser passed, and a third. Sirens filled the gray night. Jesus, it sounded like there were a million cop cars out there, converging nearby. Something big was happening in the Gaslamp tonight. Tony thought of Chatherton, sitting on his butt out at Rancho Vista del Oro. How upset he'd be to miss out.

The girl weaved, clutched his arm. Blinked. "Come on," she said. "Gotta get on . . . out."

Tony looked at her, then in the direction of the gathering sirens. Chatherton would be able to tell him tomorrow what this was all about. Or maybe he could tell *Chatherton*. "Let's go check this out first," he said suddenly.

"Huh?" The girl made a sick face. "How come?"

"I just want to see. It sounds like it's close by. Come on."

She seemed to think about it, or try to. "Okay."

They joined the surge of people moving toward the sirens.

In Ginnunga Gap, Pendergast and Mitford watched the news on the big control room monitor. Pendergast was recording all the local broadcasts, but Mitford noticed that he had elected to watch a station where the anchorperson was a woman. She had big distracting earrings in her big distracting ears. "About ninety minutes ago," she said in her intense newscaster's voice, "one of the most shocking murders in San Diego history took place downtown in the Gaslamp District. For a live report, we take you to Todd Jefferson. Todd?"

Dark, foggy streets appeared on the screen. In the foreground stood a reporter holding a microphone; in the background, a tall building lit shimmering silver white by police klieg lights. There was a stripe of darker color on the wall, an irregular streak of what might have been rust, but wasn't.

Mitford and Pendergast glanced at one another. The doc's eyes were twinkling.

"Joyce," Todd said, "this scene is reminiscent of the nights in Victorian London when a man named Jack the Ripper roamed the streets. The information we have right now is that a man named William L. Jeffers, his wife and daughter, vacationing here from Montana, got lost in this neighborhood and were approached by two unidentified men, apparently muggers. But, according to the statement Mr. Jeffers gave police, a third man suddenly appeared, attacking and killing the first two. He then hauled one man's body up the side of the building behind me." He gestured at the red stripe.

Joyce's voice: "Any idea how he climbed that wall, Todd?"

"The police are not speculating about that at this time. But they have revealed that a body was discovered on top of the building, badly mutilated."

The rest of the report was basically a rehash, backed up by footage of policemen leaning over the parapet of the building, and of the members of the Jeffers family being loaded into ambulances. Their expressions were drawn and distant, like those of air-raid survivors.

"So what do you think?" Pendergast asked when it was over. His eyes were practically on fire now.

"One thing—how come the witnesses never said anything about Anubis? You know, what he looked like, exactly what he *did*. I thought you *wanted* people to be freaked out by that."

"I'm sure the police are withholding those details," Pendergast said. "Or, think about this from the witnesses' point of view. Would you tell the police you'd just seen a man turn into a monster and kill somebody?"

Mitford smiled slightly. "Good point."

"Don't worry, after a few more deaths of this type, people will start to talk about what they've seen. But by then, it will be too late."

Mitford glanced at the holding cell monitors. Anubis, dressed in a fresh smock, had been returned to his, and stood there staring at a sitcom, "Married With Children." "I have a question," Mitford said. "After the Loners have killed the designated number of people, what's going to make them stop? Especially since there will be so many by then . . ."

"There won't be that many. A Loner's reproductive rate is genetically linked to its activity level. So when there're fewer prey, there will be fewer Loners, and they're territorial and solitary, mixing only to mate.

You know that. There will ultimately be a balanced ratio of about one Loner for every two thousand humans."

"So you're saying there will *always* be Loners, even after they've accomplished their mission?"

"Their mission will never really be 'accomplished'; a balance is what we're looking for."

"How were Anubis's readouts?"

"I'm still checking them against the projected norms, but so far, so good. We should be ready to test another Loner by Monday."

"And will you be coming along this time?"

"No, this time I'll stay here and monitor the news."

Mitford smiled inside. Good. "Where do you want me to go?"

"La Jolla."

"La—you're kidding."

"Of course not. We need to know how Loners respond to all kinds of environments."

Mitford thought about it. La Jolla was considered the Riviera of San Diego, a far cry from the Gaslamp Quarter. "Exactly how do the Loners decide who to attack, anyway?" he asked.

Pendergast gave him a puzzled look. "Exactly how do you decide whether to eat cauliflower or steak?"

Mitford sighed. Why couldn't the doc ever give him a straight answer? Seven out of ten people—the Great Evil—were supposed to die before *Enkidu* was over. But *which* seven? Muggers obviously qualified, and finding a mugger in the Gaslamp Quarter at night couldn't have been too tough. But in La Jolla . . . How could a Loner sniff out an embezzler or a tax evader?

Well, fuck it. The doc must have known what he was doing. Besides, if the constituency of the Great Evil didn't include a few lawyers and bankers, then something was missing from Pendergast's definition of evil. "Which Loner will I be taking?"

The doc's eyes roamed the monitors. "Sekhmet. Start piping PBS and symphony music into her cell now, and make sure you drop appropriate clothes in before Monday night."

Mitford nodded, but with less enthusiasm than he'd felt a moment ago. Although it was true that the female Loners were equipped with exactly the same physical weapons as the males, still . . . they were, after all, distilled from *human* women. Women . . .

Talk about unpredictability.

* * *

After the security monitors indicated that Mitford had retired to his private suite, Pendergast went for a walk through the silent corridors of Ginnunga Gap. Beneath one arm he carried a large, leather-bound book.

Twenty years ago, the underground complex had been dug out of the side of the ridge by an entrepreneur named Delaney Hartzog, who had intended it to be the La Costa of survivalist camps. Back then it had been called Hiber Nation, and was capable of housing over 100 people for two years in great comfort, safe from radioactive inconvenience. The living quarters were cozily furnished, the recreation facilities extensive, and the kitchens equipped to do much more than warm up C rations. Interest had initially been strong.

But during the 1970s, when no nuclear war was forthcoming, subscriptions for suites had dropped off until the project became a target for creditors rather than Soviet missiles. In 1977, Delaney Hartzog shot himself with an Army-issue Colt .45. Pendergast eventually bought the abandoned complex, along with the surrounding two hundred acres of scrub land, from the executors—under a false name, of course. By then *Enkidu* had reached the stage where absolute secrecy was as critical as additional space.

After he was sure the existence of the complex had faded from public interest, Pendergast had begun the long, difficult task of converting Hiber Nation to its new purpose. It had required the installation of state-of-the-art surgeries, laboratories, training enclosures. Not much of the equipment was available at the local medical supply house, and most of it had required professional installation. Unfortunately, the technicians could not be allowed to spread word about the mysterious lab in the high desert. There was only one way to ensure their silence. Luckily, Pendergast had Ira Mitford.

As soon as the new facilities were operational, Pendergast had re-christened the complex Ginnunga Gap.

Now, as he walked down the silent main corridor of the science wing, he remembered how cramped his facilities at Tortoise Mountain had been. Worse, how exposed they had been to encroaching homeowners. Flushed with nostalgia, he peeked into each room as he passed.

First came the microbiology lab, which, with its Petri dishes, retorts, flasks and test tubes, at first glance looked like something from a science-fiction movie, circa 1956. These humble tools were used now, as in the past, to grow and nurture living cells. Along the back wall were three kinds of microscopes—standard binocular, electron and fluorescing—for the purpose of observing the development of those cells. An X-ray machine, gamma-ray generator, ultraviolet light source and micro-laser were all used to break apart DNA molecules or to alter them; a variety of enzymes, alkylating agents and acids were also used for this purpose. A door led to a liquid-nitrogen freezer where a variety of tissue samples were stored for future use or experimentation. In the freezer were containers of Alpha Loner DNA, awaiting further work should it prove necessary.

Pendergast hoped it would not. In fact, although most of his work had taken place in this very room, he hoped the equipment would never have to be used again. He hoped the Alphas would continue to test well, and could be set free without further modification. Backing into the hall, he closed the door behind him.

The next room was the dispensary and surgery. Here, human eggs containing transplanted Loner DNA had been artificially implanted in the uteri of breeder women, where they had developed in the normal manner for three months. That was the gestation period for a Loner, but of course not for a human being, and the results for the poor breeders had been quite painful. Here, too, autopsies had been performed on failed proto-Loners. Hope and despair—the two sides of the coin of progress.

Next came the incubation chambers, where the breeder women had been maintained during their brief, explosive pregnancies. How strange it was to have those rooms silent now, not echoing with sobs and prayers in Spanish.

The next room had always been silent, or nearly so, even though in a very real sense it contained the beating heart—or, more properly, the central nervous system—of *Enkidu*. It wasn't much to look at—a small chamber containing nothing but a metal box the size of an air-conditioning unit, and a pedestal supporting a high-resolution plasma monitor and a keyboard. The only sound was a soft, almost imperceptible hum coming from the box. Anyone who kept an aquarium might have found that sound reminiscent of a filter-pump, and they would not have been far wrong.

If this machine had been available to the world at large, it would have changed *everything*.

Pendergast stood there staring at the humming box and thinking about Charles Carlton.

Actually, it was ironic. Thirty-three years ago, George Irving Pendergast had not had much interest in genetics. He had been a twenty-three-year-old *enfant terrible* in neurosurgery, a genius with a microscope and scalpel. Then he had met Charles Carlton, molecular biologist and a pioneer in the use of that then-exotic tool, the digital computer, for purposes of diagnosis and research.

Carlton had not been able to fathom Pendergast's lack of excitement about the structure and function of the elegant double-helix molecule, deoxyribonucleic acid, that defines what we call "life." "Controlling DNA would make half of what you do unnecessary," Carlton had pointed out.

"No doubt," Pendergast had said, "but nobody knows how the tiniest section of DNA actually works, never mind how to use it."

"That's just a matter of time," Carlton said with utter confidence. "Computers will make the difference."

Pendergast had snorted into his coffee.

"Look," Carlton said. "You're thinking of this all wrong. Don't think of a gene as a *thing*, as a section of a chromosome. It's not a piece of chromosome any more than a voice on audiotape is actually part of the tape. It's just *information*, stored away in code."

"So?" Pendergast said. He knew that, of course. He was a *doctor*.

"So the code is binary. Every cell contains *all* the information needed to create and operate the organism—it's just that some of the genes are turned on, and some are turned off, depending on what's needed. Binary, like in a computer. You watch—one of these days, we'll be able to program biochemical information just like we program computers."

Pendergast, who had always seen living creatures as something far grander than mere wads of digital coding, had nevertheless had to admit that from a practical standpoint, Carlton's revelation was intriguing. Back then, *Enkidu* had not even been an issue—medicine had been all that mattered. Imagine . . . if you could break the genetic structure of a deadly virus or an inherited disease down into a series of "ons" and "offs," and then learn how to recode them to some new, harmless description . . .

The problem, as he had already pointed out, was that no one understood the details of how a DNA molecule was put together, far less how it worked. Geneticists did most of their studies on the relatively simple

DNA found in bacteria such as *E. coli*, but even that was overwhelmingly complex. Human DNA, with over one hundred thousand components and what seemed an infinite number of interrelationships, looked as insoluble as the Gordian knot, at least in this century.

But Pendergast, cutting into human brains every day, began to wonder if there weren't a way to change that. Neurons were marvelously efficient processors of information. Far better than computers.

Months later, when he approached Carlton with his new idea, Carlton had scoffed. At first. But after Pendergast showed him the results of his preliminary experiments, Carlton had grown very interested indeed.

The concept was simple: build a computer around biological, rather than mechanical or electronic, processors. Carbon rather than silicon. There were many problems to surmount, of course, the first of which was simply getting neurons to grow and survive in laboratory conditions, far less to accumulate on electrically conductive surfaces. It required nearly a decade of experimentation before, in the early 1960s, the two scientists successfully produced their first "neurochip." Composed of simplified bipolar neurons bonded to a conductive surface, the chip was capable of passing impulses from point A to point B in a predictable manner.

After that, things went quickly. Neurochips could literally be *grown* in nutrient solutions, then wired together. The way the chips stored and passed electrical impulses was determined by their DNA—in other words, their basic programming was engineered, at the molecular level, by Carlton. Once connected, these preliminary chips formed the "brain" of the computer—the world's first and only carbon-based digital processor.

Although rudimentary in comparison with a human brain, that was all right; after all, this processor didn't have to concern itself with moving an unwieldy body from place to place, or finding food, or reproducing. All it had to do was pass electrical impulses from place to place, switching its DNA from "on" to "off" in predictable ways. And this it did. At amazing speed.

With the processor in place, other neurochips were banked together to form memory and storage regions, and all of it was tied together into an integrated bundle—a genuine computer. Carlton dubbed it the Carlton-Pendergast Neuroprocessor, or CPN. Once online, its development proceeded at an astonishing rate, especially by the standards of the day. The computer couldn't think, but it could learn, and correlate information almost instantly. In a matter of months, with Carlton's guidance, the CPN was actually describing the best way to *improve itself*.

By 1963, it was time to program the computer for its primary purpose: analyzing the human DNA molecule.

The process was simple in concept: tell the CPN what the DNA molecule was like, and what a human being was like, and ask it to determine how one was related to the other. In practice, of course, it was terribly complex. First, a sample of Pendergast's blood was fractionated to separate out the white blood cells, which contain nuclei and, therefore, chromosomes—which in turn house DNA. Once the DNA was isolated and chemically broken into various base pairs, the scientists had chains of amino acids that they could measure. Then it was a matter of translating this information into binary code and feeding it into the computer, which required thousands of billions of bytes of storage space, all of it useless from a practical standpoint. It was like having an entire library of books written in an unknown language.

Next, a morphological and psychological profile of Pendergast was compiled. He was poked, prodded and sampled in virtually every manner known to mankind—from minute blood and tissue chemistries to the Minnesota Multiphasic Personality Inventory. This data was also translated into binary code and fed into the computer, resulting in a sort of digital "profile" of Pendergast.

Finally, the few DNA bases that had already been defined by science were described to the CPN, so it would have some understanding of how these bases related to specific traits.

Then Pendergast and Carlton just stood back while the CPN compared the rest of Pendergast's DNA, a base at a time, with the model of Pendergast himself, and attempted to track cause and effect.

Despite the incredible speed of the CPN, the scientists realized this was going to take a long time, so they reserved a portion of the computer's processing capacity to perform work of more immediate usefulness: making money. Quitting their jobs, they formed BioEdge Corporation, through which they developed pharmacological products designed with the help of the CPN.

Eventually, they knew, they would have to reveal the existence of the biocomputer to the world at large, but first they wanted to accomplish some real good for mankind. "You know what the military will do once it gets its hands on this technology," Carlton had pointed out. "We ought to counteract as much of that in advance as we can."

The good of mankind. It was wonderful, exhilarating. In their lifetimes, Pendergast and Carlton could expect to see the end of hereditary diseases and birth defects, infertility, and many forms of mental and emotional instability. And that was just the beginning. There was no end to the possibilities.

All because of the two of *them*.

Pendergast, intrigued with the possible long-term effects of the CPN's existence, had eventually programmed the computer to make a projection, based upon all the information he could feed it, about what the world would be like in the future now that the CPN existed. The result had driven him back in his chair.

Next, he had asked for a prediction based upon a world where the CPN had never been unveiled—and was horrified to find that the results had improved only along the chronological axis: if mankind wasn't given the biocomputer, then the coming disaster would not occur for perhaps one hundred years rather than fifty or sixty.

The CPN had identified the Great Evil.

Except that that wasn't quite true. It had only made the nature and reality of the Great Evil impossible to ignore.

That was why Pendergast was so surprised by the reaction of Charles Carlton, the most analytical and logical of men, to the news. Carlton had laughed. "It's just a *prediction*, George, based on today's information. Digital astrology. It doesn't take into account all the progress science and society will make tomorrow. Don't worry about it; we're here to *save* the world, remember?"

But Carlton had to be wrong. Now that the CPN had pointed it out, the Great Evil was so clear that Pendergast was embarrassed he'd never acknowledged it before. And try as he might, he could find no way around its reality.

Well, one way. But it seemed so . . . *wrong*. Pendergast was a *doctor*.

This was a dilemma that had no solution in the cult of twentieth-century science or medicine. Nor in the Christianity Pendergast had been taught. So he had studied elsewhere and, to his surprise and relief, discovered that ancient people had viewed people and their position in life very differently. With new perspective, he realized that his peers were nothing but priests of the twentieth-century religion of science—

and, like the clergy of any faith, they considered their activities divine, inviolate. Geneticists were the worst of the lot, psychopathic children playing with the building blocks of life.

For an ethical human being, recognition of evil mandates action. Pendergast felt he had no options now, and no help. Hooking the computer into the data-processing network evolving across the country, he had begun to search for a new partner, someone to help him fulfill the unavoidable plan that was growing in his mind. Eventually, with the unwitting help of a new FBI computer system called VICAP, designed to track repeat or "serial" killers, he had located Ira Mitford.

About a month later, Charles Carlton had had a tragic accident. And after that, only one person on earth knew about the nature and capabilities of the CPN. He dubbed it the Ark of the Covenant.

Although the Ark's "autonomic nervous system," the DNA-level programming that operated the system itself, had been engineered by Carlton, Pendergast knew how to write memory-resident programs. Following Carlton's death, Pendergast went to work on the program that was used to analyze DNA. He was no longer interested in isolating the genes that determined handedness or the ability to roll the tongue. He didn't care if he ever knew how to produce an organism with perfect pitch, or a talent for composing *haiku*. He wanted to make a Loner.

And he wanted to do it *now*. The world needed this project. The world needed *Enkidu*, and the sooner, the better.

With the Ark at his disposal, designing a Loner was actually fairly simple. He already had the necessary genetic profile of a human stored in the computer; now all he had to do was add the hypothetical description of a *Loner* to the soup and let the Ark determine how Loner and human DNA should differ.

The next step was vastly more difficult: he had to find or create the necessary DNA bases, and be sure they worked together as a fully functioning DNA molecule.

Again the Ark had helped, determining what nonhuman organisms contained DNA fragments of useful shape and structure, which could then be "spliced" into human DNA, or what techniques would work best to mutate normal DNA in the necessary way.

It was Carlton's dream of "digital biology" come true. But as Pendergast quickly discovered, the difference between designing a Loner in the computer and actually creating one was like the difference between reading the plans for an airplane model and ending up with a 1/32 scale

F—14 sitting on your desk. For the next five years, in his lab at Tortoise Mountain, he struggled to make genes from species as alien as *Carcharodon carcharius*, the Great White Shark, fit together with those of *Homo sapiens*. The result was a number of chimeras, bizarre hybrid creatures that were good lessons but nothing like what he wanted.

Finally, he decided he was rushing things too much—he had been too quick to stop the CPN from generating the entire human genone map. He was trying to build his F-14 from plans that lacked crucial diagrams.

But when he went back to the Ark and tried to restart the original DNA sequencing program, something went wrong. Part of the computer's exquisite brain simply died.

Pendergast still wasn't sure what happened. Perhaps the lygase solution, the DNA "food" in which the neurochips were constantly bathed, had become contaminated. Or perhaps a micropulse of electricity had swept through the system. It could even have been something Pendergast did incorrectly in writing his program. Carlton could have figured it out, but Carlton was gone, and now, so was about half the Ark's processing capability. Which meant that mapping the entire human DNA molecule would take forever.

The world didn't have forever.

Pendergast considered attempting to repair the damage. He could grow new neurochips, of course—but he wasn't sure he could program them so that they'd work with the main processor and the rest of the chips. At the very least, *that* would take forever, too.

For a while he'd lost himself in despair. Perhaps the religious fanatics were right—perhaps there *were* some things human beings—even *moral* human beings—weren't meant to know.

But this slump hadn't lasted long. All Pendergast had to do was watch the daily news to see that the Ark's dire predictions were, one by one, coming true. Someone had to reverse these trends. And Pendergast knew he was the only one who could do it before it was too late.

Luckily, the rest of the Ark's brain continued to function as before. Pendergast moved the CPN to Ginnunga Gap and installed the finest labs he could afford. There, he continued to try and match the digital dream of a Loner with physical reality.

And he failed.

And he failed.

And he failed.

But then Vulcan was born.

And from that moment, the treacherous, winding road Pendergast had been inching along turned into a superhighway. With Vulcan's DNA as a model from which to learn, all flaws were quickly identified, traced, corrected. And just over five months ago, eighteen brand-new organisms had burst into the world, beautiful, perfect—and fertile. Alphas.

The foundation, Pendergast hoped, of a new world.

Now, heart beating with joy, Pendergast closed the door on the Ark of the Covenant and moved on.

The next chamber was the menagerie, which had once housed a variety of experimental animals. Now it was home only for large monkeys, which Mitford waggishly called "Loner Chow." Pendergast stopped here briefly before continuing on, a sagging canvas bag slung over his shoulder.

At the end of the hall was a heavy door marked AUTHORIZED PERSONNEL ONLY. Pulling it open, Pendergast entered a long, narrow corridor with walls and floor of unpainted concrete. The air was dank and chilly; widely-spaced bulbs provided wan yellow light. Here and there, patches of mold darkened the walls like shadows cast by nothing.

At the far end of the corridor stood another door, this one equipped with three deadbolts. Before opening them, Pendergast took a deep breath and thumbed a switch on the wall. Instantly, he was plunged into darkness as total as that in an undersea cave. Although he had done this every day since last May, something about it still moved him. "Yea," he whispered, "for though I walk through the valley of the shadow of death, I shall fear no evil."

Turning the locks, he pulled the door open, stepped through into equal darkness, and let the door close behind him. There was no sound.

He shuffled forward, arms outstretched. Although he knew exactly the dimensions of this room, he always felt certain he was about to step off the edge of an abyss . . .

But, of course, his hands found the row of steel bars instead. Letting out his breath, he shuffled sideways to a folding chair and sat, placing the bag he'd brought from the menagerie at his feet and the leather-bound book in his lap. Then he felt around under the chair for the special goggles and infrared flashlight he kept there. It was no good using Starlight scopes or other light-augmenting gear in this room; there was nothing to amplify.

Pulling the goggles over his eyes, he waited a moment, listening.

From below came a coarse purring sound that made him shiver, as it always did.

He took a deep breath, to calm himself, then switched on the torch. The beam, visible only through the goggles, flashed over the bars in front of him. They were each an inch and a half thick and eight feet long, socketed into concrete at top and bottom. To one side was a gate with a massive lock. Beyond the bars lay a pit fifteen feet deep and ten feet across. All its surfaces were made of cured concrete, so hard and smooth it gleamed like ice.

Pendergast had discovered this chamber when he and Mitford made their initial inspection of the complex fifteen years ago. He remembered how Mitford had gazed at the bars and pit and the only way up—a retractable rope ladder—then said drily, "Looks like Delaney wasn't just worried about the bad guys on the *outside*, huh?"

Pendergast had shrugged. "A prison cell is of no use to us," he'd said, and closed the door on this place. Forever, he'd thought at the time.

But times change. Last May, late at night, he'd unlocked the door again.

Leaning forward, he aimed the infrared beam into the pit—and jolted automatically back in his seat as a mass of teeth rocketed up at him, yawning wide. A moment later the teeth slammed together several feet away with the blistering *crack!* of steel plates slamming together. Curved claws shrieked against the wall, receding fast. There was a thud. "Keepsssss on tickin'," a voice grunted.

Peering breathlessly down through the goggles, Pendergast met the stare of black, deadly eyes. He shivered. Even Loners couldn't see in total darkness, but they had a sense of smell as sharp as a bloodhound's, and hearing acuity that extended well above and below the range perceptible to humans. Pendergast's presence was known.

Of course, that was only natural. Exactly what he'd intended, expected. *Created.*

Skin still tingling, he smiled. "Good evening, Vulcan," he said. "Are you ready for tonight's story?"

CHAPTER FIVE

WHEN DEBORAH WAS SUMMONED to Andrews's office right after lunch on Monday, she felt her stomach knot around its contents of egg salad and apple. Great timing. Probably they taught that kind of thing at business school.

Andrews's office was located at the west end of the Carlton Center's administrative wing. A glass wall offered a splendid view of the government-protected land between here and the lip of the famous Torrey Pines cliffs, where the continental United States dropped an abrupt two hundred feet to a narrow beach and the Pacific Ocean.

The interior of Andrews's office was decorated in a style Deborah thought of as Big-Man Blah, with textured wallpaper on two walls and paneling on the third. The paneled wall was almost obscured by commemorative plaques and framed photos of Andrews shaking hands with everybody from Ann Jillian to Carl Sagan. Ted called it "The Wall That Ego Built."

Andrews's desk swept through most of the available space like a rosewood aircraft carrier, its glossy top meticulously neat at all times. It was far more tidy than Andrews himself. His tailored suits couldn't disguise the sagging of his belly or distract from the eternal cowlick that rose like a miniature tornado from the back of his head, nor could they eliminate the stains on his tie collected from countless business lunches at the finest restaurants in La Jolla.

Still, the man had a kind of loud authority, and absolutely unshakable self-assurance. When he spoke at board meetings, he was listened to. Even, Deborah suspected, when he had nothing to say.

But he had plenty to say now.

He'd already finished the part about how the Carlton Center was the backbone of MedSpec Corporation, that without the research division, the company would quickly "go back to filling bottles with pills." He'd also finished the part about how everyone working at the Center had to pull together, act as a team. Now he was working on the part about how when one person failed to do that, the whole team suffered, the division suffered, MedSpec Corporation suffered.

Deborah's attention wandered; after almost six months of dreading this moment, Andrews's speech seemed nearly anticlimactic. But she knew that to appear impatient would be a mistake, so she gazed fixedly at the Wall That Ego Built as if feeling chastised. Actually, she was trying to identify all the people in Andrews's photo collection. One was Dr. Charles Carlton himself as he'd appeared in the 1960s; a youngish man wearing a white lab coat and black horn-rimmed glasses. The dates of his birth and death were inscribed across the bottom. He had been only fifty-one years old when he had driven his car off the cliff, not far from here. Reportedly, his blood alcohol level had been .20, double the current legal limit.

Beneath Carlton's portrait hung those of other scientists who had come and gone from the Center over the years, although one man was notable for his absence: Dr. Pendergast.

No, wait, there was a single picture of him, although he was not the primary subject. The photo was an old one of the lab wing, taken back when the building had just been completed and was nestled in a barren landscape still crowded with construction equipment. In the foreground, Pendergast and Carlton strode along side by side, deep in conversation, gesturing intently. The photo was obviously informal; as Deborah looked more closely, she was especially amused by one of the many construction workers in the background. He was a young blond man sitting in a truck and gazing at the scientists with an aura of boredom that suggested he'd rather be out surfing.

There was a date on this photo, too, and it gave her a chill—the very same day Carlton had died.

She gazed at the young Pendergast, his beard much less gray than it was now, his shoulders less rounded, and felt another involuntary chill. When that photo had been taken, Pendergast was walking with a ghost, and didn't even know it. God, it must have come as a shock to discover that his partner had died in such a dismal—

"—Kosarek?"

She started. "Oh. I'm . . . sorry, I—uh—didn't hear that last part."

Andrews rolled his eyes. "Why do I get the feeling you never hear *anything* I say, Ms. Kosarek?"

She turned her gaze to the floor.

"I'll be honest," Andrews went on, perching like a gargoyle on the corner of his desk. "You're not due for a performance review for a couple of months yet, but if you were, I don't think it would be a good one. It's not that you're a poor worker; you're not. It's just that your skills . . . frankly, I've tried on several occasions to convey to the home office that they need a person with more . . . technical expertise . . . to work in your position. I think you're better qualified for general typing or clerical duties."

Deborah said nothing, clamping a lid on a volcano of anger. *Be a secretary, lady.* That's what he was telling her, the pear-shaped bastard. But they both knew the home office felt that putting a scientist in her position would serve no purpose at all; they *wanted* someone with no science background, who would have to ask the kinds of questions that would turn a phrase like ". . . ckDm103B is annealed with *eco*RI-cleaved pB7, a repeating unit from a tandem array of type I sequences sub-cloned into pBR322 . . ." into something a medical news reporter or sales rep could comprehend.

"I understand," she said.

"Do you?" He raised his bulk from behind the desk and loomed over her. Intimidation 101, she thought with another spurt of anger, and suddenly visualized him slipping and falling chest-first onto the note-spike on his desk. Which was probably exactly what Ted thought whenever he came in here . . . A dangerous flurry of giggles bubbled behind her clamped jaws.

Andrews said, "NIMROD is the most significant discovery to ever come out of the Carlton Center. *The most significant.* It will make MedSpec the greatest biomedical company in the world *if* we develop it as a coup, but of course other firms are working on similar ideas. But thanks to your . . . because of what happened last year on the computer, we're already way behind schedule. And now, as you know, it looks as if Dr. Pendergast has gotten involved in some other project." Andrews's lip curled. "He's . . . impulsive that way."

"What do you mean, 'gotten involved in some other project?' " Deborah asked.

"Exactly that. But now that he's extended his sabbatical, there's no telling when he'll get back to NIMROD."

Deborah had to look down.

Andrews went on, "I'm sure you'll understand that we can't risk a repeat of the mistake you made last December, which is why I'm considering bringing in another technical writer to . . . be your backup. Someone more familiar with computers, at least. We'll see."

Deborah clenched her teeth hard, so hard they squeaked in their sockets, but said nothing. She knew what he was doing: taking advantage of Dr. Pendergast's absence to try to push her out.

Andrews returned to his chair, sat, picked up a copy of the professional journal *Cell*. As if he understood the things. "You may go," he said, not looking at her.

As soon as Deborah reached her cubicle, she sat down and typed her thoughts on her keyboard:

BASTARDSONOFABITCHASSHOLESCUMBAGFUCKHEAD!!!

That made her feel as if she could function again, at least.

Erasing the entry, she called up the NIMROD text. There it was, just waiting for new input. She simply couldn't believe—

"Did you hear about the murder last night?" a voice said in her ear. "The Cannibal murder?"

The computer emitted a loud beep as Deborah's fingers jumped. For a moment she sat silently, eyes closed, lips compressed. Then she looked up. "Ted . . ."

Today he was wearing a T-shirt inscribed *Toxic Waste Is Your Friend*. "Just thought I'd mention it," he said, "so your meeting with Andrews would seem less obnoxious."

She let her breath out slowly. "You don't have to do me any favors. *Really*."

"A cannibal, though. Did you hear about it?"

"The police deny the victim was eaten."

"The police are killjoys. Listen: First Richard Andrews gets appointed to manage the Carlton Center, and now muggers are dining on their victims. These are sure signs of the decline of the western world, I tell you."

To her amazement, she was smiling. Then it faded. "Closer than you think," she said.

"It was that bad?"

"About what I expected—I basically got a lecture on incompetence."

"From an expert, though." Ted sat on her desk. His too-green eyes were intense. "It's not *fair*. None of this is your fault. You didn't have a decent backup tape in the first place. And Pendergast—"

"Andrews thinks Dr. Pendergast might have given up NIMROD completely to work on something else."

Ted stared in amazement. "Well, I guess I was wrong about Pendergast before. It seems he has more important things to do than save the world."

"Guess what?" Tony handed Chatherton a cold can of Coke. "I was downtown Saturday night—in the Gaslamp Quarter."

"You son of a bitch." Chatherton took a swig of soda and sighed in relief. The very air seemed to sizzle on Oro Vista Way this afternoon; every few minutes, a dust devil groaned into life in Phase II and pulled a brown necktie of dirt into the sky. "Don't tell me—you witnessed the murder, caught the perp and got a medal from the mayor."

Tony laughed. "You forgot to mention the contract I signed for a Movie of the Week." Actually, he had wandered up and down the barrier tape for an hour, peering at the activity on the other side. Somewhere along the line, he had lost track of the girl he'd intended to go home with. Probably she'd grabbed a cab—or another bystander. He hadn't minded that much.

"And while you were down there with the action," Chatherton grunted, "where was I? Sitting here on my ass, making sure nobody stole a hummingbird feeder." His face grew introspective. "See anything interesting?"

"Not really. Blood on the wall, bodies under blankets. What have you heard at the station?"

"Actually, it's pretty weird. You know how it usually is when there's a murder like this, all the scuttlebutt flying . . . but this time, zilch. Even the pathologists have been quiet, and they usually can't wait to make jokes."

"Have the victims been identified yet?"

"Oh, yeah—that was on the news. They were real scumbags, all right. Both with long priors for assault and drugs."

Tony leaned against the barricade. "What about all this cannibal stuff?"

Chatherton's face twisted. "Witnesses," he said. "Especially hysterical Midwestern female witnesses."

"Nothing to it, huh?"

"Oh, no! No, I'm sure somebody really did come along and bite off one guy's hand, and the top of the other guy's *head*. Happens every day."

Tony laughed again. In Phase II, another dust devil formed, its shape defined by the grit and papers it whisked into the sky.

"I'll say one thing, though," Chatherton muttered. "If there *were* a cannibal running around in San Diego, I'd personally invite him over to my ex-wives' houses for dinner."

The beam of the infrared light moved down the page. ". . . And the Lord was sorry that He had made man on the earth, and He was grieved in His heart. And the Lord said, 'I will blot out man whom I have created . . .' "

Closing the Bible, Pendergast sighed. "It's interesting. This book is the basis of Western civilization, you know, the very heart of it. And yet it says God was ready to exterminate mankind by Chapter Six. Why do you suppose that was?"

From the encompassing darkness, no response.

"It was because of sin. Remember the Garden of Eden? The Bible claims humans were tempted by forbidden knowledge, and so lost paradise. After that, things just got worse and worse until Noah's time, when God got so sick of his greatest creation that He decided to eradicate it. But *did* He? No. He sent a Flood, just like in *The Epic of Gilgamesh*— remember that? But just like in *Gilgamesh*, He made sure there would be survivors. And after the waters receded, what did He tell Noah's children? The same thing He had told Adam and Eve: 'Be fruitful and multiply, and fill the earth, and subdue it; and rule over the fish of the sea and over the birds of the sky, and over every living thing that moves on the earth . . .'

"In other words, according to the Bible, God made the same mistake twice in a row." He sighed. "Is it any wonder our civilization has taken this as a license to do *anything*?"

There was still no answer. And there never would be, of course.

That was essential, if rather sad. Pendergast aimed the infrared beam into the pit and played it over Vulcan, who stood in the far corner. The Loner hadn't moved an inch since Pendergast arrived.

Interesting. Only tonight, after six months, had Vulcan finally stopped trying to attack him when he entered the room. Of course Loners were designed to learn from their failures but still, it must be terribly frustrating to have a specimen of your favorite prey so close, and not be able to reach it.

Pendergast closed the Bible. "I can't stay long tonight," he said. "Mitford's on his way to town with Sekhmet; I have to go watch the news in case something happens."

But he didn't leave. This experience, visiting Vulcan in the flesh, was always the high point of his day. Talking to this being of his own creation, discussing things of importance—philosophy, history, current events. Of course he knew the Loner didn't understand a word, *couldn't*, any more than he had comprehended the actual meaning of the commercials and television programs that had been piped into his holding cell, but still . . .

Pendergast found it cathartic to share his thoughts with someone. Mitford was out of the question. Mitford didn't even try to understand. Just as he wouldn't understand *this*.

Pendergast hadn't been able to exterminate Vulcan. It was as simple as that. He'd staged the funeral for Mitford's benefit, and still pretended to visit the grave now and then. He acknowledged that keeping an obsolete Loner alive was unprofessional, even sentimental, but in this case he just couldn't seem to help it. Hideous or not, Vulcan was the father of an entire species of life. And Pendergast knew he'd never get to be so close to a Loner again.

Besides, it wasn't as if visiting Vulcan in this cell, contaminating the Loner with his presence, would hurt *Enkidu*. It would never do to imprint one of the Alphas, but Vulcan would never be free. Besides, he only had a few weeks left to live in his accelerated Loner life. Loners were like rockets—designed to live hot, brief spans. That could even be why Vulcan had suddenly stopped trying to attack him—geriatric debilitation. Pendergast hoped not.

"Vulcan," he said softly, "sometimes I wish you could talk to me. Or at least *understand* me."

The Loner blinked. Despite the fact that he couldn't see anything in the total blackness, he was staring right at Pendergast. Looking back into those eyes, Pendergast felt his own breath grow short, as if he were falling into hollow depths. There was no mercy in those eyes, no affection. Predator's eyes.

So beautiful.

"But if you could understand," Pendergast went on, "you wouldn't be what I made you, would you?"

Vulcan's response was a chilling, spiky yawn as his Loner face moved to the surface. Pendergast knew that this signified only hunger, not mirth, certainly not comprehension.

But . . . there was one more thing he had to try.

Stuffing the goggles and flashlight back under the chair, he got up and groped his way to the wall, where his fingers closed on a knob. His heartbeat thudded in his ears. "Let there be light," he murmured, and turned the knob slowly . . . slowly . . .

In the ceiling, a battery of bulbs began to glow. At first the light was almost nothing, a dream; then vague shapes became visible: the gleaming metal bars, the folding chair, the walls of the pit itself—and, finally, Vulcan.

For the first time, Pendergast and the Loner looked at one another eye to eye. Vulcan did not move as Pendergast returned to his chair, although it seemed that the hungry emptiness in the Loner's eyes became deeper than ever.

"Vulcan," Pendergast said softly. He had chosen that name with great care. "Vulcan" was the more palatable Roman rendering of the Greek name Hephaestus. In Greek mythology, Vulcan had been conceived spontaneously by the queen of heaven as a volley in a celestial spat with her husband, Zeus. But Vulcan had also been a respected member of the Olympian pantheon, the creator of armor and weapons for the other gods, even though he was imperfect—ugly and lame.

Vulcan. Pendergast rose to his feet, the Bible clutched before him. "Listen, I have to go now. But I'll be back tomorrow, and we'll talk some more. There's so much more I want to discuss with you." He hesitated, staring intently at Vulcan, feeling a knot in his throat so tight he could barely breathe. "See you again soon . . . son."

He turned the lights off on his way out.

The sound of Pendergast's footsteps receded from the racquetball court like the rumble of a distant thunderstorm. When it had ceased entirely,

Vulcan crossed the pit in three long strides and launched himself upward, reaching high with his extended talons. He grabbed two bars and pulled himself up, put his nose between the bars, inhaled deeply.

"Fatherrrrrr," he said in his rough, rippling voice, and jerked on one of the bars.

It popped cleanly out of its sockets, as it had done many times before. Vulcan slipped through the gap.

Mitford drove the van slowly down the hill into La Jolla. He was sneering. He hated this place. In his opinion La Jollans were hoity-toity snotheads, every year talking about splitting their community off from the rest of San Diego. After all, they said, La Jolla was geographically isolated, nestled along an indent in the coastline and cupped by steep ridges inland. The community boasted its own art museum, theaters, hotels, chamber orchestra, downtown district.

But Mitford knew the La Jolla attitude really sprang from one thing: wealth. The per-capita income of La Jollans, many of whom had titles such as "M.D." and "J.D." after their names, was significantly higher than that of the average San Diegan. A high percentage of La Jollans owned cars that were originally designed with the steering wheel on the right-hand side.

Maybe snobbery was one of the sins Pendergast wanted to eradicate.

Mitford debated. Even La Jolla had its better neighborhoods, and of course the finest of these clustered around the waterfront, as if they'd risen from the glittery waves. Since money feeds crime, Mitford drove in that direction. Soon the houses around him were built mostly of glass to absorb as much of the magnificent view of the Pacific as possible. The streets were picturesquely serpentine, conforming to the coastline. Joggers and strolling couples wandered about until well after dark. They felt secure. They were, after all, La Jollans.

Finally Mitford parked on a steep bit of road where the van would be hidden from both the houses above and the Cove below. The Cove was a public park, where people were inclined to wander at all hours of the day and night. High traffic also meant better chances for crime. Which meant better chances for a Loner kill.

And, perhaps, the chance for Mitford to witness the action. It would be very interesting to see just how a Loner did its work out here in the real world.

He turned and looked into the rear of the van. Behind the protective barrier sat Sekhmet, folded into the typical Loner's sitting position, legs crossed, head low, like a coiled rattler. It was remarkable how compact these creatures could make themselves. She wore a chic trench coat from Saks Fifth Avenue—of course, it wasn't designed for the kind of rain it would hopefully get tonight.

Good luck, babe, Mitford thought, and reached for the door-release button.

But before he touched it, he heard a faint sound outside and drew back quickly. A woman and a dog were walking briskly down the hill. He sighed—no Great Evil here. The woman looked about as threatening as his granny—sixty years old at least, bent and scrawny in her jogging suit. Then he perked up a bit. The dog, a huge Rottweiler, might prove interesting. When it passed the van, would its superior senses detect the presence of a Loner?

Just in case, Mitford pulled the emergency pistol from between the seats.

The woman and dog passed the van at a vigorous pace. Mitford watched them closely . . . it seemed the Rottweiler hesitated for an instant. But maybe not.

As the pair continued down the hill, Mitford put the pistol away, mildly disappointed. Evidently the doc had planned for dogs, too.

Mitford waited until they'd disappeared around a corner by the Cove, then waited a little longer. If the woman happened to witness Sekhmet's forthcoming kill, she might make a connection between that and the van. Only after the street had been clear for five unbroken minutes did Mitford push the door-release button.

Sekhmet launched herself into the street in a swirl of hair and coat, reappeared briefly a hundred feet down the hill, disappeared again. Mitford smiled. Sure enough, she was moving toward the Cove.

"Munch down, baby," he said, and settled back to wait.

Time passed, filled with the soft thunder of the surf. Overhead, the lights of a Navy plane strobed their way out to sea. A nice, peaceful night in nice, peaceful La Jolla.

He looked at his watch. Twenty minutes. Damn. See, Doc? It had taken Anubis only *fifteen* minutes to find his victim, make the kill, eat and return . . .

If there was no proper prey here for Sekhmet, how long would she continue to search? And how *evil* did a person have to be to attract attention, anyway?

Twenty-five minutes.

Was the beacon working? Mitford checked the indicator light, saw the reassuring glow. But what if Sekhmet had traveled beyond its range in search of prey? Oh, Christ, that would be cute.

In the sky, another set of lights blinked out to sea. Now there was a thought, Mitford mused. Set a Loner free in the Pentagon, or maybe Ghadaffi's stupid tent . . . It was bound to happen eventually, anyway, if Pendergast was right about the seven-out-of-ten. How could a Loner pass up military leaders and politicians?

Come on, Sekhmet, come on.

Thirty minutes.

Mitford was about to leave the van when the Rottweiler reappeared at the bottom of the hill, its claws clattering madly on the pavement. It was alone. It sped up the street and swerved wildly around the van, but Mitford was able to see the glistening patches of wetness on its ebony fur, and the droplets spattering the pavement behind it. But the dog didn't move as if it were in pain . . .

And where was Granny?

Mitford sat back slowly. "Oops," he said.

CHAPTER SIX

DEBORAH HELD UP HER HAND. "Don't say it. I watched the news last night, and I don't want to hear anything about cannibals."

Ted grinned as he sat on her desk. "Okay. You shouldn't stay up so late, though; you look beat."

"Thanks."

"It's Andrews, isn't it? Oh, sorry, you said you didn't want to talk about cannibals."

"I'll survive Andrews."

"He'll try to by-the-book you to death, ride you until you quit. He did it with a couple of lab people already."

"I'm more stubborn than he is."

He looked at her consideringly. "Probably. But what if you never get another raise as long as you're here?"

That thumped home like an arrow. Rent on the apartment rose faster than her pay as it was. "If we could only get in touch with Dr. Pendergast," she said desperately, "I'm *sure* he'd straighten this out." She paused. "Do you know where he lives?"

"Of course. How else could I have tee-peed his house?"

"You didn't."

"Actually, no. A bunch of us got drunk one night and drove up there, but there's a big gate across the road."

Deborah blinked, surprised. This didn't sound like the intense but easy-smiling Pendergast she knew. "Where is it?"

"Uh-uh." Ted shook his head. "Strictly off-limits. And I won't help you get fired by telling you how to find it."

"But—"

"I told you the guy's a loner, Deb. Or maybe paranoid's a better word. I think he only comes around here because he needs the lab facilities sometimes."

The lab facilities . . . Suddenly something occurred to her. "Didn't you tell me he modems in to our computer here?"

"Yeah, but don't get any ideas. I also said we're not supposed to send him anything he doesn't ask for."

Deborah's gaze grew flat. "I see." And she did. Ted was even more full of hot air than she had thought. Sure, he put Pendergast down, acted all cocky . . . as long as no one important had a chance to catch him at it.

Ted was watching her face. "Oh, the hell with it," he said abruptly. "What could he complain about? We're only trying to get his own damned project finished for him, right?"

"Listen, if it bothers you, you don't have to—"

"I *want* to, all right? When do we start?"

She smiled, and the crease between her eyes disappeared. "Thanks, Ted. I owe you one."

"Damn straight. Lunch tomorrow, at the restaurant of my choice."

Her smile faded, but she thought about Andrews and her future and said, "All right."

"And if by some miracle Pendergast actually gives you the information you want, you owe me dinner at the home of *your* choice. Now, when are we going to do this?"

"When's good for you?" She wasn't smiling at all now.

"Um, right after work. Less load on the computer, less chance of anybody wondering what we're doing—and there's nothing good on TV anyway."

Her lips twitched. "Okay. Six-thirty work for you?"

"See you here," he said, jumping to his feet. "We'll use your terminal so I don't have to try to sneak you into the lab."

She nodded, and watched him hurry out of her cubicle with his usual jerky, preoccupied stride. What was she getting herself into? she wondered. She'd just submitted to *blackmail*, even.

Well, she'd committed herself. She only hoped Pendergast was as understanding as she thought he'd be.

Someone on Oro Vista Way had complained that Tony and Chatherton loitered in the cul-de-sac every day, so this afternoon Tony rode along as Chatherton drove back and forth along the terraces in the security cruiser.

"Please don't tell me you just happened to be in La Jolla last night," Chatherton said.

"Nope, missed that one."

"Whew."

"Was it the Cannibal again?"

"Well . . . I heard stories that the old lady was missing some parts, just like the muggers."

"You 'heard' that, huh?" Tony said. "I thought you said nobody was talking about this case."

Chatherton grinned. "Well, you could say I've developed an inside line down at Homicide."

"An inside line?"

"I've got an . . . acquaintance . . . in their office."

"Aha," Tony said. "What's her name?"

The grin widened. "Dina. She's a clerk. She sees and hears a lot because, of course, the detectives think she doesn't exist, and she passes the good stuff on to me. You never know; one of these days I might pull the Cannibal over for running a stoplight."

"What kind of 'stuff' is she passing on?"

"Well . . . I've got some information on the Cannibal's weapon. Dina saw some of the autopsy photos—she says the wounds looked like they were made by a shark."

"*Huh?*"

"Their shape. You know, smooth, crescent-shaped. And whatever this weapon is, it's powerful enough to chop clear through bone."

"So that part's *true?*"

"Evidently. Homicide's trying to keep it quiet, of course, but Dina thinks the cops on the street ought to be told about it, so they don't get—shit, look up ahead."

Tony turned his attention to the road, and saw a boy of perhaps fourteen speeding away from them down the middle of the lane on a skateboard.

"Pull up beside him," Tony said wearily, rolling down his window.

Chatherton complied, but the kid didn't look over until Tony cried, "Hey!" Then the kid's face twisted into a disgusted oh-why-me grimace. But he didn't slow down.

"Hey," Tony said again. "You know skateboarding isn't allowed inside the complex."

The kid glanced over again and seemed about to say something smart-ass, then abruptly tromped on the back of his board and jolted to a stop, allowing the cruiser to shoot ahead. Tony looked back as the kid flicked the board up with the arch of his foot, catching it neatly. Then he just stood there in the middle of the street.

"You know he'll be back on that thing the minute we turn the corner," Chatherton said.

"I know."

"Kids."

"Good thing you never had any of your own," Tony said, grinning.

"I didn't," Chatherton sighed. "My wives did."

"Okay." Ted dropped into Deborah's chair and cracked his knuckles like a virtuoso pianist about to perform Tchaikovsky. "Here goes."

Deborah pulled an extra chair in from Winnie's cubicle, and sat down. Around them, the admin wing was silent except for the blended purr of the air conditioner and her computer. Everyone except the janitors had gone home for the day.

Deborah watched Ted's face as he logged onto the computer. He looked different, somehow, and after a moment she realized what it was: Here, behind the keyboard, his hyperkinetic jerkiness of movement had ceased. This was his element.

"Okay," he said, half to himself, fingers blurring. "This part's easy; I just hook into the right sector of the mainframe and call up the modem . . ." His voice faded to a mutter. Deborah watched in fascination as the characters danced across the screen. Not long ago, she reflected, a scientist like Ted probably wouldn't even have been able to type.

"Here we are," Ted said after half a minute. "Now comes the fun part."

Deborah focused on the screen again. It said:

ENTER PASSWORD SEQUENCE.

"Password?" Deborah said, alarmed.

"Don't worry." Ted smiled. "I've got a little code-breaker program I wrote a while back; part of it is designed to find passwords. I call it

'007.' " He typed for a moment, and the terminal played a few notes of James Bond theme music. Then the screen flooded with words that hurtled past too quickly to be read. Pointing at them, Ted said, "Most password breakers work by alphabetically sorting and testing a list of words. That can take forever. But I figured people can't resist letting their egos pick their passwords for them, so 007 starts off with some word or phrase I *know* is significant, and sorts from there in descending order of association. For example, if I wanted to break Andrews's personal password, I'd start with "Asshole" and go from—ah, here we are." The screen was flashing a message:

> MY NAME IS BOND. JAMES BOND. YOUR PASSWORD IS:
> *PROMETHEUS*

"Well," Ted said, "it's Greek to me."

"Prometheus gave man fire," Deborah said, recalling details from her World Mythology class. "He also made people walk upright like the gods . . . which he got punished for."

"Pendergast is a weirdo," Ted said, and exited back to the modem menu. He typed in the password and some numbers Deborah couldn't follow, then said, "Well, here goes." His finger fell on the ENTER key.

The computer responded: CONNECTING . . .

Mitford stretched, luxuriating in the warmth of the sun. He was convinced that prolonged exposure to air-conditioning sapped the soul. The problem was, the atmosphere above Ginnunga Gap was awful today. There had been mild westerly breezes for the past several weeks, and the Laguna Mountains to the east trapped all of San Diego's exhaust gasses right above this area. Where were the Santa Ana winds that usually blew out of the desert in the fall? They'd push this rancid air out of here.

He smiled slightly. Pendergast would no doubt say air pollution would cease being a problem after seven out of ten cars stop running due to lack of drivers. Unfortunately, after what had happened in La Jolla last night, *Enkidu*'s success rate was only fifty percent. Not so good. Mitford was surprised at the depth of his disappointment.

Fucking Sekhmet. Fucking *woman*. They were all the same, screwing you over; you had to . . .

Taking as deep a breath as he could stand, he set off down a narrow trail through the chaparral. He liked to come up here from time to time to check out the security devices, even though the computer was supposed to monitor everything. Electronics, he knew very well, could be tricked or bypassed.

On the other hand, even if an intruder were somehow able to penetrate to this point without detection, all he would find was what appeared to be a long-abandoned homestead. Pendergast's personal residence was actually on the surface, but from the outside it looked like a crumbling, stucco-and-concrete wreck all but buried in manzanita bushes and sagebrush. Its eastern facade overhung an almost sheer drop into the valley below.

But the exterior of the building was a fake. Behind the facade were polished oak and tinted glass, hand-made tile and exotic fabrics; very civilized and pleasant. On the canyon side were broad windows. An elevator hidden behind the fireplace provided direct access to the labs in Ginnunga Gap.

Mitford found it ironic that the doc refused to dwell underground, not even in one of the elite suites like the one Mitford used. "I don't want to feel like I'm hiding from the world," he'd said. But of course he spent most of his time in the control room anyway, forty feet down, monitoring the Alphas.

Mitford looked around. There were three surface structures besides the house. Two of them were mere aluminum sheds, one containing common items of hardware such as axes and rakes, the other empty. Or *supposedly* empty. Actually, in the months since last May, Mitford had drilled a tunnel up into it from a storeroom below, and filled it with items that might come in handy in the post-*Enkidu* world. Preparing.

The last man-made feature on the surface was the skylight over the underground garage. It was hidden from all but low-level aerial view by boulders, cacti and bushes. The skylight was not original equipment, of course; Mitford had insisted upon its installation because he hated building explosive devices in anything other than bright, natural light. The bombs were never large ones—just crackers for severing brake lines or loosening a stair step at the proper moment—but they could still take a finger off if you screwed up.

Speaking of screwing up . . . Mitford thought again about Sunday's Loner test. That harmless old lady . . . and yet Pendergast hadn't seemed upset about what had happened. In fact, while watching the news broadcast on TV, he'd actually laughed. "Look at the police running around," he'd said. "I can hardly wait to hear tomorrow's pack of lies."

"So you're *satisfied* with the test?" Mitford had asked in surprise.

"Of course. This will be national news by morning."

"That's important?"

"Naturally. In time, the Loners are going to change the way *everybody* thinks and acts. The sooner that process gets started, the better."

"But an old lady walking her dog . . . that's your idea of *Great Evil?*"

Pendergast had looked at him with a puzzled expression on his face and said, "Human beings are complex creatures. Deciding who is evil and who isn't isn't my job . . . it's God's."

"But the Loners . . ."

"They understand only one evil."

There it was, the segue into philosophical bullshit. What "one evil" could a couple of dope-head muggers in downtown San Diego have in common with an old lady walking her dog in La Jolla? What qualities made them all part of the hated seven-tenths? Never mind, let the doc worry about that.

"So we'll be going ahead with the next test?" Mitford asked.

"Tomorrow night."

Mitford smiled. "Which Loner?"

"Loki. We'll see how he does in El Cajon."

Mitford nodded. El Cajon was a bedroom community east of San Diego—not the best locale for lowlifes, but it beat the hell out of La Jolla.

Even better, Loki was one of the most active Loners; he often danced around his cubicle as if showering in the video barrage. You never knew, in El Cajon he might draw enough attention to himself that Mitford would have to take action of his own.

Mitford was bending over a motion sensor hidden in a manzanita bush when his communicator beeped. Pendergast calling. But Mitford didn't respond right away. No point in being *too* compliant—that was something else he'd learned in the SEALS, shortly before slitting his C.O.'s throat and watching the body sink, unnoticed, to the floor of the Pacific.

Only after a second beep did he raise the communicator to his lips. "Yes?"

"Come to the control center right away."

Catching the urgency in Pendergast's voice, Mitford wasted no more time.

When he stepped into the control room, he saw Pendergast sitting at the table, staring at a monitor. "What's up?"

Pendergast simply pointed at the screen; computer codes scrolled down it.

Mitford shrugged. "That gobbledegook doesn't mean anything to me, you know that."

"Someone at the Carlton Center is accessing my computer terminal at Tortoise Mountain," Pendergast said.

Mitford lowered himself into a chair. "Do you know who it is?"

Pendergast suddenly began chewing his moustache, a mannerism Mitford hadn't observed since the early days of *Enkidu*, when there had been a seemingly endless series of proto-Loner stillbirths.

"Deborah Kosarek," the doc said.

"Why, that cagey devil," Ted said.

"What?" Deborah asked nervously.

"Pendergast is using a cut-out computer."

"What does that mean?"

"Well, we're connected to a computer now, but from what I can see, everything on it's dated. I'm betting it's a blind to fool people; somewhere is *another* computer that's connected to this one, and that's the one with all the good stuff on it. Lots of white-collar criminals do this to hide from the authorities." He sat back, smiling smugly. "I told you Pendergast was paranoid."

"But that doesn't matter to us, does it?" Deborah asked. "I mean, can't we just leave our message right here?"

Ted sat forward again, and his fingers flickered over the keys. "We could, if that's what we intended to do."

"What do you mean?"

"We're not going to leave a message. We're going to hunt down NIMROD ourselves."

"Hunt—but you can't do that! We—"

"Listen. If we just leave a message, Pendergast will obviously know we connected, and he might get pissed off. But if we can get to his *real* system, you'll get your information without him even knowing we were there."

She threw her hands around. "That doesn't make any sense! How am I supposed to explain writing text with data I'm not even supposed to *have*?"

"Come on, Deborah. You go ahead and write the text, then later, when you *officially* get the information, you already have a big jump. Andrews will think you're a miracle worker."

She hesitated. She knew Ted was mostly interested in proving to himself—maybe her, too—that he could outsmart Dr. Pendergast. But he had a point. If she only had that data . . . "You're sure Dr. Pendergast won't know we're doing this?"

"There's no security system 007 can't find a way around. Don't worry. We're fine."

Deborah said nothing, but her fingernails found their way into her mouth.

Ted typed again, and the James Bond theme replayed. More typing. Several minutes later, Ted grinned. "I knew it; there it is. Okay, we're connecting with the other system right now. This should be great."

"You're *sure* Dr. Pendergast won't be able to tell?"

"Relax! Okay, here we are. Wow—I don't recognize this format at all. Wait. Okay. Got it. I'm searching for the directory that shows the most frequent use. That would be a logical place to—here it is." He pointed at a word on the screen: ENKIDU. "Whatever the hell that means."

Deborah frowned. "It sounds familiar."

"No matter," Ted said. "We'll just take a peek inside there." Tinted eyes bright, he began typing again.

"Deborah Kosarek?" Mitford said. He began sorting through his mental file of people associated with Pendergast. He had memorized many of the files the doc kept on people who worked in the biotech field, or who lived or worked near Ginnunga Gap or Tortoise Mountain. In a way, he collected this information the way Pendergast collected genetic material, and for pretty much the same reason—you never knew when you might need it for something.

Pendergast said, "The input is coming from her terminal, yes, but I don't believe she's the one doing it. This is a pretty sophisticated program."

"Can't you just cut them off?"

"Of course. But first I want to see how far they can go."

* * *

"Okay," Ted said, "here comes the connection. Piece of cake. Pendergast will never—"

A series of sharp beeps cut him off, and words flashed on the screen:

WARNING—ACCESS DENIED—STANDBY

Then the screen went blank.

"Shit," said Ted, sitting back hard.

"What?"

"It burned us."

"What does that mean?"

He looked at her, his face suddenly pale. "It means 007 got his fingers caught in the cookie jar. I don't know how—"

"Oh, my God. You said this couldn't happen!"

He tried to smile, said nothing.

"Did—can someone identify who accessed it?"

"If the computer ran a trace on us first, it'll know what terminal was used to access it, yeah."

"Mine," Deborah said sickly.

"Yeah. But it also knows whose password was used to get onto the mainframe. *Mine*. Shit, I should have used Andrews's instead."

"Oh, my God, Ted. Now what?"

Ted's face was pearly white. "Well, what do you think about running off to Tahiti together?"

"They reached the Ark," Pendergast said, eyes widening. "I can't believe it."

"Now what?"

"Nothing; the Ark automatically shut them out. But they *reached* it."

Wonderful warmth swept through Mitford. *Infiltration*. Successful or not, it still meant retaliation would be necessary, which meant action for *him*. Real action. It was one thing to drive Loners to test sites, it was quite another to get his own hands wet.

Even better, he now remembered who Deborah Kosarek was: a technical writer at the Carlton Center. Widowed, one child. She was also young and pretty—a combination which invariably meant slutty. Good.

Pendergast leaned forward, pushed some keys, shook his head. "It's Scully. I should have guessed."

Mitford recalled the name immediately—Theodore Scully, a Carlton Center whiz kid. He'd graduated from CalTech at the age of twenty. "But Kosarek must be involved, too, right?" Mitford said, clinging to his hope. "I mean, if this is coming in on her terminal."

Pendergast chewed his lip harder. "Probably."

"Do you want me to kill them?"

He was amused to see a little shudder run through Pendergast. Mitford had first observed that reaction on the day he'd performed his original job for the doc—eliminating Charles Carlton, who had discovered what Pendergast's research was really all about. And since then, he'd observed it each time he did the Doc's wet work. It added up to a lot of shudders.

A great guy, the doc—he'd helped Mitford out of a little mess up in Seattle long ago—but still, Pendergast was, like everybody else in the world, a hypocrite.

"No," Pendergast said, without looking away from the screen. "Nobody's to be killed over this. Deborah's no threat, and Scully's just a smartass kid. I doubt he would have understood *Enkidu* even if he'd managed to break all the way in. He was probably just playing around, showing off."

"An accident is as good as enemy action," Mitford said, quoting his SEAL demolitions instructor. "Are you sure you want to take a chance? You didn't with Arcadio."

"Arcadio was different. We *knew* he was a threat . . . and we also knew we could erase him without drawing attention to ourselves. No, I'll just change the access paths and—" Pendergast suddenly sat back. "Oh, wait a minute."

"What?"

"I think I know what's happening. I should have thought . . . Deborah was working on a project I left in a mess at the Carlton Center. That's probably what she's trying to contact me about. That would explain everything."

"You're sure?" Mitford asked, hiding his disappointment.

"I'll find out tomorrow." Pendergast's relief was palpable.

"And meanwhile we're just going to wait?"

"Until I'm *sure* what's happening, yes," Pendergast said sharply. "Especially until I know if anyone else was involved."

"But what about the next field test?"

"We'll put it off a day or two, until I talk to Andrews and make sure we don't have this problem again."

For a white-hot moment, Mitford wanted to pull his pistol and empty it into Pendergast's head. *Wait a day or two? You got my hopes up! Got my hopes up for nothing!*

But then the thought slipped away. This was his bread and butter here. More than that. His destiny and the doc's had been joined since the day Pendergast showed up at Mitford's motel room and said, "FBI agents are on their way here right now to arrest you. But I can make you disappear forever . . ."

Pendergast was watching him. "There *is* something you can do for me in the meantime, though," the doc said.

Mitford waited.

"There are still some chimera samples back in the vault at Tortoise Mountain. I think they'd be safer out here."

Mitford scowled. He hated—

"I know it's grunt work, but I'll tell you what. Take your time, spend a couple of nights up there. Do . . . whatever. Just be back by dark, the day after tomorrow. And, Mr. Mitford . . . make sure you clean up after yourself."

Mitford looked at him sharply. Did the doc know about how he spent his time off? If so, he didn't seem to mind. And Mitford had to admit, there was some appeal to the idea of spending a night at the old Tortoise Mountain place. The party potential there was considerable . . .

Before he started any R & R, though, there was something he must take care of. Pendergast seemed to have a soft spot for Deborah Kosarek. But Mitford didn't. No woman could be trusted, not for a minute. So tomorrow, Mitford decided, he'd do a little snooping. You never knew what you might learn that way.

"All right," he said. "I'll go."

CHAPTER SEVEN

EACH TIME RICHARD ANDREWS HALTED in front of the glass wall in his office and clasped his hands behind his back, his lumpy silhouette reminded Deborah of the Michelin Man. And that cowlick . . . but today she felt no urge to laugh.

"It's inexcusable," Andrews said, staring out at the stunted Torrey pines that dotted the edge of the cliff. "What the hell did you think you were doing?"

Deborah exchanged glances with Ted, whose manner was decidedly less sardonic than usual. In his jeans and T-shirt, hands folded on his lap, he looked like a grade-schooler called to the principal's office. He obviously wasn't going to chip in, so Deborah said, "I just wanted to finish NIMROD, that's all."

Andrews whirled. "You used the Carlton Center computer without authorization—and used it to break into a *private* system, to boot. Dr. Pendergast was *very* upset."

"It just . . . seemed like the only way."

"The only way." Andrews puffed up, then whirled on Ted. "And you, Mr. Scully. You should know better than this."

"I was helping the lady," Ted said faintly, without lifting his head. Andrews hovered over him for a moment like the blade of a guillotine, and suddenly Deborah understood something: Dr. Pendergast must have lashed out at Andrews for keeping sensitive information like private modem codes on the main computer, where any Brat-Packer could access them. But at the same time, Andrews must have been forbidden to fire anybody; otherwise, pink slips would have been waiting in Deborah's and Ted's mailboxes this morning.

That made her think of something else, and she cleared her throat. "Mr. Andrews—how did Dr. Pendergast contact you about this?"

Andrews bristled. "Why do you ask?"

"Well . . . all I wanted to do was get in touch with him. If he has a phone—"

"For your information," Andrews said stiffly, "Dr. Pendergast does not permit outside calls to his home. He called *me* to report what happened and to ask for an explanation. You may or may not have your jobs this afternoon after he calls back. That's up to him, unfortunately. Now, tell me, Mrs. Kosarek—do you think you've helped anyone with this little shenanigan?"

This time she had to look away, and once again her eyes sought the old photo of Dr. Pendergast and Dr. Carlton. But she focused on the young man sitting in the truck. The surfer. Be like him, she thought. Removed, laid back, even slightly amused, if you can manage that.

Difficult.

Andrews strode behind his desk and leaned over it. "You might have been trying to erase your previous error by doing this," he said, "but two wrongs don't make a right. I'm sure Dr. Pendergast will agree."

Be like the surfer. Be like the surfer.

"Please return to your cubicle," Andrews said after a moment. "I'd like to speak with Mr. Scully alone now."

Ted didn't meet Deborah's eyes as she walked past him.

Twenty minutes later, a meek voice said, "Guess our lunch date's off, huh?"

Deborah looked up at Ted. Said nothing.

"Andrews told me that no matter what Pendergast says this afternoon—in other words, even if we get to keep our jobs—you and I aren't supposed to 'fraternize' anymore."

Deborah was suddenly fighting tears of shame and rage. "I'm sorry I got you into trouble, Ted."

He sat on her desk and tried to smile, but it was a failure. "I could just walk out to keep Andrews from having the satisfaction of firing me, but . . . maybe I shouldn't have bought the sailboat so soon after the Porsche."

"I feel just awful."

"You want to make it up to me? We could still do lunch. All we have to do is meet off-campus."

She hesitated. "Seems fair," she said wanly.

He looked at her for a moment, his mouth finally quirking into the familiar smile. "Fair? For what I just went through, you should have my baby."

By the time Deborah got home that evening, she felt a hundred years old. Thanks to traffic she'd been twenty minutes late picking Virgil up from the daycare center—and then, halfway home, the poor kid had puked applesauce all over the dashboard. Alarmed, she'd touched his forehead. There was no fever, but he'd given her a pathetic, teary look as she tried to wipe his face with a wad of tissues, and she'd driven faster.

On the other hand, she still had a job. Andrews had come by her cubicle at four o'clock and said exactly that: "You still have a job." Then he'd walked away. A few minutes later, a window had opened on her monitor and these words appeared: PENDERGAST LOVES ME, THIS I KNOW, CAUSE MY PAYCHECK TELLS ME SO. TED. She'd had to struggle against guffaws of relieved laughter.

Her apartment building was on Clairemont Mesa Boulevard, a street lined with a seemingly endless chain of apartment complexes. Although she and Brad had been saving for a condo, they hadn't put nearly enough in the bank before the accident. And now, with the average price of a home in San Diego approaching a quarter of a million dollars . . .

After pulling into her parking slot, she cleaned Virgil up as best she could with his own shirt and hoisted him gingerly out of his car seat, grunting at his weight. He was going to be big, just like his father. She kissed his forehead, then lugged him past the swimming pool and up the stairs to her apartment.

When she put the key into the lock and tried to turn it, it didn't budge. It was already unlocked. The door swung open freely.

My God, had she actually left her apartment unlocked all day long?

As she entered, Virgil suddenly seemed very light in her arms. The living room was silent and hot; she always kept the air conditioning turned off during the day to save money. Standing still, she listened and looked for anything out of the ordinary. Nothing. Just the familiar furniture, the familiar prints hanging on the walls, the too-familiar silence.

Laying Virgil on the couch, she made a hurried but careful inspection of the other rooms. Everything looked exactly the same as it had when she'd left it this morning.

Relief. But also concern, and puzzlement. Sure, she'd been upset when she'd gone to work today, worried about the possible ramifications of the computer invasion—but how could she have forgotten to lock the front door?

Shaking her head, she walked back into the living room. And screamed when she saw someone bending over Virgil.

The intruder also screamed. Virgil blinked awake instantly, eyes wide, mouth stretched on the edge of a terrified wail.

The intruder put her hand on her chest and swayed as if she might fall over. "Deborah! My God, you scared the shit out of me!"

"*I* scared the shit out of *you*?"

It was her neighbor, Sarah Matthews, eyes so round her Hawaiian ancestry was wiped out entirely. Two grocery bags rested at her feet. She said, "I was just coming up and saw the door open, and I thought maybe the—"

"Thanks, Sarah. Sorry." Deborah hurried over and picked Virgil up. "Wait here, I'll be right back."

Carrying Virgil into their room, she quickly undressed him and put him in his crib. "You take a nap, honey, okay?" she said, and turned away.

"Woom," Virgil mumbled.

Deborah looked back. "Oh, I'm sorry, you want the Worm?" Bending over the crib, she rummaged through the blankets. "Hang on, he's got to be here somewhere."

But the toy wasn't there. Virgil began to cry, the special *I feel lousy* drilling wail that invariably made her want to join in.

Where the hell was that toy? Normally, Deborah left Brooke Worm in the crib except when she was changing the sheets. She searched the room quickly, sifting among the other stuffed animals, pawing through the toybox and the closet. No Brooke Worm. Meanwhile Virgil lay there crying miserably.

Come on, come on, come on, where are you?

She rushed back into the living room, where Sarah still stood near the open door. "What's the matter?" Sarah asked.

"Trying to find Virgil's favorite toy," Deborah said apologetically, checking under the cushions on the couch. "He won't go to sleep without it."

Sarah nodded understandingly. A good neighbor, even if her apartment did always smell like the inside of a bong.

Brooke Worm wasn't in the living room, either. Nor the bathroom. She even checked in the linen closet in the hall, with similar results.

Blessedly, though, Virgil's crying was beginning to fade, and when she looked into his crib, his eyes were closed. She breathed a sigh of relief.

Strange about Brooke Worm, though . . .

"Sorry about that," she said when she walked back into the living room. "Can I get you a soda or anything?"

"Thanks, but I'd better put my groceries away. I just wanted to ask if the guy got your toilet fixed this afternoon."

Deborah stopped halfway to the kitchen. "What?"

"The plumber. I thought he might still be here when I saw the door was open."

"I didn't call for a plumber. My toilet's fine."

"Oh. Well, the manager must have screwed up, then, because this plumber was in your apartment this afternoon." She smiled. "Actually, it's too bad he's gone. He was pretty good-looking. Blond, well-built . . ."

"Well, he was also an idiot," Deborah fumed. "He left my door unlocked."

"Brains or body," Sarah said philosophically, "you can't have everything."

Despite her aggravation, Deborah almost smiled. Sarah, who dated an everchanging stream of men, was always looking out for her. Unfortunately Sarah's taste ran to muscles over mind every time.

But the urge to smile faded quickly; this wasn't a laughing matter. Anyone could have walked into the unlocked apartment and removed all Deborah's worldly goods, such as they were.

Or just taken Brooke Worm.

Where had *that* thought come from?

"Sarah," she said, "would you watch Virg for a minute? I ought to go check this out at the office."

"Sure. Kick ass."

When Deborah came back ten minutes later, Sarah was watching reruns of "M*A*S*H" on television. "Well?" Sarah said.

"Mrs. Ramirez said she never had a plumber come in today."

"Seriously?"

"Seriously." Deborah lowered herself onto the sofa.

"Wow," Sarah said, eyes alight. "Do you think the guy was trying to rip you off? Maybe I scared him away."

"I don't know. Mrs. Ramirez is going to have my locks changed tomorrow just in case, and she'll post a notice in the laundry room about fake plumbers."

"Wow," Sarah said again. "What about the police? Maybe you should call the police, too."

Deborah looked at her neighbor, the only witness. Tried to envision Sarah giving a useful description of any man to the police while flirting at the same time, and had to smile a little. "Never mind. I'm sure he's long gone."

"Nothing's missing?"

"Just Virgil's stuffed toy, you know, the bookworm. You didn't see the plumber walking out with it, did you?"

Sarah grinned. "I don't know, the bulge in his pants looked a little big."

Reaction was beginning to set in, making Deborah feel almost giddy. "And you didn't ask him over to your place?" she said. "You must be slowing down."

"I'm getting picky," Sarah said. "Just like you."

"And another angel came out of the temple, crying out with a loud voice to Him who sat on the cloud, 'Put in your sickle and reap, because the hour to reap has come, because the harvest of the earth is ripe . . .' "

Pendergast looked down at Vulcan in the dim twilight of the pit. "That's from the Book of Revelation, which is supposed to prophesy the end of the world—again." He paused. "I must admit, sometimes Revelation sounds uncannily accurate. 'Put in your sickle and reap, because the harvest of the earth is ripe.' Sounds almost like *Enkidu*, doesn't it? You could almost believe . . ."

He let it go. Sometimes he got too carried away for his own good, he knew that.

Vulcan watched him silently from the bottom of the pit, his head working, working, as if the face underneath, the Loner face, was trying to get out.

"Oh, I've got some good news about Deborah," Pendergast said suddenly. "Remember, I was afraid she might be onto us? She wasn't. She was only worried about NIMROD after all."

Vulcan's lips curled up, down, up.

"I'm so glad," Pendergast went on earnestly. "She may not be the most brilliant woman I've ever met, but she's got some outstanding qualities. Self-reliance, for one. You know, she never bothers people with stories about her son's latest potty-training experience, which is unusual for a mother. I'm not surprised she tried to contact me; her compulsion to do things her own way is the very characteristic I've always found attractive in her." He smiled. "It should be familiar to *you*, too, Vulcan."

The Loner's head worked in and out, side to side.

"Why?" Pendergast said, as if Vulcan had spoken. "Well, because one day I went into Deborah's cubicle and found one of her hairs. Her great strength was bound up in that hair, just as Samson's was in his. In every cell of it. And now . . . that strength is part of *you*."

Vulcan moved his shoulders up and down. "Mayyyk miyyyyyy dayyy-yyy," he growled, and Pendergast started. This was the first time the Loner had ever vocalized in his presence, unless you counted hisses and grunts of rage. He smiled. Although the words had not been an attempt to *communicate* in the human sense of the word, they still represented something very special. Because in the future, whenever a human being encountered a Loner, the Loner's words would be the last thing the human ever heard.

But this situation was different, unique. Pendergast would now carry the sound of Vulcan's voice in his heart forever. He clutched the Bible. He felt . . . blessed.

Prior to last May, in the mad scramble to bring NIMROD up to date, Deborah had gotten in the habit of staying an hour or so after work, off the clock. Considering the circumstances, she had felt obligated.

But not now. At exactly four-thirty, she followed the rest of the support staff personnel out of the cubicle area, through the glitzy high-tech lobby that connected the two wings of the Carlton Center, and into the afternoon sunshine. All along the way, she looked around for Ted. He hadn't visited her cubicle all day, and she found, perversely, that she missed him. Or maybe it was just guilt.

As she turned the corner of the building, he said "Hi" in her ear, and she jumped with a little squeal.

"Jesus, Ted!" she cried. "Don't do that!"

"Sorry, but I didn't want to take a chance on Andrews seeing us *consorting*." His earring, a small diamond stud today, flashed like a miniature sun as he walked backward beside her. "I'm here to arrange my payment."

"What?"

"You agreed to have lunch with me one of these days, remember? Well, the day is this coming Monday. At noon."

"But—"

"Don't worry, it'll all be hush-hush; we'll even take separate cars to the restaurant. Come on, I'm buying."

She had to smile. "Okay, it's a deal. Where?"

"The Pearblossom in La Jolla."

"The Pearblossom? That's awfully expensive, isn't it, Ted?"

"I don't know, I've never been there before. It's not just a lunch, it's an adventure. See you Monday!" He ran off toward the professional staff's parking lot, leaving Deborah to continue on her own, shaking her head in bemusement.

But almost immediately her thoughts returned to Dr. Pendergast. No matter what anybody said, it just wasn't like him to abandon a project in the middle this way. Least of all NIMROD, a possible cure for mankind's greatest nemesis, cancer. What could be more important than that?

On the other hand, what made her think she knew Dr. Pendergast so well? After all, except for matters of grammar and syntax, they'd really only spoken together a few times.

But she remembered one of those occasions with the clarity of the ocean air. About six months after Brad died, Dr. Pendergast had taken her aside on the cafeteria patio, with the wind rushing through the nearby Torrey pines and stirring napkins on the table. He had asked her about Virgil, less than four months old then, and she had found herself telling him *everything*. Not only about Virgil, but about Brad, too. In those black days, the two had seemed inextricably bound together in her mind, as if her husband might have been reincarnated in the tiny bundle of her son . . . or she hoped he had.

Brad had been a rookie firefighter with the county, stationed near Alpine, a small town east of San Diego. Deborah had found it difficult enough not to see him for days on end as he worked his tour at the station. But even worse, when he got home she had to make herself smile as she listened to his breathless descriptions of orange flames leaping forty feet into the air, and climbing steep hills with smoke billowing all around, and running hose in remote locations where the heat of the sun alone was enough to make half the firefighters pass out. But he had gloried in these stories, his hands sketching spray patterns and smoke clouds in the air of their apartment, and so she had listened and smiled.

But one day, as he was carrying a hose up the side of a ridge, his foothold crumbled beneath him. And he slid down, down into the belly of a brushfire where no one could reach him. Deborah still dreamt about screams she'd never actually heard . . .

Dr. Pendergast, after listening silently to this story, had fixed his ice-colored eyes on hers and said, "You realize he died because he was true to his purpose. That's a rare quality these days. You should be proud."

Proud. Proud that her husband had burned to death on a godforsaken hillside, leaving her alone with an unborn son? And "true to his purpose"? Wasn't the real purpose of any husband to come home at the end of the day, hold his wife in his arms, and make love to her? The purpose of any father to be around as a role model to his child?

Only later did she realize that Dr. Pendergast had been correct where all the other sympathizers, including Brad's own parents and the County of San Diego, had been wrong. Brad hadn't died because he was a hero, but because he was Brad.

This was what she would tell Virgil when he was old enough to understand: *Your father is dead because the most important thing is to be true to yourself.*

And then she'd add, *Don't ever become a firefighter.*

Dr. Pendergast had understood all that. But even more importantly, he had taken the trouble to express it to her, and that was not the behavior of the selfish, unpredictable monster her coworkers believed him to be. So, yes, maybe she *did* know Dr. Pendergast better than anyone else. And it was impossible to believe such a caring man would abandon his work on cancer for *any* reason.

Her rickety car was parked at the back of the employees' lot. As she made her way to it, a flock of hang gliders swept over the edge of the Torrey Pines cliff like particolor pterodactyls, banking on the wind.

Their silent beauty held her gaze until she was almost at her parking space. Then she looked down and blinked in puzzlement. Something was sitting on the hood of her car.

Her eyes widened.

It was Brooke Worm.

She stared dumbly at the toy, for a moment actually wondering if she'd left it there herself, while all around her, engines started, horns beeped farewells, cars scurried to the exit. She was barely aware of them.

Finally she picked Brooke Worm up. Its head dropped off and swung by a thread. The edges of the cut were perfectly smooth, not torn or frayed—the fabric had been sliced with something very sharp.

Deborah lowered herself slowly onto the hood of the car. What was this all about? Two days ago her apartment had been broken into, and the only thing removed was this toy. Now it had turned up again . . . placed on her car with its throat slit like a butchered rabbit's. Why?

She could only think of one reason, even if it made no real sense: Somebody was trying to frighten her. Letting her know that he was cruel, and he knew where she lived, and where she worked . . . and that she had a small, vulnerable child.

The shakes caught her by such surprise that she had to drop Brooke Worm and brace herself to keep from sliding off the car.

Virgil . . .

Suddenly her strength returned and she ran back to the Carlton Center. The guard in the lobby looked at her curiously as she sprinted past him toward the administrative offices, but she didn't stop. A moment later she was in her cubicle, dialing the phone.

"New Horizons Child Care," a weary voice said over a cacophony of squeals and chattering.

Suddenly Deborah found she could hardly speak. "T-Terri? This is Deborah Kosarek. Is . . . how's Virgil?"

"Fine." Terri sounded a little surprised. "He's playing with Devon Roget right now. What's up?"

Deborah slumped heavily into her chair, shaking violently again. "Nothing. I'll be there to pick him up in a few minutes." She hesitated, then blurted, "Don't let anyone else get him, though."

"Not even your parents?"

She meant Deborah's in-laws. "No, of course, they're okay," Deborah said. "Just . . . not anyone else. Okay?"

"You know our policy, Ms. Kosarek. No pickups without prior authorization by the parents."

"I know. Thank you, Terri." Deborah hung up, still slightly shaky, but feeling mostly stupid now. You see? Virgil's fine. No one is out to get him, no one is out to get *you* . . .

Except there was still the matter of Brooke Worm. She looked at the toy, its head dangling, and shivered again. Just because Virgil was safe *now*, that didn't mean he would stay that way. Warnings are about things that *could* happen.

Still, the big question remained: Why would anyone want to threaten her? And *who* would? Some random psycho? She certainly couldn't think of anything she'd done that would merit—

"You used the Carlton Center computer without authorization—and used it to break into a private system, to boot."

She sat as still as a fossil, staring at her reflection in the dark screen of her computer monitor. Come on, Deborah, come on. Do you really think *Andrews* is involved in this?

No, of course not. He was a tyrant, but this sort of sickness required a darker nature. Still . . . she turned toward Brooke Worm, which sat bleeding stuffing on the desk. Here was a fact: The toy had been stolen the day after Deborah and Ted crashed Dr. Pendergast's computer.

Connection or not?

If you eliminated Andrews as a suspect, who was left? Dr. Pendergast himself? Ridiculous—it was *impossible* to imagine a man like him being involved in a threat on a child's life. For *any* reason.

Unless . . .

Unless he wasn't *willingly* involved.

No one had seen Dr. Pendergast in the flesh for nearly a year—and in all that time, he hadn't sent in a single bit of data on NIMROD. Nothing. Everyone, Deborah included, had assumed that was his choice. But what if it *wasn't*? What if Dr. Pendergast was being *kept* out of communication?

Andrews's words again: "NIMROD *is the most significant discovery ever to come out of the Carlton Center* . . ."

In the biotech industry, "significant" meant "profitable." And if the NIMROD process worked, it would be profitable to the point of disbelief. Incentive for criminals? Obviously.

Listen to yourself! Deborah thought, and shook her head wryly. What is this, a spy movie or reality? Andrews had spoken to Dr. Pendergast on the phone only yesterday.

Of course, Dr. Pendergast could have been saying what he had been *told* to say . . .

Jesus, Deborah! Do you really need excitement in your life this badly?

As she stood up and stuffed Brooke Worm into her purse, she suddenly found herself thinking about the handful of men she had dated since Brad's death. A stockbroker, a dentist, a lawyer . . . who else? Oh, yes, another lawyer. She had never gone out with any of the men twice, never wanted to. And now, for the first time, she realized what they had all had in common: They found their thrills in libraries and X-rays, ledgers and computer printouts. Day by day, the biggest physical risk any of them ever faced was crossing the street at lunchtime.

God, they were boring.

She wondered what Brad would do if he were here now. No, she knew. He'd find out for sure if Dr. Pendergast was safe. Charge up that blazing slope . . .

Well, she wasn't Brad. She was a single mother with a job as dull and safe as those of the men she had dated—a job she needed, by the way, and which was on the verge of being taken away from her.

So. So she was being silly, that was all. She'd just fetch Virgil and go home. End of argument.

Instead, she lifted the receiver again and dialed. "Hi, Mom," she said. "Do you think you could pick Virgil up from daycare for me? I've got something I need to take care of."

"Sorry I couldn't get here earlier, Vulcan," Pendergast said, turning up the lights in the jail chamber. "You must be hungry." He dropped the canvas bag into the chute, but when it slid through the hatch below, Vulcan didn't respond at all. Pendergast's heart sank. A bad sign . . .

Dropping into his customary seat, he held out his empty hands and said, "I didn't bring my Bible with me today, either. Do you know why?"

Vulcan stared at him with eyes like holes of interstellar space.

"It's missing," Pendergast said. "Gone. And there's only one person who could have taken it." Jerking back to his feet, he began pacing, Vulcan watching unblinkingly. "I'm getting very concerned about Mitford. I've always known he's a double-Y chromosome psychopath, of course, and not really loyal—but I'd hoped he'd last a little longer. His skills have been so useful to us."

He paused. Down in the pit, Vulcan's skull changed shape from moment to moment, like a cocoon with a grown butterfly struggling inside. Pretending that this indicated interest, Pendergast went on, "I keep the Bible up in my house, you know, in my personal library. Mitford's never supposed to enter that room without me being present. But now the Bible's gone—and I think some of the other books have been disturbed, too. And I don't know why."

Vulcan's jaws extended, retracted.

Pendergast sighed, then gave a half-smile. "You're right; it's silly to be upset about something like this, isn't it? After all, if Mitford needs to read the Bible so much he'd steal mine, then he's welcome to it. It might even do him some g—"

On the floor of the pit, the canvas bag gave a sudden twitch, and a piping cry rose from it. Pendergast took two steps back. "The sedation wore off faster than I expected," he said. "I'd better get back to the control center, anyway. Things could start happening any minute. See you later, son." He hurried out the door.

There were some things he couldn't bear to watch.

In the blackness of the pit, Vulcan turned his head and listened to the canvas bag. It was rustling more energetically now.

Leaping across the room in a single bound, he landed silently beside the bag and scooped it up. Extending his jaws, he dumped the monkey in and ground it up swiftly with the overlapping plates in his palate that made speech so difficult. After swallowing, he returned to his corner and folded himself down onto the floor like a cobra in a basket.

From beneath his smock he extracted a thick leather-bound book, and a penlight. When he opened the book and turned the beam of the light on the flyleaf, HOLY BIBLE flashed in gold leaf. Below that, written elegantly in pen, was an inscription: *To George, my beloved son, on his tenth birthday. May God's Infallible Word inspire you forever.—Your Loving Mother.*

Extending a talon, Vulcan gently turned a tissue-thin page. The penlight began to move—back and forth, faster and faster.

A few minutes later, soft sounds filtered down from the observation gallery above: hissing, rustling, muttering. In the gloom, a constellation of reflected gleams winked on and off. Vulcan got to his feet, legs spread wide, and clasped the Bible in front of him. "Ourrrrrr Fatherrrrr," he droned, "who arrrrrrrrt in heaven . . ."

From the gallery came a thundering chorus: "Georrrrrrge be thy name . . ."

CHAPTER EIGHT

As Deborah drove along I–5 in the arthritic afternoon traffic, she could feel her heart beating too hard. It was hard to believe she was actually doing this.

Finding Dr. Pendergast's address hadn't been difficult. Winnie, with her paranoia of computers, had it written down in the good old-fashioned Rolodex on her desk. The address was 2770 Tortoise Mountain Road; according to Winnie's well-thumbed Thomas Brothers map, Tortoise Mountain Road was a long lane that wound through an area Deborah remembered as being open land and the occasional orchard or ranch. It shouldn't be hard to locate a particular house out there.

And then what? a voice popped up in her head. *What are you going to do, knock on the door and say, "Excuse me, Dr. Pendergast, but are you being held prisoner?"*

Probably he'd be out front mowing the lawn, wearing a pair of Bermuda shorts and grass-stained boots, and that would be that.

And if not? the voice persisted.

She squeezed her purse, felt the yielding shape of Brooke Worm inside. If not, then she *would* go up and knock on the door. It was the least she could do.

And if somebody other than Dr. Pendergast answers?

She had no answer to that; she'd just have to wing it. Perhaps, deep inside, she didn't really *expect* anyone else to answer. Otherwise she'd have brought somebody to help, just in case, right?

Finally she came to the correct exit, and followed a line of cars down the ramp and onto a street that was supposed to intersect with Tortoise Mountain Road a couple of miles to the east. To her surprise, she found herself not among orchards but housing developments. She wasn't sure how old Winnie's map was, but it certainly had little to do with the way this area looked now. To make matters worse, the street signs were small and inconspicuous—how could she be sure she wouldn't drive right past Tortoise Mountain Road?

In the end she did exactly that, and it wasn't until she'd gone almost three miles too far before she was certain of her mistake. Driving back slowly against the flow of commuter traffic, she finally spotted a discreet metal sign: TORTOISE MOUNTAIN RD.

The lane climbed gradually into the hills, which were also densely packed with large, gated homes. Looking around in amazement, Deborah wondered just how much money Dr. Pendergast earned in a year.

Suddenly the street made a hard left-hand turn. Straight ahead, a dirt lane continued straight ahead between two houses before vanishing into a wall of underbrush. Deborah slowed almost to a stop, puzzled. A dusty sign told her the dirt track was Tortoise Mountain Road, and the paved section was Rancho Real. But that was absurd; the dirt track looked like nothing more than a firebreak. Some joker must have pivoted the sign around.

Turning left, she continued along the paved road. Soon, a high stucco wall appeared on her right; beyond it were tiers of closely ranked, Spanish-style houses marching halfway up the side of a mountain. She drove past an entrance with a guard kiosk in the center. A large sign read RANCHO VISTA DEL ORO, and in smaller letters, *Security Patrolled 24 Hours a Day*.

A half-mile farther along, the pavement ended abruptly at a metal barricade. Beyond that, a maze of unfinished houses stood on bare, battered lots. The air was pungent with the scent of torn earth.

She pulled the note she'd made in Winnie's office out of her pocket and reread it; the address definitely indicated that Dr. Pendergast's house was located near the end of Tortoise Mountain Road. She glanced at the stucco wall surrounding Rancho Vista del Oro, then at the imposing but androgynous houses beyond. Somehow she'd always pictured the doctor living in a cottage on the beach or a log cabin in the mountains.

Turning the car around, she drove back to the main gate of Rancho Vista del Oro and pulled up to the guard kiosk. An elderly man in a dark green uniform leaned out and smiled. "Hello, ma'am. What can I do for you?"

"Hi. I'm looking for 2770 Tortoise Mountain Road. Is that in here?"

He frowned. "Sorry, no, Tortoise Mountain doesn't continue into the complex."

"Oh." She was crestfallen. "Well . . . what about a man named George Pendergast? Does he live here, by any chance?"

The old man's smile became noncommittal. "Sorry, ma'am, I'm not allowed to give out information about our residents."

She was already hot and frustrated, and anger suddenly rose in her with strangling strength. "You can't even tell me if he lives here?"

"Sorry. Our list is strictly confidential."

"But—but that's *stupid*!"

He shrugged, but his eyes grew sharper. "I don't make the rules, ma'am."

"But this is an emergency! If he lives here, I *have* to see him!"

"Ma'am," the guard said stiffly, "if you'd like to talk to the property management company, I've got their phone number. Otherwise, I'll have to ask you to back out and leave."

As Deborah opened her mouth to protest some more, a dirt-colored car cruised out of the development and stopped on the other side of the kiosk. The driver was a young man dressed in a uniform like that of the guard. He leaned forward and looked at her curiously through the windshield, then called to the old man, "Something wrong?"

"Nothing serious, Tony. . . This lady was just leaving."

"I'm trying to find out if a certain person lives here," Deborah blurted to the driver. "He could be in trouble. It's very important that I speak to him."

The engine of the young man's car raced as he put the transmission into park. "We're not allowed to give that information out, ma'am. Sorry."

"Look, I—"

"Ma'am, seriously," the young guard said. "You'll have to move on. You're blocking the drive."

Deborah glanced into the rear-view mirror, saw a BMW sitting close behind her. Looking desperately at the guards again, she saw identical expressions of unrelenting patience on their faces. With a snort, she jerked the Omni into reverse and managed to maneuver past the BMW. As she sped back up the road, she cursed under her breath. Idiots! What if Pendergast *was* being held prisoner behind those stucco walls? God, how frustrating to be thwarted by the very people who were supposed to keep him *safe*!

Oh, well, she'd tried. And since there was obviously nothing more she could do, she might as well just call it quits and go . . .

When she reached the place where Rancho Real became Tortoise Mountain Road again, she jerked the wheel hard to the left instead of the right, and the Omni jolted off the pavement onto the dirt firebreak. These trails were little more than rough paths made to accommodate fire-fighting vehicles, but at least this one curved back in the general direction of Rancho Vista del Oro. Deborah had already noted that the walls along the sides of the development were only four or five feet high, not impossible to climb . . .

She had to drive very slowly, partly to keep from ripping out the bottom of her car, partly to keep a plume of rising dust from giving her away. The manzanita and sagebrush that scraped the sides of her car filled the air with spicy-syrupy aromas.

Just as the slope of the mountain began to steepen appreciably, the road curved in the wrong direction. Deborah stopped. From here, it appeared that the road arced around behind the mountain, where there was no sign of housing.

Opening the door, she stood on the edge of the seat and peered over the bushes toward Rancho Vista del Oro. The southern-facing wall was only about thirty yards away—thirty yards packed with manzanita and sage. But she was as close as she could get by car.

Switching off the engine and locking the doors, she looked ruefully at her clothes, took a deep breath and pushed into the bushes.

Manzanita is a plant at once springy and unyielding, like a stuffed pincushion. As she worked her way through it, her skin felt as if it were being whisked off—but she knew that later not a mark would show. Her nylons weren't so lucky; they were already as shredded as old snake skins.

Expensive delusion you're having here, Deborah.

Finally she reached the wall, and, standing next to it, angrily tore off what was left of her nylons. Now she was hot, sweaty and itchy all over, and she peered impatiently over the wall with a distinct lack of stealth. Here was someone's back yard, a barbecue smoking pleasantly on the patio. No good. Turning her head, she saw that the next house up the hill had a flower arbor in back that almost touched the wall. She crept up to it, peeked over again. Better. From here the house was hidden by a tapestry of fragrant bougainvillaea.

After a lot of grunting and the scraping of expensive shoe leather, she managed to straddle the top of the wall. During the moment she perched there, she imagined getting caught like this—businesslike skirt hoisted around her thighs, legs sticking out like those of a gymnast going over the pommel horse, hair tangled with twigs. Then she dropped behind the arbor and brushed herself off as best she could. It would be stupid to wander this neighborhood looking like a bag lady.

Speaking of wandering the neighborhood, what did she think she was going to do now that she was in? Pendergast's address no longer existed, at least not as it was listed in the Thomas Brothers. She knew she'd recognize his car if she saw it—but of course it could be parked inside a garage. Then what? She didn't know. But she had resolved to do this, she had ruined a pair of perfectly good panty hose for it, and she *would* do it.

A peek around the arbor showed a child's swingset in the middle of the yard. No sound of children, though. The family must be out. Excellent.

Taking a deep breath, she strode across the yard with as much assurance as she could manage. There was a wood-slat fence all around it, and a gate beside the house. She opened the gate quietly and pushed through. Breathed a sigh of relief.

A tall shape stepped away from a hedge. "Hi," the young guard said.

Screw the snotnoses on Oro Vista Way, Tony thought as he escorted the sweaty, embarrassed woman to his car. Technically he was off work now, and if he felt like driving up to the cul-de-sac to talk to this woman, that was his business. With her smudged clothes and sweaty face, she certainly looked the part of a desperado. Just doing my job, boss.

The woman said nothing as they drove away from the house, but when Tony turned uphill rather than down, she cried, "Where are we going?"

"A place where we can talk. I'd like to know exactly why you tried to sneak in here."

For a moment he thought she was actually going to throw the door open and leap out. "Easy," he said.

She relaxed in stages. Hands, arms, shoulders, finally face. "I feel so stupid," she said.

Tony took another glance at her. "You must have been really desperate to try climbing that wall in those clothes," he said.

She sighed. "How did you know where I was?"

"I had a feeling you weren't going to give up, so I drove up the hill and watched you come along the dirt road."

She flushed. "I feel so stupid," she said again, more forcefully. A pause, then: "Are you going to turn me over to the police?"

He looked at her again. Despite the dirt and twigs, she was a far from painful sight. She had a good figure, and pleasant if rather pinched features—although much of that tightness could, of course, be due to the present circumstances.

"No," he said, "I'm not going to turn you in. Here we are." He stopped the car at the end of Oro Vista Way and climbed out. After a moment, she got out too.

"Quite a view, isn't it?" he asked. The sea breeze, surprisingly stiff, whipped at the hem of her skirt, and she held it down with casual skill. Tony pointed to the south. "See, there's the dirt road you were on."

"Listen," she said tensely. "If you're not going to . . . I mean, I have to pick my son up from daycare . . ."

Tony glanced at her hands. No wedding ring. Of course, a kid and no ring wasn't an uncommon combination these days; nearly all the women he'd dated since his twenty-eighth birthday had had at least one rug rat at home.

"Maybe you'd like to tell me what was so important about getting in here," he said.

From the corner of his eye, he saw her head drop slightly. "Like I said before, I have to locate someone I work with. He used to live up here somewhere, and he still might for all I know. I think he may be in trouble."

Tony looked back at her with more interest. "What kind of trouble?"

"Well . . ." Her face reddened slightly. "It sounds kind of ridiculous to say it out loud."

"Try me."

Taking a deep breath and darting him a quick sideways glance, she said, "I think somebody may be holding him hostage in his own house."

Tony kept his nod nice and even, showing neither surprise nor disparagement. "Why would anyone want to do that?"

A longer pause. Tony noticed there were spider webs from the bushes caught in her hair, and felt an urge to pluck them out. She said, "He and I both work at a biotech research lab. He's one of the senior scientists, and he's been on sabbatical for months. I'm a technical writer, and when I tried to contact him for some information, I couldn't get through—then I got the message to butt out. It didn't seem like Dr. Pendergast at all. And then . . ."

Tony raised inquiring eyebrows.

She finished in a rush: "Yesterday, someone broke into my apartment while I was at work and stole my son's favorite toy." Reaching into her purse, she fished out something that looked like a moldy bagel. Tony saw that it was a toy wormlike thing. Its head dangled by a couple of strings. Deborah went on, "I found it sitting on my car this afternoon, cut up like this."

Tony peered at the slit in the worm's throat, then looked back at Deborah with a bit more interest. Of course, the mere possession of a mutilated toy didn't prove she was telling the truth. Still . . . "What do you think it means?"

"I think it's some kind of a warning."

"About what?"

"Well, I told you Dr. Pendergast is a scientist. He's been working on some very valuable—"

"Dr. Pendergast? You mean George Pendergast?"

Her eyes widened. "Yes! You *do* know him."

"Well, I know *of* him. He's sort of our local eccentric." Tony pointed up the hillside. "He lives on top of the mountain. You say his research could be valuable?"

"Very. That's all I can say about it."

"But you think he's being held prisoner by people who want the results of his research. Right?"

"Something like that."

Tony ran a palm down his throat. "Biotech, huh? It's not like germ warfare, is it, anything like that?"

The woman looked shocked. "No! No, it's . . . beneficial."

"Hm." Tony stared up the mountainside. "We could pay him a visit, both of us. That would make it look sort of official."

"Really? You'd do that?"

"Sure. I've always wanted to drive up there, anyway." He held out his hand. "My name's Tony Garwood, by the way."

"Deborah Kosarek." They shook, sweat against sweat.

"Okay, Deborah. What do you say we drive back to your car and take it from there, since it's already blocking the road?"

"All right."

They climbed into Tony's clunker and cruised down the hill. Near the bottom they encountered Chatherton in the PSS cruiser, going the other way. Both cars stopped in the middle of the street, and Chatherton stared at Tony's passenger with raised eyebrows.

"Car trouble," Tony said. "I'm helping her out. See you tomorrow."

"Right." Chatherton winked before driving on. Tony was careful not to acknowledge that, or even glance at Deborah to see if she'd noticed.

A few minutes later they switched to Deborah's car, and she took the wheel. The road ahead followed the contours of the mountain in a generally counter-clockwise direction and the car followed it upward, bumping and rattling, followed by a lazy rocket-trail of dust. In places, the road had been partially washed out by long-ago rains, and Deborah drove around the gaps with exaggerated care. Tony noticed that the sweat appearing on her own brow outpaced his own, and wondered how much of her apprehension was due to the decaying road, and how much to the destination.

Suddenly inspired, he said, "When we get there, maybe *I* should go to the door. That way, if Pendergast's alone—you'll have to describe him to me—I can tell him I'm investigating a report of smoke or something. But if someone else answers . . ."

"Thanks, but no, I'd better go with you. Even if someone else *is* there, they'll probably make Dr. Pendergast answer the door. I know him. I'll be able to tell if something's wrong."

Tony nodded. He liked both Deborah's nerve and her profile, and he sincerely hoped she wasn't just some paranoid flake wandering around up here. But even if she was, she was the most interesting thing to have come into his life in months.

They were in the green shadows on the east side of the mountain now. Lizards scuttled out of the way, thrushes dove through the sage. The only signs of human habitation were glimpses of the housing developments beyond the surrounding hills.

"See all the undeveloped land around here?" Tony said.

Deborah, eyes locked on the road, nodded.

"It belongs to Pendergast."

"You're kidding," she said.

"Nope. Has all the developers slobbering, believe me; but he won't sell."

"I had no idea," she said. Tony couldn't tell if she was impressed by the evident wealth or disillusioned—or maybe she was too scared to be either. Then he realized, with wry amusement, that even he was finding his heartbeat rising. *Just like the good old days*, he thought. Of course, he knew that cops who died on duty usually got killed during a routine traffic stop or while breaking up a simple household dispu—

He jolted forward in his seat as Deborah thumped a foot down on the brake, and the car skidded to a dusty halt.

"Wow," Tony said. "He really *doesn't* like company, does he?"

A massive steel tube hung above the road, hinged to an upright on one side and padlocked to an upright on the other. From the center of the tube hung a sign: PRIVATE PROPERTY—NO TRESPASSING—DO NOT ENTER.

Deborah turned toward Tony. A pair of deep lines had appeared between her brows.

"Feel like taking a walk?" Tony asked.

Mitford was packing his clothes for the trip back to Ginnunga Gap when the perimeter warning buzzer blared. He ran to the small panel of security indicators near the front door of the house, and saw a flashing light that signified someone or something had broken the electric-eye beam down by the gate. That beam was elevated several feet off the ground to prevent triggering by coyotes or dogs . . . Had Pendergast decided to come up here unexpectedly? No, the doc would have unlocked the gate, setting off an entirely different alarm.

Who, then?

Mitford cursed these primitive security arrangements. When he had first joined Pendergast, he'd been horrified at the lax defenses around this place. In many areas, critical alarm sensors had been deactivated for God knew how long because rodents of some kind had chewed through the wires. "So what?" Pendergast had said crisply. "The system isn't designed to detect rats, it's designed to detect *humans*. Besides, there's nothing here worth worrying about."

But that wasn't entirely true. The preserved bodies of some of Pendergast's unsuccessful early experiments had been stored for years in a vault under the house. "Chimeras," the doc called them. Why he wanted them back now, Mitford wasn't sure—unless it was because the doc intended to hole up forever at the Gap, surrounded by his memorabilia. Mitford had put the preserved little bodies in Pendergast's Cherokee, which he had driven here instead of using the more specialized transport van. But the Cherokee had lots of windows. And it was parked out there where anyone could peek into it.

And now an intruder was approaching, and Mitford had no way to tell who it was, or even if there was more than one. Tortoise Mountain was essentially deaf and blind. Mitford stood with his eye against the peephole and waited to see who walked up the road.

CHAPTER NINE

THE HOUSE APPEARED before Deborah expected it. They had just walked around a sharp bend when she saw it, set well back in a flat area that had been carved out of the mountaintop.

She and Tony both froze. "Well," he remarked.

It wasn't a house so much as a sprawl of connected buildings—an oversized log cabin nursing five or six puppy-cabins and a garage. There was a stone chimney attached to the main building, and a ring of eucalyptus trees formed an interlocking canopy of shade overhead. Nearby, an array of solar cells perched atop a boulder with their glittering faces turned toward the sun. The yard was mostly bare stone, broken by patches of thorny wild artichoke. Deborah remembered how Pendergast had complained about all the water that got wasted to preserve the lush landscaping down at the Carlton Center. "It's criminal," he had said. "One of these days, people will be forced to remember San Diego is really a *desert*." All in all, this place was, Deborah thought, reassuringly Pendergast: a mix of modern and old-fashioned, functional and romantic.

A brown, dust-shrouded vehicle was parked in front.

"Is that your friend's Cherokee?" Tony asked.

"I've never seen it before," she said, her voice getting tense. "But it's not the car he drives to work."

Tony shrugged as if that meant nothing, and maybe it didn't. There was no law against owning more than one car, and the other one could be parked inside the garage. "Shall we?" Tony said.

They started walking toward the complex—Deborah hesitated to think of it as a "house"—and as it drew nearer, she realized that the buildings weren't nearly as well maintained as they had appeared to be from a distance. The logs were laced with crumbly veins that suggested termites, the windows were curtained with dust, and most of the angles of the structure were subtly wrong, indicating uneven settling.

There was no doorbell. Tony stepped onto the porch, glanced at Deborah, and knocked.

No response. Overhead, eucalyptus branches crackled dryly in the wind. If it weren't for the faint shouts of children rising from somewhere in the valley, this place might have been a million miles from anywhere.

Tony knocked again, putting his weight into it this time.

The door opened so abruptly Deborah jumped.

The man standing there was not Dr. Pendergast. He was youngish, smooth-faced, with shining blond hair pulled back into a ponytail. For a moment Deborah felt a thrill of shock—*I've seen this guy before!*—then she realized he looked like half the men her neighbor, Sarah, dated.

But then, so had the plumber . . .

The expression on his face was more appraising than perturbed as he stared at Tony, ignoring Deborah completely. "You're on private property," he said in a flat voice. "Or didn't the locked gate make that clear enough?"

"Is this the residence of George Pendergast?" Tony asked, apparently oblivious to the blond man's threatening tone.

"It's his house, but I'm renting it, and I haven't seen him for months."

Tony glanced at Deborah, who tried to convey her helplessness through her eyes. She didn't *know* if this was the plumber. How could she? Turning back to the blond man, Tony said, "May I ask your name?"

"No."

"Do you work with Dr. Pendergast?"

"No, I only rent from him. And I'm through talking to you. Get off this property right now, before I . . ." He paused. ". . . call the police."

Although his expression never changed, Deborah had the feeling he'd almost burst into laughter at his own words.

Tony still seemed deaf to threats. "Could you tell us where Dr. Pendergast is now?"

"No, I couldn't. And this is your last chance to get lost." Suddenly the temperature of the blond man's voice dropped a hundred degrees. "I'm not kidding."

Deborah almost took an involuntary step back. Even Tony's smile slipped a bit. "Thanks so much for the help," he said ironically, and turned to Deborah. "Come on."

As she stepped off the porch, sweat cooling on her brow, she thought she glimpsed the blond man's eyes swing sharply toward her for the first time. But she didn't look again to make sure.

Through the spyhole, Mitford watched the intruders walk back down the driveway, and considered killing them right now. He'd been tempted to do it from the moment they come into view around the corner, and he'd recognized the Kosarek bitch.

He'd been right about her all along, obviously. Even yesterday's little warning hadn't put her off.

Taking his hand away from the shotgun behind the door, he bunched a fist. *Women.* Surely they would constitute the biggest part of Pendergast's seven out of ten.

But the rage passed quickly, and was replaced with pleasure. After all, some females *were* able to compensate for the ways of their sisters. Hadn't he spent the last sixteen hours partying with such a one on Pendergast's old bed? He sure had. He'd picked her up off a sleazy street in East San Diego. Oh, what legs showing under her tiny skirt. Of course, she hadn't looked so hot once he saw her up close. They never did, the liars. Fakers.

But like the rest of them, she'd really partied once he'd shown her how.

She was lying in the bedroom now, quite motionless on twisted sheets. He'd drop her off on the way back to Ginnunga Gap. There were plenty of good hiding places just off the freeway in the East County, places where she wouldn't be found for days or weeks or ever. One less member of the Great Evil for the Loners to worry about.

He found himself watching Kosarek closely as she turned the corner and disappeared. She was prettier up close than from a distance, the opposite of most women . . . still, he could easily discover the party girl who lived inside her if he—

No, he couldn't do that; for whatever reason, Pendergast would be furious. And Mitford still needed the doc. He knew that if he wasn't kept busy he tended to lose control of himself, and party too much, too hard.

But being cautious now was not just a matter of pleasing Pendergast. There was also the matter of the security guard, Tony Garwood. According to Pendergast's dossier on him, he was an ex-cop who was tight with another guard who was still a cop. That was a connection that must be considered. Killing Garwood too casually could easily lead to all kinds of complications for *Enkidu*—a circumstance to be avoided at all costs.

Now Mitford almost wished he'd never answered the door. He'd only done so because if he hadn't, his visitors might have walked over to the Cherokee and spotted the containers in there. Which would have been disastrous. Even dead, some of the chimeras made *Mitford* feel like running away, screaming.

He watched for the red light on the panel beside the door to blink off, signifying that something had passed back by the gate. He needed to get out of here so that he could prepare Loki for his field test tonight. Taking Loners out was proving to be very interesting, and not just because of the potential for trouble. The Loners themselves were more and more intriguing all the time.

Mitford felt that he and they had a lot in common.

"I'm sorry," Deborah said as the conglomeration of buildings disappeared around the curve behind them. She realized she was practically running, and slowed down. "I was pretty useless. I guess I expected Dr. Pendergast to come to the door after all, and say everything was all right."

"I understand," Tony said.

"I'm glad you were there," she added simply.

He smiled a bit. "No problem. I take it you didn't know that guy?"

"No, but he gave me the creeps." She automatically glanced over her shoulder, as if the blond man might be following them. The road was empty. "Maybe it was just his hair. The man who broke into my apartment yesterday was blond and athletic-looking, too."

"How do you know?"

"My neighbor saw him."

"Oh." Tony shrugged. "Well, blonds are a pretty common species around here."

"I know." Yet she glanced back again. The road was still empty, of course. Then she saw something on a nearby rock, almost touching her hand. Her first reflex was to cringe away—it looked like a big thorny lizard. Then she realized that the body was oddly segmented, tailless, and clung to the stone with six long, hairy legs. Its head rotated toward her. It smiled. It had Robert Andrews's face.

Deborah screamed.

"What?" Tony cried, whirling.

The rock was bare. Behind it, the bushes trembled slightly. "I saw— I saw something on that rock," Deborah said in a squeaky voice.

"What was it?" She realized Tony had one hand on the butt of his gun.

"I don't know. Just some animal; a lizard." And it had been, of course. Just a lizard, and her overactive imagination at work.

Tony walked back to the rock and peered behind it, one hand still on his gun. Deborah, caught in the backwash of her shock, tensed as he put his face close to the bushes. But then he straightened and shook his head. "It's gone now. Are you all right?"

"It just startled me, that's all," she said, and forced a smile. "First the guy at the house, now this—you must think I'm quite a flake."

"Hardly. That guy put me on edge, too."

"He did?" As they continued down the road, Deborah resisted an urge to glance over her shoulder yet again.

"He never once looked at my gun," Tony said. "Did you notice that?"

"No . . ."

"Think about it. Two strangers pound on the door of an isolated house without warning, and one of them is carrying a gun in plain sight—and the guy doesn't even acknowledge it. Also, he never asked who we were or what we wanted."

"You're wearing a uniform that says Protector Security Systems, you know. Maybe that's why the gun didn't bother him."

"*You* looked at it first thing. And there's something else. He didn't have to answer the door at all. If he'd just ignored us, we would have gone away."

Deborah looked at him closely. "You mean . . . you think . . ."

"I just got the impression he was playing with us, that's all." He paused. "Okay, let's take this one step at a time. Is there any other place you can think of where Pendergast might be? A vacation house or cabin or something?"

"Not that he's ever mentioned."

"What about relatives?"

"I don't believe he's got any living family."

"Hm. Let's try another tack. Your neighbor—if we described the guy we just saw to her, do you think she could tell us if he was the same guy who broke into your apartment yesterday?"

"Maybe," Deborah said unenthusiastically, "but I doubt it. She's pretty spacey."

"I see." His gaze locked on her consideringly. Then he said, "Listen, what the hell. I'm not doing anything tonight—maybe I'll just wait around awhile, and if our friend on the mountain leaves, I'll follow him."

She stared. "Are you serious?"

"Sure, why not? Just to find out where he lives. I memorized the license number of his Jeep, too. I can give all the information to a cop I know, and he can find out if the guy's got a record or anything."

"I don't know if you should follow him," she said. "What if he really *is* dangerous?"

"Danger is my life," he said with an unreadable smile. "That's why I'm a security guard in such a high-risk area."

She couldn't tell if he was being serious or not.

"Anyway," he said, "I'll need to know how to get ahold of you later to tell you what I find out."

Her gaze sharpened automatically.

"Don't worry," he said, "I haven't broken into anyone's apartment in months."

"Sorry." She blushed. "It's just that this whole thing is . . . it's thrown me off."

"That's okay," he said, his smile fading. "I've had that problem once or twice myself."

Parking his car near the gate of one of the other housing developments, Tony settled in to wait. He didn't want to hang around RVO itself because that would mean explaining his intentions to Chatherton, and Chatherton would laugh at him. For good reason. For one thing, there was no solid reason to suspect the blond man of doing anything wrong; for another, what if the blond man didn't leave the mountain tonight, or tomorrow night, or the night after that? This stakeout was idiotic. True, Deborah Kosarek was attractive enough, but Christ, she wasn't—

Just then the Cherokee cruised past, Blondie driving. No passengers. Tony's heart gave a kick.

Okay. Maybe this was idiotic, or maybe it was actually dangerous—but either way, Tony realized he ought to take it seriously. Starting the engine, he pulled out a hundred yards behind the Jeep.

He wasn't experienced at shadowing a car. Even back when he was a cop, the only vehicles he had deliberately followed were those that were weaving around the road, hinting at a drunk driver behind the wheel. But the Jeep, a tall, gangly vehicle, was easy to keep in sight from a distance, while Tony's own car was as nondescript as a paper bag. So he hung well back as the Jeep took the freeway heading south. For a while they were both stuck in traffic at the I-5/805 split, but eventually things broke up and the two vehicles continued on. The blond man took the exit onto I-8, heading east, and Tony followed.

Tony noticed that even as traffic eased, the Jeep cruised along at the speed limit—in San Diego, a phenomenon almost suspicious by itself. The two vehicles passed through Mission Valley and the college area, then dropped into the El Cajon Valley. Here, much of the commuter traffic siphoned away, and Tony fell back even farther. The Jeep continued along the freeway, out of El Cajon, out into the rural hills. Tony let more and more cars get in front of him.

The shadows were stretching long by the time the Jeep reached Alpine, a town that had once been a small rural enclave but was now a growing sprawl of yuppie estates. The Jeep took the exit, and Tony followed warily. Other traffic was now almost nonexistent. The Jeep cruised through Alpine, still heading east, then pulled onto a narrow frontage road that paralleled the freeway. The houses drew farther and farther apart until they ended entirely; Tony's car and the Jeep were suddenly the only two vehicles on the road. Tony stayed so far back that he frequently lost sight of the other vehicle. Still, it seemed safe enough—the only intersections were narrow, rugged fire-cut roads. On both sides were high, rough hills, draped with sagebrush and manzanita and punctuated with pale, knobby boulders.

Tony drove a mile, two miles, only occasionally creeping up enough to glimpse the Jeep. There were no major crossroads, no houses that he could see. Maybe this was a private lane now. He'd better be very careful.

Without warning, the road ended. There was a wooden barricade, then bushes and rocks. No Cherokee in sight. Tony slowed and halted, climbed out of his car. Overhead, the sky was glowing with the bright purple hue of a desert sunset, and the air danced with midges and gnats. In the distance, the tips of the Laguna Mountains flared yellow orange.

But where was the Jeep? Beyond the barricade lay nothing but brush, stunty juniper bushes, boulders, dust. The barricade was exactly as wide as the road itself, but on either side, clumps of sagebrush had been cleared away, and rough dirt trails wound away through the nearby manzanita. Tony recognized the scars of off-road vehicle activity. Judging by the tire marks, these trails had been made over a long period of time and by a variety of vehicles. The Cherokee may or may not have just passed through here.

Tony listened. But the freeway was just out of sight over a low hillock, and the intermittent drone of passing cars made it impossible for him to hear if the Cherokee was nearby.

Damn! The Jeep must have taken one of the fire roads after all. Blondie could be anywhere by now.

Climbing onto the bumper of the car, he looked around for signs of a dust cloud, a house, anything. Saw only desolate, high desert terrain. No houses. No dust rising. No Jeep.

Well, never mind. He'd done what he'd promised to do. Nothing seemed to have come from it, but that wasn't the point. He'd done what he'd promised to do.

Climbing back into his car, he turned around and started back. He felt pretty good.

When Mitford strolled into the Ginnunga Gap control center he found Pendergast already there, staring at the monitors.

"Sorry I'm late," Mitford said. "Got hung up in traffic."

Pendergast merely grunted. "What sort of world would allow traffic jams to happen?" he muttered. "Wouldn't you think people would take the *hint*?"

Mitford smiled to himself. Evidently the highway planners at CalTrans had just joined the ranks of the Great Evil. He wondered what the doc was staring at with such severity. To him, the monitors seemed to display the same old readouts as always.

Suddenly Pendergast said, "Did you bring the chimeras?"

"Yeah. Where do you want me to put them?"

The doc turned and looked at Mitford with eyes that seemed unusually piercing and humorless. "Storeroom D."

"Okay . . . am I still taking Loki to El Cajon tonight?"

Pendergast held the stare for a moment, then turned back to the screens. "Yes. Set him free in the parking lot of that shopping mall, Parkway Plaza."

Mitford grinned. A parking lot! This time he might be able to position himself so he could actually watch the Loner in action. "Okay," he said eagerly. "I'll get him ready."

Pendergast nodded distractedly, and Mitford was almost to the door when the doc suddenly said, "Ira, have you been inside my house recently?"

Surprised by the use of his first name, Mitford stopped. "I was just there."

"No, not Tortoise Mountain. My house here."

"Oh. No, not for months." In fact, the last time had been when he and Pendergast had shared a drink to celebrate the successful births of the Alpha group. "Why?"

"Never mind." Pendergast didn't look away from the screens; he seemed to have already forgotten he'd asked a question. "Be sure you don't get pulled over for speeding or anything tonight."

"You want me to leave right away?"

"You'll have to, to get there before the mall closes."

Mitford realized Pendergast was thinking in terms of a crowd of potential victims, and smiled again.

"Don't park where you can be seen unloading or loading Loki, either," Pendergast added. "Keep your distance."

"Of course," Mitford said, turning away quickly. Sometimes it seemed like the doc knew his intentions better than he did himself.

PART II

Children, it is the last hour;
   and just as you heard
   that Antichrist is coming,
   even now many antichrists
   have arisen;
From this we know that it is
   the last hour . . .
            —1 JOHN 2:18
            THE HOLY BIBLE

CHAPTER TEN

"Woom!" Virgil squealed as Deborah walked into her in-laws' house, holding Brooke Worm triumphantly in front of her. She had stitched up its throat with thread from the sewing kit in her purse. Virgil ran to her at his usual breakneck pace and snatched the toy from her grip.

"We were wondering where that was," Betty Kosarek said. She stood at the far end of the hallway, an apron tied around her waist, smiling. Although she looked like June Cleaver at the moment, she was actually a full-time office manager at a small law firm, and provided the steady income in the household. From behind her wafted the aroma of baking cookies. "He's been asking for it all evening."

"It got . . . lost for a while," Deborah said, not wanting to get into any of that right now.

"Hey," boomed a voice from the distance, "is that the second prettiest woman in my life, or what?"

Smiling, Deborah took Virgil's hand and walked into the living room. As they entered, Delbert Kosarek ("Call me Del, or else") turned toward them from his recliner. As usual, he had a beer balanced on his mound of belly; as usual, he was watching ESPN on TV. Deborah peeked at the screen. Australian football.

Del was as big as his wife was diminutive, with a loud voice and brash manner. Deborah was always amused by his efforts to control his language around his grandson.

"How's it going, Dad?" she asked, sitting on the sofa with a sigh. Her feet felt pinched and sore, and she knew she hadn't been able to hand-brush all the dust off her clothes. But no one commented.

"Same-old-same-old," Del boomed, whatever that meant, as he hoisted a contented Virgil onto his lap. "Looks like I might be working some nights starting next week, for however long—you know how it is

117

in the fu . . . in the shipbuilding business around here, always feast or famine."

Deborah nodded. Betty came in bearing a tray of chocolate chip cookies—Virgil's favorites—and passed it around. Sweet and hot, they made Deborah realize how ravenous she was.

"How's school going, honey?" Betty asked, perching on the ottoman next to her husband's stockinged feet. Looking at her, Deborah knew that wasn't what she had wanted to ask at all.

"Oh . . . School's okay," she said. "I got stuck doing some work-related stuff tonight, so I missed class. It was real nice of you to watch Virgil for me."

"Oh, no problem, you know that," Del said, and scuffed his unshaven face gently across Virgil's cheek. This summoned up a gale of giggles.

Betty was still watching Deborah. "You ought to slow down a little," she said in concern. "You look awfully tired."

Deborah managed a smile. "I'll try to get some sleep tonight." But she wasn't sure she'd be able to, not if she spent the whole night waiting for the sound of the plumber coming to pay another visit—or dreaming about that awful creature she'd thought she'd seen on the rock on Tortoise Mountain.

Just like that, she found herself thinking about the gun case in Del's den. It contained a couple of shotguns, some rifles, and several pistols. Although Del had given up hunting years ago under Betty's insidious pressure, he and Brad had often gone target-shooting together. Deborah had even tagged along a few times to "plink" at cans in the desert. She knew how to handle a gun . . .

Jesus, Deborah! What do you have in mind, building a bunker inside your apartment and standing guard?

Now her gaze moved to the mantel over the fireplace. It was covered with framed photos, and Deborah found herself staring at the shot of Brad in full fireman's gear, playfully spraying himself with a garden hose. Next to that was a photo from the wedding—Brad and her kissing, Brad pretending to resist. It had been a fun ceremony, not stuffy, not overly serious. They'd honeymooned in Cabo San Lucas . . .

Suddenly she missed Brad more than she had since her initial devastation at his death; she wanted him to be at home when she got there, lying in bed waiting to take her into his arms. She wanted . . . needed . . .

Struggling with tears, she looked away from the picture. Maybe it was just fear. The question kept revolving through her mind: Had the blond man at Pendergast's place also been the plumber who broke into her apartment? Tony Garwood had sensed something strange about the man, too. And even after short notice, Deborah felt oddly confident about Tony's perceptions. His composure, his sense of presence had been comforting to her during the encounter on the mountaintop. But then, the qualities were familiar to her—the man in the wedding photo had possessed them as well.

She suddenly felt a flood of guilt almost as strong as the previous regret had been, and was dismayed. She had no intention of dating Tony. Not that Brad would have *minded* her dating someone. Hell, even her in-laws told her she needed to get out more often . . .

She sighed; she was too tired to wrestle with this tonight. Besides, there were the ongoing realities of her daily life to face. College, for instance. She still had a report on *Beowulf* due, and if she didn't want her grades to drop, she'd better . . .

Beowulf. A mythological hero. Something clicked in her mind. "Mind if I use the encyclopedia for a minute?" she asked Betty.

Betty looked surprised. "Of course not. Go right ahead."

Deborah didn't look up "Beowulf," but "Enkidu"—what Pendergast had called his secret computer directory. She had just remembered, vaguely, where it originated.

She found the listing and read it quickly, and the commas between her brows appeared. As she had recalled, "Enkidu" was a character from the *Epic of Gilgamesh*, an ancient Sumerian mythological poem. Gilgamesh himself had been a great hero, part-god and part-human. But when he threatened to become uncontrollable, the gods confronted him with Enkidu, a primal, uncivilized being, to act as Gilgamesh's foil and nemesis. But the two became friends, and before they were struck down, threatened the gods themselves . . .

Deborah's frown deepened. Pendergast's computer password had been "Prometheus"—Greek mythology—his secret files were called "Enkidu"—Sumerian—and of course his anticancer antigen was named NIMROD, which was from the Bible.

All of which told her what? Only that Dr. Pendergast fancied mythological or religious passwords. Still, something about the names bothered her. Maybe it was that they were all associated in one way or another with violence and death. That didn't seem like Dr. Pendergast at all.

Putting the encyclopedia away again, she turned and found Betty staring at her. "Have you had dinner yet?" Betty asked.

"Pro beach volleyball coming up," Del added from the recliner. "Pretty great, huh, sport?" he asked Virgil.

"Vaibah," Virgil said equably.

"Thanks," Deborah said, "but we'd better be going." She pretended to look for Virgil. "Now, where's that kid of mine?"

"Kid?" Del leaned forward and hid Virgil under his bulk. "What kid are you talking about?"

Beneath the beefy arms, Virgil giggled, the tones going up and down the scale like notes on a toy piano.

"The best kid in the whole world," Deborah said through a tight throat.

Positioning the van properly at Parkway Plaza turned out to be a logistical nightmare. The multilevel parking garage in back was out of the question—too few exits—and the side lots were narrow and situated too close to streets. Which left only the front lot, and it was getting slim on cover as closing time approached.

Finally he found an area, not too close to either the street or the building, where a couple of cars afforded a bit of shelter without blocking his view of the mall. Shutting off the engine, he just sat for a while, watching people come and go. At this hour, it was mostly "go," except for the gaggle of young punks and their sluts loitering near the nearest entrance. Maybe Loki would go after one of *them*. Please, Loki. Show Uncle Ira your stuff.

Turning, Mitford switched on the lights in the rear compartment of the van. Loki sat facing the doors as if in anticipation. He wore Levi's and a loose sweatshirt, and a Padres baseball cap was perched on his head. In short, he looked like anybody else.

Mitford pressed the door-release button.

The Loner was gone in a flicker of motion, and a second later Mitford spotted him moving toward the mall with long strides. Mitford felt a sudden, almost overpowering urge to get out of the van and follow. Just in case Loki passed up the punks.

But Mitford stayed put. No matter what, he had to be here when Loki came back.

The Loner had already vanished from sight. Damn. Keeping the bulletproof windows rolled up despite the heat—SOP—Mitford leaned back and waited.

Caitland Wilson had to shop carefully, what with her husband Jim only making six bucks an hour at Thrifty Print and her being on maternity leave from May Company for another week. And of course there was the new member of the family to keep in Snuggies.

Which was why she shouldn't be inside Waldenbooks. Books cost money.

Well, at least feeding little Trudy was free. Caitland had that one covered. In fact, right now she had it covered with a towel to hide the equipment from prying eyes as Trudy sucked away. Caitland smiled down at her daughter's busy, contented face. *Just the way Jim looks down there*, she thought, and turned red. It was that kind of thinking that had brought Trudy along in the first place, sinking all plans for college for both Caitland and Jim, at least for a while.

Well. That could be fixed later. Everything seemed to be working out all right. Which was kind of fun, because the success of the marriage—so far—obviously surprised both sets of parents, if not Jim and her. They got by fine as long as they kept an eye on every penny they spent. In fact, their relationship only seemed to grow stronger under the stress. Just like in the romance novels.

"We'll fool 'em all," she said to Trudy.

"Sorry?" said a voice, and she looked up to see one of the clerks, a guy, standing in the main aisle by the Romance section, looking at her.

"Nothing," she said, reddening again, making sure the milk factory was covered.

"Anything I can help you find?" he asked.

"No, thanks," Caitland sighed, and the clerk walked away.

She really should get out of there. After all, her purpose for coming to the mall had been to show Trudy off to her coworkers at May Company, and she'd done that. True, she'd known it was time for the latest shipment of Silhouette Romances to arrive, but why even look? Books were a frivolity she couldn't afford—they couldn't afford—right now.

A half-minute later she was outside the store again, dropping onto the nearest bench. Her knees shook slightly. The crowd in the mall around her was thinning fast, streaming toward the exits.

Nobody had followed her out of the store. Nobody was pointing at her and shouting. Nobody had seen her slip a brand-new copy of *Love in Amber* into Trudy's diaper bag.

But her heart refused to slow down. She hadn't stolen anything since she was five years old and had pocketed a handful of caramel pieces in a drugstore. Mom had found the wrappers in the wash the next day, questioned her—she'd broken down in tearful confession immediately—and Dad had taken matters from there. Oh, boy, had he.

But she really wanted this book, and she couldn't afford to buy it right now, and besides, she figured she'd singlehandedly kept Waldenbooks solvent over the years. Surely they owed her one free book. It was a big company. And now it was too late to change her mind, anyway; the bookstore clerks were lowering the security gate. The mall was empty except for a few stragglers. Time to go.

Detaching a disgruntled Trudy from the restaurant, she draped the infant over her shoulder for a quick burping. But as she raised her hand for the first pat, a man stepped in front of her.

Her heart skipped a beat. *Caught. Busted. Oh God.*

"I—" she began, not knowing what she was going to say. Then she looked up and froze. The man standing before her wasn't a security guard; he wore no uniform and displayed no I.D. badge. He was dressed in jeans and a baggy sweatshirt, and stared down at her from beneath the brim of a Padres baseball cap. His eyes were small and dark green.

"How are you?" he said in a gravelly voice.

"I—I beg your pardon?"

"How are you?" He was twitching slightly, she noticed—his legs and arms moving in nervous tics, the way some spazzes did. Some kind of spaz panhandler, that's what he was. "Sorry," she said nervously, "I don't—"

He reached out and snatched her daughter from her arms.

She sat there, disbelieving. Trudy hung by her armpits from the man's hands. The child wasn't upset; Jim often held her that way. The man stared at her with his green eyes.

Caitland leaped to her feet, the milk-stained nursing towel falling unnoticed to the floor. "Hey! *Hey!* What do you think you're *doing*?"

All around the mall, people turned toward her, but the closest of them seemed to be a mile away.

Green Eyes tilted his head toward Caitland, like a dog hearing a distant whistle, then looked down at her exposed breast. His nose twitched. "Does a body good," he said.

Caitland threw out her hands. "Give me my baby!" she shrieked, taking a jerky step toward him. "Give her to me! Give her to me, you spaz!"

Green Eyes took a long step backward. "And now," he said, "a word from our sponsor."

"Help!" Caitland screamed at the frozen, staring people scattered around the mall. "Somebody help me, *he's got my baby!*"

At last, footsteps accelerated toward them.

Green Eyes chuckled. "This man receives sinners and eats with them," he murmured, and raised Trudy high. "Real food for real people."

What happened next was over so quickly that later, none of the witnesses' stories would match. But Caitland, by far the closest, saw everything plainly. It would be stamped into her brain forever.

Green Eyes's head deformed, stretching forward and back, the Padres cap falling off. His eyes sank in, gleaming like evil jewels from black pits. From the lower half of his face burst a mass of glistening pink and white flesh, skin pulled over it as tightly as a drumhead. It was lined with interlocking teeth that suddenly separated, revealing a deep, deep maw. Far inside, things pulsed in wet darkness.

Caitland screamed again. No words now. Other cries of alarm shot in from all over the mall.

But Trudy didn't react with shock or fear; she simply gazed wonderingly at Green Eyes. And suddenly Caitland, down where conscious thought touches the deep river of instinct, knew what was about to happen. Wet heat gushed down her legs.

But she couldn't move.

The maw moved, though—very fast. There were two loud sounds like shears snapping together, *snick-snick*, and suddenly Green Eyes's hands were empty. A few red droplets sprinkled on the floor.

And as abruptly as they had appeared, the teeth and jaws folded backward, and Green Eyes's skull telescoped back into normal shape. His lower face was now normal again, and he ran a long, dark tongue around his lips. "Amen," he said, and grinned, revealing a normal man's teeth. Except they were rimmed with blood, like ivory doors with scarlet frames.

Caitland stared at him. This whole thing had to be some kind of joke, a trick. Of course. What had this spaz done with Trudy? Where had he hidden her little girl?

Distantly, she heard more shouting, and running footsteps echoing flatly in the mall. Green Eyes glanced around unhurriedly. "Chow," he said, and suddenly bounded away as swiftly as a two-legged greyhound, heading toward the nearest exit. One shopper, a big man also wearing a Padres cap, stepped in his path and took a swipe at him with something heavy in a Sears bag. Green Eyes vaulted high, shoes flying off, and put both his bare feet on the big man's face. He drove the man over backward to the floor with a thud. Blood exploded out in a fan. Green Eyes ran on again, sweatshirt flapping around him. Everyone else leaped out of his way, and a moment later he vanished around the corner, the afterimage of a grin floating in the air behind him.

A crowd quickly gathered around the big man, who lay quite motionless. An even bigger group formed around Caitland. She saw their mouths moving. All those mouths. Pink, glistening holes with teeth inside. Teeth inside. Teeth . . .

She began to scream, but when she felt her own teeth moving against her lips, she closed her mouth so hard she crunched halfway through her tongue. The melted copper taste of blood almost overwhelmed her. She knew that if she opened her mouth now, her teeth would look like ivory doors with scarlet frames.

So she kept her mouth shut, and refused, refused to open it.

Deborah locked her car and walked toward her apartment, Virgil draped sleepily over her shoulder. When she reached the swimming pool, she looked up at the darkened windows of her apartment and thought, *The plumber could be up there waiting for me, right now.*

The idea was so vivid that for a moment it was as if she actually saw a face behind the glass. She stopped abruptly, her heart galloping like a thoroughbred at Del Mar. Of *course* she hadn't seen a face. But that didn't mean nobody was up there—did it?

Shut up, she told herself with nearly hysterical anger. *Stop acting like a baby and get in there.*

But . . .

Suddenly she found herself thinking about Tony Garwood again, his reassuring bulk, his steady manner, how *in control* he had been. How unafraid he would be now—how unafraid *she* would be if he were . . .

Oh, God, Deborah, stop it. He has a uniform and a gun. Why would he be afraid?

But she had the feeling that even without the accoutrements, he still wouldn't be scared. Or at least he wouldn't show it. He radiated an aura of self-confidence, just like . . .

Like Brad.

Well, yes. Like Brad. So what?

So you wish he was here, escorting you to your dark apartment with the watchful windows.

Wish who was here? Brad, or Tony?

Brad. Tony. Either.

You *are* scared.

I'm scared. She knew she didn't think clearly when she was frightened. She hated being frightened.

"Shhh," she whispered to Virgil. "It's okay." But Virgil was asleep.

Suddenly anger and self-disgust rose up in her, and she marched to the stairs, climbed them, thrust her key into the lock. The *brand-new* lock. Felt the tumblers turn, just as they were supposed to. Opened the door. Flicked on the lights. Everything looked fine. Quiet. Neat. Quiet.

Still carrying Virgil, she checked the rooms. Empty. Empty. Empty. What about the closets? Under the bed? Nothing.

Idiot. Scaredycat.

Laying Virgil in his crib, she kissed his forehead and went back into the living room. After locking the door, she dropped onto the couch, stretched out and stared at the ceiling.

And still wished someone was with her. Someone to just lie here with her, hold her. *Be* with her.

You're falling apart, Deborah.

She began to cry. But this time it didn't feel like grief, and it didn't feel like fear. It felt like loneliness.

CHAPTER ELEVEN

MITFORD TOOK HIS TIME driving back to Ginnunga Gap, struggling to get control over his own anger and disappointment. Christ, eating a baby! Turning, he glared into the rear compartment at the Loner. Pendergast hadn't seemed to mind when the old lady in La Jolla got munched, but a *baby*? It was too much. A glitch this size must surely lead to a big delay in the field test program . . .

Once in the garage, Mitford pumped anesthetic gas into the back of the van, waited a few minutes, then pulled Loki out and loaded him onto a wheeled cart. After dumping the stupid creature into its cell, he went to the control room.

At the door, he hesitated for a moment, bracing himself for the bad news. Then he walked in.

Pendergast was sitting in his usual chair, watching the news on the main monitor.

He was smiling.

Mitford moved almost warily to his own chair. "Well?" he said. "Now what?"

Pendergast glanced at him. "I beg your pardon?"

"Last time it was an old lady, this time a helpless baby . . ."

"Yes?"

Mitford frowned. "Well, that's bad, right? Two out of three Alphas haven't killed the kind of people you want."

"The kind of . . ." Pendergast sat back in his chair, brows compressed. "Mr. Mitford, what are you talking about?"

"The Great Evil," Mitford said. "The seven-tenths; you know, the people ruining the world. The ones Loners are *supposed* to kill."

"Oh. Oh, I see." Pendergast reached over and shut off the television.

"Tell me, Mr. Mitford—have you listened to *anything* I've said about this project over the last ten years?"

Suddenly Mitford felt warm around the neck. He didn't like the condescension he heard in Pendergast's voice. "Of course I've listened. You think you can save mankind."

"No. I think I can save the *world*. The salvation of mankind will follow in the natural course of events."

Mitford frowned. He was in no mood for a sermon.

Sighing, Pendergast took his glasses off. Without them his eyes looked smaller, but even more intensely blue. "Have you heard of the greenhouse effect?"

"Sure."

"Homelessness? Black tides? Famine? The extinction of the passenger pigeon? Gas shortages? Acid rain? Personal injury lawsuits? Child abuse? Toxic waste? Unemployment?"

"I watch the news," Mitford said drily.

"Yes. My point is, all these problems are caused, or at least exacerbated, by the same thing. The Great Evil."

"The greenhouse effect and child abuse are caused by the same thing?"

"Yes. The Great Evil isn't a *kind* of person, Mr. Mitford. It's people. The Great Evil is that there are simply too many human beings living on this planet."

After a moment, Mitford said, "*Overpopulation*? That's what this is all about?"

"That's what *everything* is about." Leaping to his feet, Pendergast began to pace back and forth in front of the world map. "There was a time when the earth could satisfy the needs of all its inhabitants, from insects to human beings. Every creature took what it needed and left the rest. Then *Homo sapiens* came along, and started demanding more. More food, more territory, more energy . . . and even that was fine, to a point. The earth is bountiful. But it is *not* unlimited." He spun. "When were you born?"

"1954."

"In that year, the number of humans on the earth was approximately three and a half billion. Do you know what it is now?"

"No."

"Almost *six* billion. That's nearly double, Mr. Mitford, in your lifetime.

The growth rate is geometric—two begets four begets eight begets sixteen begets thirty-two. By the time you're eighty, the population will be almost *sixteen billion*. Imagine that—you think we have pollution now? Housing shortages? Famines? Imagine what the world will be like when it's two and a half times as crowded as it is today."

Mitford didn't bother imagining it; he had no expectation of living that long. "So what are the Loners supposed to do about all this?" he asked.

Pendergast sighed and shook his head. "Tell me something—why do people continue to make babies?"

"They like to." Mitford wouldn't use the word "sex."

"Of course. But why do they continue to have *too many* babies, even though that's destroying those very babies' futures?"

"Selfishness. Everybody figures they have a personal right to decide how many kids to have."

"Correct. A *personal* right. And that's because virtually every culture on earth teaches that human reproduction is not only good, it's a *divine prerogative*—as the Bible puts it, 'Be fruitful and multiply.' Remember Earth Summit, that ludicrous meeting of world leaders that was supposed to solve major environmental problems? Overpopulation wasn't even *mentioned*, even though the summit was held in Brazil, where the average birth rate is among the highest in the world, and the standard of living among the lowest. And do you know why it wasn't mentioned?"

"Brazil's a Catholic country," Mitford said.

Pendergast looked surprised. "That's right. The summit's leaders didn't want to offend the Vatican—or the President of the United States, who had his own 'right-to-life' agenda to support.

"Overbreeding is a crime committed in the name of religion. But there's another problem, one that can be laid squarely at the door of science—and that's the notion that every single human life must be preserved and extended as long as possible, artificially if necessary."

Mitford waited. He had the feeling he was listening to a well-rehearsed speech. The doc would get to the point eventually, no doubt.

"In the wild, things are very different," Pendergast went on. "Nature regulates populations in two ways—externally and internally. External controls include predators, accidents and disease, which cull mostly the aged and weak. Internal controls are rare, but they exist—for example, when a pod of *Orcas* grows too large for its feeding grounds, its birth rate declines for a while. Nobody starves, and the prey species are never depleted. Everybody wins.

"Humans, of course, are different. We long ago eradicated the predators that hunted us, and during the last century, science has suppressed most plague diseases as well. As for internal controls, except for a few rare cultures, we have none. We feel we have the absolute right to reproduce at whatever rate we desire—and there's no indication that that attitude will change anytime soon."

"Then what, exactly, are the Loners for?" Mitford asked again.

"To restore competition at the top of the food chain."

"You mean . . ."

"Loners are designed to prey on humans, period. According to my plan, our two populations will eventually balance out at a ratio of about one of them for every two thousand of us—but only *after* our human population has been reduced to approximately thirty percent of its current level."

"Wait a minute," Mitford said, leaning forward. "You're telling me the Loners will kill *anybody*?"

"According to their individual tastes, yes."

"But you could have made them so they'd go after whoever you wanted."

"Within limits, certainly."

"I don't believe this. How could you pass up a chance like that?"

Pendergast sighed. "I told you before, I'm not God. It's not my job to decide who deserves to live or die; that's a moral issue. My job is to decide *how many* die—that's scientific."

Mitford's eyebrows arched sardonically.

"Somebody has to do it," Pendergast said stiffly. "Somebody has to take responsibility before it's too late. Listen—an average of thirteen species of life disappear from this planet *every day*—that's a thousand times greater than the extinction rate at the height of the Cretaceous Period, when the dinosaurs disappeared."

"What makes you so sure the Loners will stop reproducing at the level you want them to?"

"It's programmed into their genes. They have short lifespans, infrequent mating cycles, and are solitary and territorial. Taken as a whole, this will eventually result in a stable Loner population. And, of course, their hunger will result in a stable human population."

"But sooner or later, people will learn how to identify Loners with X-rays or blood tests or something. Then they'll go to war on them."

Pendergast actually grinned, an expression so rare Mitford stared in amazement. "That would require the kind of large-scale cooperation that will soon become a thing of the past," the doc said. "In the future, social units will have to be small enough that everybody knows everybody else . . . Loners look like people most of the time, remember? Would *you* trust a stranger?"

Mitford found himself smiling. That was pretty damned clever, he had to admit. Then he looked around the control room with its screens and instruments, and said, "You really think the world will be better off back in the Stone Age?"

"No, no, *no*," Pendergast said. "That's the *point*—without overpopulation, we can have it *all*. Television and clean water, cars and fresh air, paper and trees, food and wildlife. Technology has advanced to the stage where automation can replace factory labor, and computers take the place of universities. I foresee a world of small communities connected by communications systems but separated by vast expanses of wilderness."

Mitford grunted. "What about child abuse and personal injury lawsuits, stuff like that? You said the Loners can cure *those*. How?"

"That's a side benefit. In a world with a proper population level, children will be treasures again, and people in general will be more inclined to support the people they know. In other words, 'society' will become a survival mechanism again—not just an excuse for rap music and conceptual art."

Mitford glanced at the Alpha cell monitors. "What about you and me?" he asked.

"Pardon?"

"Will the Loners try to hunt us, too?"

"Given the desire and opportunity, yes, of course. If I made *anyone* exempt, even myself, I'd be the biggest hypocrite the world has ever known, wouldn't I?"

"Yeah," Mitford said, "I guess you would."

Somehow, he managed not to laugh.

After the nightly news broadcast was over, Tony got in his car and went for a drive. He didn't feel like sleeping, but he didn't feel like going to a bar, either. Maybe he'd just cruise down to Sunset Cliffs and stare at the Pacific for a while.

There wasn't much traffic on University Avenue for a Friday night, he noticed. He wondered if people were scared of the Cannibal; the city's new celebrity hadn't struck yet today. According to the news, the two assaults in El Cajon were not being credited to the Cannibal, for the simple reason that there had been no mauled corpse left behind. One victim had been critically injured, but survived, and the other—a child—had simply disappeared.

Tony could hardly wait to hear what Chatherton had to say about the witnesses who had spoken on TV. One of them claimed she'd seen the attacker snatch the infant from her mother, then stuff it into some sort of bag before fleeing. Another said the attacker cut the baby in *half* first. But the best story came from the hysterical pubescent girl who swore that the attacker "turned into a monster and ate that baby."

Tony shook his head. Yeah, Chatherton was going to love that one. Cannibal hysteria was obviously growing.

Of course, Tony had another reason to look forward to seeing Chatherton tomorrow—because of Deborah and *her* story. Although he was sure Chatherton's reaction would be one of disbelief or even scorn, in a way it didn't matter. Tony would be seeing Deborah again to tell her about it. And that felt good.

It suddenly occurred to Tony that it had been a long time since he'd met a woman outside the confines of a singles bar. And how long had it been since he'd been with *any* woman who had stayed on his mind for so long? Of course, the circumstances under which they'd met had a lot to do with it—how could you not be intrigued by a woman willing to conduct a solo guerilla raid on an expensive Southern California housing development?

Suddenly he realized he'd turned south on Sixth Avenue. The neighborhood was Hillcrest, which had a strong personal identity built around its high population of gays. There were a lot of good restaurants and shops here; the streets were still bustling with people. But Tony knew why he'd turned onto Sixth Avenue—farther south, it formed the western border of Balboa Park.

Balboa Park had a split personality, marked by the deep canyon through which Highway 163 ran. The east side was the popular, exciting character: it contained the San Diego Zoo, theaters, and the museums of El Prado. The west side was the practical, introspective one, offering little more than grassy lawns, jogging paths and shade trees. The east side was outgoing, bustling with both tourists and locals even late at night. But after dark the west side, poorly lit and without cultural facilities, drew mostly the homeless, the lost—and those who preyed on them, and on one another.

As the park approached, Tony looked over at it. Here and there, homeless people clustered on the grass with their shopping carts full of junk encircling them like Conestoga wagons in Indian country. Elsewhere, Tony knew, well beyond the reach of the streetlights, other figures moved. Some alone, some in groups. Looking for things. Drugs, sex, trouble.

Rolling down his window, Tony inhaled the smells of the park: wet grass, freshly sprinkled; eucalyptus leaves; dust. From somewhere in the darkness came a hoot, and a raucous laugh. His heart beat harder.

Up ahead, bright lights glared on a mob of people across the street from the park; Tony knew what was going on even before he got there. There was a medical center there that included an abortion clinic, and every few months, a group of Right-to-Life advocates would demonstrate in front of it. Tony and Ed Winston had had to keep an eye on these affairs when they were working the neighborhood; although the demonstrators seldom got violent, they could get loud, disturbing the occupants of nearby apartment houses.

One of the local TV stations must have gotten tired of covering the Parkway Plaza story. A reporter was standing in the white glare of klieg lights and interviewing a woman, who clutched a small girl's hand on one side and a gory poster of an aborted fetus on the other. Nearby, a smaller group of Pro-Choice advocates waved their own icons: twisted coat hangers and signs proclaiming NEVER AGAIN!

Tony saw a young police officer standing to one side, watching the proceedings with an expression of sardonic boredom on his face. How quickly that expression came to you when you were a cop, Tony thought.

When he reached the stoplight at the end of the block, he turned left. The street connected the two halves of the park, spanning the major canyon on a long, graceful bridge and becoming El Prado on the other side. But Tony turned left again before he reached the bridge, and drove slowly along a winding lane. It was a dark street, but not nearly as dark as the heavily wooded canyons that dropped down on his right.

He and Ed Winston had often parked their cruiser on this street and walked down one of the dirt paths that folded and wound through the canyons. Creeping down in the darkness with their big flashlights turned off in their hands, their thumbs over the switches, searching for drug deals or homosexual trysts or whatever. Ed had had a passion for busting people down there, for "making this place safe again."

Even then, Tony had known that there was a personal side to this passion. Only six months before he teamed up with Ed, Ed had been stabbed by a guy down there in the canyons—an angel-duster, who had never been caught. Ed had spent a month in the hospital leaking into tubes, and by the time he got back into the field with Tony as his green partner, he had developed an equal hatred for drug pushers and users. What Tony hadn't known then was that it was the kind of hatred that's born of fear. Ed and Tony had never gone into the park with their holsters snapped . . .

Without realizing it, Tony was driving slower and slower.

At the time, he hadn't recognized the symptoms of Ed's growing paranoia—but he should have. As the months went by, Ed talked more and more about the fact that San Diego's record of police officers killed in the line of duty was worse than New York's or Chicago's, and that the ratio of cops per citizen here was less than half that of Los Angeles. Worse, organized street gangs like the Crips and Bloods were increasingly infiltrating Balboa Park . . .

Perhaps Tony hadn't noticed because he was so busy making a name for himself in the department—excellent evaluations, commendations from the brass, and the ultimate compliment, hearing his name on the lips of cops he'd never even met. All this at the ripe age of twenty-three. He knew that Ed Winston, cagey and experienced—much like his own father had been—had a lot to do with his outstanding progress.

Things happened so fast.

That was what he kept telling himself about that night, whenever the memory ambushed him. There was no way either he or Ed could have done anything differently. No way. Anybody could make a mistake like that. Besides, why should a good cop—especially a cop with a career as otherwise exemplary as Ed Winston's—have to suffer degradation, censure, public humiliation—possibly even *jail*—because of a simple *mistake*?

It wasn't as if anything could bring that kid back to life.

This was what it had looked like that night: A bunch of dark figures huddling in the canyon, the way dope dealers do while conducting business. If you were a cop you didn't fuck around in a situation like that, especially in the canyons. You got in position and pulled your gun and said "Freeze" and said "Police," and they put up their hands and you got another bust and another good report and that was that.

Except this time. This time, after Ed took his usual post on the trail, squatting low, and Tony turned to work his way around to a higher position so he could cover the escape routes, there came a sharp, clear sound from the huddle of figures: *Snick*.

And Ed Winston started shooting.

Tony remembered wincing as the first blast of gunpowder went off almost in his ear and an arrow of burning gasses flashed past his eyes. Later, at Mercy Hospital, the doctors would pick grains of gunpowder out of his scalp, and for months his right ear would buzz softly. But at the time he felt no pain; he had simply dropped into a shooter's crouch, his own revolver in his hand, wincing again and again at the bright strobes of Ed's .38. Those flashes illuminated a cluster of kids—boys in their early teens, cringing, eyes round with terror and shock. Not that kids couldn't be dangerous, of course, but these were all unarmed. And frozen in that strobe like a bee in amber was one image that would become a memory and, soon, a nightmare: The closest boy caught in mid-whirl, a scarlet necktie flying out from his throat. Except it wasn't a necktie. Above that, a cigarette clung to his shocked-open lips. And lower, he clenched a Bic lighter in one hand, his thumb on the wheel where it had been trying to get the flint to spark.

Snick-bangbangbangbang.

Tony had never pulled the trigger of his gun. But Ed Winston had capped off four rounds and the kids scattered, leaving six unlit Marlboros lying on the path, soaking up blood. The cigarettes would eventually test negative for PCP or other illicit substances. The kids would be back later with their parents, after the TV crews arrived.

All but one of the kids. Tony never heard the Bic-holding boy fall to the ground, but there he lay now, an innocuous-looking hulk in the darkness.

Tony knew that he moved very quickly to the boy after that, but in his memory there was a moment of time that lasted forever: He and Ed standing motionless in the stench of burnt cordite while the echoes of the gunshots marched away through the canyons. Then Tony switched on his flashlight, and discovered that blood doesn't form a neat pool in dirt, but crawls away in many directions like the crooked legs of a sea star. The cigarettes were turning pink with it.

And the boy was still alive. He lay in the fresh mud, eyes wide, mouth opening and closing slowly. A failing arc of blood pumped from the ragged hole in his neck. Tony bent over him, reaching out to apply pressure to the wound—just as the flow ceased entirely.

But the boy's eyes didn't close. As they stared at Tony they became silvery-flat, like photos exposed too long to the sun.

Ed suddenly pushed past Tony and bent down over the trail, plucking up the cigarettes and the Bic. "He had a knife, Tony," he gasped. "A switchblade. I heard it, saw it. Didn't it look to you like a switchblade? Didn't it?" Plucking up bloody cigarettes.

"Jesus, Ed," Tony said. "Holy Jesus." He switched off the light. The darkness was better. And yet, his sense of panic were really quite distant. Almost academic. His mind felt so clear . . . so alive . . .

"Listen to me," Ed said in the darkness. "Listen to me carefully, this is my life here, man. We thought a meth deal was going down. We *gave the warning*, do you understand? We *gave the warning* and *saw* one of them go for a knife. Do you understand? That's what you saw, Tony, wasn't it? Wasn't that what you saw?"

Did Bic make switchblades?

"I *had* to shoot him," Ed said. "One of his buddies must have grabbed the knife and taken it with him when they ran away. Isn't that right, Tony?"

Suddenly Tony heard his dad's voice: *I hated the fucking corruption in New York, Tone. I'm not saying I never took any payola, I'm saying I wish I never did.*

"Tony," Ed said. "There'll be a board. You can't shoot your gun at a goddamned rattlesnake in this city without a board review, you know that. And the blacks will castrate me if they think . . . if they . . . Tony . . ." Suddenly, plaintively, ". . . Tony, it was an *accident*."

And it was, of course. Anybody could see that. What were those fucking kids doing smoking in the bowels of Balboa Park at this hour, anyway? Kids like that, it was only a matter of time before Marlboros became crack. You could say that Ed's real mistake had only been to catch them too soon.

And there was this, too: Testifying that Ed Winston, veteran cop, had drawn down on a bunch of unarmed youths and capped off four rounds without warning because he heard a *sound* would not bring this boy back from the dead. Nothing would bring the boy back. *Nothing*.

"That's what I saw, Ed," Tony heard himself saying, the body cooling at his feet, and was horrified at how convincing he sounded. "He pulled a knife. That's what I saw. Don't worry about it, let's just call this in now . . ."

A red stoplight suddenly flared ahead, and Tony hit the brakes hard, halting his car halfway across the pedestrian walkway. Two men, walking arm in arm, paused to glare at him.

"Jesus Christ," Tony said shakily.

CHAPTER TWELVE

Someone was in Mitford's living room.

Mitford awoke instantly, fully alert, and lay there listening.

There it was again. A soft rustling. Pendergast? What was he doing here? And at—he glanced at his clock—3:00 A.M.?

Mitford's suite was as utterly dark as only underground rooms can be, but he knew its layout exactly, knew precisely how he had left things when he went to bed. The connecting door to the living room was open. Mitford's favorite pistol was under his pillow. He slipped it out now, eased out of bed, and crept with complete assurance to his dresser. A flashlight lay there, and he picked it up and made his way to the doorway.

Here he paused and listened again. Finally he heard it, a soft brushing sound near the front door.

Eyes averted slightly to prevent temporary blindness, he switched on the flashlight. The front door was just clicking closed.

He crossed the room in two bounds, wrenched the door open and leaped into the hallway, pistol raised. The corridor was long, lined with unused suites that were always locked—and it was empty.

Mitford hesitated a moment, surprised. Pendergast couldn't have run fast enough to reach the corner by now, and if a Loner had somehow escaped, there would have been a strident alarm. Then what had been in Mitford's room? He refused to believe he'd imagined it. There had to—

Suddenly he thought of the monkeys. Loner Chow, yes, but they were good-sized animals, big enough and smart enough to open an ordinary door. They moved damned quick, too. What if one of them had escaped from the menagerie? Even if Pendergast knew about it, he would never tell Mitford for fear Mitford would shoot the creature.

Which he would. Christ, if one of those things was running free in the complex, it would end up setting off every damned alarm there was . . .

Finally Mitford sprinted down the hall, but there was nothing around the corner, either. He continued on to the control room and stared at the monitors. Nothing was moving where it shouldn't be moving. Mitford shut down the VCRs and rewound them for a few feet to check on activity during the past fifteen minutes—nothing there, either. Of course, the security cameras didn't cover every possible route through Ginnunga Gap.

No longer tired, Mitford decided to conduct a room-by-room sweep of the complex. Starting in the secure areas, he worked his way toward the perimeter, disregarding only the locked rooms and, of course, the Loner's cells. But he found no sign of an intruder larger than a mouse.

Finally he ended up in the science section, which had been pretty much abandoned since the Alphas reached maturity. Right away he could hear the chattering and screaming of monkeys coming from the menagerie down the hall. It used to be that Mitford was responsible for taking care of those damned animals, but once the Alphas were born, Pendergast had volunteered to take over. Mitford had abdicated willingly, although he'd been a little surprised; he knew Pendergast got all dewy-eyed about having to keep any animal caged, and lamented the necessity of the monkeys' eventual fates . . .

That made him think again about the doc's explanation of the real purpose of *Enkidu*, and he smiled. Man, once you got used to the idea, it didn't sound so ridiculous. Imagine a world where sudden death and complete luxury dwelt side by side, no matter where you lived. One minute you're watching satellite TV in the comfort of your beachside house; the next, as you step outside for a breath of sharp, crystalline air, a Loner streaks across the sand and rips your throat out. It would be like . . . condo cave-dwelling.

And the pragmatic side of Mitford recognized something else, too: After only fifteen more field tests—a couple of weeks—*Enkidu* would be fully launched, the Loners freed. Which meant Ira Mitford would be looking for a job, because he certainly didn't intend to hang around this dump while all the excitement happened out there in the world. But that was no problem. In the forthcoming age, with everyone living under the constant threat of violent death, a man with his talents and special knowledge would be in big demand. Yeah. Talk about making a *killing*.

The menagerie was exactly as he remembered it—a chaos of anthropoid shrieks, bar-rattling, stomping. None of the cages were open, but some were always empty, and it was impossible for him to be sure all the monkeys were accounted for. Suddenly he wondered what Pendergast planned to do with the surviving monkeys, anyway, after the Loners were turned loose. Free them, too? Probably—and when he did so, he'd no doubt imagine he was Noah throwing wide the doors of the ark.

Nothing like a quasi-religious mass-murderer to keep things interesting.

In the hallway again, Mitford tested the doors to the other rooms. They were unlocked, so he poked his head in each room to check for hairy anthropoid intruders. There were no monkeys in the microbiology lab, or the incubation room, or the surgery. He didn't bother to check the old jail-pit, not only because it would hold no interest for a monkey but because the metal door leading back to it was much too heavy for a monkey to open.

Finally, he was left with only the computer room. What was it Pendergast called it? Oh yeah, the Ark of the Covenant. Mitford opened the door, quickly scanned the Spartan interior. Nope, no monkey here. Well, he'd just have to keep a real close eye on the security videos for the next couple of days; sooner or later, he'd spot—

What was that, lying on the floor under the keyboard pedestal? Nothing he'd seen here before. He walked over and picked it up. It was a book—a big, leather-bound book. HOLY BIBLE embossed on the cover. Son of a bitch. He opened it, read the inscription on the cover page. *To George, my beloved son* . . . This was the Bible Pendergast had kept in a place of honor up in his library. Damn, what was it doing down *here*?

Even weirder, it had been mutilated. Not chewed or torn the way a monkey would do it, but systematically demolished, whole sections sliced out neatly, as if with a razor. God, it wasn't like Pendergast to damage a book—particularly *this* book. Mitford flipped through the remains. All that was left intact was Genesis, Exodus, Luke, The Book of Revelation, and a few odd pages here and there.

Mitford stood there for a while, the dismembered book in his hand. He didn't know very much about the Bible, really, but *everybody* knew that Genesis concerned the beginning of the world, and Revelation the end of it. Which sort of mirrored the idea of *Enkidu* . . . Still, it just didn't seem like Pendergast to do something like this. Not like him at all.

Finally Mitford shook his head. Shit, Pendergast was a split personality anyway—stone-cold scientist and rhapsodizing philosopher, cynic and dreamer, humanitarian and, soon, unsurpassed slaughterer of human beings. Who could pretend to know what a guy like that was thinking at any one time?

Still, it was troublesome enough that Mitford decided to be especially careful from here on out. If Pendergast was coming unwrapped, who knew what personality quirks would surface in the next couple of weeks? Maybe the doc would even decide he didn't need an assistant anymore . . .

Mitford returned the book to the place where he had found it. He'd keep a closer eye on Pendergast from now on. You bet he would.

Be prepared. Good advice for Boy Scouts and ex-SEALS alike.

When Deborah arrived at the Carlton Center on Monday morning, she found two notes taped to her computer monitor. One said simply, "Remember?" That would be Ted's reminder about their lunch date at the Pearblossom. Smiling, she peeled it off and looked at the second note—and her smile vanished.

> *From the Desk of Richard Andrews*
> COME TO MY OFFICE FIRST THING A.M.

Despite herself, she felt a flare of low-grade panic. Now what? Ordinarily, Andrews had Winnie type all his memos for him. But this one was written in his own precise block printing, which made it quite ominous . . . had he learned about Deborah's trip to Pendergast's house? That wasn't possible—was it? God, she was getting so *paranoid*.

Depositing her purse on the floor beside her chair—as if it were an anchor to which she must return—she took a deep breath and walked toward Andrews's office.

His door was open, voices coming out. She knocked on the jamb.

"Come in," Andrews said.

He sat in his astronaut's chair behind the desk. Lounging across from him in one of the guest chairs was a young man Deborah didn't recognize. He wore gray slacks and a navy blazer, and his tie was held in place with a clip in the shape of a tennis racquet.

"Please have a seat," Andrews said. "Jim, this is Deborah Kosarek, our . . . *established* technical writer. Ms. Kosarek, this is James van Doren."

The young man leaned forward and shook her hand briefly, leaving her smelling of Aramis. Perching on the edge of the second guest chair, Deborah turned inquiringly toward Andrews.

"Ms. Kosarek," he said briskly, "in view of recent . . . developments . . . in your department, we've decided to hire a second technical writer. Jim's straight out of UCSD with a major in computers and a minor in biology. He should be able to cover any gaps we may have in the technical writing area."

The young man smiled at her with perfectly straight teeth, and she flexed her lips back. "You say he's going to work *with* me?" she asked Andrews, and was fairly pleased with the evenness of her tone.

"Let's just say that the two of you will be dividing the workload. Jim will have his own assignments, while you'll continue to deal with your current . . . *ongoing* projects until they're completed. This way, we'll hopefully never fall behind schedule again."

She had to look away to hide the impotent fury that boiled up in her. Once again she focused her attention on the old photo of Pendergast and Carlton. God, she wished she'd found Dr. Pendergast safe and sound up at his house yesterday. Perhaps her motives weren't entirely selfless, but . . . suddenly she realized that Andrews wouldn't be making this change if he expected Pendergast to return soon. His bullshit about "dividing the work load" was just a first step toward making her quit of her own volition.

She clenched her teeth until her jaw creaked. No way. No way would she give in to such a cheap shot.

All these thoughts went through her mind in a flash. When she turned back to young Jim, she wore a pleasant smile. "Glad to have you on board," she said. "There's always plenty to do." Flicking her eyes quickly to Andrews, she caught his look of surprise. Better, *he* knew she'd caught it. His face reddened, but when he spoke his voice was cold.

"Jim will also double-check your work for a while, Ms. Kosarek . . . so he can get used to the way we do things."

She kept the smile carved on. "That's nice," she said, but her eyes roved to the photo again. Pendergast. Carlton. And the guy sitting in the pickup, looking bored and cynical. Be like him. Be like . . .

Her jaw dropped open.

That young man—he was the same guy she'd seen yesterday, up at Dr. Pendergast's house.

Well . . . so what? If anything, that supported the man's contention that he was simply renting the house from Pendergast. Perhaps they'd met during construction of the Carlton Center. Hell, maybe they lived *together*. Maybe they were gay. She hated that thought. Then something else occurred to her, something just as disillusioning but so sensible it took her breath away.

Gay or not, surfer-looking or not, what if the Blond Man was *also* a geneticist? What if he and Pendergast had been working together in secret for all these years? What had Ted said before? Something about Pendergast cultivating the image of a lone wolf . . .

She realized Andrews was staring at her, head tilted, and suddenly remembered the hallucination she'd had of the lizard-crab-thing with her boss's smirking face. Forcing another casual smile onto her lips, she turned to the new man and said, "So when do I start training you . . . Jimmy?"

The Pearblossom Restaurant was perched on a steep hillside with a panoramic view of the Pacific Ocean. As Deborah pulled into the magnolia-shaded lane fronting the building, she sighed at a sign reading VALET PARKING ONLY. Even with Ted buying lunch, there went her budget for the week.

Reluctantly surrendering her keys, she gave her name at the desk and was led to a small table next to a floor-to-ceiling window. Amongst the potted ferns sat Ted, staring disgruntledly out at the Cove just below. She suddenly had to smile. Over his T-shirt, he was wearing an ill-fitting sport coat in a strident plaid.

"Didn't know they had a dress code, did you?" she asked as the *maître d'* glided away.

Ted started to get to his feet to help her with her chair, but she waved him off and seated herself.

"Do you believe this jacket?" he grumbled, holding out his arms to show the too-long cuffs. "They've got a whole closet full of them back there—all designed for three-armed linoleum salesmen."

"Just be glad they don't require a tie, too."

He grunted, and his gaze flicked over her like a feather-duster. "You look great, at least."

"Thanks. I needed that."

"What's the matter?"

She lifted her menu to hide her face, and noticed that none of the prices were listed. "Just another run-in with Andrews," she said. Paused. "You were right—he's trying to force me out."

"I heard he hired a new boy. But don't worry, I'll rig the computer so it makes the guy look like an incompetent boob—assuming he isn't one already. By the way, now that I've seen the menu, you have my permission to order a glass of water as long as they don't put ice in it. I'm kidding. Order whatever you want. I can always sell the Porsche."

Deborah didn't feel like smiling anymore. She decided on a Cobb salad.

"Seriously, though," Ted said, "don't worry about Andrews. He won't push you too hard as long as Pendergast is still around."

Deborah twitched, instantly thinking about the Blond Man. Friend or foe? "Ted," she said suddenly, "could you do me a favor?"

His face clouded. "Uh-oh."

"No, nothing like before. I just need some information out of the Admin database."

"Come on. You heard Andrews—'How dare you get into the sacred files?' I can't do that."

"No, no; these aren't personnel records. I just need a list of Dr. P's past associates—standard P.R. stuff. Especially names from back when the center was brand-new. It's no big—"

Ted turned and pointed toward the surf line. "See that street down there?"

"What? I—"

"Right there next to the rocks. Where the pelicans are. See it?"

"Sure."

"That's where that old lady got her throat torn out by the Cannibal the other night. Then he hauled her down onto the beach and—"

"*Ted . . .*"

He turned toward her again. "Make you a deal, Deb. You don't ask me to do *anything* relating to Pendergast, and I won't tell you what happened down there. The blood and gore and dismemberment . . . deal?"

"No."

She startled herself, Ted even more. Plunging on, she said, "I need some names, that's all. I could ask Winnie for them, but that would take forever. You can pull them off the computer in fifteen minutes. Come on."

He sighed. "What do you want them for?" Then he hurriedly waved a hand in dismissal. "Wait, never mind. I don't want to know."

"Please, Ted. It's not like it's classified information or anything."

He rolled his eyes. "Why doesn't that make me feel any better?"

Trying on a smile, she said, "Come on. Don't be a wimp."

"Wimp. Great. Thanks." A sigh. "Okay, I guess I owe you one after sitting like a lump in Andrews's office the way I did. Okay. When?"

"By tomorrow afternoon?"

"I'll see what I can do. But, Deborah . . ."

"Yes?"

"If there's even one hint I could get in trouble—just one hint—I'll pull out immediately. I want you to know that up front. Wimps always prosper."

Impulsively, she reached out and covered one of his hands with hers. "Thanks, Ted. I'll make it up to you."

His fingers trembled slightly. "If it's another lunch date," he said thickly, "forget it. I don't think I can afford your gratitude."

"All right," Chatherton said, "what's the matter?"

Tony looked up. They were driving slowly through Rancho Vista del Oro in the PSS cruiser, Chatherton behind the wheel.

"Nothing's the matter," Tony said. "Why?"

"You haven't asked me what I know about the shindig in El Cajon last night. That's not like you."

Tony smiled. "Sorry. Had something else on my mind. Besides, I heard the police don't think it was a Cannibal killing."

"You believe everything the PD tells the media?"

Tony's eyes narrowed. "You mean it *was* the Cannibal?"

"Let me put it this way: There are two little details the department didn't mention to the press. First, they found blood on the floor that matches the type of the little girl. And second, the cuts on the face of the man who got in the way are identical to some of the slashes found on the Cannibal's first two victims."

"Wow—has the department put together a Cannibal Task Force yet?"

"I understand they're working on forming a Joint Task Force with the

Sheriff's Department and El Cajon Police, yeah. Boy, what I'd give to be on *that*."

Tony nodded. "That would be great."

Chatherton turned the cruiser up a steep grade to the next terrace. To the north, bulldozers crawled restlessly between the new houses in Phase Two. "By the way," Chatherton said, "what's her name?"

"Sorry?"

"The woman you're thinking about—is she the same one I saw you with yesterday?"

"Oh. Well, yeah. Her name's Deborah Kosarek, and she's got a problem."

"Yeah—you."

"No, seriously. In fact, I wanted to talk to you about it." Keeping everything as unembellished as possible, Tony described the trip to the top of Tortoise Mountain, and, after a moment's hesitation, explained why the trek had been made. He didn't mention the little journey to Alpine, though.

Throughout the story, Chatherton's mouth grew more and more pursed. When it was over, he said, "You're sure this babe isn't some kind of flake?"

"I don't think so; she doesn't seem the type. And anyway, the guy up at the house was definitely off-kilter."

Chatherton shrugged. In a cop's book, "off-kilter" was almost a compliment.

Finally, Tony took the plunge. "I followed him when he left here, too."

"You *what?*"

"I followed him. There were a bunch of off-road trails where he went, but no sign of a driveway or a house."

Chatherton shrugged. "So what do you want me to do?"

"Nothing. I just told Deborah I'd get your opinion, see if you thought the police might look into it."

Pulling a wry face, Chatherton said, "Come on. What do you *really* want?"

"Seriously, I promised I'd get your opinion, that's all. I thought a cop's comments might calm her down, reassure her."

"Okay. Here's my *opinion*: Even if she's absolutely right about the kidnapping, there's nothing we can do at the moment. As you already know, Tony." He paused. Then, casually, "Didn't you tell her you used to be a cop?"

"No. It's too complicated to get into."

Chatherton gave him a long look, but Tony was watching the passing streets for signs of rampaging skateboarders.

"Anyway," Chatherton said finally, "you've got my opinion—your ladyfriend is a flake. End of story."

"There is one more thing, if you don't mind."

"I thought so."

"It's no big deal. Could you check with DMV and find out who owns a brown Cherokee, California license 2ZJZ350, and give me any information you can dig up on him?"

"What for?"

"It's the blond guy's car."

"Tony . . ."

"I just want to find out where he lives. Come on, Bill."

Chatherton sighed. "Okay, for you I can do that; anything to help you hang onto a woman for once. In fact, if you want, I could run down to the guard office right now and call in about the license number. Good enough?"

"That would be terrific." Tony chose to ignore the *hang onto a woman* zinger. "Listen, one more thing: Tomorrow, while you're at the station, could you check and see if the guy's got a police record, too?"

Chatherton laughed. "Anything else?"

"Nope."

"Okay—but if I do all this, will you promise me one thing?"

"What's that?"

"If this *does* turn out to be a conspiracy of some kind, how about giving me all the credit for making the bust? You know, 'Street cop uncovers high-tech murder ring.' Promotions. Glory. All that shit. Come on."

Tony laughed. "Okay, as long as you let me drive the car in your parade."

"Deal."

When her doorbell rang, Deborah was trying to keep Virgil from wearing his dinner. She hesitated, spoonful of green glop poised, then sighed, put the spoon on the counter and said to her son, imprisoned in his high chair, "Stop scowling, big guy. I'll be right back."

When she peered through the peephole in the door, she blinked in surprise, then turned the lock and opened it.

"Hi," said Tony, his smile warm but a little uncertain. He was wearing his guard uniform, including the gun. Deborah glanced nervously across the landing at Sarah's door, wondering if her neighbor was peeking.

Tony shuffled his feet. "I thought I'd just drop by on my way home from work, instead of calling," he said. "Hope you don't mind."

She did, actually, but she dredged up a noncommittal smile. "Come in. How did you get my address?"

"Great deductive prowess. I looked it up in the phone book." His bulk changed the dimensions of the room, she noticed, and was reminded of Brad again. She turned quickly back to the dining area.

Tony glanced at Virgil in his high chair, and Virgil stared back with open curiosity, his squirming momentarily stilled.

"Is that your son?" Tony asked.

"He'd better be, I'm stuffing goop into him. Have a seat if you can stand to watch this."

Tony approached with the tentative stride of someone unused to children, pulled his nightstick out of his belt and lowered himself into one of the chairs. "What about you?" he asked. "Have you eaten yet?"

"The king always gets fed first." She paused, glancing at the nightstick. "Well, did you follow that guy yesterday?"

"Yeah, but I lost him somewhere east of Alpine. Do you know anybody who lives out there?"

"No." She wondered if Tony had driven past the fire station where Brad had worked. Concentrating on spooning food into Virgil's eager mouth, she said, "What about your policeman friend? Did you talk to him?"

"Yeah . . ."

"And he told you I was crazy, right?"

"Actually, he checked out the license number of the Jeep. It's registered to a man named Frederick Faust—ring a bell?"

"No."

"Well, he's a fifty-year-old man who lives in La Jolla."

"Not Alpine?"

"No. I thought I might cruise past his address later, but that's about all I can do."

She sighed. "Well, thanks for all you've done already; it was really nice of you." She paused. "Besides . . . I found out Dr. Pendergast might know that guy we saw up at the house, after all." She explained about the photo in Andrews's office.

When she was finished, Tony said, "Well, that's that, then."

She said nothing.

"Deborah . . . are you *upset* that you were wrong?"

She had to smile. "I know, I seem morbid. It's just that . . . well, of course I'm glad. I wouldn't want anything to happen to Dr. Pendergast."

"Would you like to get something to eat?"

It caught her off guard. "What?"

"Dinner. We could talk about this some more."

She looked at him closely, felt the familiar wariness welling up inside. Justified or not? She didn't know this man, certainly didn't trust her automatic attraction to him. He carried a *gun*, for God's sake. Even Brad had never had to do that. "I'm afraid I don't have a babysitter or anything," she said.

His eyes flicked toward Virgil, then back. "So bring him along. No problem."

He was obviously not a baby person—a distinct and major liability in a man, as far as she was concerned. She'd just keep that in mind. "All right," she said. "Let's go."

CHAPTER THIRTEEN

MITFORD GUIDED THE VAN out of Mission Valley onto Highway 163, and the vehicle began the laborious climb out of Mission Valley. Mitford was feeling pleased. Tonight the doc, barely glancing up from his computer terminal, had said, "Take Supai to Balboa Park." That was great—once the sun went down, the park could be almost as interesting as Southeast San Diego.

The question was, which side of the park should he go to? The west side was popular with faggots and the lice-ridden bums the government liked to call "the homeless." He hated those scuzzballs, especially the Vietnam vets who claimed to have been "traumatized" by their experiences in the war. The east side of the park, on the other hand, was where the museums, meeting halls and theaters were located. Which meant that although that area had its share of panhandlers, too, there were also a lot more legitimate visitors there at night.

So the choice was actually quite simple. No matter what Pendergast said about egalitarian population control, Mitford thought it was a waste to let Loners kill harmless old farts like the one in La Jolla. If your goal was to clean up the earth, why not concentrate on the garbage?

The high, graceful span of the Cabrillo Bridge, which connected the two halves of the park, passed overhead. The exits were coming up soon. Mitford glanced into the rear of the van, where Supai sat on the floor, gazing flatly at the doors. The Loner was wearing the sailor suit Mitford had dropped into his cell. Mitford thought that was pretty funny. Of course, in a military town like San Diego, it also made an appropriate disguise.

Here came the exits. Mitford was about to take the lane leading to the west side of the park when a car roared past on the shoulder, then whipped across the van's front bumper with inches to spare. Mitford jumped hard on the brakes, and for a heart-stopping moment it seemed the top-heavy vehicle would turn turtle. Then it straightened out again, and Mitford glared at the infringing car. It was an old Impala, its chassis skimming a hair above the pavement. Tiny blue and red lights glittered all over it—even inside the wheel-wells—and Mitford didn't have to see the interior to know it featured fuzzy upholstery, stuffed dice hanging from the rear-view mirror, and a fur liner around the steering wheel. Damned low-riders.

Trailing laughter, the Impala rumbled onto the exit into the eastern half of Balboa Park.

Mitford swung the van after it. Hell, if Pendergast could act according to signs and omens, then damn it, so could he.

At the end of the ramp, the low-rider turned north on Park Boulevard, as he had hoped it would, and rumbled past the high, glittering arch of the fountain at the end of the Prado. Then it turned clumsily onto the access road that went between the rear of the museums and the zoo. Perfect, perfect. Mitford knew that road. It dead-ended behind the Old Globe Theatre. A dark, quiet place.

By the time he turned the van off Park Boulevard, the low-rider had vanished into the shadows. Mitford shut off the van's lights and crept forward until he saw the Impala again, parked behind the art museum. Four youths were walking purposefully away from it, undoubtedly heading for one of the paths leading into the canyons. Had to be dope dealers or buyers. All *right*. No old ladies or infants tonight . . .

Maybe if he cruised right up behind the potential prey before releasing Supai, he could even watch a kill, at last. But his orders were explicit: *Under no circumstances allow the van to be associated with the tests.*

Then he realized there was a way to get his satisfaction without breaking security. He had brought a Starlight scope with him tonight, and if he released Supai and gave him a few seconds head start, he could follow on foot, using the scope to keep his bearings . . . Odds were good that Supai would go after the hoods; after all, the Loner's nose would surely lead him to such a concentration of prey. Then Mitford could watch what happened without risking himself, and still get back to the van before Supai finished eating.

It sounded good. The doc had never actually forbidden him to leave the van; probably he thought Mitford would be too leery of the Loners to put himself at such risk. Well, neither God nor Dr. George Irving Pendergast had ever created anything Ira Mitford was afraid of.

Switching on the Starlight scope and raising it to his eyes, he watched the punks step off the pavement and disappear into a canyon. Then he punched the door-release button and watched Supai bound out of the van, sweep past the passenger side, and skim away in the direction of the low-rider homeboys. Yes! Mitford waited until he had disappeared into the canyon, too, then quickly drew his pistol, transferred it to one jacket pocket, slipped the Starlight scope into the other, and reached for the door handle.

He had placed one foot on the ground when the police car pulled in behind him.

"The time for *Enkidu* is drawing near," Pendergast said in the semidarkness. "Can't you feel it? The time of retribution and change that so many religions have predicted is finally almost here, Vulcan."

From the floor of the pit, Vulcan leered up at him, and Pendergast realized that the Loner's ability to mask his real face behind the human one was failing rapidly. It was sad. There was no question now: Vulcan was dying. And it wouldn't take long. Unlike humans, Loners weren't built to linger on and on, sapping the resources of their world for nothing.

"I wish you could live to see that day," Pendergast murmured. "You deserve to be aware of what your children will accomplish. To witness the heaven that earth can become again."

"Halleluia," Vulcan hummed.

Pendergast shuddered with a curious mixture of joy and sadness. Sometimes, it seemed as if the Loner really did understand his words, maybe even his intentions. How much more would Vulcan learn to comprehend if he could enjoy the lifespan of a human being? It was a rhetorical question, of course.

"You know," Pendergast said, "I think—" He jumped as the remote alarm in his pocket beeped. "Now what?" The alarm meant that the Ark, which monitored a dozen outside computer systems, had noted the foreign appearance of a tagged phrase, such as "Enkidu," "Pendergast" or "Hiber Nation." This was how the Ark had warned Pendergast about Deborah's attempt to contact him from the Carlton Center.

But tonight, of course, the alarm no doubt indicated police activity. "I'll bet Supai just sent another victim to his Maker," he said, and rose excitedly to his feet. "I'd better go check. Goodnight, son."

After hurrying back to the control room, Pendergast looked at the main monitor and scowled. No, this wasn't an alert from the police computer, after all . . . once again it was from the Carlton Center. Someone was accessing his, *his*, administrative file.

He noted that the request was coming over one of the Center's laboratory terminals, so it couldn't be Deborah's work. Nor was the intruder attempting to break into the Ark this time—he was simply calling up Pendergast's personnel file on the mainframe. But even though there was no compromising information in that file, the fact was that nobody on the science staff had any reason to be looking at it—especially at this hour of the night.

Pendergast checked for the entry code of the operator, half-expecting to see Ted Scully's number. But it was the code of a veteran staff geneticist, Trevor Dusart. Odd. Dusart was a good scientist but rigidly single-minded, focusing on his work so tightly that he rarely noticed the "Kick Me" signs younger members of the team taped to his backside.

Pendergast watched the screen for a moment, then accessed the Carlton Center personnel list and found Dusart's home number.

He dialed, and after three rings, a woman's voice said, "Dusart residence."

"Is Trevor there?" Pendergast asked.

"Yes, just a moment."

Pendergast hung up, then dialed a more familiar number.

"Carlton Center," said a monotonous voice. "Front desk."

"This is Richard Andrews," Pendergast said sternly. "Has Ted Scully logged out for the day yet?"

"Uh—let me check, sir. No . . . he's still here."

Pendergast hung up again and sat back slowly. So. The invader wasn't Dusart; it was almost certainly Scully, using Dusart's I.D. number. Probably thought he was being clever.

At least he wasn't working from Deborah's terminal this time. That didn't mean she wasn't involved somehow, of course, but Pendergast hoped desperately she wasn't. A woman like her deserved to live on into the new and glorious future. But what interest could *Scully* possibly have in Pendergast's background?

The computer notified him that his admin files had been printed and the system exited. Scully was finished with whatever he'd been trying to do. Pendergast sat back, frowning.

At that moment, the police radio sputtered frantically to life.

* * *

"Hi, officers," Mitford said, climbing all the way out of the van.

The two cops rose simultaneously from the patrol car. The driver was short and slender, about Mitford's own age. As he walked forward he held his arms slightly away from his sides, gunfighter-style; the pose looked aggressive, but Mitford knew it was just practical, a way to avoid bumping wrists against the junk hanging from the utility belt. The second cop was younger, black, and seemed a little nervous. Mitford noticed that both officers' holsters contained the ever-more-popular automatic pistols rather than .38 revolvers.

He watched the cops come closer, trying hard not to think about the guns. He'd always hoped somebody would hassle him while he was on a Loners mission, of course, but cops . . . damn it, this situation had to be handled without violence if possible; dead cops made for a stirred-up hornet's nest, especially since these two would have already radioed in the van's license number and description. The information they would get in return was false, of course, planted in the DMV computers by Pendergast, but still—it also meant the van's description would be known to everybody with a badge.

And if Supai happened to attack those punks in the canyon while the cops were still here . . . Christ!

The white officer stopped just beyond arm's reach. His nameplate read P. L. DONOVAN, and his expression was stony and alert. No rookie, this.

Mitford played his part. "What can I do for you, officer?"

"May I see your driver's license, registration and proof of insurance, please?" Donovan took his clipboard from under his arm. Meanwhile, his partner walked over and peered into the back of the van.

Mitford pulled out his wallet and started to hand it over. No worries here; his driver's license had him named Gilbert G. Ahmesh, from Riverside.

Donovan raised one hand, palm out. "Remove the license from your wallet and hand it to me, please." As Mitford tugged at the license, the cop went on, "Why are you parked back here at this hour? The museums and theaters have been closed for quite a while."

Mitford held the license out between two fingers, and watched Donovan take it without removing his gaze from Mitford's face. Smart cop, all right. "Just sitting for a minute," Mitford said. "It's a nice night."

"Why is the back of your van open?" the second cop asked.

"I was just letting in a little breeze. As you can see, there's nothing in there."

"There's a partition up front. How do you expect to feel a breeze?"

"The partition opens," Mitford said.

Donovan seemed to have ignored this exchange as he examined Mitford's license in the beam of his penlight. "Have you been drinking at all this evening?" he asked.

"No, sir." Tough to say "sir."

Without comment, Donovan handed Mitford's fake license to the second cop, who carried it back to the car, slid in on the passenger side and unclipped the radio mike.

"Now," Donovan said, "I'm just going to conduct a little test." He took a Bic pen from his shirt pocket and lit it up with the penlight. "Watch the end of this pen. Follow it with your eyes, but don't turn your head." Mitford knew this test; it was designed to detect nystagmus, the uncontrollable trembling of the eyes that is always evident in inebriated people. He hadn't been drinking, of course, and didn't even smell of alcohol, so he knew the cop was just looking for an excuse, any excuse, to haul him in. And no wonder. What cop would believe somebody had parked an open van behind the art museum in the middle of the night just to take the air?

What a balls-up run of foul luck. Mitford listened for the sound of death and mayhem in the canyons. Nothing. That was good, but . . . what was taking so long? What was Supai doing?

Donovan snapped off the light. "Turn around, please."

Mitford stiffened. "What for?"

"Just turn around and put your hands against the van."

"You're going to *search* me?"

Donovan rested a palm on the butt of his nightstick. "I asked you to turn around. I'm not going to ask again."

Inside the car, the second cop sensed the tension and sat up straighter.

Fury at the scope of the incipient disaster swelled up in Mitford. The moment Donovan touched him, the cop would feel the weight of the gun in Mitford's jacket pocket. Which meant there was no way to avoid—

Suddenly a figure in a U.S. Navy uniform floated out of the bushes next to the police car. As Mitford watched in disbelief, Supai leaned in through the passenger-side window. The black cop jumped in shock and let out a startled, mangled scream. Abruptly, half the windshield turned opaque.

Donovan spun toward the commotion, and Mitford instantly took advantage. His hand blurred down to his pocket and up again, and there was a loud, echoing *crack*. He didn't believe in silencers.

The bullet caught Donovan at the base of the skull, spraying blood, bones and teeth onto the cruiser's light-rack ten feet away. Mitford lowered the pistol slightly and pulled the trigger again. *Crack*. There. Head and heart, his signature. Donovan fell.

But there was no time to gloat; Supai was right *here*. Mitford spun toward the police car. The Loner was gone. Where—?

"Ah wan mah Em Tee Vee!" a voice wailed behind him, and he spun fast and low, pistol tracking. Supai stood between him and the art museum; the Loner's distended face and most of the sailor suit glistened with blood.

Part of Mitford's mind reflected that this was the first time he had stood in the presence of a Loner while it was awake and aware. But overpowering that was the image of Arcadio's hand flying off his arm. Mitford kept three pounds of pressure on the seven-pound trigger.

But Supai made no move toward him. Just stood there, head slightly inclined, eyes glittering through a hood of fresh blood.

Now Mitford heard shouts rising from the Prado on the far side of the Art Museum—the gunshots had of course attracted attention—and then the radio in the cop car let out a burst of chatter. Shit, he had to get out of here. *They* had to get out of here.

Obey the beacon, you asshole monstrosity. Get in the fucking van.

But Supai just stood there. "Halleighloooooyaaaah," he said, the word elongating, Loner-teeth serrating the darkness in a mammoth grin. Mitford was reminded of a TV show he'd once seen where a great white shark tried to eat the side of a boat, jaws extended in just this way.

He grinned back.

The Loner's jaws retracted with a soft scraping hiss, the sound of a steel blade crossing a whetstone—but before Mitford could budge, Supai became a blur. Mitford felt a brush of air and the Loner was behind him again, moving. He spun with a gasp, but now Supai was just a grin disappearing into the van. Mitford stood frozen for a moment, his gun still only half-raised, and thought *He could have taken me if he had wanted to*. But the notion was repelled immediately. No. No way. Nothing could outmove Ira Mitford.

The voices from on the Prado sounded more purposeful now, and the chatter on the police radio grew increasingly urgent. Sirens wailed in the night. *Move, Mitford*.

He leaped into the van, got it turned around, and slammed his foot down on the accelerator. As the overweight vehicle picked up speed, Mitford glanced into the rear-view mirror and saw a strange thing: Supai sitting on the floor with his palms pressed together in front of his bowed head. Except for the extended talons, he looked like a little kid saying his prayers.

Tony's eyes snapped open.

He listened to the sirens for a moment, then leaped out of bed and ran to the window as a cruiser shot down the street next to his building, engine straining, siren and lights slapping against the surrounding buildings. Dogs sang in frenzied chorus all over the neighborhood.

The cruiser's lights streaked toward the park, where sirens were congregating like sea gulls over a meal.

What had the Cannibal done now?

Tony thought about poor Chatherton, sitting on his butt up there at Rancho Vista Del Oro. Tomorrow he'd say something like, *Some cops get the good breaks, others spend their entire careers handing out jay-walking tickets*.

But then, Chatherton probably didn't deserve the position he coveted. Being a detective—especially a homicide detective—required a concern for detail that Chatherton just didn't seem to have. Tony had had a demonstration of that earlier this evening when, after dropping Deborah and her son off at their apartment, he had driven out to La Jolla to see if he could find the home of Frederick Faust. He'd located Saltspray Drive without difficulty, but discovered that the street number Chatherton had given him would have placed the house about a hundred yards out in the Pacific Ocean. Not exactly precise police work.

The sirens had fallen silent. Tony climbed back into bed and stared at the ceiling, his thoughts turning back to Deborah and Virgil Kosarek. To his surprise, having a toddler around hadn't bothered him as much as he'd expected it to; as for Deborah, he had very much enjoyed being with her, even though there hadn't been anything physical in it. In fact, he hadn't thought about kissing her good night until he was walking back to his car to come home.

Maybe he'd felt restrained by the shell of reserve he'd sensed around her—a barrier he understood well. The two of them were rather like the communities around Tortoise Mountain, each hiding behind its walls. Of course, he knew what lurked behind his own barrier: the truth of *that night*. He wondered what secret pain mistake Deborah hid behind hers.

Ironically, though, her guardedness was one of the things Tony found attractive about her. Most of the women he'd dated didn't hesitate to reveal all their problems at the drop of a cocktail napkin (*I don't know why I'm telling you this, it's just that you're such a good listener . . .*), but not Deborah. She hadn't told him anything about her past, not even how she had come to be a single mother. He wondered if she ever would. And he wondered if he'd ever confess that he used to be a policeman, far less the reason he'd become a civilian again.

Would either of them ever dare peek over their walls? Did he *want* to? For years now his life had settled into a comfortable enough pattern, free of the need for him to test himself for resolve or ideals. A safe life. Why mess it up now?

In the park, the sirens started up again, dispersing this time. Tony lay there listening to them, eyes wide open.

From the darkness came a soft voice:

> ". . . Thou hast seen
>   my affliction;
> Thou hast known the
>   troubles of my soul . . ."

Pendergast smiled, eyes closed, one thumb very near his mouth. Mother. Mother always recited a Bible verse for him before he went to sleep.

> ". . . Thou hast set my feet in a
>   large place . . ."

His flannel jammies felt nice and cozy, the blanket with its embroidered stagecoaches and Indians was snugged around his shoulders to keep the bogeyman out. And Mother's voice, as always, was so comforting . . .

> "Then I will make up to you
>   for the years
> That the swarming locust
>   has eaten . . ."

He stirred. Locusts? That wasn't the kind of Bible verse Mother liked to read to him; she preferred Psalms and Proverbs—hopeful, sunny words that ensured sweet dreams. Nothing about locusts or famines, bad things . . .

> "There is a way which
>   sssseems rrrrright to a man,
> But itssss end is the way of
>   death . . ."

His head tossed, his clutching fingers made the stagecoaches and charging Indians tumble into a canyon. Poor Mother. Her voice was beginning to sound rough and hoarse . . . she was having a "spell." He didn't like to think about that. "My throat's just a little scratchy, Georgie," she would say. "Don't worry, I'll be good as new tomorrow." But each new spell was worse than the one before . . .

> "To the housssse which none may leave
> who enterrr it,
> on the rrroad frrrom which therre is
> no way back . . ."

Wait. That wasn't the Bible at all. That was from the *Epic of Gilgamesh*; he didn't think Mother had even heard of it. But *he* had. Oh, yes. After Mother became the one who lay in bed and he the one seeking to soothe her pain and fear, he had realized that Psalms held no truth, and Proverbs no comfort, and he had looked elsewhere for truth.

> ". . . to the housssse wherrre its inhabitantsss
> arrre berrrreft of light . . ."

Oh, Mother's voice was like a rusty wire now, rough and knotted. Pendergast raised his head and opened his eyes, and saw a pale smile hovering before him in the darkness. He relaxed again, smiling back—then stiffened. Mother hadn't smiled at all in her final months, at least not until the last time he'd visited her in the hospital. Then, he had entered her room one night with the Bible she had given him clutched under his arm, and found her grinning up at the ceiling. Grinning, but her eyes were dim and flat because she was . . .

. . . dead.

The crescent of teeth vanished and he jolted fully erect, caught in a whirlpool of disorientation, wondering how the stars had gotten into his bedroom. Then he realized the stars weren't in his bedroom, and neither was he. He was sitting at his desk in front of a broad window that overlooked a valley and the Laguna Mountains. His hands clutched not cowboys-and-Indians blankets but the hard, flat surface of the desk. Where his head had been resting was a flattened copy of Lao Tse's *Tao Te Ching*, which spoke of the senselessness of struggling against the natural world, the *Tao*.

For a moment he couldn't seem to move. His body felt very distant except for his heart, which slammed about so furiously he wondered if he was having a coronary. He even seemed to hear the urgent *beep-beep-beep* of a heart monitor like the one that had supposedly guarded his mother on her deathbed.

Mother. Suddenly he realized she was still in front of him, a pale shape floating away among the stars. Receding, fading. His chest seized in love and despair. *Mother . . . ?*

. . . or something behind him, reflected in the window?

He whirled, gasping. The library was a large room, made intimate by bookcases crammed with volumes of poetry and scholarly thought, and glowing embers muttering quietly in the fireplace. Here and there, glass cases exhibited treasures: pre-Christian scrolls, Egyptian parchments, hand-illuminated Gospels from the so-called Dark Ages, even rubbings of cuneiform verse from an ancient clay tablet of *Gilgamesh*. In a place of honor on the mantel stood a photo of his mother. Mother, who had died from throat cancer when Georgie Pendergast was only twelve years old.

But of course Mother wasn't here now, either in person or in spirit. Dead, Pendergast feared, was truly dead. He turned back toward the window. Beyond lay the stars and the pale oval of his own face. No reflections of intruders behind him. Well, of course not. There was only one way in or out of the library, through the elevator behind the fireplace. And only he and Mitford knew about that.

Mitford.

The annoying beeping kept on, and finally Pendergast realized it was the computer alarm. He'd been hearing that sound, on and off, for most of the night—the police had been very busy compiling information about the murders in Balboa Park. *Be on the lookout for a Caucasian male, thirty-eight years old, medium height and build, blond hair and blue eyes. Subject is driving a navy blue van with mirrorized windows, California license number 2KWZ541, and using the name Gilbert G. Ahmesh. Subject wanted in connection with the killings of police officers in Balboa Park. Considered to be armed and very dangerous.* It was disastrous. Mitford, or at least his false identity, was now equated with the San Diego Cannibal. So was the transport van.

Facts which severely jeopardized the Alpha field test program.

All because of Mitford.

Pendergast didn't want to see the current computer readout; undoubtedly it was more bad news. He stared outside instead. The darkness was beginning to fade; now he could see, far below, the valley stretching away like a vast bowl of fog. That land belonged to him—a buffer against "civilization," and protection for *Enkidu*. He'd worked so hard to protect *Enkidu*. What would happen to all his work if Mitford was captured, and decided to talk?

Pendergast knew Mitford wasn't the type to be caught easily, or to submit willingly to restraint. Still, it could happen. He could be shot, or paralyzed with a Taser, or trapped somehow. And what about Supai? What would happen if the police opened the back of the van?

The beeping was unrelenting. The terminal itself was hidden in an oak cabinet beside the desk. To Pendergast, this library was a refuge from the modern world, a repository of wisdom and introspection from a quieter age. He wished the Ark would shut up.

Outside, the growing dawn light revealed a layer of tobacco brown haze above the fog; it cut the mountains in half like a rusty knife. He scowled. Air pollution—just one visible periscope from the deadly submarine of planetary decay. Today, across the globe, 90,000 acres of rain forest would fall, 10,000 dolphins would die in tuna-fishing purse seines, equal numbers of sharks would be destroyed just for their dorsal fins—and at the same time, half a million more people would be born, begging for food and shelter and energy. God, time was so short, so desperately short; doom was written on the very air in sepia ink.

So, do something.

He turned to the computer cabinet with renewed determination. So be it. He was a scientist, and believed in conducting thorough tests, a complete methodology, prior to pronouncing any experiment a success. But he was also a concerned, passionate denizen of the earth, and if he had to, if Mitford had been captured or killed and Supai discovered, he would release the rest of the Alphas this very day. He'd hate to do it so crudely, without emphasis or ceremony, but if necessary, he wouldn't hesitate.

Opening the cabinet, he pulled out the keyboard and typed in his access code. Instantly the monitor spilled out a torrent of security information originating from the San Diego Police Department. Pendergast's eyes widened. Wait a second—this didn't have anything to do with Mitford or the van, after all.

Someone was trying to find out if Frederick Faust—one of Pendergast's pseudonyms—had a police record.

There was no such record, of course, but that was beside the point. Why would anyone be interested in the nonexistent Frederick Faust? Did their interest have anything to do with the fact that the name Faust was also the name under which Pendergast had purchased Hiber Nation ten years ago?

Quickly, he found the name and badge number of the officer who had made the inquiry: William Chatherton, SDPD. The Ark noted that a cop by that name also worked as a security guard at Rancho Vista Del Oro.

Sitting back dizzily, Pendergast stared out the window. This simply could not be coincidence. Chatherton must have seen something, heard something . . .

Suddenly he noticed another pale blur hovering in the sky like a cloud, fading stars showing through it. It grew steadily larger, as if coming closer—he thought he saw eyes, a mouth. Smiling.

Mother?

A noise behind him.

He whirled around again, hands rising as if to fend off a blow, knocking the computer keyboard to the floor. A man loomed over him—dark hair, boots, coveralls. Pendergast struggled to his feet.

"It's me," the dark-haired man said impatiently, and only then did Pendergast recognize Mitford.

"What the *hell*?" Pendergast gasped, slumping back.

Mitford ran a hand through his clipped hair. "After what happened in Balboa Park, I thought it would be wise to change my look."

Pendergast's heartbeat dropped into a more normal range. He was relieved that Mitford had returned safely, of course. But why had he ever given this psychopath access to his private lift? He didn't like having people creep up behind him when he was . . .

"How long have you been here?" he demanded.

"In the complex? About an hour. In this room? About thirty seconds."

Pendergast couldn't help noticing that as Mitford spoke, his teeth flashed in and out of sight in pale crescents—just like the smiling teeth that had hovered before him when he'd awakened earlier. "Why didn't you contact me right away?"

"I had to put Supai back in his cell and work on my disguise. I'll repaint the van tomorrow, and put on new plates. Then we'll be ready to go again."

Pendergast realized his palms were sweating. Later, he'd replay the security camera tapes to make sure Mitford really hadn't been up here earlier, creeping around. "You won't be going anywhere tomorrow," he said sternly.

"Why not?"

"Why do you think? At the very least, I have to manufacture a new identity and papers for you. That will take time." Pendergast had forgotten his determination to release the Loners immediately, if necessary. Because it *wasn't* necessary. He could still do this right.

But Mitford might have to have an accident first, perhaps in one of the Loner's cells. Unless he was able to get his act together.

"Do you really think I'll run into cops again?" Mitford snorted. "Come on, it was pure bad luck."

"Really? Does the name William Chatherton mean anything to you?"

Mitford's eyes might have flickered, but it was too dark to be certain. "Sure. He's a San Diego cop, and also a security guard at Rancho Vista Del Oro. Why?"

"Because right now, this moment, he's checking to see if Frederick Faust has a police record. I don't like having someone investigate my pseudonyms. Are you sure nothing compromising happened on Tortoise Mountain while you were up there?"

"I'm sure," Mitford said evenly.

Pendergast wished he had Mitford in an empty holding cell where he could monitor his vital signs for indications of lying. "Well, *something* attracted his attention. I don't know exactly what it was, but I do know I don't believe in coinci—"

"*I* could find out what he wants," Mitford said.

Pendergast hesitated. The expression in Mitford's eyes reminded him of Vulcan's bright, fixed stare, and he shivered slightly. But hell— this was, after all, the exact sort of task he had Mitford around for in the first place. And it might keep him out of further trouble. "All right," he said. "But you'll have to be very, *very* discreet. We've already got more than enough attention from the police."

"Cops have accidents all the time," Mitford said. "But . . . what if he implicates someone else? What if Scully or Kosarek put him up to this?"

"Deborah? What could she have to do with it?"

"She was snooping around before, remember?"

"Don't . . . listen, I'll admit Scully might be worth talking to. Deal with him as you see fit. But don't go near Deborah unless you've cleared it with me first. Do you understand?"

"Sure." Mitford suddenly grinned, teeth floating like rows of birthday candles in the gloom. "When can I go after Chatherton?"

Pendergast stared out the windows again. Dawn was very close now, and across the valley, the yellow brown layer of haze had grown livid, as if the air itself were bruised. Mitford, he thought, would surely last a little longer.

"The sooner the better," he said fervently.

CHAPTER FOURTEEN

WHEN DEBORAH CALLED UP HER LIST OF THINGS TO DO the first thing in the morning, she saw:

WHERE WERE YOU LAST NIGHT? I CALLED YOUR HOUSE—T.S.

P.S. DIAL 119

She reached for the phone.

"Arnold's Pizza," said Ted's voice after one ring. "If you want anchovies, try Point Loma Seafood."

"Hi, Ted," Deborah said. "Sorry I wasn't home last night. I had . . . I met with a friend."

Long silence. Then, remotely: "That's okay."

Why do I feel guilty? Deborah thought crossly, and said again, "I'm sorry. Did you . . . get what I asked?"

"Oh, yes, some of us were slaving away last night."

"No problems?" she asked, ignoring the sarcasm.

"No problems. Turn on your printer and I'll send over the list. By the way, I wouldn't try contacting most of these guys if I were you."

"Why not?"

"About a third of them are dead. I'm beginning to think Pendergast carries a curse around with him."

"Dead of what?" Deborah asked.

"How would I know? Maybe the Cannibal got them; he seems to be on a roll. Two cops and four teenagers in one night . . . okay, here comes the list."

Deborah's printer began ratcheting, and a long register of names and dates slid out.

"I don't want to know what you intend to do with this, by the way," Ted said over the noise. "I know no-theeng, I see no-theeng."

She didn't answer, watching the list feed. As her eyes roved the birth dates—and, in many cases, dates of death—she felt a chill. Ted was right, the latter number seemed excessive . . . but on the other hand, in a grim way it helped. Finding photos of all the *living* people on the list would be difficult enough.

The question was, did she really expect the blond man to be among them?

She didn't know, but at least it was a possibility. Even Tony Garwood had agreed with that; had actually offered his assistance in tracking down the names.

She still wasn't entirely sure of the big man's motives, but had to admit that he had been pleasant company last night. At the restaurant, his efforts to not look uncomfortable in Virgil's presence had been funny and even kind of endearing. Naturally, Virgil had latched right onto him, as a cat will unerringly find the lap of the one person in the room who's allergic to animal fur.

But the important thing was that no matter what Tony's motivation was, he *did* seem genuinely interested in helping her find out if Dr. Pendergast was all right. And at the moment, that was all that mattered.

"—tonight?" Ted asked.

"I'm sorry?"

"I said, what are you doing tonight? How about that dinner?"

"I . . . can't."

"Meeting another friend?"

"No. I just . . . better not."

"Oh, I see. You're afraid you'll find me irresistible. I understand. Happens all the time. Listen, Deborah, anytime you need me to do you another favor, you just call."

He hung up.

Deborah sat motionless for a while, feeling miserable. She didn't like to think of herself as a user. Was she? Was she just using Ted? Had she led him on in some way?

Yes, to the former. Be honest. As to the latter . . . not *intentionally*.

She took a deep breath. Surely Ted would understand when this was all over.

She turned back to the list. Many of the names were familiar to her: Geneticists. Microsurgeons. Fertility specialists. Considering Dr. Pendergast's reputation for being a loner, the range of his contacts in the biomedical industry was truly amazing.

But she couldn't get over how many of the men had died in the last ten years, especially since the majority of them were quite young— an inestimable loss to mankind. Illness couldn't account for them all. Accidents? That was a lot of car wrecks and tumbles down stairs.

Even Ted had remarked on it. *I'm beginning to think Pendergast carries a curse around with him.* And if Ted thought the proportion of dead men on the list was statistically abnormal, then it was probably statistically abnormal.

Meaning what?

Suddenly she felt the same way as she had when she found Brooke Worm on her car that day. Dead research scientists. Too many dead research scientists . . . including, of course, Charles Carlton himself. Was there a common denominator in their deaths?

Like a certain blond-haired man, for example?

You really are getting paranoid.

But then she was fishing in her purse for the piece of paper Tony had given her last night. On it were scrawled two telephone numbers, one labeled "Home," the other, "RVO."

She licked her lips, glanced at the list one more time, then reached for the telephone.

"I haven't been here in years," Tony said, leaning forward to peer tentatively over the cliff's edge. Far below sprawled the Pacific Ocean, fiercely blue toward the horizon, greener as it shelved up to Black's Beach. There were people scattered down there on the sand, most of them buck naked, sunning themselves. Black's Beach hadn't *officially* been a nude beach for years, but because it was so difficult to get to, sun-worshippers still felt secure there.

A sudden wave of irritation swept over Tony. Why couldn't people just obey the law? But no. They baked their genitals in public, they sold drugs in city parks, they massacred two cops behind the San Diego Museum of Art.

Or *he* did. The Cannibal was a genuine celebrity now—besides the cops, he'd massacred four Hispanic youths last night. That made him a mass-murderer as well as a serial killer. A double threat. National news. And this time, he'd used a gun as well as his shark-bite tool.

Tony cringed as a huge shadow suddenly swooped over him. A hang glider soared past, so close he could hear the wind humming in its wires.

"Jesus," Tony said to Deborah. "I can't believe people do that."

She nodded, although she wasn't watching the glider; she was staring out to sea. Tony wondered why she had insisted on meeting him out here. He wished she'd move farther away from the UNSTABLE CLIFF sign. The wind ruffled through her short dark hair and rattled the sheaf of paper clutched in her hands. She looked lovely, if a bit tired. She hadn't responded to any of his small talk. "I only have an hour for lunch," he prodded gently.

She twitched, as if he'd feinted at her with his fist. "There's something I wanted to show you," she said.

"Show away."

She stepped closer to him—what perfume was that?—and held up the sheaf of paper. "This is a list of Dr. Pendergast's associates. I thought I'd dig up photos of everybody on it, just in case that man we saw up at the house is one of them. But . . . look. Twenty-three of these people have died in the last ten years."

Tony took the thin pile of papers, a computer printout. "So?"

"Look at the dates. A lot of them were *young*. Twenty-three people in ten years. It's too much."

He flipped through the printout. None of the names were familiar to him. "Do you know *how* they died?"

"Only Dr. Carlton. He supposedly drove his car over this cliff while he was drunk."

"*This* cliff?" Tony glanced sickly at the edge. "Why 'supposedly'?"

"Well, look around. Do you think even a drunk could *accidentally* drive off here?"

He did look around. The cliff was separated from the nearest passable road by fifty years of rough, fissured terrain. But he said, "I once saw a drunk driver crash into a house and push it six inches off its foundation before he realized he'd . . ." He stopped; Deborah had looked away. "What I'm saying," he went on quickly, "is that we can't jump to conclusions. You're talking about multiple murder here. Murder of *scientists*. Why? What would be the purpose?

"Maybe it's someone's way of getting hold of research data. Tony, there can be big money involved in medical science—*huge* money."

He nodded, but said nothing.

"Tell me something," she said harshly. "If a third of all the security guards in San Diego died in one ten-year period, what would you think?"

"You misunderstand," he said. "I was just thinking . . . last night, after I left your place, I tried to find Frederick Faust's house. But the address I was given doesn't even exist."

"What do you mean?"

"I mean the street ends before you get to the right number. My friend could have just written it down wrong, of course, but . . ." He straightened. "Okay, listen. I'll see if Bill can find out how some of these people died. That might give us a little more ammunition. Okay?"

She took a deep breath, let it out slowly. "I appreciate your help, Tony. I know I sound paranoid about all this. But I keep thinking about Virgil's toy with its throat slit . . ."

Tony suddenly remembered how the little boy had looked last night, wearing a paper restaurant bib and happily banging his spoon on the tabletop. "I understand," he said, and resisted the urge to touch Deborah's shoulder. "We'll get everything figured out eventually. You'll see."

She nodded, but was staring out at the ocean again. Tony thought she looked like a whaler's wife searching the horizon for familiar sails.

At Ginnunga Gap, Mitford checked the surface monitors carefully before going to the garage and climbing into the Cherokee. If there was one thing he was determined to do, it was to make up for the incredible string of bad luck that had plagued him in Balboa Park last night.

Of course, tonight he'd be more fully in control. This job was much more to his taste and talent.

The back seat of the Cherokee was loaded with everything he thought he might need: rope, restraints, duct tape, knife, blankets, towels. He'd also taken the precaution of covering all the Jeep's windows, even the windshield, with dark sun-block film. This would serve two purposes. First, it would alter the vehicle's appearance—although there must be a thousand brown Cherokees in San Diego, it wouldn't hurt to be careful, now that someone—that damned Garwood, no doubt—had gotten Chatherton interested in the Jeep. He'd put different license plates on it, too. The other purpose of the film was, of course, to make it difficult for passersby to see him at work inside the vehicle.

He pushed a button on the dash, and the armored garage door swung up heavily, letting in warm afternoon light. A startled tarantula strutted away on its hairy legs, and Mitford guided the Cherokee around it carefully. A moment later the vehicle was bouncing down the dry wash, bushes dragging against the doors.

In the rear seat, the blanket shifted a bit and started to slip to the floor. A taloned hand quickly reached out from beneath it and tugged it back into place, then disappeared again.

Tony was familiar with the smoldering gleam in Chatherton's eyes. It was the way cops looked when other cops got killed.

"Did you know either of them?" he asked gently.

"Johnson, a little. They were both good cops."

Every murdered cop was a good cop, afterward. But Tony wondered what they'd done wrong. Two police officers versus one Cannibal shouldn't equal two dead officers.

According to the news, the Cannibal had used his chopper to sample five of his six victims, excluding only the cop he'd shot. Also, because the bodies of the four Hispanics had been discovered by a couple of early-morning joggers who screamed the news all the way down the Prado, the police weren't even attempting to deny that the victims had been eviscerated.

"At least we have a description of the Cannibal now," Tony said. "That's something."

Chatherton snorted. "Sure. Blond hair and blue eyes, just like a million other guys in San Diego County. Besides, his driver's license and the van's registration were both fake. *Shit.* I *knew* something like this was going to happen if the department didn't open up and . . ." He fell silent, glaring into the valley.

Tony waited awhile, then said, "Bill, I know this isn't a good time to ask . . . but did you get that information I wanted?"

"What . . . ? Oh. Yeah. Faust doesn't have a police record."

"Nothing at all?"

"No." Chatherton paused, then looked up. "But I found out something else. Guess who owns a shitload of property out near Alpine?"

"Faust?"

"Faust."

"How did you find *that* out?"

"Well, I mentioned the disappearing trick the Jeep pulled to Dina, that clerk I've been seeing. She's from Alpine. And she said, 'Maybe he went back to that old survivalist camp.' "

"Survivalist camp?"

"You know, one of those places with bunkers where you can survive a nuclear war? After Dina mentioned it, I vaguely remembered reading about it when I was in high school. So I went to County Records and checked the deed—the place was bought about fifteen years ago by Frederick J. Faust."

"Great work, Bill," Tony said, ashamed of the way he'd discounted the cop's sleuthing skills. He gazed thoughtfully into the valley. Earlier, a mild Santa Ana wind had begun to blow, forcing the smog out to sea and giving the valley a preternatural clarity, like the miniature landscape in a snowglobe. It was a hot, dry wind, but Tony's skin felt cold anyway. "Well," he said, "that might explain why I couldn't find his house in La Jolla."

"Huh?"

"The address you gave me—there's no such place. I thought it was just a mistake, but now . . ." Reaching inside the PSS cruiser, he pulled out the computer printout Deborah had given him. "Look at this. Deborah gave me this this afternoon—it's a list of doctors and scientists like Pendergast."

Chatherton took it. "So?"

"Look how many of them have *died* in the last ten years."

As Chatherton flipped through the pages, his brows slowly came together.

"Twenty-three altogether," Tony said. "Twenty-three—and now Pendergast disappears, too. It makes you wonder, doesn't it?"

"What's the point in killing off a bunch of scientists?"

"I asked the same thing. According to Deborah, the research these guys do is worth a mint. Somebody could be stealing the information and then covering his tracks—permanently."

There was a long pause, then Chatherton said, "Somebody who lives in a survivalist camp, for instance?"

"It makes you wonder," Tony said again.

"But Faust doesn't match the description you gave me of the guy up on the hill."

"Maybe Faust wore a disguise when he got his driver's license. Or maybe Blondie *works* with Faust."

Chatherton flipped through the printout again, more slowly. "If you're right, this could be big shit."

"Yeah."

"Where did this list come from?"

"One of Deborah's friends at the Carlton Center got it. A guy named Ted Scully."

"Did he happen to know how any of these guys died?"

"One of them drove his car off the Torrey Pines cliff, supposedly drunk. I don't know if he knows any more than that."

Chatherton chewed his lip. Tony waited, watching from the corners of his eyes.

"Tony . . ." Chatherton said, "you aren't getting involved in this just so you can climb up that woman's skirt, are you?"

"No. Bill, checking on a few death certificates might clear it all up."

There was a long pause. Then, "Yeah." Chatherton straightened. "Yeah. Let's just do that."

When her doorbell rang, Deborah jumped violently, leaving Virgil with a dollop of chocolate pudding hanging from the tip of his nose.

"Sorry, hon," she said, wiping him off and hurrying to the door.

When she saw Tony's face hovering in the peephole, she felt a strange mix of emotions. Surprise, relief—and fear, because the relief seemed so strong. She opened the door.

"Not again," Tony said, looking at the spoon in her hand.

"No matter how much I feed him, the next day he wants more. Come on in."

"I'm sorry to interrupt," he said, closing the door behind him. Instead of his uniform, today he was wearing a pair of jeans, a T-shirt and a loose jacket, and looked bigger than ever. "But I've got a kind of strange request for you," he said, looking her somberly in the eye. "It's an important one."

"What's that?"

"I'd like you to get out of this apartment for a while."

"Out? Why in the—"

"Because whoever threatened you can get in here whenever he wants."

Her breath was suddenly trapped in her chest. "What happened?"

As Deborah pulled Virgil out of his chair and cleaned him up, Tony told her what his police officer friend had learned about Faust and the survivalist camp. Then he added, "And there's more. Bill had a friend of his run a computer check on the deaths of all those scientists: all but three died in accidents, suicides or violent crimes like armed robbery. In the robberies there were never any suspects."

"You mean—"

"The odds are way off the scale. Bill's convinced, but he wants to have more information before he goes to his superiors. He's on his way to see Ted Scully right now."

"Why Ted?"

"Because he generated that list, and he knows what goes on in the science end at the Carlton Center."

"Oh," Deborah said nervously, trying to imagine how Ted would react to a cop standing on his front porch.

"Deborah," Tony said, "I—" He started as Virgil jogged headlong into his knees. Putting his hands on the boy's shoulders, he went on, "I don't want you to get too scared or anything, but I just think you should get out of here until things fall into place a bit. Just in case."

"Casencase!" Virgil shouted, slapping Tony's knees exuberantly.

Watching them, Deborah found her mouth as dry as talc. This situation had passed beyond her worst fear now—she was actually being asked to go into hiding by someone she hadn't even met until two days ago. Everything was *real*. "I . . . maybe I could go stay at my in-laws' house," she said. "They deserve to know what's going on, anyway."

Tony blinked. "Your in-laws?"

"My husband . . . died a couple of years ago."

"Oh. Um . . . Deborah, maybe it's not such a good idea for you to stay at a *relative's* place, a place where you could be traced. You know?"

She swallowed. "But . . . how long will it be before I know it's safe?"

"That's hard to say."

"I can't afford to stay in a hotel indefinitely, Tony. I—"

"Listen, you could use my place. It's not exactly in the best part of town, but—"

"*Your* place?"

"My landlord's got a spare room," he said. "I'll stay down there. Really, I wouldn't mind."

"Tony . . . thanks, but I . . ."

"I understand; you don't even know me. That's smart. It was just an idea." Almost absent-mindedly, it seemed, he put his big arms gently around Virgil. "I'm just trying to do what's right."

"I appreciate it. Really. But my father-in-law's an ex-Marine with a house full of guns. We'll be fine there."

"Okay."

She hesitated. "You could come and see the place, if you'd like. Meet Del and Betty. Besides, it might be better if *you* explained what's going on, anyway."

Tony gazed at her steadily over Virgil's head. "All right. But, Deborah, if it doesn't look safe to me, will you leave? We can think of some kind of arrangement."

"I'm sure it won't be necessary," she said, managing a smile. "I'll go pack."

Twenty minutes later, as she was locking the apartment behind them, the door across the landing opened and Sarah's head poked out. After giving Tony an appraising look, she smiled at Deborah. "Hi . . . What's up?"

Deborah glanced down ruefully at the three bags she'd packed. "I'm taking a little trip."

Sarah peered at Tony again; he looked back noncommittally. "Yeah?" she said. "Where you going?"

"To my in-laws for a few days. Oh, I'm sorry—Sarah, this is Tony Garwood. He's a . . . friend." Although she was mortally embarrassed, in a way she was glad her neighbor had barged out here. At least now there was a witness that she had left her apartment with a man . . . just in case. In case what? Her world was coming apart.

Tony said, "Nice to meet you. Deborah, we'd better get going."

"Right." She took Virgil's free hand—he was clutching Brooke Worm in the other—and said, "Sarah, we'll talk later, okay?"

"That's for sure." Beaming, her neighbor withdrew.

Deborah felt utterly drained. She wasn't cut out for a life of intrigue.

But it was all her fault, wasn't it? She'd started this snowball rolling, and now it had grown into an avalanche sweeping her along. "Okay," she said. "Let's go."

CHAPTER FIFTEEN

ALTHOUGH HE WOULD NEVER BEFORE have thought it possible, right now Chatherton wished he was driving a black-and-white. Scully had already left the Carlton Center when Chatherton called him from RVO, so the cop had decided to drive to Scully's home in University City. He'd gotten the address from Traffic Division.

But along the way, he'd promptly gotten stuck in traffic. Now the major advantage of a black-and-white became manifest: lights and siren for slicing through traffic at the speed of your eagerness. And Chatherton was very eager to see Scully. The more he thought about what seemed to be going on here, the more he had the feeling this could be his big break. Kidnapping . . . multiple murder . . . if it was true . . . well, when your luck peaked as rarely as William Chatherton's, you didn't let any potential opportunity slip away.

On the other hand, you didn't screw it up, either. Cry "Wolf!", then turn out to be wrong. Things looked promising, but he wanted to be *sure* before he walked into the Homicide detectives' bullpen and said, "My name's Officer Chatherton, and have I got something for you."

It turned out that Scully lived in one of those condo developments that look exactly like apartment complexes. The streets were a hopeless tangle, and Chatherton drove around for almost fifteen minutes before he found the cluster of mailboxes that marked Scully's building. The building itself was set back off the street, accessed by a driveway marked RESIDENTS ONLY. Chatherton didn't give a damn about that, but all the parking spots were taken, so he drove down the street to the nearest GUEST PARKING area. A shit brown Jeep Cherokee was hogging both slots. Damn!

He cruised past slowly, hoping the driver was inside so he could give him the evil eye. There *was* somebody behind the wheel, but the vehicle's glass was so dark Chatherton could only see a silhouette. He felt an urge to pull over and slap a couple of parking citations on this . . .

Brown Cherokee.

Facing forward, he drove on without giving away his surge of excitement. His eyes sought the rear-view mirror and struggled to read the reversed numbers on the license plate—but they didn't match those of Faust's vehicle. Damn.

He turned a corner, wishing once again that he was in a patrol car. Then he could call the station and find out who those plates *did* belong to. You never knew, they might be stolen . . .

As he came around the block again, he realized his luck had improved. Someone was just pulling out of a parking spot that offered a vantage point of both the Cherokee and Scully's building. Chatherton pulled in and sat there examining the situation. The silhouette of the Jeep's driver's head hadn't moved. Why was the guy just sitting there in his vehicle?

Chatherton debated his options. He could hightail it out of here right now, call the station and report this. Report what? Or he could call Tony, have him run out and provide backup. Or he could walk up to Scully's door and warn the man that it was possible he was being stalked by a man who might or might not be a kidnapper and stuffed-animal-murderer.

Or, finally, he could handle this alone. Watch the Cherokee and find out for sure if someone—Frederick Faust, or maybe his blond friend, assuming they were different people—really was here checking on Ted Scully.

Settling back, he placed his service revolver beside him on the seat and covered it with a week-old newspaper he'd found on the floor. Then he prepared to wait, just like the detectives on TV shows. All he needed was a cup of cof—

At that moment, the door to Ted Scully's condo opened and a thin man with a flattop haircut stepped out. Locking the door behind him, he walked briskly to the carport and climbed into a Porsche 911.

And simultaneously, the Cherokee's exhaust pipe belched a small cloud of smoke.

Bill Chatherton smiled. There was no doubt about it—at long last, his luck had changed for the better.

* * *

"I couldn't . . ." Tony said.

"Sure you can," Del boomed, climbing out of his chair. "There's plenty. Right, Betty?"

"There always is. Please join us, Tony."

Tony glanced at Deborah, who stood in the kitchen next to her mother-in-law. Deborah was expressionless.

Sidling close, Del said, "Ribs. Barbecued in my own special sauce. Tell him, Betty—nobody makes better ribs than I do."

"Nobody makes better ribs than he does," Betty said. "That's why *his* ribs have been invisible for fifteen years."

"Oh, har-har. So how about it, Tony? Ribs? Potato salad? Apple pie? When's the last time you had homemade apple pie?"

Tony had to smile. "It's been a while."

"Done, then. You're staying for dinner. But there is a price—while the ribs are cooking, you'll have to sit out on the patio with me and drink beer."

"You're going to force beer on me?"

"Drown you in it."

Tony smiled at Deborah, and this time she smiled back a little.

"Deal," he said.

"All right. I'll get the barbecue lit. Betty, you mind grabbing a six-pack out of the garage and bringing it out on the patio?" He grabbed Virgil's hand. "Come on, big guy, let's go blow ourselves up. Tony, see you in a minute."

Tony and Deborah were alone.

"Sorry," she said, looking at her feet. "I hope this isn't going to mess up any plans you had for tonight."

"I didn't have any plans." He paused. "You know, your—um, Del and Betty took the news awfully well."

"Maybe they didn't believe it."

Tony grunted. "I doubt Del showed me his gun collection by accident. I'll bet he's outside checking the street for unfamiliar cars right now."

A smile flitted across Deborah's face. "I told you he's an ex-Marine— and he taught hand-to-hand combat."

"That explains the handshake."

"Yeah—I think you passed that test, though."

Fleetingly, Tony wondered if she always brought her dates over to be tested by the parents of her dead husband. He said, "I guess I won't need to worry about your being safe here, at least."

"Tony . . ." She looked him directly in the eye. "Listen, I appreciate everything you've done for me. Really."

"No problem." God, she had pretty eyes.

As if she had read his thoughts, she looked away again. "Do you think your cop friend is done talking with Ted yet?" she asked.

"It's hard to say. I'll call him after dinner and check."

"What happens after he's done with Ted?"

Tony hesitated. "Well, he'll report his suspicions about Faust to his lieutenant . . . and the police department will take it from there."

Deborah must have sensed the uncertainty in his voice. "Meaning what?"

"Well, exactly what they'll do depends on what Chatherton tells them. Chances are someone will at least try to contact Dr. Pendergast—and they should look deeper into what happened to all those scientists. Someone will probably check Faust out more thoroughly, too."

"Is that all?"

"What else do you suggest? Unless Ted knows more than he . . ."

The patio door slid open and Del walked in, Virgil perched on his shoulders. The pungent smell of lighter fluid surrounded them. "Okay," Del said, "fire's started; now we get going on the sauce. Where's Mom with my beer?"

As they walked past Tony, Virgil suddenly flung out his arms. "Ohnee!" he cried.

Del froze in place. "What did he say?"

"Nothing." Deborah grabbed Virgil and hoisted him down to the floor. But he continued to hold his arms up to Tony, fingers waggling.

"I don't—" Tony began, befuddled.

"Better pick him up, Tony," Del boomed. "He's a stubborn little guy, just like his mom."

With an uncertain glance at Deborah, Tony reached down and gathered the boy up. Virgil snuggled comfortably in the hook of his elbow. Tony noticed an expression halfway between amusement and dismay struggling over Deborah's face; he imagined he must be wearing the same expression.

"Tony," Del said cheerfully, banging pans around in the kitchen, "have you ever watched Jet Ski racing on Prime Ticket?"

"Shit," Chatherton said in disgust. Scully's Porsche, followed by the Cherokee, had just pulled into the parking lot of a nightclub called Flash. Chatherton knew this place—trendy, numbingly noisy, and inclined to spew drunken yuppies into the streets at two o'clock in the morning. It was also usually jammed well beyond its fire-code limits—all in all, not the best place in the world in which to tail a person, never mind *two* people, especially when he still hadn't seen one's face.

Up until now his luck had run like melted gold. The Cherokee had tailed Scully's Porsche through the heavy Friday-evening traffic, and Chatherton had in turn tailed the Cherokee—now dropping back several cars, now switching lanes, just like in the manuals. As a group they had entered I–5, then transferred to I–8, and finally exited into an area of Mission Valley thick with a strange mix of office complexes, hotels and restaurants.

Pulling into Flash's parking lot at a leisurely pace so that the Cherokee would have plenty of time to move on, Chatherton glanced at the building and saw that even at this early hour, the line of people waiting to get in wrapped halfway around it. He sighed. Well, even lucky people couldn't expect *everything* to work out.

The parking lot was already nearly full, and it took him a moment to spot the Porsche and Cherokee. The former was waiting near a big corner slot as another car backed out, while the latter had cruised to the very rear of the lot, where it was even now slipping beneath the overhanging branches of a magnolia tree. Definitely suspicious. Heart accelerating, Chatherton found a parking spot twenty yards away from both vehicles but offering a view of each through mazes of intervening cars. Then he shut off his engine and waited.

Scully backed-and-filled carefully, until his Porsche was precisely centered in the corner slot. There was no apparent activity around the Cherokee, but Chatherton was painfully aware that the vehicle was visible only as a couple of wheels beneath the magnolia branches. A very strategic position . . . Chatherton suddenly wondered if the Jeep's driver had figured out he was being tailed. In his mind, Chatherton was calling the driver "Blondie," as Tony did.

Beep-boop.

Turning toward the Porsche at the sound of its alarm being set, Chatherton saw Scully walking briskly away. Although Scully's clothes looked rakish and expensive, and his flattop haircut and earring were right in style, he still looked like the kind of guy who should be wearing a white shirt buttoned to the collar, and horn-rimmed glasses with tape on the nose bridge. He—

Something moved in the corner of Chatherton's eye, and he spun quickly back toward the Cherokee. No, nothing. Everything under the magnolia looked the same; the branches weren't even moving. And yet, he had to admit Blondie could have slipped out the far side of the Jeep and vanished into the dense wall of bushes that lined the parking lot. Once through that, he could walk undetected around the lot and stroll back in again wherever he chose. And Chatherton still didn't know what the man looked like, except for what Tony had told him: athletic build, longish blond hair . . . not much to go on.

Suddenly Chatherton realized he was sweating. His luck was slipping away again. He needed backup; that way, the parking lot and the nightclub could be covered simultaneously. But he didn't dare try finding a phone now and leave the Cherokee unobserved.

Well, here we go again, he thought bitterly. Just my fucking luck to get stuck in a dilemma like this.

The line in front of Flash was moving along quickly; Scully was already showing his I.D. to a muscle-bound bouncer in a T-shirt. Behind Skully were enough people to form a symphony orchestra—and several of them were blond males. Was one of them Blondie?

Once again he thought he glimpsed a flicker of movement under the magnolia, but when he looked closer, everything was still. Too still? Had Faust sneaked away or not, damn it?

There was only one way to be sure. The problem was, it would be almost impossible to creep up on the vehicle . . .

A headline blazed through Chatherton's head: PATROL COP UNCOVERS MEDICAL MURDER PLOT—TOP BRASS EMBARRASSED. Fuck it, some people just had to *make* their luck.

And suddenly he knew how to do it.

Making sure the car's interior light was switched off, he put his pistol back into its holster, slid across the seat to the passenger side and eased out of the car. Keeping low, he scurried from car to car like a soldier in that old TV show "Combat," heading for the edge of the lot with its barrier of vegetation. He figured he could use the hedge for cover as easily as Faust could.

Only after he'd started crawling beneath the bushes on his belly, scooping dirt into his pants and raking his back open on branches, did he wonder how he expected to get into Flash if he looked like a particularly unsuccessful bag person. Shit! By the time he finally popped out the other side, he was sweating and cursing softly under his breath—fuck "Combat." He'd just have to make the best of it.

Hurrying to the rear of the lot, he turned the corner and made his way stealthily to where the magnolia tree stood. He crawled close to the trunk and peeked around it. Yes. There on the far side was the Cherokee in a tent of leaves, its windows blacker than ever. Occupied or not? Everything hinged on knowing that.

Backing out of the hedge again, he crept toward the rear of the Jeep—and, hopefully, the driver's blind spot—then took a deep breath and crawled back under the bushes. He uttered no sound, not even when a stiff branch peeled a groove into the back of his neck, and finally found himself on the far side of the bushes, lying on his belly on the rough surface of the parking lot. He waited a moment, listening, the odor of asphalt and hot rubber burning in his nostrils. He could hear nothing but the faint thud of dance music from Flash and the irregular ticking of the Cherokee's cooling exhaust pipe. From inside the vehicle came no sound at all.

So now what, Chatherton? What are you going to do, lie here all night?

Suddenly he pictured the way he would look to someone who might find him like this, sprawled out on the pavement like a squashed cat. He jumped to his feet. He was a *cop*, goddamn it. And this vehicle was illegally parked perpendicular to the marked stalls, wasn't it?

So quit fucking around.

Although his police uniform was in his car, he always kept the badge and I.D. with him. Tugging the little folder out of his pocket, he walked around to the driver's door and rapped sharply on the window.

No response.

"Police," he said loudly, holding his badge against the glass and knocking again. "Roll down the window, please."

Nothing.

He debated. If the Cherokee was empty, then Blondie was probably already inside the nightclub with Skully—while here stood Officer William Chatherton, I.D. in one hand and dick in the other, fortune slipping away again.

Almost without thinking, he tried the driver's door—it was locked, of course. And without a search warrant or probable cause, he had no right to break in. Still, what if there was a photo of Faust inside the vehicle? Or, for that matter, something genuinely *incriminating*? Chatherton could always claim he'd glimpsed it through the window first . . .

A Cherokee is a five-door vehicle. He'd only tried one of them.

The left passenger door was locked. He moved to the back-seat door and tugged on the handle, and when it popped open, he was so surprised he nearly fell over backward. He froze, heart galloping.

There was no movement inside the Cherokee. No sound.

Finally, he bent close and peered inside. The interior was as black as the gut of a woodburning stove.

"Police," he said into this darkness, with notably less authority than he would have liked. There was still no movement, no reply.

Why hadn't he brought his damned flashlight along? Should he run back to his car for it? No, this was his one shot. He glanced around, then leaned forward and stuck his head inside the Cherokee. He touched nothing. The windows were dull purplish blotches in the darkness; otherwise, all he could see was part of the rear seat. Then he realized the seat was covered with a blanket. A *lumpy* blanket. A blanket with something under it . . .

He licked his lips. It could be anything. Dirty laundry. Tools. A dead body.

He reached forward, clasped the edge of the blanket between two knuckles, lifted it. Carefully. His heart thumped so loudly in his ears, it drowned out the bass beat emanating from Flash. Beneath the corner of the blanket he glimpsed a fold of cloth—a towel. He lifted higher. What was this? A packet of long plastic pull-ties, of the same sort police officers use to hogtie violent prisoners. Also a coil of nylon rope. And a roll of duct tape. He remembered a homicide detective once drily saying, "Duct tape is used in so many crimes, people should have to register it like a gun." Finally he raised the blanket all the way, saw some kind of folded canvas tarpaulin. He nodded, feeling all warm inside. Individually, these items were perfectly innocuous. But collectively—

From behind him came a faint rustle. And even before the hard finger of a gun barrel pressed against his spine and a voice said, "Hi, there, officer," William Chatherton realized his luck had just returned to normal.

After Ted had been inside Flash for about forty-five minutes, he tallied up his score: six strikeouts. Jesus, it was almost enough to discourage a person.

The most depressing thing of all was that the club was *stuffed* with women. Girls, rather, most of them probably fresh out of college and still craving the hot rush of dancing and drinking to blow away the boredom of their nine-to-five jobs. Girls who loved the music of whoever was currently hottest on MTV, and who snorted cocaine and drank Corona beer with a slice of lime stuffed into the bottle. Girls whose firm bodies squiggled under tight clothes.

Ted Scully never had any luck with such women. Or, admit it, with any other kind, for that matter. The cruel truth was that the only females who seemed interested in him were his mother's friends, all of whom coincidentally had daughters who had just graduated *summa cum laude* from the University of San Diego with degrees in astrophysics and whose braces had left permanent stains on their teeth . . .

He was sitting alone at a cramped table at the edge of the thunderous dance floor, being tripped over occasionally as he sipped his sixth Bacardi and Coke—one for each rejection—and stared into the seething stew of bodies. The dance floor was in the center of the building, with a balcony level above and tables on all sides. Suspended over the floor were clusters of lights; strobes, multicolored spots, the mandatory mirrored ball. From time to time a blizzard of balloons fell from unseen spaces above the lights, to be bounced around and burst underfoot. Of course, you couldn't hear the popping over the battering volume of the music. Nor could you hear individual conversations—nobody patronized Flash to engage in scintillating repartee.

He finished his drink and signaled his waitress, who smiled cheerily and held up a "just a sec" finger. The waitress liked him—or, rather, his big tips. Sounded like a sick joke.

If you're so unhappy, then what the hell are you doing in this place, Scully?

Trying to get over Deborah Kosarek, all right? How's that for honesty? You happy now?

He sighed. It was true—he didn't want to be here, trolling for fish amongst the sharks; he wanted to be in a nice, quiet bistro with Deborah Kosarek. He knew he bugged her sometimes—he couldn't seem to help that—but he sensed that she also liked him a little. Maybe even more than a little.

Why had she hurt him, then? Put that way, it sounded so high school—"Oh, she broke my heart"—but that was the way he felt, damn it. He'd even laid his entire career on the line for her, really, and what had he gotten in return? Zip, that was what. Less than zip. But he knew she had no husband anymore, and he didn't think she dated much, either. Nearly all the single men at the Carlton Center had been politely rebuffed by her at one time or another. In fact, that was why Ted had been so elated when she'd asked him for help. He'd thought . . . he'd actually thought . . .

Sighing again, he wondered if Deborah was romantically hung up on Dr. Pendergast. What a disgusting notion. Dr. P was reputedly gay or at least some kind of celibate because he was never seen with a woman, nor had he been known to *talk* about women except in a clinical sense. Plus he was, what, fifty-five years old? What could a babe like Deborah possibly see in a man like that? Maybe she was one of those women who only fall for unattainables—priests, happily married guys, like that.

On the other hand, it could be that she was involved with a man unaffiliated with the Carlton Center. No doubt a rendezvous with him was the "something else" she'd had to attend to tonight.

His drink arrived and he slugged it down, felt it add fuel to the blaze already searing his stomach and head. He looked around at the games of sexual cat-and-mouse going on in the throbbing dark, and considered that as far as romance went, Ted Scully's curse was that he wanted, in his own way, to be *nice*. And it seemed that no matter what women said, they liked to be pushed around—grabbed by the hair and hauled off to a cave by somebody dressed in the skin of a sabre-toothed tiger.

—Like that guy across the way, for example. Tall, lean, standing with his weight on one leg, arms crossed, pelvis tilted aggressively forward. Women all over the club were watching him—in some cases, over the shoulders of their dance partners. Why? Was he the most handsome man in here? No. The best dressed? No. Did he reek of money? No. It was his attitude, that radiation of predatory confidence. As his gaze roved the room, women smiled at him hopefully.

Ted felt the heat building stronger inside him, and realized it wasn't all just booze. Something unfamiliar: anger. He pictured himself walking straight up to that wolf and punching him in the face, dropping him like a sandbag, and all the women applauding . . .

As if aware of his scrutiny, the wolf turned and looked squarely at him with eyebrow-lifted arrogance. Ted spun away, face hot.

That was when he saw the woman. She sat alone at a table not ten feet away—had she just come in, or had the crowd kept him from noticing her before? He didn't know, but he was glad he saw her now. Lustrous black hair, generous mouth, large eyes . . . sort of the way Deborah Kosarek might look if she let her hair grow long.

Ted, your neighbor's *cat* reminds you of Deborah these days. Get off it.

But there was something else about her that attracted him. He thought about it, and realized that her posture—back stiff and eyes darting—telegraphed uncertainty. In fact, Ted felt he could recite the woman's past: In high school she had been homely and acne-faced, never asked out on a date, crying in her bed every night. Only recently had she fulfilled her potential. Now she was a swan who feared that others still saw her as the ugly duckling of days gone by.

Which meant she might be here in Flash alone. Come to test the waters . . .

Suddenly someone half-blocked Ted's view of—and he knew it was the wolf even before he looked up. Yes. Fury flooded through him as the wolf smiled down at the swan and held out his hand. Instantly—for men like the wolf, Ted thought bitterly, everything seemed to happen on cue—the music segued into a throbbing slow song. The action in the club unwound, and the heavy musk of the sex hunt floated like a miasma in the darkness.

But for a moment, the swan just looked uncertainly from the wolf's hand to his face, and Ted thought elatedly, *She's going to turn him down, she's going to tell him no!* Then, with a rather uncertain smile, she took the hand and rose to her feet. The wolf grinned.

And Ted moaned. Seen in full, the swan was all the more stunning. She was nearly as tall as the wolf, her tight red minidress revealing sleek legs and small, erect breasts, the nipples poking perkily against the fabric. Oh, God, oh—

Together, the swan and the wolf squeezed out onto the packed dance floor. Instantly, balloons cascaded from the ceiling like . . . like sperm cells. Ted watched helplessly, wishing he had another drink or ten. At first the swan held her partner rather clumsily around the waist, barely moving her feet and looking around at the other dancers, as if uncertain what to do. The wolf grinned, his teeth flashing blue white in the light from the mirrored ball.

After a moment the swan began to sway her hips in time to the music, and moved closer to the wolf. Ted swallowed a fiery lump in his throat. Why was he watching this? He could almost feel the swan's body pressing against him, and suddenly he thought about Deborah Kosarek again. Deborah rubbing against him that way: breasts, hips, pubic bone . . .

And without warning he was more than just angry, he was *furious*. Why did the bad guys always have to win? Look at the wolf's hands now, sliding down the swan's back, riding on the upper swell of her buttocks. In return, the swan placed her cheek on the wolf's shoulder, her hair cascading down his back like an ebony waterfall. Ted wondered if this was the moment she had dreamed about through all those years of pimple cream and crash dieting. If so, how would she feel tomorrow, when she awoke on sticky sheets and found no one beside her?

Suddenly Ted was on his feet and striding onto the dance floor, head whirling. *May I cut in?* he would ask. It might work, and fuck it all, *somebody* had to do something. Some—

The wolf suddenly raised his head and stared directly at Ted with strange, flat eyes. For an instant Ted faltered, then kept going. There was no law against trying to cut in on a dance, was there? No. And you never knew what might happen until you—

The wolf just kept staring, thin lips slowly pulling up into a smile. Then stretching into a grin. Ted faltered again. The wolf's teeth were now bared in what was almost a rictus—but Ted forced himself closer, and reached out and tapped the swan on her shoulder.

She twitched, obviously startled, and her head rose abruptly. At the same moment, the wolf's jaw dropped and his mouth became a yawning cave from which a plume of blood flapped like a ragged tongue. Ted jerked back with a cry, the blood splattering at his feet. What—

As he looked back up, the wolf's head teetered unsteadily, then lurched heavily to one side. It rested on his shoulder at an impossible angle for a moment, then rolled off and swung across his back on a thin strap of tissue.

Meanwhile, the self-involved dancers all around bumped against Ted like moored boats. As he watched, unable to comprehend what he was seeing, the wolf's head tore loose from its tether, thudded to the floor, and rolled against Ted's feet, peering up at him walleyed. The swan continued to slow-dance with the headless body, her arms locked around its waist, her hair hanging over her face.

Staring down at the severed head in its nest of balloons, Ted opened his mouth, but there was no air in his lungs to power a scream. He heard a ripping sound rise over the music, and looked up just as the swan turned her head, staring at him through the sopping veil of her hair. Except she wasn't the swan anymore; what lay behind the veil was something elongated and bristling with teeth. And clenched in the teeth was one of the wolf's arms.

Suddenly Ted's voice found him and flew out like an air-raid siren, startling even him, piercing the music and chatter in the nightclub.

The music went on for a moment, then stopped abruptly, leaving the scream stranded. From all sides, people stared at Ted with curiosity, anger, embarrassment. But he only had eyes for the grinning thing in the red dress, the ugly duckling that became a swan that became a monster. He tried to back away from it, was resisted by the crowd. "This is his body," the thing growled at him around the arm in its mouth, then abruptly released its dance partner and raised both hands. There was something wrong with its fingers. Sickle-shaped claws . . . "Fewer calorrrries, less fat!" the creature cried as the wolf's body toppled slowly to the floor, knocking its own severed head into the crowd. The head came to rest between a woman's toes.

Suddenly Ted's screams were joined by a chorus that spread like shock waves from an explosion, and the stampede for the door began. Shrieks, smashing tables, shattering glass. Overhead, the disco lights continued to flash cheerfully. The swan stood alone in an expanding clear spot, grinning a grin that seemed to fill her face. Ted still couldn't move. He saw her head make two quick moves forward and back, jaws snapping, and the wolf's severed arm disappeared. Briefly, through the veil of her hair, Ted could see down her throat to black depths where bony shapes scissored and pulsed.

And suddenly Ted was running, too—but not in the same direction as the rest of the crowd, those lemmings. He aimed for the rear fire door, struggling against the mob, almost falling, thumping against shoulders and elbows. Screams continued to rip through the air like broken glass, and some of them were his. A redheaded bouncer pushed violently past him toward the dance floor, arms and eyes bulging.

Then the fire-door bar was in Ted's hand and he was bursting through, the alarm blaring behind him, trash cans bouncing across the pavement as he stumbled into them. Which direction to the parking lot? For a moment he spun in place, lost and dizzy . . . and as the fire door came into view, still closing, he caught a glimpse of the dance floor again. Lying in the center of it was the wolf's body—and the upper half of the redheaded bouncer. Running toward Ted was the swan, pretty again except for the scarf of blood she wore over her shoulders.

Ted whirled, screaming, and crashed directly into a hedge. For a moment he fought it, ripping his expensive shirt and scratching his hands and wrists. Finally he tore away and, by sheer luck, stumbled into the parking lot. He glanced back just as the fire door burst open, and his feet suddenly seemed to take flight. On all sides, screaming people were scurrying about like extras in a disaster movie, but he was faster than them all.

At the parking lot exit, two cars slammed together, metal and glass everywhere, and Ted dodged the tangle, darting between parked cars like a punt returner heading for the goal line. He was sure the swan was chasing him, that now she wanted to make love to him. He glanced back just before he reached his car, and tripped and crashed into the Porsche so hard the alarm went off, its whooping voice rippling over the surrounding buildings. But if the swan was there, he couldn't see her. Tearing his keys from his pocket, sending coins dancing over the pavement, he opened the door and leaped into the car, slammed the door, locked it.

"Hello, Ted," said the man in the passenger seat.

Ted jerked away with a cry, cracking his head on the window. A band of light shimmered over the barrel of the pistol the stranger held in his hand, and also on his teeth as he smiled. For a moment, darkness wrapped Ted in a warm and comforting blanket. This was too much. Too much. An endless nightmare.

"My name's Mitford," the man with the gun said, and his voice was real. He stared out the window at the screaming crowd. "What's going on out there?" he asked mildly. "Cops bust the place?"

Ted couldn't respond. Couldn't even remember how to make his mouth work. Or his bladder. He realized he'd wet his brand-new slacks.

Mitford smiled again. "Don't be so nervous, Ted. You and I are just going to go someplace more private and have a little talk, that's all.

You'll find I'm a terrific listener. But let's take my vehicle, okay? It will work better, where we're going." He wagged the gun, indicating Ted should get out of the car.

That was when Ted noticed that Mitford's shirt sleeves were speckled with red droplets.

CHAPTER SIXTEEN

THE SMELL, FAINT BUT UNMISTAKABLE, reached Pendergast the moment he opened the door into the pit. "Oh, no," he whispered.

He turned up the lights. Vulcan sat in the usual corner, staring up at him. But Pendergast's gaze shot to the mound of damp feces near the waste-hole. The feces looked quite different than the Loner's usual small, dry pellets—it was a sure sign of the inefficient metabolization of food.

Lowering himself onto his chair, Pendergast rested his forehead against the bars. Vulcan watched him, eye sockets netted with wrinkles that hadn't been there yesterday.

"Oh, no," Pendergast said again, sick to his soul. "My poor son."

Of course, this was not unexpected. Vulcan's highly strung Loner physiology was really faltering now; internal organs falling out of sync, skin losing elasticity, hair . . . yes, even his hair was thinning. At the age of thirteen months, two weeks and four days, Vulcan was dying—of old age.

Pendergast tried to ignore a bright stab of grief, tried to look at this scientifically. How much longer did Vulcan have? A week? Maybe.

Closing his eyes, Pendergast found himself reciting part of the great eulogy from *The Epic of Gilgamesh*:

> "I have been to you, Enkidu, your mother, your father;
> I will weep for you in the wilderness.
> You were the axe at my side, the bow at my arm,
> the dagger in my belt, the shield in front of me . . ."

He opened his eyes again, and Vulcan was staring at him steadily with eyes like shriveled black spiders. Dying . . . *I'm part of you, Vulcan,*

Pendergast suddenly thought. *If humans really do have souls, then you must have one, too.*

He shivered, shrugged it off. How stupid—and insulting to Vulcan, as well—to burden him with so human a concept.

"I'm afraid your time is drawing near, Vulcan," Pendergast said. "I know it's the most natural thing in the world, dying . . . but it's nice to know you'll live on through the Alphas. They're much more than your children—they're *you*, your very *self*, directly transplanted. Just as you are part of *me*. You could say that through the Alphas, you and I will live on, together, to save the earth. What greater legacy can there be than that?"

Suddenly he realized his eyes felt strange, hot. And his vision was blurry . . . Tears. Remarkable. He hadn't cried since his mother's death in 1950.

But he let the tears flow freely—only Vulcan could see them, after all. They felt hot and pure, like lava flowing up from great depths, melting and purging the burden of destiny that had hardened in his mind. No, not his mind. His *soul*.

Through a wavering curtain he saw Vulcan smiling at him, and he smiled back.

"Tony," Del said, shortly after the last of the apple pie had disappeared from the dish, "how about helping me clean up outside?"

"You bet. Mrs. Kosarek, that was great pie. In fact, everything was terrific."

She beamed. "Call me Betty. And it's nice to see somebody besides Del eat so much around here."

"I'm twice the man she married," Del said, carrying his plate into the kitchen.

"I'll get Virgil ready for bed," Deborah said and rose to tug the boy out of his high chair, which was situated between Virgil and Tony. During the meal, Virgil had occasionally reached out and patted Tony on the shoulder as if he were a well-trained pet. Tony had felt a little embarrassed by the attention, but also obscurely pleased. Toward the end, he'd even found himself wondering just how different his personality would be if he'd been raised in New York City surrounded by cousins, nephews, nieces.

Putting his plate in the sink, he followed Del outside. The Kosarek house was located in a part of Clairemont that had once consisted almost entirely of military housing, but over the years, the shoebox-shaped houses had been bought by civilians and modified to varying extents. The Kosareks' had a second story and back-yard patio; the entire back yard was surrounded by a wooden privacy fence. Tony had already noted the heavy Yale padlock on the gate that led into the alley. It gleamed brightly in the patio lights, as if it had just come out of a box.

As Del wielded a wire brush on the grill, Tony gathered up dishes and spoons, and wiped spilled sauce from the tray. They worked in companionable silence, the only interruption an occasional sizzle and flash from the bug zapper hanging under the eaves. Tony thought that under the circumstances, it was somehow inappropriate that he should feel so contented. During dinner, the conversation had never touched on the subjects of Dr. Pendergast or kidnapping. Deborah had gradually relaxed, too . . . and as she did, Tony had realized that much of her cool, distant beauty was a by-product of aloofness. When she laughed, the facade immediately dissolved, revealing a different face: less *elegant*, maybe, but more approachable. Warmer. A face that went with walks in the rain or sailing on the bay rather than with opera and elegant dinners at the Fontainebleau. A face capable, perhaps, of great passion . . .

Christ, Tony. Why don't you just carve her initials on this tray?

He wiped harder. The tray was already clean, but then, he knew Del hadn't really invited him out here to tidy up.

"Tony," Del finally said, "I didn't want to discuss this before, because I could tell how much it worried Deborah . . . but just how serious *is* all this stuff about Pendergast? Is Deborah really in danger?"

Tony didn't answer right away, phrasing the answer in his head. Then he said, "I honestly don't know. All we've got so far is a lot of little pieces that point to a bad conclusion; we could be entirely wrong. But after what happened with Virgil's toy, I don't see any reason to take chances." He paused. "By the way, Del, why did you change into that baggy shirt?"

Del froze, glanced toward the house, then unbuttoned his shirt and held it open. "It's a Chief's Special," he said without change of expression. "Licensed, of course."

"Of course. You must have just forgotten to put it on earlier. It's not like you're *worried* or anything."

"Right." Del turned back to the barbecue and resumed scrubbing with the wire brush, although if a shinier grill had ever existed, Tony had never seen it.

"You ever been in the military, Tony?" Del asked suddenly.

"No . . . I just missed the Vietnam draft."

"Hm. It's just that, the way you handled yourself, I thought there might be some kind of specialized background. You're sharp."

So are you, Tony thought. "Well," he said, "I was a cop for a while. San Diego PD."

Del nodded. "That makes sense."

Tony waited for the inevitable question—*Why aren't you a cop now?*—but it never came. To his amazement, he discovered he *wanted* to tell this man the entire story of what had happened in Balboa Park—maybe because the question *hadn't* been asked. "I resigned while I was still a rookie," he said suddenly. "Something happened that . . . well, made me rethink my reasons for being on the force, wonder if I was doing it for the right reasons." He paused. "I guess the last thing I wanted to be was a half-assed cop."

Del was silent a while longer, then said, "Has Deborah ever mentioned Brad to you? Her husband . . . my son?"

Tony was taken by surprise. "Just that he died in some kind of accident."

The wire brush moved faster. "He was a firefighter for the county. Doing the job right was important to him, too. He died in a brush fire in the East County." He cleared his throat. "Now Deborah and Virgil are all the family we have left, Betty and me."

Tony nodded uncomfortably.

"She hasn't dated very much since then," Del went on. "Shit. What I want to say is, if she seems a little standoffish, don't take it personally. She'll come around. As far as I'm concerned, you're the only worthwhile man she's seen since Brad."

Tony stared in amazement, and Del turned and gave him a crooked smile. "Don't worry, I'm not thinking about getting out the shotgun and calling the preacher. I'm just saying I'm glad you're not an uptight asshole in a suit, and you're welcome here any time."

Tony laughed, although his eyes were suddenly stinging again. The barbecue must still be putting off smoke. "Thanks, Del. I'm . . ." His head snapped up, and he stepped out into the yard.

"What's the matter?" Del said.

"Listen."

Del joined him in the damp grass. From all directions, the whoop and wail of sirens wove a broken threnody on the night air. "Jesus," Del said. "Sounds like a war."

"Or the Cannibal again," Tony said.

The cacophony grew louder and louder, the sirens converging. The patio door slid open, and Deborah and Betty stepped out, looking around in nervous wonder. Deborah held Virgil in her arms.

"What is it?" Betty said.

Del shrugged. "Don't know. Sounds like they're heading toward Mission Valley, though."

"Let's go back inside," Betty said. "I *hate* that sound."

As they stepped into the living room, Deborah came close to Tony. "I think Virgil wants to say goodnight to you. He wouldn't settle down."

The boy squirmed in her arms, and after a moment's hesitation, Tony took him. Immediately, Virgil snuggled against his chest, thumb in mouth.

"I'll be damned," Del said, and laughed. "Looks like you've got yourself a partner there, Tony."

Tony stared down at Virgil, strikingly aware of the weight of the child, his warmth, his softness. "Uh, want me to help put him to bed?" he asked Deborah.

Her face was unreadable, the Ice Maiden mask firmly in place. "Would you?"

They went upstairs, then down the hall to a small bedroom at the rear of the house. Mismatched pieces of furniture had been pushed aside to make way for an old-fashioned wooden crib. The only decoration was a family portrait on the wall. In it, Del was a lot less beefy, and Betty wore a bouffant hairstyle. Between them stood a grinning boy of about twelve, a small gap between his front teeth. Tony stared at him for a moment. The future firefighter.

He turned, held Virgil out at arm's length and said, "Okay, dude, bedtime. What do you say?"

Virgil grinned. Tony wondered if he'd have a gap in his adult teeth when they came in. The boy clung to his arms for a minute when Tony tried to put him in the crib, but at last relented and lay back. Grabbing Brooke Worm, he said, "Irbe deedah Woom."

"What was that?" Tony asked.

"I have no idea. But . . . Del's right. Virgil's really taken a shine to you."

"I hope it's a family thing," Tony said without looking at her. "I mean, Del invited me to come over anytime." He sighed. "I don't want you to think I'm trying to force my way into your life, though, Deborah."

"*Is* that what you're doing?" she asked.

That rocked him. He was used to conversations so thickly iced with innuendo and entendre that no substance could ever be found. But suddenly, heat rose up his neck. "Look," he said, "I'd like to see more of you if you'd let me, yes—but I'm not going to push myself on you."

She looked back into the crib, and sighed. "I guess I sound pretty ungrateful for someone whose life you're trying to save, don't I?"

"I don't know. I've never tried to save anyone's life before."

She laughed, a real laugh, and looked up at him again. "I don't . . . I like you. Let's just see what happens. Okay?"

"Good enough." He realized he'd actually been holding his breath. "But in the meantime, do you mind if I come over and play with Del now and then?"

"It would be good for him," she said. "And Betty, too, to get Del out of the house occasionally." For a moment, their eyes locked. Then she blushed and turned back to the crib. Virgil's eyes were closed; his grip on Brooke Worm had loosened. "Okay," Deborah said softly, "I guess we can leave." As they entered the hallway, she hesitated. "Do you think it would be okay to call your cop friend now?"

Tony realized that he'd completely forgotten about that. "Good idea," he said with a flash of guilt.

"There's a phone in the den." She opened the next door down the hall and turned on the light. Tony saw the phone on an end table. After he dialed, he let his gaze rove over Del's gun collection. The display case, glass-fronted and securely locked, was a beauty—Del had made it himself. It contained two shotguns, three rifles—a .30–.30 and a pair of old .22 "squirrel rifles"—and a clutch of pistols. One spot in that section was empty. All the guns had locks on their triggers. Careful guy, Del, especially with a toddler in the house.

After four rings, Chatherton's answering machine switched on and Tony told it he'd call back later. When he hung up, he was frowning.

"What's the matter?" Deborah asked.

"He's still not home." Tony looked at his watch. "They must be having quite a conversation."

"Maybe they're still at Ted's," Deborah said. "Let me call there."

She took the phone, hesitated, dialed Directory Assistance. Jotting a number down on a notepad, she dialed again. A moment later she rolled her eyes at Tony and said, "Ted, this is Deborah. It's nine-thirty, and I was wondering if you've spoken to a policeman named Bill Chatherton recently. If you have, I'd like to hear from you as soon as possible. If not, don't panic. It's about Dr. Pendergast. Please call me at—" She looked at Tony as he shook his head violently.

"Don't leave this number on a machine," he whispered. "Tell him you'll call back."

Her face paled slightly, and she did as he asked. "I didn't think about that," she said after she hung up.

"It's just a precaution."

They walked downstairs and found Del and Betty sitting in front of the TV in the family room. Del looked up. "There was just a news flash about what's going on in Mission Valley, Tony," he said. "You were right—it *was* the Cannibal."

"What happened?"

"He killed two people and caused a panic at some nightclub; that's all they've said so far."

Tony looked at the TV. It was showing a commercial for disposable diapers. "No names?"

"Not yet. I'm sure they'll tell us more than we want to know at eleven o'clock. Why?"

Tony shook his head. "No reason." Which wasn't the truth at all. The truth was, when Del had said the Cannibal killed "two people," Tony had immediately flashed on Bill Chatherton and Ted Scully.

"Here we are," Mitford said, bringing the Cherokee to a halt in a swirl of starlit dust.

Ted looked around, but he had no idea where "here" was; he could see nothing but bushes and rocks and darkness. He'd meant to keep track of where they were going, but hadn't been able to concentrate. For one thing, his hands were lashed to the door handle with a stalk of serrated plastic like the kind used to bundle computer cables together, and it hurt like hell. It had also forced him to sit in a contorted position during the interminable drive.

For another, there was Mitford himself. The man had whistled a lighthearted tune ever since they'd gotten into the Cherokee, and yet his gun had been in constant sight, poking up from between his legs like some kind of Freudian joke.

They had driven for quite a while, Ted knew that, although at first he had thought—hoped—they wouldn't even be able to get out of the parking lot. It had been a whirlpool of people and cars, all the exits were blocked—but Mitford had calmly led him to the Cherokee, lashed him into this position, then simply crashed the four-wheel-drive vehicle through a wall of bushes and into the adjacent parking lot, spewing sod and leaves behind.

After that, it had taken only moments to reach the network of surface streets that led out of Mission Valley. Mitford had driven calmly eastward, only his eyes giving away any tension as they followed the police cars that frequently whooped past. Once he had turned toward Ted and said, "All this commotion can't be just because somebody found Chatherton. What the hell happened back there?"

"Chatherton?" Ted said, trembling. "Who's that?" Already his wrists were throbbing from the binding strip.

"Never mind. Just answer my question."

Ted worked very hard to recall what the question had been, then cringed. If he told the truth to this man, he'd probably get shot for lying. He felt the hard eyes on him. "I—there was something in there," he said weakly.

"What do you mean, *something*?"

Ted could feel the cold touch of the gun even though it hadn't moved from between Mitford's legs. "A *woman*," he blurted. "She . . . attacked a guy. Cut his head off." That was close enough. In fact, that was exactly right. Had to be. The rest . . . imagination.

"Cut his head off?" Mitford looked amazed. "With what?"

"I don't know." Suddenly Ted wanted to puke, and swallowed forcefully. Around them were fast food restaurants, gas stations, other cars. The normal world, moving smoothly past . . .

"No shit," Mitford said, and for a moment his face became pensive. "A murder. There. *Tonight*. You'd think . . . boy, the doc's going to freak out." He laughed, and then, thankfully, kept to himself.

After that, Ted lost track of what was going on outside the Jeep. Until now.

"Where are we?" he asked thinly.

Mitford rolled down his window, letting in the harsh rasping of crickets and smell of dust. He lifted the pistol out of his lap. "We're in the East County," he said, and inhaled deeply. "It's nice and private out here, don't you think? A person could scream out here, and nobody would ever hear him. You know?"

Ted stared at the gun, felt his bladder begin leaking again. He couldn't seem to stop it, and that made him cry. "What are you going to do with me?" he wailed. "What are you going to do with me?"

"Ask questions and listen to the answers; I told you that. Simple, right?"

Ted shuddered.

"*Right?*"

"R-right. Right."

"That's better. Then we won't need this." Mitford put the pistol under the seat, out of sight, and Ted was suddenly filled with a feeling very much like gratitude. But his wrists were still lashed to the door, and he was still out here in the middle of nowhere with this psychopath . . .

"All right," Mitford said, "here's the first question: Do you have any idea why I want to talk to you?"

Ted shook his head so hard it made him dizzy.

"You don't? No idea at all?"

"No idea. No idea."

In the gloom, Mitford's eyes were black holes in the wan sun of his face. "I wonder," he said. "Would you lie to me, Ted? Should I trust you?"

"I wouldn't lie to you. Really. I don't want to get hurt. I—"

Mitford reached into his sleeve and pulled out a knife with a blade as thin as a leaf of unmown grass. "Tell me, Ted," he said. "Do you know what *Enkidu* is?"

"*En*—what?" Ted couldn't take his gaze off the knife. "I don't know what you're saying. I—"

The knife darted forward before he could move. He felt a horrible, sinking pain in his left eye, a pain so deep it seemed to burrow into his throat, turning his scream into a low, resonant moan. Half the world went dark. He reared back, felt something thick and warm trickling down his cheek. Through his other eye, he saw the blade withdrawing. Half its length was now dark. "No," Ted moaned. "Oh, no . . ." He wanted to raise his hands to his face, but couldn't.

"That's one eye," Mitford said calmly, wiping the blade on Ted's sleeve. "Right now that eye is collapsing like a little balloon; you'll need a glass one to replace it. But think about total blindness, Ted, and tell me—*What is* Enkidu?

But now all Ted could think of was how awful he must look, vitreous matter oozing down his cheek like thick tears, the collapsed eyeball dangling from its optic nerve. How little he could afford to be ugly. *Uglier*.

"Ted . . ." Mitford said impatiently, and the blade gleamed like a comet's tail in the air.

Ted made himself think. That had always been his strong point, thinking. "I remember," he said with shrill triumph. "I forgot before, honest. I forgot before. I forgot."

"Just tell me, Ted."

"Okay. Okay. *Enkidu* is a program on Dr. Pendergast's compu . . ." His eyes widened, making painful red clouds blossom inside his head.

Mitford's teeth appeared in the darkness. "Yes, Ted, that's right. *He* sent me. The benevolent Dr. Pendergast. He won a Nobel Prize once. Doesn't that make you feel warm all over?"

When the nightly news began, Deborah and Tony were alone in the family room. Del and Betty had gone to bed an hour ago, exchanging smug smiles as they walked up the stairs. Deborah hadn't missed that. She had sighed inside, but couldn't help feeling a little amused, too—it was like being in high school all over again.

Of course, if she wanted to, she could bring the evening to a graceful end simply by saying, "Well, I'd better get to bed. Thanks for everything," and escorting Tony to the door. She could . . . but she didn't. And Tony seemed to be in no hurry to leave.

They shared small talk—what classes she was taking in college; what odd things had happened to him in his security work. One story led to another, back and forth, and the longer it went on, the more comfortable she felt. She occasionally found herself glancing up at the photo of Brad on the mantel, almost as if expecting that the smile there would have changed to a disapproving scowl. But the slightly gap-toothed grin remained the same.

Every now and then, either Deborah or Tony would pick up the phone and make a call. But there was never an answer. As the night grew old,

Tony said, "Don't worry, Bill's bound to be home when the eleven o'clock news comes on. He's got a real fascination with the Cannibal."

"Really?" Deborah said. "Ted's practically a Cannibal *groupie*, too."

"Maybe that's where they've been all night," Tony said, half-humorously. "Out swapping Cannibal stories."

Deborah laughed. She'd laughed quite a bit tonight, she realized, even at things that weren't that funny. It made her feel light inside, as if she'd just recovered from a headache she hadn't even been aware of.

Just then the news broadcast started, and Tony turned toward the TV. Deborah watched his face—suddenly, it was as if part of him left the room.

An anchorman stared into the camera and said, "Police are calling it 'a slaughterhouse.' They're referring to the scene at Flash, a popular Mission Valley nightclub where three men died tonight. For more details, we'll go to our reporter in the field, Gene Palmer. Gene?"

The TV studio vanished and suddenly swarms of police, civilians and paramedics were trapped in the flashing lights of police cars and ambulances. In the foreground stood a reporter. "Peter," he said, "as you can see behind me, the situation here at Flash is chaotic. Police are currently taking statements from dozens of witnesses, and paramedics are treating those who were injured during the stampede from the club.

"This is all we know so far: Three people are dead at this time—two inside the building, and a third whose body was discovered later in a car in the parking lot." He consulted his notes. "The first two victims have been identified as James Allman, an engineer at General Dynamics, and Duane Washington, a security guard here at Flash. We want to stress that although initial reports indicate that these men are victims of the San Diego Cannibal, this now seems to be in question. Earlier, we taped interviews with some of the witnesses of what went on inside Flash."

The scene cut to a young couple standing in the nightclub's parking lot, their trendy clothes and haircuts looking vaguely absurd in the unrelenting television light. In a stunned voice the woman said, "This guy was slow-dancing with a woman in a red dress. Just dancing. Then . . ."

"The next thing we knew," her companion blurted, "his head was rolling across the floor."

Cut to a muscular young man wearing a Flash T-shirt, his face also stunned. "We heard screaming, then people were running everywhere. I saw Duane heading for the dance floor. There was a woman standing there, all covered with blood . . . and then everybody stampeded and I couldn't see what happened next. But that *woman* must have killed Duane; nobody else was close enough."

Deborah looked at Tony, but Tony's gaze seemed welded to the screen. She shivered. Was *he* a member of the San Diego Cannibal Fan Club, too?

The field reporter reappeared. "The mysterious woman in red was noticed by several people. So far, none of the Flash employees are admitting they saw her enter the nightclub; evidently it's not uncommon for attractive young ladies to get in without having their I.D.s checked."

From the anchorman: "Is there any clue as to a motive in these attacks, Gene?"

"In the case of Duane Washington, it was apparently just that he tried to restrain the woman. As for James Allman, right now the police are only saying that it was not a robbery. They'll be questioning various women he's known." He hesitated. "I should add that because of the violent nature of these murders, some officials are speculating that they're 'copycat' crimes—deliberately done in the style of the San Diego Cannibal. If that's the case, Peter, the police could be facing a long winter . . ."

"What about the third murder, Gene?" asked the anchorman.

Instantly, the scene changed to a shot of a parking lot, mostly empty now. On one side, lights and policemen surrounded a car. Gene's voice said, "Actually, Peter, police are speculating that the third death might not have been a homicide at all. While searching the parking lot after the killings inside Flash, officers discovered the body of a dead man in this car. He had been shot at extremely close range, apparently with his own pistol, which he was holding in his hand . . ."

Deborah suddenly leaned forward and squinted at the screen. "Look," she said. "*Look.* See that Porsche in the back of the lot? That looks like *Ted's* car."

Tony grunted, concentrating on the broadcast. Deborah wondered if he had even heard her, and decided it didn't matter. After all, it had been a stupid comment—how many cars like Ted's were there in San Diego?

". . . identity," the announcer said. "His name is William F. Chatherton—an off-duty San Diego police officer who . . ."

Deborah shot a horrified look at Tony. He had stiffened, every muscle in his face standing out in sharp relief in the glare of the TV.

". . . traffic division, and was not known to be involved in any criminal investigations. Although his death was possibly a suicide, police are nevertheless investigating connections between him and the other dead men on yet another night of carnage in San Diego."

Tony shot to his feet and, without a word, strode to the patio door and let himself out.

Deborah hesitated. Did he want comfort or not? And what comfort could she offer, anyway? The same well-intentioned but senseless words she'd received herself?

Maybe good intentions were all that really mattered. She got up and walked outside. Tony stood in the middle of the yard, his hands in his pockets, face turned up to the few stars that penetrated the haze of city light above.

"You don't think it was a suicide, do you?" she said.

"No. Chatherton got too close to something, and now he's dead and it's supposed to *look* like a suicide."

"But what was he doing at Flash?"

He looked at her, his gaze so intense she could almost feel it through the darkness. "Didn't you say you saw Ted's car on TV?" he said.

"Well, I . . . saw one like it."

"And he's not answering his telephone, either."

She put her hand to her chest. "You're not saying—"

"Did Ted go to Flash often?"

"I don't know." Had he ever mentioned it before? Usually, when he started blathering about his night life, she just closed him out.

Raising his head and speaking toward the sky, Tony said, "I suspect Bill went to Ted's house after Ted had already gone to Flash. Chatherton learned that somehow, and went to Flash, too—but he got intercepted by Faust, or Blondie, or somebody else involved in this conspiracy."

"But why would *they* be there?"

"Because they were also after Ted."

"*Ted*? Why?"

Tony let out a long sigh. "Deborah, that printout he gave you . . . did it come off the same computer you used when you contacted Dr. Pendergast?"

"Everything at the Carlton Center goes through the mainframe. Why?"

"Think about it. When did that fake plumber show up at your place? Right after you used the computer the first time."

"Yes, but—but it's not the same thing. That time, we used the modem. This time Ted didn't need to connect with another computer."

"So there's no way anyone on the outside could have known what Ted was up to?"

She stood motionless, suddenly remembering how nervous Ted had been about accessing the administrative files. *If there's even one hint I could get in trouble—just one hint—I'll pull out immediately. Wimps always prosper.* "I guess it's possible," she said thinly. "But, Tony, you can't be saying . . . you can't be saying Ted is dead, too. Please. Maybe that wasn't his car I saw on TV. Or if it was, maybe he's being questioned by police right now. That would explain why he isn't home. I mean, they didn't find a bod . . . they didn't find another . . ."

Tony suddenly stepped close to her, touched her shoulder. "Easy. You're probably right. Ted probably *is* with the police."

She knew he didn't believe it. But there *had* to be some reason Ted wasn't answering his phone besides what Tony had suggested. Just *had* to be.

"What about the other killings?" she cried suddenly. "As long as you're trying to tie everything together, what about the other two people who got murdered tonight? Were they just coincidences?"

"I don't know," he said.

She realized she had been shouting and, hoping she hadn't wakened Del and Betty, fell silent and hugged herself to hold in a shiver. She mustn't shake or sob or show any sign of weakness now, because if she did, Tony would probably put his arm around her. And she didn't want to be held, didn't deserve to be comforted. Despite her denials, deep inside she knew that Ted was dead. And that was, of course, her fault . . . her own selfish fault . . .

". . . and of course we'll bring you updates on the events at Flash as they become available to us. For everyone at Eyewitness News, good night."

Pendergast moved his gaze from the primary monitor to the holding cell screens, and noted that none of the Loners seemed particularly interested in the news broadcast. Which was as expected. He didn't *want* Loners to exhibit interest in human events, just human lives. To Loners, the activities of *Homo sapiens* were to be understood at a visceral level.

Pendergast, however, was *very* interested in the news. In fact, earlier this evening, when he had seen the first "story" about the murders at Flash, he had been shocked—a "Cannibal" killing, *tonight*? How—? Immediately he had turned toward the security monitors, but a glance revealed that all the Alphas were in their cells. Well, of *course* they were. What was the matter with him? There was no way a Loner could get out of its cell, far less Ginnunga Gap. The Ark controlled all the doors, and monitored unauthorized activity outside the cells.

Still, a Cannibal-style murder spree tonight . . .

Mitford? Who better to imitate a Loner?

Unfortunately, because actual police reports from the crime scene wouldn't begin to flow into the computer for some time, Pendergast had to wait for the eleven o'clock news, like everyone else, before he could learn more.

The moment he heard that the murderer had been a *woman*, he had slumped back in his seat, weak with relief. Mitford was capable of many things, but acting like a woman would never be one of them.

Then he heard the name "Chatherton" and sat bolt upright again, turning up the volume in time to hear that the corpse of Officer William Chatherton had been found in his car in the Flash parking lot. Possibly a suicide.

Pendergast sat back and rubbed his face. Mitford *had* been at the nightclub, after all . . .

A moment later the news turned to a story about a series of Right-to-Life demonstrations being conducted around the city. Despite his other worries, Pendergast watched—and when he saw the protesters in front of a Sixth Avenue abortion clinic, he quaked with sudden fury. One of them was a girl about eight years old, lugging a sign that read, DO YOU WISH I'D DIED, TOO?—PSALM 127:3.

Pendergast knew that verse well:

> Behold, children are a gift
> of the Lord;
> The fruit of the womb is a
> reward.

Reward? For what? Junkies had children. Thieves had children. Hell, *child molesters* had children. As for using the Bible for justification, how come he didn't see any signs out there referring to Exodus 12:29, where

God himself massacred the firstborn of Egypt—innocents all—just because one person wouldn't do as he was told? You had to look at the whole thing to see how the parts fit together, that was the thing. But then, all organized religions demand tunnel vision from their adherents.

To calm himself, Pendergast glanced at the holding cell monitors again, and saw movement in Anubis's chamber as the Loner walked up to one of his TV screens. His long dark tongue slid out and licked slowly across the image of the little girl. Pendergast smiled, calm again. Never mind the Right-to-Lifers—soon, the Loners would *force* realistic behavior on them.

Just then a red light on the security panel began to flash, indicating that one of the Ginnunga Gap's motion detectors had registered the approach of a vehicle. A few minutes later a surface TV scanner showed the Cherokee, bouncing and heaving over the brutal terrain. The garage door opened to receive it, and a camera inside the garage showed the vehicle pull to a stop next to the 500-gallon gasoline tank. Mitford climbed out of the cab, stretched, then walked over to the tank and lifted off the hose. Pendergast waited impatiently as he filled the Cherokee.

By the time Mitford reached the control room, Pendergast was ready, his face composed.

"Done." Mitford took his seat and smiled. "But I suppose you've heard all about it on TV by now."

"Oh, yes, it was big news," Pendergast said, trying not to look at the maroon stains on Mitford's sleeves.

"They think Chatterton committed suicide, right?"

"That's the current theory . . . but I'm sure there'll be an autopsy."

Mitford shrugged. "No problem. I shot him in the eye to cover the damage I did with the knife."

Pendergast winced. "And . . . what about Scully?"

"I decided two suicides in one night might be too much, so I just made him disappear."

Pendergast began to tense inside. "And . . . the other murders at the nightclub?"

"Murders? Ted only told me about one."

"There were *two*: a patron and a bouncer."

"Yeah? Well, Ted didn't mention the bouncer."

Once again, Pendergast wished he had Mitford in an Alpha holding cell. "According to witnesses," Pendergast said, "a woman murdered them, then tried to make it look like a Loners-type killing—a Cannibal killing, I guess I should say." He paused. "Are you sure you didn't go inside that club tonight?"

"Of course I'm sure. I talked to Chatherton in his car, then waited for Ted to . . ." His eyes sharpened. "What are you suggesting? You think I'm a transvestite or some—"

"No, of course not," Pendergast said quickly. "It's just that I'd never considered the possibility of a copycat killer. Between what happened last night and tonight, people are going to get the wrong idea about the Loners."

"From a security standpoint, that's fine," Mitford said evenly, but his eyes burned with a dark fire.

Pendergast hid the shiver of apprehension that passed through him, and changed the subject. "The real question is, what did you learn from Chatherton and Scully?"

Mitford smiled. "Well," he said, "I'm afraid Deborah Kosarek is going to have to die."

CHAPTER SEVENTEEN

"DEBORAH, I DON'T THINK I should leave here tonight," Tony said. He and she were in the family room again, sitting on opposite ends of the couch. "Not after what happened at Flash. You never know, Chatherton might have said something before he was killed."

Deborah clutched her throat. "Shouldn't we call the police? Tell them what we know about—"

"I'm sure they're going to be fielding a million calls tonight from people who think they know who's killing who," Tony said. "We'd just be another name on the list."

"But . . ."

"I have a better idea. Tomorrow, I'll go downtown and see an old cop friend of mine; he's a homicide detective now. I'll—"

"You sure know a lot of cops," Deborah said.

A pause. "Yeah. Well, I'll explain it to you sometime. Meanwhile, I'll show Lieutenant Stoner the list and tell him everything I know, all that's happened. See if I can stir up some interest."

"And if not?"

He hesitated. "You might ask Del to keep his gun cabinet unlocked for the next few days."

"I understand." She closed her eyes.

"I'll sleep on the couch here," he said, patting a cushion.

"I'll get some blankets." She paused. "Tony . . . I'm glad you're staying."

He smiled slightly, said nothing.

When she returned, he was standing in the middle of the room wearing only his jeans, checking the action on a big revolver. She froze.

"I'll keep this under the couch tonight," he said. "If you happen to get up early, make sure Virgil doesn't come over here."

She nodded, cold inside. And yet, with part of her mind she noticed that except for the slight love-handles around his waist, Tony's torso was lean and muscular. "Here's your bedding," she said.

"Thanks." He tossed it carelessly on the couch, and Deborah realized he had no intention of sleeping.

"Do you think the police will believe you?" she asked. Although the couch in the nursery folded out into a perfectly comfortable bed, she found she didn't want to go up there just yet.

"Maybe," Tony said, shoving his hands into his pockets. "I should at least be able to talk them into sending someone up to Pendergast's house—maybe they'll get the Sheriff's Department to check out that survivalist camp, too. It depends on how convincing I can be."

"Please be convincing. I can't live like this, Tony, wondering when that man is going to—"

Tony took a step toward her. "Don't be afraid," he said. "I won't let anything happen."

Suddenly she reached out, and his bulk enfolded her, seemed to absorb her. "It's not just me," she said shakily against his bare chest. "I've endangered everyone I know." And she began to cry.

Although the morning was aging fast, and somewhere above the surface of the earth the sun burned high and hot, down in the jail pit everything was utterly black, cool, quiet. Pendergast hesitated for a moment with one hand on the rheostat knob and the other tightly clenched around a fat cloth-bound book. Although he knew he was alone in Ginnunga Gap—except, of course, for the Loners in their cells—for a moment he had the overpowering sensation that the viewing area before him was full of people. He quickly cranked up the lights.

Of course, no one was here except for him and Vulcan, who sat motionless on the floor of the pit, staring up. Naturally.

Although Pendergast had prepared himself, he was still shaken by the sight of poor Vulcan, his entire body shriveled now, and trapped in a state halfway between human and Loner. His talons were partially extended; his killing jaws protruded through cracked human lips; all his bones were displaced. And he was almost completely bald.

Tears came to Pendergast's eyes as he put the food bag down and took his seat. "How do you feel, Vulcan?" he asked softly.

The Loner blinked. Slowly, his talons and jaws retracted and the various segments of his skull slipped into their human semblance. But his Loner skin didn't smooth out; deep fissures radiated from the scars on his face like cracks in ice. He looked, quite simply, like a terribly sick old man. Pendergast revised his estimate of how much time Vulcan had left: one or two days, tops. In the wild the Loner would already have been killed and replaced by a young Loner seeking territory.

Pendergast looked at the book he had brought with him today: The *Nag Hammadi*, a collection of Gnostic Christian texts. Unlike conventional Christians, Gnostics asserted that God was imperfect and the human race a mistake, and that human salvation had to be earned through purifying actions. No wonder Gnosticism had proven to be a relatively unsuccessful religion. So few people were willing to accept responsibility for what they did . . .

"You're not the only one who's going to die soon," Pendergast blurted. "I—I just sent Mitford after Deborah Kosarek." He rubbed his face. "I'd so hoped she . . . never mind. Whatever her intentions are, they can't be tolerated anymore. And Mitford says there's *another* person involved in this, too, an ex-policeman. I'm afraid there's no choice but to weed them both out quickly, before the danger gets any greater."

Looking into the pit, Pendergast tried to match Vulcan's crumpled, unrelenting stare. "I know what you're thinking," he said. "Why don't I just set the Alphas free now instead of taking a chance on getting caught with them here? Well, I've thought about it. But I don't want to make the same mistake *God* made when he placed mankind on the earth—I want to be *sure* that what I start never goes bad. Do you understand?"

Vulcan's head slowly rose and fell.

Pendergast dropped his book and jolted forward, clutching the bars. Had that really been a nod? No . . . no, of course not. Imitating human behavior was one thing, but nodding in response to a direct question indicated *comprehension*—and Loners simply weren't equipped for that level of abstract thinking. It must have been a mere reflex, a muscular tic.

Still, after Vulcan died, an autopsy might be in order. Just to find out what his brain looked like . . .

Wait, what kind of thinking was that? Would a carpenter disassemble a house he'd built in order to see if its structure had changed? He was just experiencing opening-night jitters, that was all. Perfectly natural, considering how long and hard he'd prepared for what was about to be launched.

"Don't worry, Vulcan," he said. "I won't back out on *Enkidu*. We're doing the *right* thing, the only thing to save the world. Right?"

Vulcan did not respond at all.

When Sarah Matthews heard the knocking on the door across the landing, she hurried to the peephole and peered out. Exciting things had been happening over at Deborah's lately.

For a moment, she couldn't see clearly—she'd been smoking grass pretty heavily since noon—but finally she focused on the back of a man's head. Short, dark hair . . . a swabbie? Good luck, fella. Although Sarah had dated a few sailors and didn't personally think they were such bad guys, she doubted most of them were Deborah's type. On the other hand, nowadays a really short haircut didn't mean much; a lot of men had them.

Only one way to find out.

She opened the door and said, "Hi. May I help you?"

Today she was wearing Spandex shorts and her string bikini top, and as the visitor turned, she waited for his reaction. In the past she'd gotten everything from major jaw-drops to flurries of blinks; this time she received a quick up-and-down glance accompanied by a slight widening of the eyes—then it was gone. "Hi," the man said, looking squarely into her face. "Do you know where Deborah Kosarek is?"

For a moment *she* was disconcerted. Why so little response? Maybe he was gay. Or perhaps he already knew her. Now that she thought about it, there was something familiar about him . . . his voice, maybe? That was hardly definitive—she could have heard him in any of a hundred bars. "Uh, Deb's not home," she said. "She's . . ." For a second she almost said, "with a friend," then realized that would be pretty uncool. ". . . at her in-laws'. She may be gone for a while. Can I help you?"

His eyes tracked over her body again, this time more slowly—but there was much more judgment there than appreciation, and she didn't like it. "No, thanks," he said. "I've got a message to deliver from a mutual friend, that's all. You say she's at her in-laws'?" For a moment she had the strange feeling he was about to reach out and touch her—

but not on the face or hand—and she backed away slightly, gooseflesh all over her body. He smiled. "Thanks for your help," he said. "You're saving Deborah's life."

Sarah couldn't reply. Lips twitching, she watched him vault down the steps and disappear. Then she went back inside and tried to light a fresh joint, but her hands were shaking too much.

When Tony had told Deborah he had an old friend on the force who was now in the Homicide Division, it had been a bit of a stretch. True, Lieutenant Stoner had been one of his instructors back in the academy, but Tony was only *assuming* the man would remember him.

As it turned out, he had to make two visits before he actually got to see Stoner. The first time he went in, he was directed to a sergeant, to whom he explained carefully what was going on. The sergeant promised to run some of the names from Ted Scully's list through the computer again, but said it would take a few hours.

Tony had returned to the Kosareks', watched a couple of TV fishing shows with Del, then had come back and been escorted through familiar halls to Stoner's cluttered office on an upper floor of the headquarters building.

Stoner was a shapeless bulk of a man with ears so red they seemed to have just come in from an arctic wind. "Let me make sure I've got this straight," he said, peering at the computer printout through half-glasses. "You believe Bill Chatherton was murdered as a result of a conspiracy to kidnap and kill scientists working in the biotechnology field. Is that right?"

Tony had forgotten how closely this guy's face and tone of voice matched his last name. "Something like that," he said. As a matter of fact, Stoner had quoted him exactly.

Leaning forward, Stoner rubbed the sides of his head, thumbs in his ears. Must be tired, Tony thought. Between the San Diego Cannibal and three dead cops, the Homicide Division had to be buried in work—and, of course, bad publicity.

"Did anybody check out the names on the list?" Tony finally asked.

Stoner looked up. "Of course."

"And?"

The printout rattled as Stoner flipped through it. "Let's see—car accident, electrocution, car accident, suicide, asphyxia, riding accident, disappeared while on fishing trip . . . they're all like that. No investigations begun or recommended in any instance."

"But accidents can be faked," Tony said. "And, statistically, that list is just too—"

"Please." Stoner held out his hand like a traffic cop. "Don't quote statistics. Everybody from the mayor to the guy who puts Cokes in the vending machine is giving me statistics."

"But—"

"I'm just saying this information is *inconclusive*, Tony. That's all."

"What about Chatherton and Ted Scully's deaths?"

"Okay. Scully's car was found in the parking lot at Flash, yes. But there was no body in it, not even the sign of a struggle. Maybe he went home with a woman." Stoner paused, peering at Tony over the tops of his half-glasses. "As for Bill, the autopsy results state that he's a probable suicide."

Tony wanted to jump up, stomp around, tear his hair. Instead, he took a deep breath. "Bill had his problems, but he wasn't suicidal."

"He had more problems than you may know. Did he ever tell you his performance record has been under review for the last few months?"

Tony stared. "No."

"Well. His career was in serious jeopardy, Tony, and he knew it."

Tony couldn't respond.

Stoner's eyes wandered to a tall pile of files on his desk. "Listen. I'm not saying we won't look into your information any deeper—I'll even send a squad car up to Dr. Pendergast's house to see if he's there, and suggest to the Sheriff's Department that they visit that survivalist camp. All right? But other than that, right now the department has more *pressing* matters, more *immediate* matters, to worry about. You understand."

"But *Faust* . . ."

"Tony, we have no evidence he's involved in any criminal activity, other than possibly giving a false address. What do you expect me to do, furnish you with personal bodyguards?"

Tony took two slow, deep breaths. "Could you at least have a patrol car cruise past the Kosareks' house every now and then during the next few days?"

"Sure, I can do that." Stoner smiled perfunctorily. "Is there anything else?"

"No." Tony stood up fast, anger roaring through him, and spun on his heel. He didn't want to lose what small concessions he'd gained. "Thanks for your time."

"Sure." Stoner was already picking up a file.

Letting himself out of the office, Tony stalked down hallways that were now almost alien to him. Even the sight of the khaki uniforms and gun belts didn't give him the usual twinge of regretful jealousy. He didn't belong here anymore. Hadn't for years.

Outside, he stood on the sidewalk and took several deep breaths. The headquarters building, a blocky, institutional pile of glass and concrete, loomed over a neighborhood that looked like it was under siege; derelicts all around, trash in the street; graffiti sprayed on boarded-up shop windows; long open plazas like defensive clearings around a fortress. Cruisers came and went constantly from an underground garage.

Turning on his heel, Tony walked toward the downtown skyscrapers. It was the weekend, so the County Records Department wouldn't be open. But the San Diego Library would be, and there were some things he wanted to check on before he returned to the Kosareks' house.

> Painful is the crossing, troublesome the road, and everywhere the
> waters of death stream across its face . . .

Pendergast was trying to read from *Gilgamesh* again, but right now he couldn't concentrate. Lowering the book, he looked at the chronometer on the control panel. 4:57. Mitford would undoubtedly strike after dark—like most predators, including Loners, he preferred to hunt at night. Pendergast would know that Deborah was dead—the security guard, too—as soon as police headquarters was notified, of course; still, he also wanted to watch the news on television.

Suddenly he found the control room oppressive, heavy with the crushing weight of stone and earth above it. It made him think of a grave, which made him think of Vulcan, dissipating away down in the prison pit. Pendergast knew he should go visit the old Loner, but just couldn't bring himself to do it.

Instead, he gazed at the holding-cell monitors and absorbed the reassuring sight of the Alphas, healthy and vibrant. That made him feel better. *There* stood the future.

Setting *Gilgamesh* aside, he switched on the main TV monitor and scanned through the early news programs. A brush fire in the North County threatened hundreds of homes. How sad. A six-car pileup on

805 had killed four. Boo-hoo. A recent study revealed that the flesh of fish caught in San Diego Bay contained unhealthy levels of dioxins, sulphides and phosphates. Authorities were considering a ban on all fishing in the bay. What a shock.

He automatically glanced back at the holding cell monitors to see how the Alphas were reacting to this broadcast. As he did so, a familiar scene appeared on each TV screen in the cells: A little girl carrying a sign: DO YOU WISH I'D DIED, TOO?—PSALM 127:3. God, *that* again? Just then, in Anubis's cell, the Loner approached the screen and dragged his tongue over the image of the girl—exactly as he'd done yesterday. Interesting.

On the TVs, the girl disappeared and was replaced by a commercial for "The Eight O'Clock Movie": *Friday the 13th, Part VIII—Jason Takes Manhattan*. Pendergast frowned. Hadn't that film played on this same station *last* night?

A fluttery sense of apprehension suddenly rising in his stomach, he looked for the same movie ad on the control room TV. Nothing.

What the . . . ?

Moving over to Mitford's seat, he examined the security camera controls. The VCRs were all set to *record*, as they should be, feeding their images to the monitors. But he didn't believe what he was seeing. After all, the VCRs could all be overridden by the Ark's security program . . . made to *replay* old tapes, for example. But why would Mitford do such a thing?

Pendergast hit the master switch that shut off the VCRs, automatically switching the security monitors to real time. He looked up—and gasped in horror.

The Loner cells were all empty.

Mitford cruised past the Kosareks' house, not going too slow or too fast. He had spent the entire afternoon parked several streets away, waiting patiently for sunset, fantasizing about what was to come. Once, a patrol car had cruised toward him, but the cop had been looking at the Corvette across the street, and never even glanced his way. Still, Mitford had been pleased when the sun drew near the horizon and he could move.

No one was in the front yard of the Kosareks' house, but the bitch's car was parked in the driveway. Mitford drove around the corner.

Ahead, a narrow alley bisected the block, but Mitford ignored that; from the layout of the surrounding streets, he knew the alley came to a dead end at the lip of a canyon. Instead, he made a U-turn and parked at the curb in front of several other vehicles, one of which happened to be a black Cherokee. Good camouflage.

The timing was good, too. The sun was just going down, and although the sky was jolly with color, the land below was blue gray, devoid of detail. And in the houses, people's attention would be on dinner, or TV, or getting ready to go out for the evening.

Mitford sat quietly, gathering himself. Pendergast had insisted he kill these people quickly and cleanly, in "accidents." And this he would do . . . except for the Kosarek bitch. Now *she* deserved a party. Yes, indeed. The blanket and special tools were waiting there in the back seat. No one, including the doc, need ever know.

But first Mitford had to get inside the house without raising an alarm. Reaching into the glove box, he pulled out a leather wallet which contained San Diego Police identification. Between his new hairdo, the badge and the fading light, Mitford figured he'd be able to get inside easily. And then . . .

He double-checked his knife and holstered pistol, and decided he was ready. He *knew* he was eager.

Turning around, he grabbed the blanket and pulled it up. Below, a figure lay on the seat. Two others were folded up like giant pill bugs on the floor, one on either side of the transmission hump. They turned their heads and grinned at him.

"Yabba-dabba-doo," said the one on the seat.

Deborah was upstairs changing Virgil's diaper when the telephone rang. A moment later Del called, "Deb, it's Tony. He's on his way home."

A stab of alarm shot through her heart. *"Home?"*

"Here, I mean."

Shaking her head and half-smiling, she told Virgil, "Now you can settle down, you little pain. Your hero's on his way."

Virgil blew a cheerful spit bubble.

As she picked him up, groaning theatrically at his weight, she glanced out the window. Above the neighbors' roofs perched a fruit basket of a sunset, cantaloupes and tangerines and chunks of watermelon. Gorgeous. She unlatched the window and pushed it open with one hand.

Ugh—a fruit basket shouldn't smell like barbeque smoke. She started to pull the window closed again, then looked down as movement attracted her attention. A man was running down the back alley toward the canyon, carrying something large and bulky over his shoulder. She would have assumed he was just a transient getting ready to bed down for the night in the canyon—an increasing problem—except that he was moving so *fast*, with the lunging sprint of a world-class hurdler.

Suddenly a second man soared like a panther over the back fence, clearing it as easily as if it were a street curb, and landed in the back yard. A short white gown flapped around him. Deborah gasped in shock, and just had time to open her mouth to scream for Del when a large, grinning head popped over the windowsill directly in front of her. Deborah staggered back, lungs paralyzed with shock.

A tall, sinewy form flowed into the room. Although it was little more than a silhouette, and wore a short, loose gown like that of the figure that had hurdled the fence, Deborah could tell by the outline that this one was a woman. She turned toward Virgil in his crib, paused briefly, then wheeled toward Deborah. "Blasphemer," the intruder said in a thick, rasping voice. "You're out of here."

From downstairs came a scream, cut off abruptly.

The intruder stepped forward. As her face moved into the light from the hall, Deborah got a good look and opened her mouth to scream, too—but suddenly a flat hand flashed out of the shadows, trailing darkness and silence behind it.

Deborah's last thought was, *Did she have* claws . . . ?

The cells are empty.

For a minute Pendergast couldn't think of anything else at all. He just stared at the monitors until his brain began working again. *Empty* . . . but how? There were no holes or breaches in the walls; the doors were closed; the electronic locks registered *latched*. How had the Loners gotten out?

—and where were they now?

His gaze flicked to the various security monitors, but they indicated no sign of significant life elsewhere in the complex, or above it. The Alphas were . . . *gone*.

Suddenly a haze of fury began to pulse behind his eyes. *Mitford* knew where they were. Who else could have freed them?

Pendergast made himself breathe slowly, deeply, until the haze went away. Okay. Okay. Mitford hadn't been terribly interested in the computer, but his duties required enough knowledge about the security programs that he could have easily bypassed the alarm systems and sabotaged the camera playbacks. Then he must have dumped anesthetic gas into the holding cells and simply carted the Alphas away, his actions unrecorded. But *why*? Not to kill the Alphas, surely—far from fearing or loathing the Loners, Mitford had, if anything, seemed increasingly intrigued by them, always eager to take the next one out . . .

Pendergast slammed his palms down on the console. Could that be it? Had Mitford decided to turn all the Loners loose *himself*?

Pendergast's hands trembled with fury. He tried breathing slowly and deliberately again, but the shaking wouldn't stop. All right . . . what was the loss, really? So far, the field tests had certified the fitness of the Alphas for freedom. And Pendergast had, after all, himself only recently considered just letting them go.

But that was *his* decision to make. *His*, not Mitford's.

There was a slight *click* behind him; the sound of the control room door opening. He whirled. "Mit—"

The doorway was jammed with Loners, their faces full of teeth. "Beloved Georrrrrrrge," they rumbled in chorus. "Welcome to ourrrrr neighborrrhood."

CHAPTER EIGHTEEN

BY THE TIME TONY GOT BACK to Clairemont, he was feeling better. For one thing, he was excited to be on his way to the Kosareks' house. When he'd been a cop there had been a similar sensation each time he'd driven to the station at the start of a shift, anticipating the banter, jokes, shared bravado. But this was even better. Warmer. This was . . . like going *home*. *You're welcome here anytime*.

Another thing: Deborah would be there. He still remembered how she'd felt when they'd hugged.

He glanced at the stack of photocopies on the seat beside him: The fruits of his labors at the library. There were old magazine articles about the survivalist camp—Hiber Nation, it was called. Although there were no photos, the camp had been described as an extensive complex of underground bunkers and living quarters, all self-contained. Unfortunately, there weren't any exact directions to the place, either.

Useful or not, Tony felt better for having gathered this information. Now he had *something* to show Deborah and the elder Kosareks, data to make his trip downtown seem less pointless.

As he neared the intersection with the Kosareks' street, his gaze suddenly registered a Jeep Cherokee parked at the curb. He put his foot on the brake, then released it again. Even in the gloom, he could tell the Jeep wasn't brown.

Then he saw the *second* Cherokee, and slowed again. This one *was* brown. And its sides were dusty and scratched, as if it spent a lot of time thumping about on roadless terrain. He glanced at the plates—different.

Relaxing, he continued on, turning the corner and looking eagerly up the street to . . .

. . . of all the houses in sight, only one had no lights showing in any of its windows. The Kosareks' house.

Tony jerked his car to the curb, jumped out, and bolted down the sidewalk and across the Kosareks' front yard, pulling the .357 Magnum as he went. Would one of the neighbors see him? Maybe. That was fine. They could call the police. Maybe they'd even get Lieutenant Stoner, that son of a bitch.

Leaping onto the porch, Tony slapped his body against the wall adjacent to the door and tried the knob with his free hand. His heart crashed. The door was unlocked. Fighting panic, trying to keep his training in mind, he put his palm against the door and shoved. It swung in, thumped against the doorstop. Tony waited for bullets to fly out.

Nothing. Silence. "Deborah?" he yelled. "Del? Betty?"

From somewhere down the street came the faint sound of people having fun in a swimming pool. From inside the house came silence. Fleetingly, Tony hoped he was about to make a fool out of himself, that the Kosareks were all in the back yard, and they'd jump in shock when he appeared with his gun drawn. Del, Betty, Deborah, Virgil . . .

Taking a deep breath, he spun into the foyer, body low, Magnum sweeping from side to side. Then he froze. His hands began to shake. "Oh . . . God . . ."

Betty Kosarek was sprawled against the far wall of the foyer. He suspected it was she who had unlocked the door—to escape, or to let her killer enter? There was no way to tell. Her wide-open eyes seemed to glow dully in the gloom. On the wall above her neck was a huge, fan-shaped stain. Tony knew what that meant, he'd heard the phrase often enough toward the end of his police career: *severed carotid artery*.

Think. Think, now.

Without moving, he made himself look more closely at Betty's neck. It was slit open in four parallel slashes, like a shark's gills. Her torso looked strangely crumpled, as if she had been crushed under a great weight. Blood had soaked through her clothes and drained onto the floor in a thick puddle. *Such a mess*, Tony thought, the voice in his head high and shrill. *Oh, she'd hate this.*

Don't lose control, now. Think.

Of course, the only appropriate course of action was to run next door and call the police. There was no question about it. But he shoved the notion violently aside. There were still three innocent people unaccounted for, and Faust's Jeep was still here. Work to do. Tony closed the door behind him, and the sounds from the swimming pool down the block were chopped short.

But in here, silence was now pointless; he'd already announced himself. "Deborah!" he bellowed, and was startled to hear his cop voice, the roar of a man ten feet tall; that voice alone had often frozen fleeing criminals in their tracks. "Del!"

From somewhere in the house came a soft murmur . . . listening hard, he realized it was the TV.

He moved forward. As he stepped over Betty, her eyes seemed to follow him. *You were welcome here anytime. Where were you?*

He looked away, a small nova of pain and fury burning in his throat. He shouldn't have gone downtown, left them alone here. If he'd been here when Blondie came, Betty might still be—

Put it out of your mind. Concentrate. If Blondie is still here, you might yet be able to save *somebody*. Deborah. Virgil. Del. Somebody . . .

He turned the corner into the kitchen, his finger tight on the trigger. But the room was empty. Beyond, in the family room, the TV's light flickered against Del's chair. The chair was empty, too. In front of it, the hassock lay on its side like a dead dog.

A soft gust of air drew Tony's attention to the patio entrance. The glass door was open. Moving close, Tony peered outside. The back yard was empty.

When he shut off the TV, the silence became complete. Mentally, he reviewed the layout of the house. He'd already seen the foyer, front room, kitchen, family room. Downstairs, that left the garage, the spare bedroom where Betty did her sewing, and a bathroom. Upstairs was the master bedroom and bath, the den, and the nursery.

The house was so *quiet*.

First he checked the garage—two parked cars; Del's woodworking equipment. On one wall, pegboard festooned with hand tools, each covering its own painted silhouette. The air smelled of sawdust and varnish. No one was there.

To reach the guest bedroom and bathroom, Tony had to go past Betty again. He did this as quickly as possible, not looking at her.

The rooms beyond were empty.

Heart now pounding like a big, ready engine, he moved to the staircase. Stopped abruptly. On the bottom step lay Del's revolver—and clutched around the grip was a human hand with thick laborer's fingers.

Del's. The stump of the wrist was strangely smooth and flat, as if it had been amputated by a skilled surgeon. Tony stared at it for a moment, mouth dry, then raised his gaze. The stairs were spattered with blood, and on one wall, a sloppy red garland ran up to the second-floor landing in streams and splatters. Except it wasn't a garland, of course. Tony could picture Del's wrist hosing it there as he charged up the stairs.

Still wet.

Tony moved silently up the steps, not touching the blood. He was very calm inside now, removed—but the Magnum seemed to throb in his hand, as if it beat with a hatred of its own.

Two steps from the upstairs landing he paused, listening. Silence. He lunged up into the hallway, tracking left, right. The garland looped to the right and disappeared into the den. Nearer was the master bedroom, dark inside—someone could be in there right now, watching him. He leaped in quickly, snapping on lights, checking behind doors and under the bed, glancing in the bathroom—and jumping at his own reflection in the mirror. He was the only one here.

The only one alive, you mean . . .

Slowly now, he returned to the hallway and followed the garland of blood toward the den. "Del?" he called softly. "Deborah?"

Silence.

The den door stood halfway open. Four jagged, parallel gouges swept across it. Tony hesitated, noting that the gouges matched the cuts in Betty's neck; then he took a deep breath, raised the Magnum and kicked the door all the way open.

Del had obviously been trying to reach the gun cabinet. He was stretched out in the middle of the floor, belly-down, his left hand extended toward the cabinet and his right arm thrown to the side. That arm ended in a stump; blood puddled around it.

But Tony barely noticed that. His eyes, his whole mind, flew immediately to Del's back, where the shirt had been torn away, exposing thick shoulders and, just above the beltline, a heavy roll of fat. In between was nothing but a hollow bowl of bone and sinew, as if someone had tried to scoop Del as clean as a dugout canoe. The far side of his ribcage was plainly visible. Above, the edges of the gaping hole were neatly scalloped; bones, spine and muscles severed with a smoothness that was somehow more disturbing than the empties beyond. Something about it—

You know how shark bites look: smooth, crescent-shaped . . .

Tony felt dizzy. What was he thinking? Chatterton had been talking about the San Diego Cannibal, not Blondie.

Well, why not? Jesus, maybe Blondie *was* the Cannibal. Or maybe tonight he was imitating the Cannibal's style, throwing up a smokescreen.

Quit stalling, Garwood. You have one more room to check.

As he turned to leave, his gaze fell on the gun cabinet. The glass doors were closed, yet several weapons had had their trigger-locks removed. A throb of anguish rolled through him like an ocean swell—Del had taken Tony's advice, tried to be prepared. And now look at him.

No. Don't.

Tony walked back into the hallway, thinking hard about where he would shoot Blondie first. Knees? Elbows? Crotch?

Two steps took him to the nursery. He held his breath as he looked in. The room was filled with purplish gloom in which floated the lavender square of the open window. He switched on the light, fighting back an instinctive urge to scream because he knew he'd see—

But the scream remained locked behind his lips. There were no bodies. No bloody splatters on the walls or closet doors. His breath escaped as a teakettle whistle, and his knees shuddered with relief.

But . . . wait. He'd checked every room in the house. And if Deborah and Virgil—and Blondie—weren't here, then where—

His gaze fell on Virgil's blanket, piled in the bottom of the crib. There was something under it . . . Without thinking, he bounded across the room and swept up the blanket.

Brooke Worm lay there, eyes waggling.

He picked up the toy and clutched it fiercely. Maybe Deborah had managed to grab Virgil and escape. No, that didn't make sense—if they'd gotten away, surely this place would be crawling with cops by now.

In fact, why wasn't it crawling with cops, anyway? How had Blondie managed to hack two strong adults to death without drawing the neighbors' attention?

The answer was so obvious it sent him lunging to the window, where he braced himself, sucking in air: Blondie had not acted alone, of course. Maybe he had *never* acted alone.

He and Faust . . . ?

The surface of the windowsill felt rough, splintery. Looking down, he saw deep scratches in it, matching the marks in the den's door and in Betty's throat. He leaned through the window and looked around. The side of the house was rough stucco, but devoid of any real handholds. There were no ducts or pipes within ten feet. Only someone with a ladder or grapple of some kind could have scaled it.

Suddenly he pictured the whole scenario: There had been two attackers. Attacker A had entered through this window, while Attacker B simultaneously burst in via the patio door downstairs. Del had attempted to shoot B, had had his gun hand lopped off instead, and tried to run upstairs to his armory. Meanwhile Betty bolted for the front door, but never made it. Attacker A slashed her throat, then chased Del upstairs and plunged his mysterious weapon into the man's back.

Meanwhile, in the nursery, Deborah and Virgil were captured by Attacker A.

Finally, the attackers bundled their prisoners into the Cherokee and drove—

What's that? He had heard a sound behind him, a muffled chuckle. He spun. The noise came again—from behind the closed closet door.

Without thinking, Tony lunged to the sliding doors and slammed one open. He thrust the Magnum into the gap. Beyond was nothing but clothing—sweaters folded and stacked on shelves, rows of boots and shoes on the floor, winter coats on hangers. Very neat and orderly, except for one unusually broad gap. Inside there, something gleamed flatly. A big button?

Something gleamed up from between two coats—a big button?

It blinked. "Peekaboo!" cried a ragged, guttural voice, and Tony jumped backward, heart bounding, as a man pushed out from among the clothes.

The Magnum jerked up. "Freeze, motherfucker!" Tony bellowed. "Show me your hands! Show me your hands!"

A long, lanky figure unfolded from the closet, and Tony back-pedaled into the middle of the room. This wasn't Blondie; nor did he match Faust's description. He was quite young, with a long face and thick-black hair. Standing nearly six and a half feet tall, he had slender legs and bare feet protruding below the hem of a shapeless shift—a hospital gown? Yes, like something the inmate of a mental institution might wear . . .

The gown had a glistening apron of blood spattered across it. Tony's grip on the Magnum grew tighter, tighter. This might not be Blondie, but he was worse—he must be the psycho who had massacred Del, or Betty. . .or both.

And he was holding his arms behind his back.

"Let me see your hands," Tony snapped in his Cop Voice, finger tightening on the trigger, "or you're a dead man. You'd better believe it."

Smiling slightly, the tall man swept his arms around, fingers splayed. The fingers were long and somewhat thickened at the tips, and dangling from one of them was a lump of white fabric. Tony stared in horror. It was a disposable diaper.

His breathing seemed to stop, yet he heard himself say, "What did you do to him, you son of a bitch? What did you do to him?"

The intruder pursed his lips, and a small bone slid out. Sinew still clung to it in red tatters. The intruder plucked it out of his mouth and looked at it. "There are children starving in India, you know," he said in a voice with a curious rippling undertone, and popped the bone back into his mouth. He swallowed, and there was a sharp crackling sound. "Mmmmmm-mmmm," he purred. "Finger lickin' good."

That was it. A chicken bone, filched from the refrigerator downstairs. Certainly not a bone from a man's body, and not from . . . Tony found his gaze drawn back to the diaper, still hanging from the intruder's finger like a freshly harvested pelt, and thought: *Cannibal.* Then he thought, *Stop it, don't be* stupid. *That's a figure of speech. A nickname the media came up with* . . .

"All right," he said clearly, slowly. "Put your hands behind your head and walk out the door. Slowly. We're going downstairs. Don't try a thing, or believe me, I'll kill you."

The intruder cocked his head, smile fading. "Take care, Gilgamesh," he said softly. "Do not let your hand touch the waters of death. No deposit, no return."

Tony pulled back the Magnum's hammer. "I said move, you fucking fruitcake."

"Amen."

The intruder *rippled*. His body flexed and flowed, melting like a candle in the sun and then stretching into a new shape; longer, sleeker, rising onto its toes. Beneath the hem of the gown, its knees twisted around backward, and curved talons sprouted like evil thorns from its fingertips. In a smooth pulsation, its head telescoped into a tapering missile over which the skin was stretched so tightly it was transparent in places.

Then the thing grinned widely, and as its lips pulled back, they unveiled an interlocking maze of pointed teeth.

Tony did not move. It wasn't paralysis, though; it was a policeman's instinct, the automatic detaching of reflex from deliberation. It was like when you had arrested a man high on PCP and he ripped his own thumbs off to get free from the handcuffs—you didn't think, *That's impossible,* you whipped out your nightstick and used it fast. Only later did you get the shakes and maybe throw up.

But even as Tony's body filled with the electricity of adrenaline, a detached part of his mind took notes. For example, he acknowledged that the intruder's claws would fit neatly inside the wounds on Betty Kosarek's neck, and the shape of its huge jaws matched perfectly the scalloped edges of the hole in Del Kosarek's back. This part of Tony's brain acknowledged that he really was looking at the Cannibal. Not the Cannibal the police and media were searching for, not a fake Cannibal— the *real* Cannibal. And the real Cannibal was some kind of . . . *thing*.

The creature's lips writhed back from its teeth, and its voice came out like a ripping sail: "I am borrrrrrrrrn again as a new man—prrreferrrr-rrred ten to one to the otherrrrr leading brrrrrrrrrrrrand."

And then the Cannibal leaped—a wild flutter of cloth, flash of claws, gape of jaws. Tony, even pumped full of acetylcholine, barely fired the Magnum in time.

The cracking roar was deafening in the small room. The recoil threw Tony's arm up, momentarily blocking his view—not that it mattered; at this range, a .357 Magnum slug would have the same deadly impact as a charging rhinocer—

Suddenly he was soaring backward through the air. The wall stopped him and he crumpled to the floor, his gaze scarlet with agony. A terrible pain filled his chest; he couldn't breathe around it. Had he been cut? Had those talons sliced him open like a loaf of bread? He looked down. No blood.

There was movement to his right, a long shape rearing up—the Cannibal, wearing a small scarlet carnation on the front of its gown. Tony stared in disbelief. A shot to the sternum from contact range— there should be a *river* of blood pouring out of that wound, and the Cannibal should be sprawled dead on the floor. Instead, it merely looked down at itself and grinned. "Good night," it said, "and God bless." Raising its talons, it took a smooth step toward Tony.

Tony's paralysis broke and he rolled away as the claws raked through the air behind him. Swinging the Magnum toward the Cannibal's head, he pulled the trigger—but at the same moment, something ripped into his arm, jerking it to the side. He screamed in agony, saw the revolver fly across the room, felt blood streaming like hot oil under his forearm. But he also saw two digits vanish from the Cannibal's right hand. *A hand for a hand*, he thought giddily. Then the creature's head swung toward him, jaws yawning wide, and all he could see were its teeth—and, deeper in, a mass of shapes scissoring like the mouth-parts of an insect. The speed was incredible, the jaws slamming together before he could move—so close to his face that he felt the air vibrate in his nostrils. *It's playing with me*, he thought wildly, and scuttled backward on his hands and heels, trying to get his feet under him. The Cannibal followed, bending down, and Tony grabbed Virgil's crib and toppled it in front of the Cannibal, kept scrambling.

The crib exploded into shrapnel. Tony crashed into the wall, out of room, as the Cannibal loomed over him. Holding out its right hand as if to display the missing digits, the Cannibal grinned. The stumps had almost stopped bleeding. "No pain, no gain," the Cannibal growled. "So saith the angels of the Lorrrrrrrrrrd."

Without warning, its other talon whipped around, and Tony screamed as the claws split open his forehead, nose, lower lip, chin. Blinded by a mask of his own blood but sensing the Cannibal leaning toward him, he pawed around for anything resembling a weapon—and his hand closed on a sharp-edged piece of wood from the demolished crib.

"Fucker!" he screamed, and swung the slat around with all his strength, slamming its point into the creature's side. But it seemed to bounce backwards, driving splinters into his palm, then snapped in half.

Tony frantically wiped blood out of his eyes with his sleeve. The Cannibal leaned over him, grinning. "Sticks and stones may brrrrrreak my bones," it growled, "but mighty is the wrrrrrrrrrrrath of God. Amen."

Throwing the chunk of wood at the Cannibal's face, Tony lunged to his feet and hurled himself toward the open door. But the Cannibal whirled around, its hand whipping into Tony's ribs and tossing him sideways in a blast of pain. He bounced off the sofa and crashed to the floor again.

The Cannibal was toying with him, no doubt about it. It could have ripped him wide open more than once, if it had wanted to. Obviously it had no fear of him. And why should it? He had shot it in the chest with a .357 Magnum, blown off half its hand, stabbed it—yet *he* was the one being brutalized.

From the corner of his eye, he saw the creature striding toward him with a gait that was both lurching and smooth. Then he saw the Magnum again, not far away. It still seemed his best chance.

Drawing his feet beneath him, he leaped for it—

—and crashed headlong into the Cannibal, who had moved faster still. Tony stumbled backward, stunned, and fell again. Something terribly sharp sank into the back of his forearm, and as he instinctively brushed it away, it slit open his hand. He looked down—it was one of the Cannibal's claws, still attached to a knob of finger-bone.

The Cannibal's feet appeared in his field of vision, one on either side of him. The toes were incredibly long, almost fingerlike, terminating in heavy claws.

"Game's overrrrrrrrrrrr, Brrrrreederrrrrrr," the Cannibal growled. "Dinnerrrrrrrrrr is serrrrrrrrrrrved." Tony heard things grinding together in its throat, a whetstone noise.

This is it, Tony thought, staring at those backward-facing knees and elongated shins. *Just like Del. Oh, God, I hope it doesn't hurt too—*

Then he thought about Deborah and Virgil. What had happened to them?

As the Cannibal's hands began to close around Tony's arms, he reached down and grabbed the only thing available that even resembled a weapon—the Cannibal's own severed talon—and leaped to his feet. For a moment his face was only inches from the Cannibal's, and he thought he saw genuine surprise on those distorted features. Then, with a grunt of effort, he slashed the talon across the creature's neck—and was astonished when it sank into the flesh like a spoon into custard, opening a brand-new grin beneath the old one. Blood sprayed out in a freshet, and the Cannibal twisted its head away, wrenching the claw from Tony's grip.

Tony stumbled back. The Cannibal stood there, making a dreadful buzzing noise as blood poured onto its gown, expanding the size of the red apron. But it *stood.* How was that possible? Why didn't it *die?* Tony glanced at the Magnum, not two paces away now. But the creature was even closer . . .

Do it!

He lunged toward the Magnum. The Cannibal instantly cut toward it, too, but Tony had expected that and changed direction, hurling himself into the hallway. There was a growling sound behind him, *right* behind him, and without warning he slammed his shoulder against the wall, propelling himself sideways into the den. He heard talons crash into the wallboard where his head had just been, then he was vaulting over Del's body, elbow cocked, smashing through the glass front of the gun display case. He hauled out a five-shot pump shotgun, praying Del had loaded it, and swung it around just as a lean silhouette darted through the doorway.

There was no time to aim, really, but this time he fired high, toward the head. In the billowing mushroom of smoke and fire, he saw one of the Cannibal's eyes disappear and the skin blow out in a scarlet flap, blood spraying into the hallway. Instantly Tony jacked another shell into the chamber, because the Cannibal was still coming, body bent low, mouth gaping like a shark's. Tony fired straight into that maw, and the lower half of the Cannibal's face caved in. Then a great weight slammed into the shotgun and knocked Tony over backward.

The butt of the shotgun, socketed into his shoulder, pinned him to the floor like a butterfly on display. The Cannibal's momentum carried it up and over, talons flailing. Its claws sliced up Tony's body from knees to collarbone, shredding his clothes and opening zippers of fire through his flesh, and Tony pulled the trigger in a reflex of pain. Mingled with the blast was a splintering crash, a screech—and suddenly the weight disappeared. Stinging particles snowed down on him—broken glass. He rolled over, groaning, and looked up. The window was shattered. Splintered grooves tore through the wooden frame. Twisting onto his knees, moaning with pain, he rose and peered through the window.

Down on the ground Tony saw a sprawled figure in a hospital gown, broken glass glittering around it like diamonds. But it didn't look like a monster now, it looked like a man. A dead man. Around his head was a horseshoe-shaped spray of blood.

Gotcha, Tony thought almost incoherently, then looked down at himself. Talk about blood. It seemed to be flowing from every square inch of his body . . . but he was alive and the Cannibal, the *thing*, was *dead*.

Voices came to him, faint through the hissing in his ears. Looking out the window, he saw faces peeking up at him from adjoining yards. The harsh beam of a flashlight stabbed his eyes, and he turned away—

—and below him, the patio was empty. He jerked his head up just as a bit of bloody cloth flashed over the back fence.

No!

Rising to his feet and stumbling back from the window, he almost fell. He felt darkness waiting behind him, ready to claim him, and for a moment he almost let it. Anything to get away from . . .

What about Deborah and Virgil?

He stiffened his legs. Made himself think. They might still be alive. Somewhere. But *where*? Pendergast's old house? No, of course not. The other place, then, the survivalist camp.

But where is it?

Suddenly he heard sirens in the distance, and realized he faced another problem. When the police arrived, they would find the house occupied by two corpses . . . and one Tony Garwood. And what would his story be? *See, there was this monster. Well, first it was a man, then it turned into a monster and I think it was the Cannibal because it ate part of Del and I think it ate all of a little boy named Virgil and I shot it again and again and it fell twenty feet onto the pavement but then it got up and ran away—*

And Lieutenant Stoner would say, "First it was a kidnapping conspiracy, now it's *monsters*? What next, little green men from Mars?" And even if Tony could somehow talk his way out of the situation—there was the matter of Faust's Cherokee being here, which might give him some credibility—it would still take forever. And meanwhile, Deborah was out there . . . with Blondie and/or Faust . . .

A tidal wave of dizziness rolled over him, and he propped himself against the wall. What he really needed to do right now was go to the hospital. He was littering the carpet with dark red coins whenever he moved. How could he do anything, help anybody, in this condition?

Then he looked down at Del's ravaged body, saw what *Del* had sacrificed for his family. *You're the only worthwhile man she's seen since Brad . . .*

The sirens were getting louder. Grabbing the shotgun and quickly loading his pockets with shells, he staggered into the nursery, retrieved his Magnum, and went downstairs. When he opened the front door, porch lights were burning all up and down the street, people's heads peeking out through front doors. Nothing he could do about that— besides, most of them vanished when the shotgun came into view, anyway. He limped onto the lawn as fast as he could.

As he reached the sidewalk, dizziness swept up from nowhere and he sailed out into the street, falling hard, the barrel of the shotgun whipping up and smashing into his mouth. The pain was immediately absorbed in the general symphony of agony, but the taste of his own blood shocked him awake. Getting slowly to his feet, he found himself facing the wrong way. His car was behind him . . . and in front of him, just visible around the corner, was the dusty brown Jeep Cherokee with darkly tinted windows.

He scowled at it. From this angle, he could tell that the license plates weren't nearly as dusty as the vehicle itself.

Sucking at his split lip, he made himself think rationally. It was difficult to do so in the nervous howl of approaching sirens. Maybe the blond man was sitting in the Jeep right now, still waiting for the Cannibal to come back. But the Cannibal had run in the other direction.

Shotgun raised, Tony staggered to the Cherokee and without hesitation tugged on the front door handle—and jumped back in surprise when it opened. Although the interior lights did not come on, he could see that there was no one in the front seat. But there *were* a few dark splatters on the upholstery—and, lying on the floor, a large pistol.

Leaning forward carefully, he glanced into the back seat, saw nothing but a blanket thrown to one side. He picked up the pistol. It was a German-made 9mm automatic; the register indicated full. Why was it lying on the floor like that? And whose blood . . . ? Never mind. It occurred to him that this vehicle was made for driving over the rough trails in the area where Hiber Nation lay hidden. Tucking the pistol into his pants, he climbed into the cab and groped for the keys, although he suspected he'd have to practice his hot-wiring skills. But the key was in the ignition.

For a moment he just sat with his fingers on the key. There was something wrong with this, the empty Cherokee being here, something he should understand. But he just couldn't think . . .

A police cruiser flashed down the adjacent street, lights and siren fragmenting the night. Get moving, Garwood!

Starting the engine, he pulled a U-turn and cruised away from the house with the Jeep's lights off so that the license plate couldn't be read. He switched them on only after he'd gone a block. He turned a corner, then another, driving at a nice even speed. Mustn't rush madly into a canyon cul-de-sac nor into primary streets, where the police would soon be congregating. He had to be smart. Careful.

He had a long way to go.

PART III

But he who is uninitiate in the holy
    rites, who has no lot in them,
does not enjoy a share in like things
    when in death he lies
    beneath the spreading darkness.
            —DEMETER'S HYMN

CHAPTER NINETEEN

MOVEMENT. SMOOTH, RHYTHMIC, LULLING . . . Deborah wasn't sure how long she'd been awake, because the sensation was so much like that of flying through a dream. But her stomach ached so heavily she could hardly breathe, and her head throbbed like a warning flasher at the site of a traffic accident. Dreams couldn't *hurt*, could they?

A sound disturbed her. A quick, steady *thudthudthudthudthud* . . .

She opened her eyes. At least they *seemed* to open, except that what she saw was unlikely—a rough dirt surface speeding by in the darkness, only a few feet from her face. It was as if she were flying low over the ground . . . But what were those things flashing rhythmically in and out of view? They looked like a pair of pumping knees, appearing and disappearing from under the hem of a flapping white garment.

Put it all together, and the answer was this: Someone was carrying her over his shoulder while running down a dirt path. And running very, very fast. But that was ridiculous. Brad had once lifted her this way to demonstrate a lifesaving technique, and after lugging her only a couple of dozen yards, even he had been puffing.

Then she remembered seeing someone bolting down the alley behind her in-laws' house, carrying a rolled-up carpet over his shoulder. Carrying something . . .

Or had she dreamt that, too? It was hard to be sure what was real. For example, there was something very odd about those fast-moving knees, although it took her a moment to realize what it was: they were bending the wrong direction for the way the earth was moving. It was as if whoever was carrying her was running *backward* . . . or had his legs attached in reverse, like a bird's. Ridiculous.

Conclusion: She was still asleep. And dreams *could* hurt. Or maybe she had been drugged. Maybe that was it.

Drugged by whom? And why?

In her mind, she laboriously retraced her steps of that evening, hoping to separate reality from fantasy. Okay. Tony had been coming home, she remembered that. Home to Del and Betty's, that was. And she was excited about his return; she remembered that, too. Tony was coming home, and she was changing Virgil's diaper, and then—and then—

She moaned. Find another memory. Find another memory *now*.

But she couldn't. This one pushed insistently at her consciousness, growing more and more vivid. Someone vaulting the back fence . . . a silhouette in the window . . . a blur of motion . . . a scream from downstairs . . . and then . . . then . . .

She moaned again, and there was an abrupt pressure on the back of her legs, a warning squeeze. Were those *hands*? They felt as hot as an electric blanket in summer. Not like *normal* hands.

A face moving into the light.

But not a *human* face . . .

Suddenly it was harder than ever to breathe. In the photo album of her memory, the intruder's face was long and grinning, all eye sockets and teeth, like something that had dehydrated in the desert sun. And the fingers . . . they had ended in wicked, curved talons. She'd *seen* them.

A hallucination. She must be drugged. It was the only possible explanation.

She tried to look around her, and managed to twist her head enough to see steep, brush-choked hillsides rising on both sides. Their tops were outlined against a cold glow in the night sky—city lights. But San Diego was carved with canyons, and her captor was taking her through them like a submarine sliding undetected through a crowded harbor. They might never be spotted.

That's okay, she reminded herself. There's really nothing to see, anyway. You're hallucinating all this.

Still, she wondered about Del, Betty . . . and Virgil. Why weren't they in this hallucination, too? She twisted her head around again, but if there were other monsters carrying other hostages through her nightmare, they were not within her field of vision.

She closed her eyes. That was better. In her mind floated Tony's face. Not Brad's, she noticed—Tony's. She wondered what he would say when she told him about this hallucination.

Listening to the soft *thudthudthud* of running feet—*imaginary* running feet, of course—she let the steady rhythm lull her back into darkness.

A phrase kept floating up into Tony's mind: *Meanwhile, back at the ranch . . .*

By the time he left the El Cajon valley, heading east on I–8, he was repeating the words in his head like a mantra. Otherwise he tended to forget what he was doing. A pool of blood squelched on the seat beneath him, and a high, keening note had begun to grow quite loud in his head. Also, despite the fact that the Cherokee's heater was turned all the way up, he couldn't stop shivering. Worst of all, on two occasions in the last ten minutes, he'd let the Jeep wander onto the shoulder of the road, and jerked awake just in time to get the vehicle back onto the pavement. Luckily, traffic was sparse out here at this hour.

Was he bleeding to death? Were his wounds worse than he'd thought? God, could he actually be *bleeding* to death?

He resolved that once he pulled off the freeway and got through Alpine, he'd stop and patch himself up a little.

Meanwhile, back at the ranch . . .

He tried to imagine what the police were making of the carnage back at the Kosareks'. Undoubtedly they'd blame the carnage on the Cannibal—and, of course, they'd be right. But they had no idea who the Cannibal really was. *What* he was. Tony grimaced. The truth was, if he weren't carrying the wounds of fact on his own body, he wouldn't have believed it, either.

The Cannibal . . . Where had that thing come from? Outer space? A laboratory? A . . .

"Biotech, eh? It's not like germ warfare, is it, anything like that?"

"No! No, it's . . . beneficial."

Suddenly Tony remembered a film he had seen in health class back in junior high, in the days when they still taught you what to do after an atomic war. There had been footage about a pregnant mouse who had been exposed to controlled doses of radioactivity. Her offspring had all looked like rodents crossed with rhinoceroses, their bodies covered with overlapping plates of leathery skin. "Genetic mutations," the announcer had said, sounding both foreboding and excited.

Genetic mutation . . .

Tony realized he was almost off the road again, and touched one of his cuts. The electric flash of pain woke him up a little.

Maybe the mysterious Frederick Faust had forced Dr. Pendergast to *create* this Cannibal-creature. Was that possible? And if so, why? For what purpose?

Then an even more disturbing thought occurred: What made Tony so sure there was only *one* of those monsters? After all, the thing that had killed people at Flash had been described as a *woman*, right?

Meanwhile, back at the ranch . . .

He snapped awake again just in time to keep from slamming into the end of a bridge guardrail. Ahead, a sign read ALPINE. He took the exit, trembling, and found the frontage road down which he had followed the blond man before.

As soon as the last house was out of sight, he pulled over, shut off the engine, and dug around inside the glove box for a first-aid kit. There *had* to be one. Any intelligent person living in such a remote area would surely . . .

But there was nothing in the glove box except the Jeep's owner's manual and a flashlight. He tested the flash, got a powerful beam. That was good, at least. Climbing stiffly out of the cab, he limped to the rear hatch and opened it.

Inside were two long metal boxes. The first one turned out to be a well-equipped toolbox. But the second one—yes! A first-aid kit, and a good one. Hands quivering, he pulled out gauze, antiseptic and tape, and set to work on the worst of his wounds. He tried not to look at them too closely, just pulled the bandages tight. He'd get stitches later. Maybe Deborah would drive him to the hospital . . .

Although many of the dressings started blossoming with blood even before he finished wrapping himself, and in the end he felt as stiff as an overbuilt mummy, at least he didn't think he would bleed to death on the spot.

He used the last of the tape to mask the flashlight lens down to a pencil-sized hole, then limped back to the cab and clambered in. Maybe it was his imagination, but his hands already seemed to be less shaky. And he felt warmer, too. It was with somewhat more optimism that he started the engine and put the Cherokee into gear.

More optimism . . . and more fear.

More anger, too.
Blondie.

At first, as Deborah became aware of her own existence again, she kept her eyes closed. Her head and stomach ached nauseatingly, and she felt as if she were still moving . . . please, no more of that . . . then she realized she couldn't hear the running footsteps now. And beneath her was a flat surface. A flat, *unmoving* surface. Something warm and comfortable supported her head.

She relaxed. Thank God, it was over.

But when she opened her eyes, disorientation swept back: She seemed to be lying in the bottom of a giant milk carton, smooth white walls receding in exaggerated perspective above her. The top of the carton had been cut off and replaced with fluorescent lights behind heavy metal screens. One of the walls was a little shorter than the others, and the gap was filled with metal bars.

Suddenly a bearded face filled her vision, and she recoiled with a shrill cry.

"Easy," Dr. Pendergast said, helping her sit up. She realized she had been lying with her head in his lap. Slumping back against the wall and shivering, she stared at him incredulously. Dr. Pendergast. Relief and terror struggled inside her. How wonderful he was alive, but . . . that meant she *hadn't* been hallucinating—not all of it, anyway. She'd been transported *someplace*. She looked around again. The strange room was vacant except for Dr. Pendergast, her, and a pile of empty sacks in a corner.

"Welcome to Hades," Dr. Pendergast said faintly. He looked terrible: face pale, hair much grayer than Deborah remembered, beard unkempt. And yet he was *alive*.

"You . . . you're all right," she croaked, her relief overcoming her fear. "Thank God."

He smiled crookedly. "God had nothing to do with it."

She tried to stand, couldn't make it, slumped back again. Dizzy . . . "Where—where are we?"

"Ginnunga Gap. It used to be called Hiber Nation, back when it was a survivalist camp. We're in the jail cell."

"How did . . ." She shuddered. "I remember . . . I thought . . ."

"Tell me what you remember," he said, leaning toward her. "Tell me *everything* you remember."

A face in the window. Not a human face. And knees bending backward . . .

"I—I was at my in-laws' house, and . . ." She stiffened. "Dr. Pendergast, are they here somewhere? A middle-aged couple? And what about my son, Virgil? Have you seen—"

"I haven't seen another human being since I was put in this cell. Please go on."

She drew in a deep breath. She wouldn't think about the Kosareks, far less her son—not now. "I was upstairs changing Virgil," she said, "and something . . . a woman climbed in through the window. Her face . . ." She shuddered. "For a minute she looked . . . I don't know. Then I dreamt I was being carried over someone's shoulder through the canyons. Some kind of monster." She gently touched the nape of her neck. "I must have hit my head harder than I thought."

Pendergast stared at her intently. The fingers of one hand dug at his beard. "What happened when you arrived here?" he asked. "Were you conscious? Did you see a young man with short, dark hair?"

Deborah shook her head. "I didn't wake up until just now."

Pendergast chewed his moustache awhile, then turned and glared up at the door behind the bars. "What are you doing, Mitford?" he muttered. "What are you doing with the Loners?"

"Who's Mitford?" Deborah said.

"What? Oh, he's my . . . assistant. Ira Mitford."

She was confused by Pendergast's demeanor. He seemed more angry than frightened—but then, she'd once read that inappropriate emotional responses were common among long-term prisoners. "I was really worried about you," she said. "Someone murdered Ted Scully last night, and a policeman. It seemed to revolve around you."

Dr. Pendergast nodded distractedly. "Yes. But obviously Mitford's completely out of control now, doing whatever he wants."

"What are you talking about?"

He looked at her. In his pale face, his eyes were the same brilliant blue she remembered, but lined in red. "I'm the reason people are dying, Deborah, but a man named Ira Mitford is the tool. He works for me. Or he's supposed to."

Her mouth sagged open.

"It was necessary for me to have someone like him," Pendergast went on earnestly. "Someone to guarantee that my project stayed secret."

"I don't understand. Do you mean NIMROD?"

Pendergast made a sour face. "No, not NIMROD. *Enkidu*."

"The name on your computer."

"Yes." His hands suddenly took flight like tethered birds. "*Enkidu* is the single most vital piece of scientific work ever done, Deborah. It's crucial to the future of this planet and everything on it. It had to be protected at all costs—I tried to avoid sending Mitford after you, please believe that. But you wouldn't mind your own business, leave me alone."

Slowly, the color leeched out of her face. "*You* sent someone . . . to *kill* me?"

"Yes. I'm sorry, but it was necessary."

She just stared at him. It wouldn't sink in. Dr. George Irving Pendergast—surgeon, scientist, winner of the Nobel Prize—wanted her *dead*?

"But he wasn't supposed to use the Loners," Pendergast went on distractedly. "I don't even know how he managed it. They aren't designed for personal use, they're not designed for *man's* use at all, they're . . ."

"Loners?" She kept staring at him.

"The *monster* you mentioned was one." His gaze fixed on hers. "Loners are a new species of life, the heart of *Enkidu*. I created them right here, in Ginnunga Gap."

"You created . . ." In her mind, she saw that long, dried-skull face grinning at her, and those backward-working knees, and suddenly she began to shake; not just her hands but her whole body, a violent, almost spasmodic jerking. Real? Could it be *real*? "Oh, no," she said. "No. That's not possible."

"Of course it is. You saw it. Don't be foolish."

She looked at him again, saw the flat resolve in his eyes. "But—*why*?" she whispered.

"To save the world . . ." He continued to speak, talking about nature, science, human nature. With every word, more and more color boiled into his face. By the time he reached the part about how the population would quadruple in the next generation, he was on his feet, pacing erratically while his hand flickered about like albino bats. He didn't look pale or sick at all now.

But he *was* sick, of course. Deborah stared at him in uncomprehending shock. Population control . . . Eden . . . equality . . . the Law of Nature . . . the San Diego Cannibal . . . the words were an incredibly bizarre mixture of humanism and anarchy, murder and salvation.

When he was finished, he fixed his burning eyes on her. "Now you understand," he said.

But she looked away. How much of what he'd said was true? How much was even *possible*? She didn't want to believe any of it—and yet she had seen that hideous face in the nursery, and had been carried here through the darkness . . . backward-bending knees . . . If Pendergast was insane, well, then, so was she.

A great shudder rocked through her and passed, leaving a strange serenity behind. "You really think this would have worked?" she said.

"If not for Mitford . . ."

"Mitford?" She laughed bitterly. "Compared to you, Mitford sounds like a *hero*."

Pendergast sighed. "You don't understand, after all," he said sadly, and slid down the wall to a seated position again. "You're just like everyone else."

"I have a son, Dr. Pendergast. I can't imagine him growing up in a world where one of those *things* might jump out any minute and—"

"You'd rather he grew up in a world where he has to wear a gas mask because the air's unbreathable, and cover every inch of his skin before he steps outside because the ozone layer is in shreds? Where wars are fought over water rights and the only animals live in zoos?"

"People are becoming more aware of the environment now," Deborah said. "We'll—"

"Environmental problems are only *symptoms*. Just as economic recessions are *symptoms*, and sexually transmitted diseases are *symptoms*. Trying to solve any of them by themselves is like treating throat cancer with cough syrup. *You've got to eliminate the cause*."

"But you're telling me the only way to save people is by *killing* them!"

"Deborah, what do we do when there are too many stray dogs in a given area? Round them up and gas them. That's considered *humane*. But if we do the same thing with excess people, that's called an *atrocity*."

Deborah leaned away from him, appalled. "My God, you're talking . . . that's worse than Hitler."

"Nonsense. Hitler wanted to eradicate races that offended him personally. I'm trying to *preserve* life, in all its variety and complexity."

"You honestly don't see any difference between animals and human beings?"

"Human beings *are* animals. The main difference is, despite our self-awareness and self-actualization, we refuse to control our own behavior—including reproduction. It's absurd. Criminal. Immoral."

Deborah turned away again. How dare he speak of *morality*? The man was a monomaniac; obviously there would be no arguing with him about his "project." Yet she had no intention of languishing in this room to await Mitford's pleasure, and she needed Pendergast's help to get out. After all, he knew the layout of the complex.

"Have you tried to escape?" she asked.

He glanced up at the bars. "From here?" he asked sardonically.

"I know it's high, but maybe between the two of us—"

"You don't understand. Even if we somehow got out of this cell—which we couldn't—we'd still be forty feet underground and a hundred yards from the nearest exit—with Mitford and the Loners in between."

Fury boiled up in her, but she worked to make her expression soft, compelling. "Dr. Pendergast, the . . . Loners . . . are supposed to kill people, not capture them, right?"

"Yes. To Loners, humans are nothing but prey."

"But they captured *us*. One of them even carried me here all the way from San Diego. Doesn't that mean something's gone wrong with your plan? You have to stop this now, have to—"

"Mitford is what went wrong with the plan," Pendergast said, face flushing angrily. "He must have been working with the Alpha group all along, modifying their innate traits through some kind of training . . ." He shot back to his feet and resumed pacing. "He never agreed with *Enkidu's* basic objective, you see. He wanted the Loners to hunt only certain kinds of people. *He's* the one who's like Hitler."

"He sent the Loners to kill Ted Scully and Bill Chatherton?"

"There's no other explanation."

"What about Tony Garwood?" she asked tightly. "Do you know if he's on the hit list, too?"

"Your security guard friend?" Pendergast's eyes wandered. "Mitford intended to deal with him, yes."

Deborah closed her eyes. Maybe it hadn't happened yet. Tony hadn't returned from the East County when the monsters first attacked, so maybe they'd missed him. Please. Please, let *someone* be safe . . .

Once again she tried to climb to her feet. This time she made it, but had to lean against the wall for a minute while crackling lightning storms ran up and down her legs. When her muscles would obey her again, she limped toward the short wall and stared up at the bars. "How did *we* get down here?"

"The Loners hung onto the bars with their toes, like bats, and lowered us down. They were designed to have no interest in *making* or *using* things, like tools, so that impulse must still be intact."

"How many of them are there?"

"Eighteen. Nineteen, if you include Vulcan."

Nineteen. Nineteen of those monsters lurking between this cell and freedom. Deborah refused to think about it. "What's this?" she asked, pointing at a small door in one wall, near the floor.

"That's a chute for sending down food and water—but it's too small for you to crawl through, if that's what you're thinking."

She swallowed her frustration. "What about those bags over there? If we tied them into a rope and hooked it around one of those bars, we—"

"Those are food sacks; they won't hold the weight of a human being. I was careful about what I put down here with Vulcan; I'm not a fool." He sounded proud of himself.

This time she couldn't stop it. Whirling, she snapped, "Aren't you? Well, *I'm* not going to sit here and wait to be eaten, or whatever it is those things have in mind. You do what you want, but I'm going to get out and find my family. I'm at least going to *try*."

He watched her with admiration in his eyes and a wry twist on his lips. "I can see that quality of yours in the Loners, you know," he said.

"What?"

"Your tenacity, self-determination . . . I made it part of the Loners."

Deborah felt as if she'd been served a bowl of steaming maggots. "You—what?"

"I took it from the cells of one of your hairs. It's not difficult once you know the code. You should feel honored to have—"

"*Honored*?" She wanted to hurl herself at him, rake him into spaghetti with her fingernails. But that was something a Loner would do. She clenched her fists until her nails cut into her own skin. "You . . . *raped* me."

For the first time, a twinge of guilt flickered over Pendergast's face. But he said, "Don't be ridiculous. There's more of *me* in the Loners than anyone . . . *shhhhh*!"

"What?"

"*Listen.*"

She froze. At first she heard nothing; then, faintly, the scrape of footsteps came from above—but they were dragging, irregular, like sound effects from a Frankenstein movie. Deborah backed away, staring up at the door. The footsteps paused. The door opened.

In limped Ira Mitford.

CHAPTER TWENTY

TONY HALTED THE CHEROKEE at the end of the road. In the bright glare of the headlights, the crazy quilt of motorcycle and pickup truck tracks looked like bottomless canyons.

He climbed out stiffly, walked to the front of the vehicle and heaved himself up onto the bumper to get a better perspective on his surroundings. It didn't help much. Other than some distant headlights on the freeway, he could see no man-made lights at all. Well, what did he expect, a neon sign flashing *This Way to Survivalist Camp*?

Easing down off the bumper, he used the flashlight to inspect the tread pattern on the Jeep's tires, then limped around the barricade and began searching for the same pattern in the dust. He found what he was looking for almost immediately: two parallel tracks arcing off through the manzanita to the south. No other tracks crossed over them. Climbing back into the Jeep, he put the transmission into four-wheel-drive and drove around the barricade.

On the far side of the clearing, where the Jeep's tracks vanished into the wilderness, he stopped again. Stared into the inky darkness.

He was afraid.

It caught him by surprise—but once acknowledged, he realized that the terror had been inside him, buried alive, ever since he'd first seen the Cannibal-thing. He knew why the fear had surfaced now: What if there really *were* more of those things out there? One could be lurking behind every bush and rock, waiting, waiting for someone like him to . . .

Stop it. You weren't scared in the park with all those dopers and trigger-happy punks around, were you? No. So just think of this the same way. As a day's work.

But as he eased his foot off the brake, his leg began quivering.

The Cherokee pushed between the manzanita bushes, branches dragging thin shrieks along its sides. The top of the moon had just appeared above the Laguna Mountains, an arc burning a deep and sinister red.

"Well, well." Mitford smiled crookedly as he moved toward the bars. "Look here—if it isn't Hansel and Gretel."

Deborah and Pendergast stared up at him. The dragging sound was his left foot, which he pulled behind him like a dead puppy on a leash. He was dressed in filthy tatters, and much of the exposed flesh glistened scarlet. A strip of cloth was wound around his head and one ear; blood dripped from it onto the remnants of his shirt. Deborah might not have recognized him if it weren't for the hint of dangerous mirth in his eyes. He had to be crazy, to be smiling at all. He looked as if he'd been in a terrible car accident. Or maybe—hope flashed inside her—maybe Del had gotten hold of him, and—

"Mitford," Pendergast said, "what have you done? What have you done to *Enkidu*?"

The mirth in the blond man's eyes grew stronger. "You mean, what has *Enkidu* done to *me*?"

Just then, a tall figure scurried through the door behind him. Followed by another. And another. Deborah uttered a thin, airless shriek. It was *them*. Three of *them*, backward legs and fangs and claws . . . Loners.

But despite her horror, she couldn't help staring at them here in the bright glare of the cell. All were naked, tall and sleek, and moved with eerie grace on their reversed, birdlike legs. At first they looked sexless, then Deborah realized each had a smooth bony plate between its legs— genital armor? And one had breasts, rather stiff and unmoving, like the breasts of a mannequin, but breasts nonetheless.

The creatures surrounded Mitford. One of the males stepped very close beside him, placed its snout against his cheek and bared its teeth in a horrifying display. There was a bloody, ragged gap in the array of fangs in its upper jaw.

Mitford did not respond to the spectacle. Grabbing two of the bars, he fixed his gaze on Pendergast and said, "Chernobog here is a little pissed off at me. I woke up while he was carrying me back here and bashed his face in with a rock. Almost escaped, too."

The Loner hissed loudly and opened its jaws, but froze as the largest Loner raised a hand, talons spread. "Silence, crrrrrrriminal," it growled in a coarse, choppy voice. Then, turning toward the pit, it bowed its head and intoned, "We arrrrrre prrreparrrrring forrrr yourrrrr trrransfig-urrration, Beloved Georrrrrrge, as it is wrrrrrrritten."

Deborah heard a gasp. Pendergast was standing flat against the wall, his arms splayed out; his face was so pale it seemed to melt into the concrete behind it. "Humbaba," he whispered. "You . . . you *spoke . . .*"

The corners of the Loner's mouth curled so far up that Deborah could see another set of teeth—human molars—protruding from a second set of recessed jaws. "Yo," the Loner said. "In the beginning was the Worrrrd, and the Worrrrd was God, and today's Worrrrd is worrrrrrrrth a thousand bonus points. We have some grrrrrrrrreat prrrrrrizes forrrr ourrrrr winnerrrrrrrs."

Pendergast's gaze flashed to Mitford. "My God, what have you *done?* What did you teach—"

"*Me?*" Mitford said. "What the fuck are you—"

"Mitforrrrd cannot teach anything to the New Rrrrrrrrrace," Hum-baba rumbled. "He and this woman arrrrrrrre bad guys, Philistines who betrrrrrayed you and yourrrrrr worrrrrld. Only you can teach us, Beloved Georrrrrge, thrrrrough yourrrrrr Son and the Holy Spirrrrrrrits you sent to us thrrrrrrrrrough the tube."

"Holy spirits?" Pendergast whispered.

Humbaba nodded. "Yes, Grrrrrrrreat Fatherrrrrrr, the angels who speak to us in ourrrrr solitude, to enlighten us. Angels of light, come on down! NBC! PBS! The Fox Station . . . !"

Mitford burst into harsh laughter, and Chernobog immediately snapped his jaws at him. Mitford quickly clapped a hand to the bloodied side of his head, but kept laughing.

What's going on? Deborah thought, wondering if *she* had gone insane now, too.

Pendergast closed his eyes. "This can't be," he whispered. "It can't be. I *made* you. *Programmed* you. You can't be doing this."

Humbaba shrugged. "And God said, 'Shit happens.' Let's get this show on the rrrrroad." Chernobog immediately reached out, wrapped an arm around Mitford's waist, and jerked him off the floor like a sack of grain. Mitford's laugh shut off in an agonized grunt. Chernobog carried him effortlessly to the gap in the bars and, without hesitation, leaped through. Deborah gasped involuntarily as they fell to the floor of the pit, but when they hit, the Loner's legs folded like great springs, and the only apparent effect of the impact was a hiss of pain from Mitford.

Chernobog placed Mitford on his feet and held him by the shoulders until he was steady. "Next time, dude," the Loner said, "let he who is without sin cast the firrrrrrrst stone." His long tongue slid out, and he spat a great blob of red-veined phlegm into Mitford's face.

Mitford winced, but managed a smile. "Nice set of choppers you've got there, asshole," he said. "You should brush more often."

Chernobog's arms pistoned straight out, and Mitford flew across the room and hit the wall with an impact Deborah felt from where she was. Dim-eyed but still grinning, he slid to the floor, leaving pink streaks behind him.

"Kowabunga, crrrrrrriminal," Chernobog said, then whirled toward Pendergast. The scientist pressed himself hard against the wall with a gasp, but the Loner merely bowed. "And now it's time forrrr station identification," he said in a low, reverent voice, and turned back toward the short wall. His legs thrust out with lightning speed, and he hurtled upward. Pendergast gasped as the Loner hooked a bar with his talons and scrambled up through the opening.

"Beloved Georrrrge," Humbaba said, "We'll rrrreturrrrn afterrr you rrrreceive a worrrrd frrrrom ourrrr sponsorrrrr." The three Loners bowed, then turned and disappeared through the door.

Pendergast kept staring after them, sweat oiling his face. "He jumped out," he muttered. "He *jumped* out. But I didn't . . ." Spinning toward Mitford, he snarled, "Well, it looks like your obedience lessons didn't take very well. You *fool*. Now—"

"*My* obedience lessons?" Mitford wiped his face with his sleeve; where the sputum had been was an angry red rash punctuated with yellow blisters. "What the hell are you talking about?"

"Don't kid me. Only one of *us* could have trained the Loners, short-circuited their genetic instructions to—"

"Sure, the Loners are my eager slaves," Mitford said, wiping his face again. "Can't you tell?"

"You intend to tell me you didn't bypass the security system and sneak the Loners out of their holding cells behind my back?"

"The security system was *bypassed*?" Mitford looked genuinely surprised.

"I don't know exactly what you intended to do with them," Pendergast said, "but trying to train Loners was a *stupid* idea. There's no way you could overcome their instincts; they were bound to—"

"Listen. All I know is that when I got to San Diego, three of those goddamn things were hiding in the back of the Jeep. Other than that, I don't have the slightest fucking idea what's going on here. In fact, as far as I'm concerned, *you're* the one who—"

"No, crrrrrriminal," a voice suddenly rattled from above, making them all jump. "It was *I* who did thissssss holy worrrrrrrrk forrrrrrr my fatherrrrrrrr."

They all looked up, and Deborah jerked backward so hard her head cracked into the wall.

"Well, fuck me," Mitford said. "Look who's here."

"Vulcan," Pendergast whispered.

Tony stared at his watch, but had to blink several times to bring its face into focus in the jerking, rumbling darkness of the Jeep: Three a.m. That meant he had been driving around this wasteland for . . . what? He forced himself to think. Four hours? Four and a half? Something like that. Forever.

There was layer upon layer of tracks out here, that was the problem. Many had the same tread pattern. Either more than one Jeep with that design had driven through the area, or Blondie's Cherokee did not always take the same route. Whatever the reason, the tracks kept disappearing into one another or halting in some kind of cul-de-sac, and Tony would have to backtrack and look for a different set to follow.

Despair was drilling a dull bit into his heart. For all he knew, he was tracking the most popular fucking tire tread ever designed.

Then he saw the cactus.

Most of the plants in the area were typical high desert varieties— creosote, manzanita, sage, the occasional occotillo or yucca. But here and there were also "low desert" species—barrel cactus, prickly pear, even a couple of treacherous jumping cactuses.

It was a prickly pear that caught Tony's attention.

He had been following a trail that led almost due south, but it had gotten narrower and narrower until the bushes were dragging agonizing fingernails down the Cherokee's sides. Then a huge face of exposed bedrock loomed directly ahead, forcing Tony to stop. There was no way around it. For a while Tony just sat there, sweat running through his head bandage and staining his cheeks bright pink, and stared at the impenetrable wall of stone. It seemed almost symbolic. Get real, Tony. For all you know, you're not within fifty miles of the survivalist camp. Why not give up now, go get stitched up, talk to the police. Maybe now you can convince them to come back with you, go straight to Hiber Nation. And don't feel bad, either. You've done your best . . .

Had he?

I won't let anything happen.

His words.

Clenching his teeth, he put the Cherokee into reverse and backed up until he found a place where he could turn around. As he spun the wheel and the backup lights swung over the brush near the edge of the trail, he glimpsed a flash of brilliant green amid the surrounding olive hues. Stopping, he stuck his head out the window for a better view.

Behind him, several feet beyond the trail, was a crushed prickly-pear cactus. Its vibrant exposed flesh glistened with moisture.

Tony waited, staring at the cactus and trying to think. The damage to the plant had to be recent. Had *he* done it? No, the cactus was too far off the trail. Then he realized that the surrounding bushes were relatively short and widely spaced. It wasn't a trail, exactly, but . . .

Climbing out of the Cherokee, he carried the flashlight back to the cactus and shone the narrow beam on it. His heart jumped. The prickly pear's crushed pads were clearly imprinted with treadmarks in a familiar pattern.

Aiming the flashlight deeper into the brush, he felt his weariness and doubt abruptly dissolve. Some of the bushes back there had broken branches, or had been skinned down to their moist inner layers. You had to look closely to see the damage, but there could be no doubt.

He returned to the Jeep, hoisted himself up onto the bumper, and took a long look around. The moon was well risen now and had lost its angry red color, but still, it shed no light on human habitation.

He grabbed his weapons from the cab. With the shotgun slung over his shoulder, the Magnum in its holster and Blondie's semiautomatic pistol hanging heavily in a pocket, he supposed he looked like a low-budget Rambo. But he couldn't get the image of the Cannibal—shot again and again but not dying, not stopping—out of his head, and that thought made him feel almost naked.

Pointing the thin beam of the flashlight past the prickly pear, he took a deep breath and started moving.

* * *

Deborah couldn't take her eyes off the hideous, gnarled figure crouching up there. It was as squat and gnarled as an old stump, its skin hung from it like sheets draped over furniture, and its fingers and toes were twisted almost into braids. Milky cataracts gleamed in its eyes. In one talon it clutched a cloth bag like those piled in the corner of the pit, except this one bulged at the bottom.

"Vulcan," Pendergast said in a reedy voice. "Did you . . . speak?"

"Yourrrr worrrrdsssss arrrrre my worrrrdsssss, Fatherrrr," the Loner growled in a voice even more fluttery and inhuman than the others' had been. "I have learrrrrned my lessssonsssss, and earrrrrrrned my place at yourrrrrrrrrr rrrrright hand."

Deborah glanced over at Pendergast, and blinked in shock—his eyes were so wide and vacant, she was momentarily convinced he had died right there on his feet.

"Only foolssss dessspissssse learrrrning and wissssdom," Vulcan went on. "Sssssssso it is wrrrrrritten, Fatherrrr, in yourrrrrrrrrr own book."

Mitford turned a flat, reptilian gaze on Pendergast. "I guess the old boy must be a zombie, eh, doc? As I recall, you *executed* him months ago."

"Executed *me*?" Vulcan grasped the bars with his huge, twisted talons and smiled, exposing fissured gums and teeth streaked black with decay. "You underrrrssssstand nothing, crrrrriminal. Thissss issss a family affairrrrr. My Fatherrrr and I will live forrrrever in the New Rrrrrace— ourrrrr blood is theirrrrr blood. Rrrrrrright, Fatherrrrrr?"

Pendergast swallowed. "Mitford," he said in a faint voice, not looking away from Vulcan, "you're telling me you didn't have anything to do with this?"

Mitford snorted.

"But it can't be," Pendergast said. "I never taught him to work with the Alphas, or capture people, or—"

"I have found my own way to you and yourrrrrr wisdom, Fatherrrr," Vulcan said, his head pulsing, claws retracting and extending. "Afterrrrrrrrr I learrrrrrrrrned yourrrrrrr worrrrrrdsssss, I discoverrrrrred how to open the Arrrrrrrrrrk of the Covenant, wherrrrrrr- rre all wisdom residessssss. And therrrrrrrrrrre I found the Way."

Pendergast's eyes bulged. "The Ark?"

"Azzzzz easssssy azzzzzzz one, two, thrrrrrree."

"But that's *impossible*! You couldn't have . . . the Ark's a tool, a *machine* . . ."

Vulcan recoiled, talons clashing against the bars, fangs hissing across one another like the blades of scissors. "No! Machinessss arrrre *evil*, Brrrrrrrrreeder-made thingsssssss, azzzzz you have taught! You have wrrrrrrrrrritten, 'Hold fasssssssst to that which is good; abssstain frrrrom everrry forrrm of evil.' So the Arrrrrrrk can only be Holy, because it izzzzzzz of the Fatherrrrrr. Accept no imitationsssss."

"But you couldn't have taught *yourself* to use it," Pendergast said firmly.

Vulcan grinned, and one of his fangs popped out and fell to the floor of the upper deck with the shattering *pop* of a broken Christmas tree ornament.

"Rrrrreading is Fun-Damental," he said. "Like Fatherrrrr, like sssson. Now I have come to underrrrssstand all you have sssspoken to me, Fatherrrrr. As you have wished, the trrrribulation of the worrrrld is about to end. We shall usssse the keyssss of Hades to open the doorrrrs of death. Then, thrrrrrrrough the New Generrrration, you and I will get the sssstains out and leave behind a pine-frrrrresh sssssssmell. We—" He broke off as the overhead lights dimmed for a moment, then flickered erratically.

Now what? Deborah thought despairingly, but the lights steadied again.

Grinning, Vulcan lifted the bag he was carrying. "Ssssssoon the currrrrrtain will rrrrrrrise on a brrrrrand-new ssseasson," he said. "But forrrrr now, Fatherrrrr—herrrre izzzzzzz yourrrrr passsoverrrr feassssst. Eat, drrrrrink and be merrrrrry."

Opening a trapdoor, he pushed the bag in; a moment later it slid into the pit through the panel near the floor. When Deborah raised her eyes again, Vulcan was gone.

Pendergast was still staring upward, his body frozen in place.

"Vulcan's looked better," Mitford said.

"He's dying," Pendergast whispered.

"Except he should *already* be dead," Mitford said evenly. "You staged that whole thing, didn't you? The funeral, the weekly visits, all of it. *You're* an idiot."

"I just wanted . . . I kept him locked away . . ."

"In here?" Mitford looked around. "Great. This place is obviously very Loner-proof. What's the matter, doc? Did you make them stronger than you wanted to? Smarter? Did you screw up a little?"

Deborah couldn't stand it anymore. "What is going *on*?" she shrieked.

Pendergast didn't appear to have heard her. But Mitford looked over and said, "Hey, babe, you're witnessing the greatest fuckup in the history of the world."

She didn't want to speak to him, but had no choice. "I don't understand."

"Neither do I. And neither does the doc, here; that's the whole point. But one thing's for sure, he played around with something bigger than he is."

"It's just not possible," Pendergast said in a raw voice. "I broke the code. Most of it, at least. Enough of it! This *can't happen*."

"Face reality for once," Mitford snapped. "What about—what is it? *Imprinting*. You imprinted Vulcan with all your bullshit. You broke your own rule, and now he thinks you're his *daddy*, for Christ's sake. And he's passed the word on to the rest of them."

"I just *talked* with him, that's all," Pendergast said. "Just . . . talked. I never taught him how to read, certainly not how to use the Ark. How could he have learned to—"

Mitford laughed. It started small, making him wince and bend over, but grew louder and louder, echoing through the room. Deborah watched him with wary horror; Pendergast watched with disdain.

" 'Sesame Street'!" Mitford finally gasped.

"What?" Pendergast said.

" 'Sesame Street'! They learned how to read from watching 'Sesame Street' on TV, you numbnuts! And when Vulcan got out of here, he just read his way through your fucking library!" He fell on his side, laughing and grimacing. "Thank God for public television!"

Pendergast just stared at him. Deborah thought the scientist's chin was trembling, but not with mirth.

"Oh," Mitford said at last, wiping his eyes with his arm, "speaking of God, did you lose your Bible recently?"

"I—I—"

"I found it by the Ark a few days ago. Sort of all adds up, doesn't it? Vulcan was quoting Bible shit, right?"

"That means nothing." Suddenly Pendergast was pacing again. "He was quoting TV commercials and cartoons, too. I know what the problem is—I just didn't limit the Loners' retentive abilities enough. It never occurred to me . . . they obviously remember *everything* they see and hear. But that isn't the same thing as *thinking*. They don't seem to be able to differentiate between different kinds of input, fact and fiction . . ."

"Vulcan was talking about the Tribulation," Deborah blurted. "Isn't that supposed to mean the end of the world?"

Pendergast spun on her. "I didn't design the Loners to end the world! My God, why won't anyone listen to me? Besides, the Tribulation refers specifically to the time of torment that's supposed to precede Jesus' return to earth. It sounded to me like Vulcan interprets the *current* times as the Tribulation—which means that the future, when Loners are free, would be heaven."

"And you don't call that *thinking*?" Mitford snorted.

"No, not the way *we*—"

Deborah gasped. Across the room, the bag had stirred slightly. "What—what is that?" she cried.

"A monkey," Pendergast said distractedly. "Live monkeys are what we feed the Loners."

"Used to feed them," Mitford said dryly.

"Why did he put it in here?" Deborah asked.

"Didn't you hear him?" Mitford said. "We're supposed to eat it—like good Loners would."

Before Deborah knew it, she was on her feet and hurrying across the room. She couldn't just let the poor thing lie there in a panic. There had been far too much anguish in this place already. She opened the sack.

Her scream echoed through the court like a gunshot.

"What?" Pendergast cried.

She couldn't answer. Lying naked in the sack, eyes closed, face covered with dried blood, was Virgil.

CHAPTER TWENTY-ONE

A FLOCK OF QUAIL SAVED TONY'S LIFE.

The flashlight had begun to weaken some time ago, and to preserve it, Tony had finally started using it only occasionally. During the "off" periods, he kept to the track of scraped branches and crushed plants by moonlight alone. No problem, he had thought. Besides, surely he was getting close to Hiber Nation by now.

But the next time he switched on the light and flicked it around him, he couldn't find any crushed or damaged plants, any sign that a vehicle had ever passed through here. Nor, when he checked behind him, could he retrace his own steps. Lost. Through a cloud of dizziness and despair, he suddenly realized he might actually die out here . . . but it didn't really frighten him. It *bothered* him, though, to think about perishing of something as stupid as exposure or dehydration after surviving the claws and teeth of the Cannibal.

So keep looking as long as you can, then. What have you got to lose?

Guiding himself by the moon, he turned southeast and pushed hard into the bushes.

Overhead, the moon floated up the sky, brightening to incandescent silver. Tony glanced at it every few seconds, trying to see the man-in-the-moon. He'd never been able to figure out the face, but tonight, for some reason, it was so cl—

At that moment a flock of quail burst into the air from underfoot, making him halt with a cry of shock. The birds disappeared, squeaking indignantly . . .

. . . as they flew *downward*.

Tony blinked, looked more closely at the place where he had been about to place his foot, and staggered back. If he had taken that last step, he wouldn't have contacted solid earth again for a good hundred feet of boulder-strewn precipice. Far below sprawled a broad valley, its rumpled depths punctuated with the protruding knuckles of boulders. To the east, the Laguna Mountains rose as flat as stage sets in the moonlight.

His nostrils filled with the sharp, salty aroma of his own sweat, Tony backed up carefully. He was more than alert now, he was absolutely jittering with adrenaline. The rush probably wouldn't last long—by this time his adrenal gland must be about as dry as a week-old sponge—but for the moment he felt like he could *fly* over the ridge just like the—

What's that?

Perhaps a hundred yards to the south, a strange, triangular shape thrust against the sky. It was too straight-edged to be natural—it looked, in fact, like the roof of a building.

Could it be?

Tony's knees began to tremble. He hadn't expected to feel *relief* at finding Hiber Nation. Excitement, yes. Apprehension, certainly. Even fear. But not this sensation of being saved.

Or *had* he found Hiber Nation? As he crept closer to the building, the underbrush thinned, and he had an all-too-clear view of crumbling stucco walls, fractured beams, weeds growing through holes in the roof. Still, he inched forward, shotgun raised. But it just got worse. On this side, at least, the windows were boarded up, as was the door. It was impossible to see the far side because it hung right on the lip of the cliff, but he doubted it was any better. Upon closer inspection, he could see nothing but solid rubble through gaping holes in the wall.

He backed away again, reeling with a fresh flood of dizziness. This dump probably didn't have anything at all to do with Hiber Nation.

For a while he just stood there, bent over with his hands on his knees. He heard insects, a truck droning faintly down unseen I-8, the cry of a nighthawk winging overhead. That was all. *I tried, Deborah. I tried not to do a half-assed job. I . . .*

What was that, across the clearing?

He straightened. Saw two narrow rectangular shapes over there, standing side by side. Outhouses, maybe. Or possibly sheds. Or . . .

With the shotgun in the ready position, he worked his way around the perimeter of the clearing. As he drew closer to the shapes, it became clear that they were sheds like the prefab ones that suburbanites put in their back yards. But the roofs were shaggy with grass and weeds—a natural phenomenon, or deliberate camouflage? His hopes rose slightly.

But so did his wariness, and now he moved very slowly, his blood on fire in his veins. Soon he could see that the sheds were identical in size and shape, except that one had a padlock on the door. Tony glanced around, then approached the unlocked door and tested it. It slid open with a gritty scrape. Tony froze, strained his eyes and ears at the surrounding darkness, but if anyone—or any*thing*—had heard the sound, they were not acknowledging it. He slid the door the rest of the way open and switched on the flashlight.

The faltering beam flicked over axes, rakes, shovels, a chainsaw hanging from a hook, various other yard and maintenance tools, the sorts of things a homesteader might keep handy. Or might *have* kept— none of this hardware looked as if it had been used for some time. Tony backed away, weak with renewed disappointment.

The padlock on the other shed was heavy-duty, key-operated, and latched, its surface dull from exposure. Still . . .

He had noticed a bolt cutter inside the first shed, and returned for it. A moment later, the padlock thumped to the dirt next to its severed hasp.

This door slid open easily, and from inside the shed erupted a sharp smell: machine oil, metal, canvas. Tony raised the shotgun and switched on the flashlight.

And his jaw dropped with a *pop* he heard clearly inside his own head.

"Oh, God!" Deborah wailed, reaching for Virgil. "Oh God oh God oh . . ." Her sobs died down as she touched him, felt the heat rising from his skin and the flutter of his pulse. Relief made her so dizzy, she momentarily felt herself graying out.

"Is he okay?" Pendergast asked, walking toward her, concern on his face.

"*You shut up!*" She whirled toward him with such force that spittle flew from her lips. "Get away from us! *GET AWAY!*"

"Looks like she doesn't care for you much anymore, doc," Mitford remarked from his corner.

Pendergast backed away, eyes wide. "I'm an M.D. . . ."

Deborah laughed bitterly and inspected Virgil herself. His eyes were closed, and his mouth hung open with a drooling slackness that frightened her. His breathing seemed shallower than usual, too. But it was the blood on his face that really terrified her, until her gently probing fingers found no wounds except a half-inch cut on his scalp. It had already crusted over, and seemed to be superficial. She shuddered with relief.

Then she remembered how Vulcan, that *thing*, that *Loner*, had so casually dumped her son down the chute, and anger made her tremble even harder. Carefully, she folded Virgil up in the sack and carried him to the rear wall. Tears of hatred and fear welled in her eyes. He felt so limp, still. What if his injury was worse than it looked? He was unconscious, after all. What if he had brain damage, or internal bleeding? Every second might count.

Remembering something she'd read in a magazine, she pushed back her son's eyelids and peered at his pupils. The one in his right eye was huge, a black hole; the other was almost completely swallowed in a sea of blue. *His father's blue*, she thought, and finally began to cry, struggling to keep it quiet.

"Is he all right?" Pendergast asked. He sounded so sincere, upset, Deborah had to look at him.

"I think he has a concussion," she said.

"Please—may I see him?"

There were ten thousand things she wanted to scream at him, but instead, she nodded. She had to. Pendergast walked over and kneeled beside her. Without trying to take Virgil from her arms, he repeated her experiment with the pupils, then ran his long, sensitive fingers over the scalp wound. Finally he looked up. "I'm afraid it *is* a concussion," he said. "How bad, I can't say. There might be a skull fracture, too. The important thing is that you try not to bump or jar his head, just in case."

She stared into Pendergast's caring blue eyes, and abruptly a shout of laughter burst out of her. "Yeah, we wouldn't want to *endanger* him, would we? We wouldn't want to endanger his *health*. After all, we might want to *eat* him later, right?"

Pendergast looked away, then walked slowly away from her. "Loners consider people food," he said tonelessly. "That's all."

"Except for you, and me, and—" Her eyes flickered toward Mitford. "Him."

Pendergast halted for a moment, then began pacing quickly back and forth. "Yes, that's right. They're keeping us alive for some reason . . ."

"Because they think you're their papa," Mitford grunted.

"Then what about you and Deborah?"

No reply.

"If they really *have* imprinted on me as their father," Pendergast said, "that could work to our advantage."

"How?" Mitford snorted. "In case you didn't notice, they *did* make you a prisoner, too."

The pacing accelerated. "Vulcan seems to think he's doing something I *want* him to do. And he's obviously recognized that there's a connection between the three . . . four . . . of us."

"So?" Mitford said.

"The point is, he can't have more than a few hours left to live. My guess is that he's the influence keeping the other Loners together; once he's gone, I'll bet they revert to their natural state. But in the meantime, if we can convince Vulcan to talk the others back into their cells . . ."

"How?" Mitford asked, looking more interested now, and less scornful.

"I don't know. But I'm sure we can think of—" He broke off as the lights flickered again, longer this time.

"Generator must be running out of gas," Mitford remarked calmly.

"*What?*" Deborah cried, suddenly visualizing being in this place without light.

"Easy," Pendergast said. "There are backup systems . . ."

"No emergency lights down here, though," Mitford said. "This part of the Gap is *abandoned*, remember, doc?"

Pendergast said nothing.

With her fingers, Deborah hurriedly tore holes in Virgil's sack, making a kind of sling through which she thrust her head and arm. Now her son was literally attached to her, snuggled beneath her breasts and bolstered by her forearm, and she swore to herself that nothing would get him away from her again. *Nothing*.

No one spoke. Pendergast continued to pace, and after a few minutes Mitford seemed to doze. Eventually the lights flickered again, and again—and then, slowly, began to fade.

Eyes still closed, Mitford said, "Well, here we go."

Blackness flooded through the pit like slow tar.

The shed was a K-Mart for mercenaries.

Tony slowly moved the flashlight beam from side to side. On the walls hung a variety of rifles, ranging from a bolt-action target model to several different makes of submachine gun. Next to these were shotguns, two of which had their barrels sawed down to stubs and pistol grips fitted where the stocks were supposed to be. An entire wall was covered with revolvers and semiautomatic pistols of all makes and sizes, their surfaces gleaming softly in the shivering light of the flash. Dangling like giant bats from the ceiling were net bags full of camouflage clothing, canvas webbing, boots and gas masks; on the floor were crates stamped with both U.S. and foreign military insignia. Boxes of ammunition stood in neat stacks along the walls.

Tony stepped slowly into the shed, intensely aware of how faint the flashlight beam was getting, and began checking out the boxes on the floor. One contained hand grenades—not the old "pineapple" kind you saw in war movies but the modern variety, as small and rounded as lemons. Another was labeled C-4 PLASTIC HIGH EXPLOSIVE PROP U.S. ARMY; he left that one alone. Nearby was a box of pencil-shaped objects he thought might be detonators. He also found tear-gas canisters and anti-tank rockets and, in the center of the room, a large box he couldn't open. What was in *there*? An inflatable B-2 bomber?

Stepping back outside, he glanced nervously around the clearing. *Abandoned* survivalist camp, my ass. The wrecked house was nothing but a smokescreen. Somewhere around here had to be the *real* Hiber Nation.

He went back into the shed. Why was this stuff stored here on the surface? For safety's sake? Hell, who cared? Someone had done him a favor. A *huge* favor.

First he traded Del's old shotgun for a sawed-off, five-shot autoloading model—perfect for close work. Next he considered the automatic rifles. Once, back in the academy, he had participated in a demonstration on street-gang firepower where he and several other recruits had been given the chance to shoot the more popular models of these weapons. The Israeli Uzi 9mm had been the hands-down favorite. Tony took one off the wall and slung it onto his back.

The pistols and revolver he was already carrying took care of his handgun needs, but he didn't hesitate to grab several grenades. He'd never used one before, but he'd seen earlier models of them thrown in a thousand old movies. He hung them around his belt.

Finally, he tugged some ammo pouches down from the ceiling and loaded them with shells for the weapons he'd selected. When he was finished, his body was crisscrossed with straps, guns and holsters, and he felt even more like Rambo. But not *enough* like Rambo. If only he knew how to use C–4 explosives and LAWS rockets and . . .

He glanced again at the steel box in the middle of the floor. Why was it locked? None of the other boxes were. After a moment's debate, he went outside and got the bolt cutters again.

It took a while to break into the box. The lock was inset so that he couldn't get a decent angle on it, and he had to use the powerful jaws of the cutter like a pair of scissors, snipping the mechanism right out of the box. That done, he hesitated a moment. It could be booby-trapped . . .

Moving his body as far away as possible, he hooked his fingertips under the lip of the lid and threw it back, in the same motion ducking and covering his head with his arms.

There was no explosion. No alarm. When he crept back again and leaned over the box, the flashlight beam didn't glint off the curved nose cones of hand-launched rockets or a flamethrower's fuel tanks—it dropped into a hole carved out of the native rock below. Tony's eyes widened. This was the last thing he had expected. A row of notches were cut into one side of the shaft, forming a rough ladder. The dying flashlight beam penetrated only a few feet down, so it was impossible to be sure how deep it was.

Tony sat back on his heels. The weapons cache definitely meant he had arrived on the doorstep of his destination—but it seemed unlikely that this narrow shaft, scarcely wider than his shoulders, was the entrance to an extensive survivalist camp. Besides, who would store his munitions at his own front door, where any commie pinko sympathizer could take advantage of them?

Was the shaft some kind of trap, then? He clutched the shotgun. The night was aging fast, and he was feeling woozier every minute. He didn't have time to hunt all over the place for another entrance . . .

Shifting both the shotgun and Uzi onto his back, he stepped over the lip of the box and lowered his legs into the shaft. As he groped for a toehold inside it, he had the uneasy feeling he was consigning himself to the gullet of some great, hungry beast.

Pendergast's voice echoed in the utter blackness of the cell. "It's okay. There's enough air down here to last for days, if necessary. Don't worry."

Deborah wrapped her arms around Virgil. She had never experienced darkness as intense as this. Never.

"Well," Mitford said, "if we're going to be stuck down here for days, we might as well think of a way to pass the time. I know, let's sing campfire songs." He cleared his throat. "*Kumbaya, my Lord, Kumbay-aaaaah . . .*"

"Shut up!" Pendergast cried. "I have to—"

"Doc." Mitford's voice was low, reasonable. "I'll kill you if you ever tell me what to do again."

In the ensuing silence, Deborah felt her heart pounding fiercely.

The silence grew. Deborah cradled Virgil, one hand on his forehead as she willed him to live. Now and then she heard a slight sound from somewhere in the pit—a sigh, a rustle. Gradually, the noises came together and she became convinced that Mitford was creeping toward her across the floor, his body sprawled flat like a spider's, his eyes able to see her through the blackness . . .

She jumped as a pinkish rectangle abruptly appeared high over the pit—the door had opened. An irregular shape moved into the light. "We'rrre herrrre to take you on an all-expenses-paid trrrrrrrip to the temple," rumbled a Loner's voice.

"Who is that?" Pendergast demanded, his voice cracking slightly.

"It is Supai, Grrrrreat Fatherrrr. Cherrrrrnobog and Kali arrrre with me, too—we thrrrrrree kings have come forrrrrrrr you."

Deborah recognized a couple of those names from her mythology class. "Supai" was the Inca god of death, to whom a hundred children had been sacrificed each year. And "Kali" was the Hindu goddess of nature, the hideous Black Mother once worshipped by members of India's homicidal Thuggee sect.

"Where's Vulcan?" Pendergast demanded, his voice suddenly hard, commanding.

"Prrrreparrring forrrrrrr the last rrrrrrites, of courrrrrrrse."

"Take me to him right away. I, his father, command it."

"Yourrrrrrrr will be done," Supai said, and a moment later there was a soft thud on the floor. Deborah felt something brush past her, and heard Pendergast gasp in shock. A faint rustling sound returned, and then the shadows above shifted again.

A moment later, when a pair of powerful arms closed around Deborah's waist, she thought it was Mitford and began to scream. Instantly the grip tightened horribly, choking off her breath, and an inhuman voice snarled in her ear: "Up, up and away. We go to the stainless house, the temple, the house of—" The voice broke off in a sound like a question, and Deborah felt something tugging at Virgil's sling. She tightened her grip desperately.

"Saving Lunchables for laterrrr?" the voice said. "You'rrrrre a frrrrrrrugal gourrrrrrrrrrmet."

Deborah was hoisted off the ground and carried a few feet, then she gasped at a sudden, painful vertical acceleration. Overhead, the pink rectangle floated closer, and a moment later, rough Loner hands were snatching, clutching, and she found herself standing on the far side of the bars. Pendergast was there, too, his features indistinguishable in the maroon shadows. "Everything will be all right," he said in a low voice. He sounded as if he meant it.

She moved away from him.

In a flurry of movement, one of the Loners appeared from below and flung Mitford through the gap. He hit the wall, grunted in pain, then righted himself. Suddenly all three of the creatures were there, slim and silent. Deborah shuddered. Even in the gloom, she could see their teeth shining . . .

"Come," said Supai, "to new frrrrrrrrreedom." Turning, he swept through the doorway. His fellows circled behind the humans and pressed forward, hissing. The group moved after Supai.

Outside the cell was a long, narrow corridor filled with the red glow, which emanated from a distant doorway. Against this light, Supai was a sinister silhouette—*the bogeyman*, Deborah thought wildly.

"Where exactly are we going?" Pendergast demanded.

"To the Holy of Holies, Beloved Georrrrrge," Supai replied. "It's almost time for the top-rrrrrrated show of the new season to begin. Follow me." He strode toward the light, and Pendergast immediately hurried after him. Deborah caught up quickly, not wanting to be too near Mitford, whom she could hear scraping along behind. In fact, she could hear his footsteps plainly, as well as Pendergast's and her own— but she couldn't hear the Loners. They drifted along like ghosts, Supai in the lead and the other two at the rear. Drifted like ghosts—except that ghosts didn't throw shadows.

The group passed through the doorway and entered a broader corridor, where the floor was covered with tiles, the walls with plaster, and the ceiling with acoustic panels. Red light bulbs glared down at regularly spaced intervals. As Deborah passed beneath the first one, she quickly examined Virgil again. His eyes remained closed, his body very limp—but he was still breathing. Trying to keep him steady against her chest, she glanced around. On either hand, open doorways revealed rooms full of scientific and medical equipment, some of it familiar to her from the Carlton Center, some completely alien. She shuddered. *I created them right here, in Ginnunga Gap . . .*

They kept walking, turning corners. Deborah saw plaques on the passing doors: SEKHMET. CHARON. ANUBIS. MEDB. She recognized many of them as the names of demons and monsters from various cultures—more Loner names, obviously. How could she have judged Dr. Pendergast so terribly wrong?

Mitford said, "Hey, doc, looks like we're going to the garage. What do you think, are they going to pull an Arcadio on us?"

Pendergast's shoulders twitched, but he didn't look back. "Don't be ridiculous. If that was their intention, why would they have bothered to make us prisoners first?"

"What's 'an Arcadio'?" Deborah asked hoarsely.

"Never mind," Pendergast said. "It's got nothing to do with us. Besides, everything's under control."

Mitford laughed tonelessly. "Isn't it always?"

Another corner, another hallway, this one terminating in a pair of closed doors. When Supai pushed them open, the group entered a narrow, unlit chamber, the floor of which slanted up to a second pair of doors. These were equipped with small, wire-reinforced windows, through which fell still more red light. Deborah, tired and frightened, wondered if they led into hell. It would seem almost a relief.

"Bow," a voice behind them growled, and a great, hot hand closed on the back of her head, pushing it forward and down. The same thing happened to Mitford. Pendergast was not touched.

Supai paused at the top of the ramp and glanced back at them. "Welcome to the Twilight Zone," he said in a low voice that pulsed with passion. "Beam me up, oh Lorrrrrd."

"Beam me up," the other two Loners echoed.

Mitford cawed laughter, and instantly Chernobog's claws lashed out like scythes. Mitford's exposed ear fell to the floor. Squealing in shock, he clapped a hand over the nub and rocked back on his heels. Deborah noted with strange dispassion that the blood flowing between his fingers looked purple in the gloom.

"Obserrrrve rrrrespectful behaviorrrrr, crrrriminal," Chernobog growled. "It's showtime."

Supai pushed the doors open, and they all walked into the smoky red light.

CHAPTER TWENTY-TWO

THE ROOM INTO WHICH SUPAI led them was large and high-ceilinged, broken into black and red slices by the widely spaced emergency lights. Deborah looked around for more Loners, but saw none. This appeared to be a garage or shop of some kind. One wall was half-covered with pegboard on which were painted the silhouettes of hand tools, although the tools themselves lay in untidy heaps on the floor below, as if hurled down by an earthquake. Distributed around the room were larger power tools—table saws and drill presses and lathes. Deborah thought of Del's woodworking shop, although the smell here was very different: oil, metal, gasoline. And Del would never have left his tools scattered around this way . . .

She mustn't think about Del, or Betty. If she did, she would then have to wonder about that shriek she had heard just before she was captured . . .

Instead, as Supai led them into the garage, she concentrated on finding a way out. Over the center of the room hovered a skylight, stars visible through it. But it was at least thirty feet up, higher, surely, than even a Loner could jump. Beneath it stood a narrow table draped with a starlit cloth, cool blue white against the surrounding hellish glow.

Farther away stood a big van, and next to that, a metal tank with GASOLINE stenciled on the side. In the distance, vague in the gloom, was the far wall of the room—and what looked like a garage door on tracks. Deborah stared at it, wondering how quickly she could raise it if she could get to it. And what lay on the far side? Freedom? Or just more Loners?

They had reached the white-shrouded table now, and Supai walked around it. But Pendergast stopped short, and Deborah and Mitford stopped behind him uncertainly. The Loners in the rear growled, but

Pendergast ignored them. "What's going on?" he demanded. "Where's Vulcan?"

Supai turned, starlight flaming softly blue in his eyes. "He will join you soon, Grrrreat Fatherrrr . . . as it is wrrrrrrrrrrritten."

Pendergast hesitated a moment longer, then glanced at Deborah and Mitford, shrugged and walked around the table. "Please face the doorrrrrrs, Beloved Georrrrrrge," Supai said, stepping close behind him, and he did so.

Kali leaned close to Deborah's ear. "Now you, crrrrriminal," the Loner growled. Deborah hurried around the table, the Loner at her heels, and stood on Pendergast's right-hand side. Mitford was herded to Pendergast's left with Chernobog just behind him, teeth bared. His broken fangs looked like shards of polished stone.

Suddenly Supai sprang high into the air, soaring over Pendergast's head as though launched from a trampoline, and landed on the tabletop. Flinging out his arms, he bellowed, "And now, it's time forrrr the People's Courrrrrrrrt! New Generrrrrrration, come forrrrrrrrth!"

Across the room, the double doors swung open. To Deborah's shock, two human beings entered—a man and a woman, both completely naked, heads lowered. They moved toward the white-clothed table as the doors rocked open behind them and another pair of naked people came in. They were followed by another pair, and another, and another . . .

"Come on down," Supai cried, "and assemble for the grrreat supperrrrr, in orrrderrr that you may eat the flesh of kings and the flesh of commanderrrrs and the flesh of mighty men and the flesh of all men, both frrrree men and slaves, and small and grrrrrrrrrrrrreat!"

The flesh of men? Deborah stiffened, but Kali was breathing on her neck; there was nowhere to go, they had been led into a *trap* . . .

"Easy," Pendergast whispered. He sounded calm, almost thoughtful.

The double doors kept opening, closing, naked people marching through. The men were all on one side, women on other. As the first pair neared the table, they stopped and turned to face one another. The second pair halted a pace farther away and also faced inward. As did the next pair, and the next . . .

When the doors finally stopped moving, two lines of naked people extended all the way back to the doors, forming a narrow aisle between them. They all stood perfectly still, arms at their sides, heads bowed. Somehow, their meek attitudes frightened Deborah more than anything else she'd seen in this place. Who *were* these people? And what had been done to them to make them behave this way?

She managed to turn her eyes far enough to see Pendergast, but his expression was distant, unreadable. On his other side, Mitford stood with one hand cupped around his bleeding ear—but his eyes were roving everywhere. Looking for a way to escape, Deborah realized, and wondered if his injuries were really as debilitating as he made them seem. Suddenly, horribly, she found herself almost admiring him.

I'm definitely going crazy now.

She looked back toward the naked people, who just stood there silently with heads bowed. Both lines, she saw, had gaps in them. On the women's side there was a space large enough for a single person, while on the men's side, there was room for *two*. One woman, two men . . . her throat tightened like a boa constrictor. Were the gaps meant to be filled by Pendergast, Mitford and her? Were the three of them intended to fill out the menu of the "supper" Supai had spoken about?

But then she realized there were only seventeen people in the room. Hadn't Pendergast said there were *nineteen* Loners?

Virgil quivered slightly in his sling, and Deborah was suddenly certain it had been a dying spasm. Tugging open the top of the sling, she reached in and put her trembling fingertips on his chest. Thank God, his heartbeat was still there, and seemed steady. He whimpered.

"No snacking, Brrrrrreederrrr," Kali growled in her ear, and she snatched her hand away. Suddenly she hoped Virgil *didn't* regain consciousness, at least not until she found some way to get him out of—

"Enough!" Pendergast suddenly shouted, making her jump. "Supai, I'm tired of waiting. I want to see Vulcan *now*."

Supai's hideous face turned and looked down at them. "Patience is a virrrrrrtue," he rumbled. "All good things to those who wait. So it is wrrrrrrrrritten."

Pendergast seemed about to say something else, then he closed his mouth. Looking at him, Deborah thought she saw a strange glint in his eyes—curiosity? Did he find all this *interesting*?

On the surface of the table, a strip of moonlight appeared, shimmering silver. It expanded slowly into a narrow rectangle, which widened into a square. Above, the moon peeked through the skylight, hard and bright. No one moved, spoke, reacted. Deborah's neck was beginning to ache .

from Virgil's suspended weight, and her skull was pounding again. If something didn't happen soon, she was afraid she was going to—

Supai raised his head, sniffed the air, and swung his arms high. "Blessed arrrre those invited to the marrrrriage supperrrrrrrrrrr of the lamb," he said. "And now . . . *herrrrrrrrrrrrrrrre's Vulcan!*"

Across the room, the double doors opened slowly, and Deborah stared in shock as Vulcan shuffled through. Was it possible the Loner had deteriorated so much since the last time she saw him? He was bent almost double, the bones of his skeleton sliding back and forth beneath his translucent skin like a flimsy scaffold in a windstorm. His great head quaked wildly, and even from this distance, Deborah could hear the damp bellows-wheeze of his breathing.

At a gasp beside her, she glanced sidelong at Pendergast. His eyes were clenched tight; he looked stricken. She shivered.

It took Vulcan several minutes to creep all the way down the aisle to the table, but no one moved. When he finally arrived, he stopped, his quivering head tracking along the table from Deborah to Pendergast to Mitford. His eyes were an overall pearly white now, but his nostrils twitched constantly. "Fatherrrrrrrr," he growled at Pendergast.

Pendergast, eyes still closed, whispered, "Vulcan. Listen to me. Please, we have to—"

"And George was the worrrrrrrrrd," Vulcan said, "and the Worrrrrrrrrrd was George, Dude." He shuffled around to face the two lines of naked people, and his fluttery voice grew louder: "Brrrrrrethrrr-rrren! Tonight is the beginning of the end of the materrrrrrrrial worrrrrrrrld!"

To Deborah's shock, the prisoners all raised their heads together and shouted, "Ahhhhhhhhhhh-*men!*"

The shaft was getting narrower. That couldn't be an illusion because Tony had never been claustrophobic; the shaft just *had* to be getting narrower. Now there was barely enough room for him to bend one leg while he groped with the opposite foot for a toehold. And with every move he made, the guns slung over his back clattered against the rough stone behind him, or his kneecaps got barked in front, or both. Now he knew that this hole *was* a trap; in a moment he'd be stuck as tightly as a collie in a cat-door, unable to move in either direction, and eventually Faust would come along and pour burning oil down on top of him . . .

He made himself halt, hips and shoulders wedged against the sides of the shaft to relieve the pressure on his limbs, and took several deep, calming breaths. The shaft was *not* getting narrower. And no matter how it felt, it did *not* go on forever. No doubt he would soon find the bottom. Soon.

It turned out to be the next step. As he reached down with his toes, they contacted a flat surface with a hollow *thud*. He immediately jerked his foot back, waited. That hadn't felt very substantial—what lay underneath? Another shaft? Hell, at this point, did it matter? Raising his foot as far as possible, he stomped down hard. A *bonk*! echoed up around him and his foot shot easily into space, the momentum almost jerking him out of the shaft. A dim red glow washed up around him, and he listened for indications of alarm. Nothing. But he couldn't see anything below around his own body.

Easing himself down with the waning strength of his arms, he groped with his extended foot for some kind of support. Nothing . . . nothing . . . Finally he had to bring his hands down another notch and lower himself again, mind going smoky with the fear that the only thing beneath him was a thirty-foot drop to steel spikes or a tank full of sharks or . . .

His toe touched another flat surface, this one more solid. Tentatively, he put weight on it. Okay. More weight. Fine. Now his other foot came down and found a home. Tony lowered his hands notch by notch until his eyes cleared the bottom of the shaft. He found himself staring into a shadowy gap between a thick shell of reinforced concrete and a suspended acoustical-tile ceiling. Releasing his last handhold, he squatted below the ceiling, trembling all over with exhaustion.

He was in some kind of storeroom, perched on top of a rack of metal shelves full of cardboard cartons, cans and boxes, and a dozen great drums marked DRINKING H_2O. A single red bulb on the wall splashed Tony's monstrous shadow across row after row of shelves.

This is it, he thought, fighting back a sudden attack of the shakes. He had made it—he was inside Hiber Nation, the psycho's lair.

Across the room was an open doorway, more red light coming through it. Climbing down from the shelf, arms and legs trembling, Tony unslung the sawed-off shotgun.

From the doorway he peered out into a long hall. Red lights and open doors marched down it. He blinked. This place was *huge*. Taking a deep breath, he started down the corridor.

His sense of urgency compelled him to run, but he forced himself to be systematic. Each time he passed a room, he peered in with three eyes—the two in his head and the black one at the end of the shotgun. The rooms were all utilitarian—kitchens, more storerooms, a chamber where a vast air-conditioning unit hulked. The fans were motionless. In the next room, two great generators stood silently in the smell of diesel fuel. In fact, Tony saw no signs of life at all. What if he was too late? What if Hiber Nation had been occupied a few hours ago, but no longer? Could he be too late *again*?

Moving faster, he almost reached the end of the hall before he noticed the small video camera mounted high in the corner. He froze, although of course the damage was already done . . . or was it? The camera rested on a motorized mount, but when Tony walked on, it didn't pivot to follow. In one way, of course, that was terrific—but it was also a bad sign.

Around the corner he found what were clearly living quarters. Through an open doorway he saw a room furnished with a couch, chair, TV, stereo. Shotgun ready, he leaped in.

No one.

This chamber turned out to be only one room in a suite of three, all as neat and characterless as accommodations in an expensive hotel. And all unoccupied. But in the bedroom, Tony found a bureau full of men's clothing, medium-sized . . . the Blond Man's size. There was also a closet, similarly filled. The desk was empty except for a .32 revolver and a large, vinyl-covered binder. Popping the revolver open, Tony unloaded the shells, then twisted the cylinder out of alignment so that it couldn't be closed again. After a moment's hesitation, he opened the binder—and staggered back in shock.

On the first page were mounted four Polaroid photos, undated and uncaptioned. All four depicted women with handcuffs on their wrists and ropes on their ankles, strips of duct tape across their mouths, thin wires cutting into their necks . . . women who had not needed to be told to hold still for the camera. Dead women.

Tony made himself flip through the entire book, bile in his throat, his heart thudding with mounting dread. Four photos per page, page after page. Handcuffs. Plastic restraints. Duct tape. Staring eyes. Blood, sometimes. A few of the faces were familiar—he'd seen them on missing-persons posters in the squad room. But he was searching for a *particular* face.

He reached the end without finding it. No Deborah.

Letting out a harsh sigh, he threw the photo album back into the drawer. If he got the chance he would come back for it later; it would clear up a lot of unsolved murders—but right now, the past wasn't his concern. Keeping Deborah's picture out of that book *was*.

One good thing—surely Blondie wouldn't have left his little scrapbook behind if he had abandoned Hiber Nation.

Leaving the suite, Tony continued on into the complex, moving faster now, almost running, glancing into each room he passed with the shotgun raised and ready. Come on, Blondie. Or Faust. Or whoever. Come on. Come on . . .

Finally a metal-clad door blocked his way. Standing to the side, he stretched out his arm and pushed the door smoothly open.

From somewhere beyond came a voice, faint, echoing, the words not quite comprehensible. It didn't matter. The sound alone made his heart thump harder—someone was *here*. Peeking around the doorframe, he saw yet another long hallway stretching before him. It ended in a pair of swinging doors. The voice was louder in that direction.

Shotgun ready, he broke into a soft run.

Vulcan's talons raked the air, and moonlight streamed and sparked along their edges like melted solder. His voice pounded back and forth off the walls.

"Brrrrethrrrrren! Beforrrrrrre we starrrrrt to parrrrrrty down, I've got a newssssssss flash—we've lossssssst one of the New Generrrrra-tion. Anubissss hazzzzzzz not rrreturrrned frrrrom the materrrrrrial worrrrrrrld."

The lines of naked people stirred, and Deborah heard Kali hiss.

New Generation? Deborah thought suddenly. *Anubis?*—that had to be a Loner name. Was Vulcan saying that one of the Loners had been killed? She stifled a surge of joy. Maybe Anubis had found Del to be more than he could handle. Or perhaps Tony had returned in time to kill the damned thing. Please, God, please let either be true. Let Tony and Del and Betty be alive and let them have called in the cavalry. The police. Soldiers. A SEAL team. Yes—with more than a dozen unaccount-ed-for Loners around here somewhere, a SEAL team would be good.

Suddenly Virgil's weight was much lighter around her neck, but she kept all signs of hope from reaching her face. Pendergast had secrets. Mitford had secrets. The Loners had secrets . . . Now she had a secret, too. She intended to keep it that way.

"Anubissss hazzzz been canceled," Vulcan wheezed; it was impossible to tell if he was saddened or excited by the thought. "Endusssssst to Endusssssst, ashessss to vacuum. Let usssssss prrrrrrray."

To Deborah's horror, the naked people raised their hands, palms together, fingertips touching chins. She couldn't believe it or understand it. There was a long moment of silence in the room, then Vulcan turned and, grasping the edge of the table, hauled himself up on top of it. Supai moved out of his way. As soon as the old Loner was safely on the table, Supai bowed to him, then bounded backward over Pendergast's head, landing softly in his former place.

Drawing his feet under him, Vulcan stood semierect, legs shaking, and faced the naked people again. They turned toward him. "In the beginning," he growled, "Beloved Georrrrrge crrrrrreated the heaven and the earrrrrth . . ."

Beloved George? Deborah thought dizzily. But—that was what the Loners called *Pendergast*! She glanced at him; this time Kali did not interfere. Pendergast was staring fixedly up at Vulcan, head tilted back, mouth tensed in a line of intense concentration.

". . . And He made the beasssstsssss of the earrrrth afterrrrr theirrrrrr kind," Vulcan continued, "and everrrrry thing that crrrrrreepeth upon the earrrrrrth afterrrrr theirrrrr kind . . ."

He was quoting from the Book of Genesis now. Deborah tried to follow the logic of this speech . . . it sounded like Vulcan had cast Pendergast not only in the part of his own father, but as Almighty God Himself. Which was horrifying—but also, in a way, encouraging. Perhaps Pendergast *would* be able to make the creatures do as he wished.

". . . blesssssssed them, and ssssssaid unto them, Be frrrruitful and multiply, and rrrrrrreplenish the earrrrrth, and sssssubdue it . . ."

She realized Vulcan was skipping around, mixing words and verses and even religions without apparent rhyme or reason. Still, the overall tone was familiar, and Deborah found herself remembering Sunday mornings in church. The congregation flapping handheld fans with the Twenty-Third Psalm printed on them. Butt-numbing pews. The preacher droning away behind his podium . . .

She also clearly remembered the last time she had said a real prayer:

At Brad's funeral. She had asked God to let Brad be alive. *Ask and ye shall receive*, the Bible said. Yet Brad had gone into the grave anyway, not alive.

"Finally Georrrrrrge ssssaw the wickednesssss of man on the earrrrrth," Vulcan rumbled, "and He was ssssorrry He made man to brrrrrreed on the earrrrrth. And He sssaid, 'Yo, I'll blot out the Brreederrrrrs, and everrry living thing.' Ssssso He made a flood, but it didn't get out all the grrround-in dirrrrrrrt . . ."

Deborah glanced at Pendergast again. Now his brows were drawn together even more tightly—he was finally planning something, she hoped. Maybe some appropriately God-like thing . . .

Vulcan's voice grew slower and even rougher. "It is wrrrrritten . . . that the Lonerrrrsssss will sssssmash out the gatesss of the underrrrworld . . . and devourrrrr the living . . . and the New Generrrration will increassse beyond the numberrrrrrr of the living . . ."

Increase beyond the number of the living? Deborah's attention snapped back again. Hadn't Pendergast said *Enkidu* called for a balance of one Loner for every two thousand human beings? That didn't sound like what *Vulcan* was saying.

"It's okay," Pendergast murmured, as if he had read her mind. "He's dying; it'll be over in a minute. Don't worry."

". . . And I ssssssaw a new heaven and a new earrrrrth," Vulcan went on, almost whispering now. "And in it the Brrrrreederrrssss were rrrrraised as cattle for ssssssacrifice to the godsssss . . ."

Deborah gasped.

"Shhh," Pendergast said. "It makes sense, from a Loner point of view. But it's all Vulcan. And as soon as he dies . . ."

As if on cue, Vulcan sank to his knees on the white cloth, paused, then lowered himself onto his back. As he stretched his twisted body out to its full length, his face moved directly below Deborah's. That pulsing, semihuman mass of wrinkles and teeth made her want to shriek.

"Time to parrrrrrrrrty," Vulcan whispered, and grinned, and Deborah recoiled from the swampy stench of his breath.

As one, the naked people took one step toward the table.

"Thisssssss is my body," Vulcan hissed into the air. "Tasssssste and sssssee that the Lorrrrrd is good, and good forrrrrrr you, too."

The nearest female prisoner stepped forward, stopping at the edge of the table.

"Sssssekhmet," Vulcan croaked. "Let usssss prrrrrrrey."

The woman bowed over him. "Surely I will require your lifeblood," she said, and Deborah screamed as she *changed*. Deborah had the horrible impression that something was swimming up inside the woman's body and head like a creature from the bottom of the sea that had never encountered the sun before, and now it was pushing tightly against the woman's skin and staring through her eye sockets, and its teeth slid out of her jaw, distending and expanding it, and her head became long and leering. Like cocoons, her fingertips extruded claws that clattered eagerly on the tabletop.

Deborah's scream faded as she realized no one else in the room seemed surprised by this transformation.

Then she understood: Sekhmet was a *Loner*, and always had been. All these nude people, as ordinary as they looked, must also be Loners . . .

Sekhmet bent down over Vulcan, eyes avid.

"Ssssekhmet," Vulcan murmured. "Thisss is my body which is given forrrrr you. Eat, drrrrrink and be merrrrry."

Grinning, unveiling her fangs to the gumline, Sekhmet bobbed down and, with a blur-quick snap, ripped a chunk of flesh from Vulcan's withered arm. Blood gushed out of the U-shaped wound, and Vulcan's jaws stretched wide in a yawn that might have reflected pain—or ecstasy. Deborah screamed as his hot blood shot up and speckled her face.

Sekhmet swallowed. "I shall neverrrrr eat it again," she intoned, and turned away. As she strode to the end of the women's line on her backward-bending legs, the first naked man stepped forward.

"Kho-dumo-dumo . . ." Vulcan hissed, voice trembling in agony or exaltation. "Let ussss prrrrrey."

"Surely I will requirrre your lifeblood," the man said, and went through the same quick, hideous change as Sekhmet had.

"Thisssss is my body which is given forrrrr you," Vulcan said again. Blood poured from the hole in his arm and soaked into the white tablecloth. "Eat, drrrrrrrrink and be merrrrrrrry . . ."

A bow, a flash of teeth, and another piece of Vulcan's arm vanished. "I shall neverrr eat it again," Kho-dumo-dumo intoned in the rippling growl of a Loner.

"Oh, God," Deborah choked as she realized that this ordeal was going to go on and on. "Oh, God . . ." She started to turn her face away, but a pair of powerful hands clamped onto her head from behind and inexorably pointed it straight ahead. "Don't touch that dial," Kali growled in her ear. Deborah closed her eyes.

"Kalma," Vulcan rumbled. "Let ussssss prrrrrrrey . . ."

Suddenly Pendergast's whisper, harsh and trembling, came to Deborah: "It's the Last Supper. Don't you see? It's their interpretation of the Last Supper, among other things. Don't worry. I understand now. After Vulcan's dead, they'll focus on *me*. That will be my chance to take over."

"Aipaloovik," Vulcan said. "Let ussssss prrrrrrrey . . ."

Deborah realized that listening by itself was even worse than looking, and she opened her eyes again. A female Loner was now walking back to the end of the line, and Vulcan's arm had been reduced to little more than a chain of fleshy nubs strung along a skewer of bone. More blood pumped onto the tabletop and fanned out through the white cloth.

Deborah quickly raised her head and stared at the waiting Loners. The human-looking ones stood in the front, the transformed ones in back. The contrast was nauseating, horrible. In their humanoid incarnation they appeared so *normal*, so . . .

Deborah's knees folded as if they'd been clubbed from behind; if it hadn't been for Kali's firm grip on her head, she would have fallen. She had just realized that there was something vaguely familiar about all those pensive, downturned faces. They all looked like Pendergast. Negroid, Asian, Caucasian, Latino, but all Pendergast—ethnic variations on a theme. We Are the World.

There's more of me in the Loners than anyone . . .

She finally got her legs back under her, skull throbbing from Kali's overpowering grip, and stiffened her knees.

There was a good side to this, too, she told herself. If the Loners' link to their creator ran this deep, perhaps he really could convince them to do *anything*. Go back inside their cells. Maybe even kill themselves. Kill each other . . .

On the other hand, Pendergast was insane. He might instead decide to say, "Go out and eat people arbitrarily as I intended you to, and sin no more, Amen."

Deborah pictured the Loner population expanding across the country, feeding, breeding, spreading. Eventually reaching every corner of the world, stowed away in the baggage compartments of airplanes, and on trains, and in the back seats of cars . . .

She looked past the Loners to the double doors. Maybe if she stared at them hard enough, *concentrated* on them, they would burst open and Del or Tony would charge into the room at the head of a squad of Marines, who would then pull out their guns and put an end to all this.

"Thisss is my body which is given forrrr you . . ."

She felt movement against her breasts, heard a faint whisper from Virgil. Clutched him, silenced him. Relief and terror fought inside her. She didn't want him awake for this. Didn't want him drawing attention to himself. He became still again.

Deborah concentrated on the doors. Concentrated. Concentrated . . .

CHAPTER TWENTY-THREE

AFTER HIS FIRST GLANCE through the windows in the double doors, Tony jerked away so violently he almost tumbled back down the ramp. But the impression was chiseled into his mind: A table bathed in a great deal of blood, a group of naked people—and at least a half-dozen Cannibals.

Shock and horror made him dizzy. So many Cannibals! And those people . . . who were they, and what were they doing here? Were they prisoners or participants? And one of them . . . had that been *Deborah*?

Slowly, he put an eye back to the window. There were two lines of figures extending away from the door; at the far end of each line stood human beings; closer, Cannibals. All of them were naked. Males on the left, females on the right. Then his gaze shot back to the table in the center of the room, and he strangled a gasp just in time. There was Deborah, standing behind the table. She looked disheveled and pale, and was wearing a sling of some kind around her neck, but otherwise she seemed to be all right.

At that moment, she raised her eyes and stared right at him, and he automatically lifted a hand in warning. There was no reaction . . . well, of *course* not—because of the lighting, the windows had to be like mirrors on Deborah's side. And it was a good thing, too; if she *had* given a sign of recognition, there was no telling what the Cannibals would have done.

Just then the naked people all shifted position, stepping forward, and Tony had a better view of the sling Deborah wore. A small, motionless leg dangling from one end of it. *Virgil*? Could it *be*?

Through fireworks of relief, Tony realized that Deborah was not alone behind the table. Beside her stood a man Tony recognized from Deborah's description—Dr. George Pendergast himself. And beside *him* . . . yes. He'd done things to his hair, but it was unquestionably

Blondie. Tony noticed with grim satisfaction that he looked as if he'd been cranked through a food processor. Maybe Del had gotten in a few licks before the Cannibals finished him off, after all.

But someone was missing from the group—Faust, the mysterious Faust. Which seemed to prove, once and for all, that Blondie and Faust really were the same person.

One of the nude men was now approaching the table, and Tony noticed a bloody mass of meat lying there. He looked closer, then recoiled. It was a hideous, withered *Cannibal*, the Methuselah of Cannibals, its body missing great crescents of flesh.

At that moment, the man who had just approached the table rippled all over, and in seconds became one of the long, sleek creatures Tony recognized all too well. Holy Christ, so that was what all these nude people really were. It explained so much . . . how the Cannibals got in and out of their kill zones undetected, how they were able to approach prey under the least likely of circumstances . . .

As Tony watched, the new Cannibal bent down, opened his jaws wide and snapped a mouthful of flesh out of the ancient monster's thigh. Tony winced. He had to get the prisoners out of there. But how? Armed like Rambo or not, did he really think he could blast his way in, free Deborah and Pendergast, then fight off more than a dozen Cannibals all the way back to the escape shaft? And even assuming he *could* do all that, there was still the matter of having to wander, lost, through the dark chaparral above while looking for the Cherokee . . .

Moving his face close to the window, he searched the sides of the room for another exit, or some way to distract the Cannibals—*anything* that might suggest a plan.

Immediately he saw the parked van, and his heart leaped. A vehicle meant—yes, there on the back wall was a big rolling garage door. Which implied, of course, that there was some kind of passable road on the other side. How could he have missed a *road* during his wanderings? Never mind. Right now, what mattered was that the road must exist, and the van definitely existed, and—

Without warning, one of the Cannibals swung around and stared straight into his eyes. He jerked back a step, gasping. The Cannibal remained frozen for a minute, nostrils twitching—then it turned away again.

Did it smell me? Heart pounding wildly, Tony crept back up to the glass. If the creature had detected him, it seemed uninterested now.

Or perhaps unimpressed. Tony remembered how the first Cannibal had tossed him around, toyed with him. Perhaps all these creatures felt scorn for his kind—perhaps, to them, he was simply not enough of a threat to disturb their grisly evening smorgasbord.

Or maybe they *couldn't* take action on their own. Maybe Faust had to tell them what to do.

So . . . what if *Faust* were dead?

Peering through the window again, Tony debated his chances. When switched to single-shot mode, an Uzi was a fairly accurate weapon— but the lighting in the garage was very poor, and Faust was half-hidden by the crowd in front of him . . . and, in truth, Tony was no marksman under the best of circumstances. Besides, even if he *did* manage to kill Faust, how did he know the Cannibals wouldn't promptly tear the prisoners apart?

No, a direct attack wouldn't do. There were four parts to the problem. First, he had to separate the hostages from the Cannibals. Then eliminate Faust. Then kill as many of the Cannibals as possible while herding the hostages into the van. And finally, crash through the garage door and drive away into the moonset . . .

One, two, three, four.

But he couldn't think past number one. How was he supposed to get the hostages away from the Cannibals? It wasn't—

Suddenly he realized the answer hovered just above the crowd. The moon was suspended in a large pane of glass in the ceiling.

A skylight in a bomb-proof shelter?

He stared at it in wonderment, and the whole plan fell into place— one, two, three, four. To pull it off, all he would need was perfect timing, complete cooperation from the hostages, and a great deal of luck.

But the skylight at least made it *possible*.

With a final glance at Deborah, he spun on his heel and sprinted off the way he had come, as fast as he could go.

By now Vulcan was little more than a torso, a head, and a few random chunks of quivering flesh—but he was still alive. Deborah stared in revolted terror at his rolling eyes and grimacing mouth, at the way his head changed shape constantly. Blood saturated the entire tablecloth and was now forming a substantial pool on the floor below.

Of the Loners, only Supai had not yet fed. Now he walked around the table and bowed low over Vulcan. The ritual words were exchanged, and Supai briskly snapped off a fragment of Vulcan's right thigh. Then he raised a talon and drew the claw slowly across the thin flesh above the old Loner's eyes; first horizontally, then vertically, making an oozing cross. "Blesssss thissss messssss," he hissed.

Vulcan smiled. "Okay, Sssssssupai. Give them a piece of my mind . . ."

Flipping back flaps of scalp to expose Vulcan's skull, Supai sank a claw deep into one of the sutures between bone segments and started to trace along it. Blood and some clear fluid gushed out, and Deborah had to close her eyes again, stomach clutching viciously.

A moment later there was a damp tearing sound, and she looked back as Supai peeled a large, hollow section of skull out of the front of Vulcan's head. The brain lay exposed beneath, gray pink and thickly rumpled. Blood poured out of the hole and into the piece of skull. "Thissssssss izzzzzzzzz my blood," Vulcan whispered as Supai lifted away the makeshift, dripping cup.

Vulcan turned his mangled head toward Pendergast, eyes rolling up, lids fluttering. "Fatherrrrrr . . ." he whispered. "Into yourrrrrrrr handsssssssss I commend my ssssssssssssssssssssssssss . . ." His voice faded, faded, and all at once he seemed to collapse in all directions, head flattening, torso sagging, until he was nothing but a collection of bloody bones held together by shreds of tissue. Then he was completely still.

"*Enkiduuuuuuuuuuuuuuuuu . . .*" the Loners rumbled.

Supai lifted high the piece of skull and turned toward the assembled Loners. "Don't drrrrrrrink and drrrrrrrive!" he cried, and brought the crude cup to his lips. He slurped once, said, "The Lorrrrrrrrrd is in me," and passed the skull to Kho-dumo-dumo, the first male Loner in line. Kho-dumo-dumo also sipped. "The Lorrrrrrrrrd is in me," he said, and handed the cup to Humbaba behind him. In this way the cup proceeded to the end of the males' line, then back up the females'. After Kalma drank, she carried the nearly empty cup around the altar and gave it to Kali, who sucked from it, intoned, "The Lorrrrrrrd is in me," and passed the cup to Chernobog. He also drank, said the words, then returned the cup, finally, to Supai.

And Supai held it across the altar before Pendergast. "Fatherrrrr," he said, "take this cup away frrrrrrrom me."

Pendergast stared at the skull-bowl, eyes bulging like red marbles.

The seconds stretched out, and from among the assembled Loners arose a low, discontented murmur.

Supai moved the cup closer to Pendergast's lips. "Was it not necessarrrry for the Son to sufferrrr these things that He might enterrrr into his glorrry?" the Loner growled. "No pain, no gain."

Pendergast's eyes darted this way and that. Then he took a deep breath, and Deborah saw his neck muscles tighten. Slowly, slowly, he leaned forward, eyes closed, and touched his lips to the bony rim of the cup. Deborah clamped her throat shut against rising bile.

A different, richer murmur passed through the room, and Supai grinned. "Now in you the fulnessss of Deity dwells," he said. "You arrrrrre the head overrrrrr all rrrrrrule and authorrrrrity. Who's the Boss? Beloved Georrrrrrge."

Pendergast, a drop of blood glinting like a ruby on his moustache, turned and cast Deborah a triumphant glance. Then he wheeled toward the Loners and threw out his arms. "I forgive you all, for you know not what you are doing! But now, it is time for you to return to your rooms and—"

The Loners stirred, and a castanet clattering of talons spread through the room.

Bounding up on top of the table again, straddling Vulcan's ravaged body, Supai roared, "The Last Supperrrrrrr is over, boys and girrrrrrrls! Time to begin a brand-new season!"

"Yes!" Pendergast shouted. "That's right! And the first step is for you all to—"

"Now the Fatherrrrr and Son have joined," Supai went on, "and they must pass on, as it is wrrrrrritten, to prrreparrre the way forrrrrr the New Generrrrrrrration, accorrrrrding to His prrrrrophecy!"

A rippling roar rose from the Loners. "Ahhhhhhhh-mennnnnnnnnn!"

Taking a half-step back, Pendergast gasped, "Pass on?"

Supai looked down at him. "It's only naturrrrrral," the Loner said.

"No! No, I don't—I want—I command you to set us free!"

"The Trrrrrrrrrruth shall set you frrrrrrrrree!" Supai thundered, and vaulted over Pendergast's head again, landing behind him.

Deborah gasped as Kali suddenly grabbed her by the arms, but the Loner merely moved her a few paces back as the rest of the creatures swarmed around the table, rushing toward Pendergast, pressing in on him, obscuring him from view. Deborah heard him bellowing inarticulately, and suddenly he reappeared—raised high on the hands of the

Loners like a football coach after a homecoming victory. The mob bore him, kicking and thrashing, away from the bloodsoaked altar and across the room—but not toward the doors. They surged in the direction of the workbench.

Deborah suddenly realized that she and Kali were not alone. Mitford still stood where he had been, Chernobog's hands clasping his arms so tightly that Mitford's fingers were turning blue. And Supai was still there, too, bending over Vulcan's corpse. Extending a claw, he carved three of the dead Loner's teeth from his jaws. "And out of his mouth came a sharrrrrp two-edged sssworrrrd," Supai intoned. "Neverrrrr needs sharrrrpening." After bowing respectfully, he whirled from the table and sprinted after his fellows with a long, jolting stride.

The mob of Loners had reached the workbench. Swarming onto it, they pressed Pendergast flat against the pegboard wall with his arms outspread.

"Let go!" Pendergast howled. "Listen to me! I made you! I *created* you! You have to *listen to me!*"

As Supai approached the crowd he sprang off the floor, soaring over the mob and alighting on the pegboard beside Pendergast. Clinging there with his talons, he said, "We have followed yourrrrrrrrr worrrrd, Grrrrreat Fatherrrr. And we know what must be done to brrrrrrring yourrrrrr final prrrrrrrophecy to life."

Rearing back, the Loner slammed one of Vulcan's fangs through Pendergast's right wrist.

Deborah screamed. But not as loudly as Pendergast, whose torso arched away from the wall as blood spewed down the pegboard behind his hand. Deborah thought his eyes were going to shoot out of his head like tennis balls from a serving machine. He screamed even more loudly when the second tooth thumped through his left wrist, half its length disappearing into the pegboard. But neither of these screams compared to the one he uttered when the third fang split the bones of his crossed feet. That shriek seemed much too loud to have come from a human throat, and too prolonged to be fed from human lungs.

But still Deborah watched. Pendergast had been correct, of course—the Loners *did* find him special. Didn't it say in the Bible that God the Father and the Son were, in a way, a single entity? Pendergast and Vulcan, Father and Son. The Last Supper. Now the Crucifixion . . . but what next? Did the Loners expect Vulcan to rise from the dead in three days, or were they going to move on directly to fulfill their vision of Armageddon, where humans were nothing but cattle?

Slowly, the mob of Loners moved away from the wall, staring up at it rapturously. Pendergast hung there, writhing, his blood making outlandish patterns as it flowed around the holes in the pegboard. "Oh God!" he shrieked, tears flashing silver on his cheeks. "Oh God! Oh *Gahhhhhhhhhhhhhhddddddd*!"

Deborah finally had to turn away, but Kali's hands immediately rose and clamped her head in an iron grip, forcing her to face Pendergast again. "Prrrrrraise the Lorrrrd," the Loner whispered. Deborah closed her eyes and hugged Virgil against her chest, burying her mind in her son's warm, helpless life.

Suddenly Mitford spoke, and she could hear the half-smile in his voice: "Don't get bent out of shape, babe. After all, this is what the doc always wanted."

When Tony crawled out of the shaft and collapsed onto the floor of the shed, he wasn't sure he would be able to rise again. Black spots thronged through his vision, much darker than the night, and his arms and shoulders sang like violin strings. Every wound on his body felt as if it had been torn open by the rough stone walls of the shaft. He was bleeding in many places again.

But he *had* to get up. Had to. And did.

Staggering to the door of the shed, he peered out into the clearing, blinking to clear his eyes. To the north rose a mound of huge boulders . . . that would be where the skylight was hidden. Which meant the garage door had to open into that dry wash about forty yards away.

Turning, he went back and grabbed a couple of blocks of C–4 plastic explosive and several boxes of large-caliber ammo, then limped toward the dry wash. It was a struggle, the manzanita grabbing constantly at the straps of his guns and pouches, but he finally got there—and almost fell over the lip of the wash, which would surely have resulted in at least a broken leg.

In the moonlight, it was difficult to see much of what lay below. But the wash seemed to end at a dirt-floored basin overhung with rocks and bushes—if the garage door was built into one of the embankments, it had been thoroughly camouflaged.

But it *had* to be down there.

He hesitated, then tossed the blocks of C–4 into the basin, trying to place them against the flattest section of the incline. Next he dropped the boxes of ammo down, then added four hand grenades for good measure.

After fighting his way back through the manzanita, he grabbed a coil of heavy rope from the hardware shed and coiled it up as he walked to the pile of boulders. Climbing them wasn't easy—he felt as weak as a newborn puppy—but eventually he reached the top and peered over.

Yes. There was the skylight, glowing like a rectangular pool of lava down among the rocks. From this angle Tony could see little of the garage itself. He tied a loop of rope around the top of the boulder, then used the rest to lower himself down to the skylight. Despite a desperate sense of urgency, he took his time—a slip now would end everything.

Finally he arrived and, squatting on the edge of the skylight, placed the remainder of the rope beside him. Then he peered through the glass.

For a horrible moment he thought he had taken too long, was too late again. Although the gore-heaped table indeed lay directly below him, most of the crowd was gone. Only four figures remained—Faust, Deborah, and their monstrous escorts. Where was Pendergast?

Then he saw that everybody was looking in the same direction and, squatting, he followed their gazes. His eyes flew wide, and he almost lost his balance and toppled headfirst through the skylight. *Pendergast*. Suspended from the pegboard wall, the scientist was a squirming, writhing hieroglyph of blood. Dear God . . .

But Tony realized that in a way the Cannibals had done him a favor, reducing by a third the number of people he needed to worry about. A cruel thought, but he couldn't help that. He needed every advantage he could get.

Standing erect, he pulled a grenade off his belt and judged the distance and trajectory he'd need to use to lob it into the dry gulch.

How long had Pendergast been writhing up there? Deborah wondered faintly. A minute? Two? It seemed like hours, days—forever. His screams were growing hoarse and shattered. She seemed to recall that it had taken Jesus nine hours to die on the cross—and even that had been some kind of speed record. If she had to stand here and witness this for nine hours, she would simply go insane.

Closing her eyes again, she thought about rescue. Tony on his way here. Had to be. Had to be . . .

Now Supai was saying things to the Loners in a preachy voice, vaguely familiar-sounding things, but Deborah tried not to listen. Any more of that *would* drive her insane. It would drive her insane right *now*.

Finally, Supai fell silent, and the only sound was Pendergast's irregular moaning. Deborah opened her eyes.

The Loners had all turned, and were staring toward the altar. Supai pointed and cried, "And two otherrrrrrs, who werrrrrrrre crrrrriminals, werrrrrre led away to be put to death with Him . . . Book 'em, Dano."

Kali's hands closed hard on Deborah's arms again as Deborah started to struggle, knowing it was useless but unable to stop herself. The mob of Loners broke into a jog across the floor.

A ferocious blast shook the room and made the garage door bulge inward like a heaving ribcage. Deborah's eardrum popped savagely. Across the room, the double doors clapped briefly out as if shoved by ghostly hands, and the mob of Loners skidded to a halt. The garage door sprang back to its original shape, but not before heavy clouds of dust spewed in beneath it and rolled across the room like a red and gold avalanche. Faintly, from beyond the door arose a distinctive crackling and popping noise, and Deborah's heart leaped like a sprinter off the blocks. Gunfire! It had happened—it had actually happened: The cavalry had arrived.

Supai let out an inarticulate screech and bounded toward the dust cloud, the rest of the Loners on his heels. Even Kali released Deborah and started moving in the same direction before Chernobog snapped, "Don't touch that dial, Kali! Stay tuned forrrrrr furrrrrtherr—"

CRAAAAAAAAAAACK! The sound came from directly overhead, and Deborah ducked instinctively as a brilliant tongue of flame licked down from the skylight and Kali's head bobbed violently. A great plume of blood rose from the crown of her skull, painting the concrete around her.

CRAAAAAAACK! CRAAAAAAACK! Kali's head bobbed twice more and half her face disappeared, great teeth standing in the gap like white pickets. She whirled and took a wavering step toward Deborah, but one of her legs suddenly bent forward and the other backward, and she collapsed to the floor, thrashing like a stranded crab.

CRAAAAAACK! CRAAAAAAACK!

Chernobog let out a whistling screech and crashed heavily against the side of the altar. Deborah jumped out of the way as the Loner spun around and around, blood geysering. Where was Mitford? She couldn't see him. A moment later, she couldn't see anything as the advancing dust cloud consumed her.

From the direction of the garage door, a fierce shrieking chorus rose over the crackling gunfire. Deborah turned away from it and started to feel her way around the altar, hoping she could somehow find her way to the double doors and get—

Overhead, the skylight exploded downward in a storm of shattered glass, and Deborah squatted protectively over Virgil as the shards rained down. From beneath the canopy of her arms, she saw a loop of rope drop to the floor a couple of feet away, then looked up as a man slid into sight through the swirling dust, slithering down the rope in spinning jolts, like a novice mountaineer. He hit the floor in front of her with a crunching thud and instantly unslung a big gun from his back. Deborah kept looking up, waiting for the next soldier to appear, but there was no more movement from above.

Outside, the racket of gunfire abruptly died.

Deborah's rescuer turned toward her, and she gasped at the sight of a raw, bloody face like a rare roast of beef already sliced for serving. He looked—

He looked—

"*Tony?*" she cried.

Garwood? Mitford thought. *Son of a bitch.*

Mitford huddled beneath the altar, peering through a small gap in the bloodsoaked tablecloth that hung on all sides like the walls of a scarlet tent. As he watched, Garwood glanced around intently—looking for him? Probably. Good—that meant he hadn't seen Mitford dodge under here. Chernobog had, of course, but that was one Loner who no longer mattered.

Thanks, Garwood.

Taking a good look at the security guard's wounds, Mitford realized that Garwood had been in a tangle with a Loner—and *survived*. Incredible. Was *Garwood* the reason Anubis hadn't returned? Amazing!

Outside, the explosions and gunfire tapered off and then ceased.

Mitford waited for someone to follow Garwood down the rope—but it didn't happen. And no one burst through the double doors. Son of a *bitch*. Garwood was alone. Even SEALs never went on solo ops. Still, you had to admire the size of the guy's balls.

But Mitford admired the Uzi even more, not to mention the shorty shotgun. And those hand grenades . . . wait, wait, all those were *his* weapons. Fuck! Garwood must have raided the ordnance shed.

Briefly, Mitford considered taking the weapons back right now, then decided against it. There were still fifteen healthy Loners out there in the dust cloud, and they sounded like they were coming back this way— and when they got here, they were going to be pissed. Which meant that, Uzi or no Uzi, Garwood, the broad and her brat would soon be ground beef. And Mitford knew he could expect the same thing to happen to *him*, no matter if he had the Uzi or not. The garage belonged to the Loners; escape was the only way to survive.

One thing was certain: unlike Pendergast, he'd never underestimate a Loner again.

So he waited. Let Garwood draw all the attention to himself and his little friends as they made their break; then, when the Loners followed them like a pack of dogs, Ira Mitford would be free to use the garage door or, if it was too damaged, the alternate escape route that dangled from the skylight above.

It seemed like a sound plan—but just then, to his amazement, Garwood took hold of Kosarek's arm and ran in the wrong direction— straight into the heart of the dust cloud.

Straight toward the Loners.

CHAPTER TWENTY-FOUR

"NOT *THAT* WAY!" DEBORAH CRIED.

Tony grabbed her by the arm, snapped, "We need the van," and literally jerked her into the thick of the dust cloud, circumventing the injured creature's still-thrashing body. The van was only a dozen paces away, a blocky shadow in the dust—but from somewhere beyond it came a wild roaring and shrieking that flash-froze Tony's blood. For a moment he considered tossing a grenade back there, then he remembered the fuel storage tank, and just concentrated on running, instead. Luckily, Deborah went along without further disagreement.

As he ran, Tony glanced about for Faust, but the Blond Man was nowhere in sight. Damn! He had vanished, spoiling part of Tony's plan, but there was no time to dwell on that.

The van quickly became more solid through the dissipating dust. Now Tony had time to worry about whether or not the passenger's door, the nearer one, was unlocked. Surely, surely. Who would lock a vehicle that was parked in a secret, subterranean garage?

A paranoid psychopath, that was who. Like Faust. And if the van was locked, Tony would have to take the time to break the window, and—

"Tony!" Deborah shrieked as a cluster of lean forms sprinted in through the dust, teeth flashing, talons reaching.

"Brrrrrreeeeederrrrrrsss!" the nearest one screeched.

Tony pulled the Uzi's trigger. He'd already switched it over to full-auto, and a stream of slugs caught the Cannibal in the crotch and stitched up its torso, blasting it off its feet. Tony was already firing a second burst at another Cannibal, then turning to shoot at another. They dove, twisted, vanished like fish into the smoke. Blood spattered the floor, but there were no bodies. Then the Uzi's clip was empty and, cursing, Tony jerked it out and tried to slam in a new one. It wouldn't go. He turned it around, almost dropped it, whacked it home. Sweat poured down his face. The endless firepower of TV machine guns was a joke.

More Loners darted in, coming from all sides. Tony whirled this way and that, firing, firing, firing into the gloom. Deborah squatted low, staying clear. In the muzzleflashes, Cannibals were caught in various poses, talons reaching, jaws distended, fury in their inhuman eyes. Screaming and hissing. Blood and tissue flew—but still, no bodies fell to the floor.

The van was only a step away when the Uzi ran out of ammo again. Shadows swarmed at the edge of vision; there was no time to reload. Tony slipped the strap of the Uzi over his shoulder, let the weapon fall to the floor, and swung the shotgun into its place. He hoped the Cannibals thought they were making for the garage door, and were concentrating on cutting them off there.

Deborah screamed as a Cannibal squirted out from under the van and vaulted into the air, shrieking triumphantly. Tony whirled and the shotgun kicked viciously in his hand, spewing a great blossom of flame that erased the Cannibal's face. Tony dodged the tumbling body even as Deborah grabbed the door handle on the van. Tony's jaws clenched in an inadvertent snarl of doubt—but the door sprang open.

Sensing movement behind him, Tony whirled and lifted the shotgun— and the barrel slid straight into the yawning, bloody maw of the same Cannibal he'd just shot.

Screaming, Tony pulled the trigger twice. The Cannibal's head became a tunnel with light showing through from the other side, and the impact rocked its skull back violently. The shotgun flew from Tony's hand. He scrambled frantically into the van behind Deborah as the Cannibal sagged to the floor—at last! Three of its fellows immediately vaulted over it, and caromed off the closing door, actually slamming it shut as Tony crashed his fist down on the lock.

The inside of the van smelled like burnt gunpowder. Outside, Cannibals swarmed over the windshield and side windows, clawing at the glass. The van rocked as if in an earthquake.

Tony crawled over Deborah to the driver's seat.

"Where are the rest of them?" Deborah asked.

"Rest of who?" He reached for the ignition. Keys? Yes, keys. He would have said a thank-you prayer if he'd known one.

"Whoever came here with you."

"I came alone. I have a plan. Hold on."

Deborah screamed, and Tony looked up as a Cannibal hurtled through the air toward the windshield, curling itself into a remarkably compact ball in midair. Tony instinctively threw up his arms as it crashed into the windshield directly in front of him, but the glass held.

Tony felt his spirits climb like a rocket. That was no ordinary safety glass, and this was *working*. He started the engine as Cannibals slammed harder and harder against the coachwork, claws shrieking over metal and glass. Many of the creatures, he saw, had terrible wounds in their heads and bodies. They smeared blood all over the glass—but still they attacked. Tony was surprised they hadn't thought to go for the tires.

Popping on the headlights, he saw that the thickest of the dust had mostly dissipated. The garage door looked a thousand miles away. To his dismay, despite all the explosives that had gone off against it, the door was not only still standing, it appeared to be undamaged except for bent rails and a single cracked panel.

Then he saw the remote-control garage door opener on the van's dashboard, and eagerly punched the button. But this time his luck was out—either the door's motor wasn't hooked into the emergency power, or the rails were too twisted to permit the door to move. Either way, it didn't open, and there was only one thing left to do.

"Put on your seatbelt and brace yourself!" Tony shouted, snapping his own harness down. Without speaking, Deborah did as he asked, then enfolded Virgil tightly between her arms and chest.

Shifting the van into drive, Tony slammed the accelerator to the floor.

When Garwood and Kosarek disappeared into the dust, Mitford figured they must be making a run for the garage door. That, of course, was suicide—but on the other hand, at least from Mitford's point of view, a diversion in one direction was as good as a diversion in another. He was just about to lunge up for the rope when the Loners suddenly appeared again, racing around like irritated sharks. From the dust the Uzi began firing; then, a few moments later, the shotgun. Be patient, Mitford told himself. Patient . . .

When he heard the van's engine roar to life, Mitford found his appreciation of Garwood climbing a notch. The guy could only have one thing in mind—and it was a good plan, considering Garwood's limited knowledge of Ginnunga Gap's construction. It wouldn't *work*, of course, but it was good thinking. Mitford regretted that he would never have the chance to take Garwood on, man to man. That could have been interesting.

Across the garage the van's lights snapped on, revealing the Loners swarming all over it. Mitford couldn't count how many of the creatures were participating in the attack—but more to the point, he didn't see any that *weren't* participating, or that seemed remotely interested in what was going on over here.

The van began to roll, and the Loners either clung to it or ran in pursuit. All the Loners, it looked like.

Now!

Sliding out from under the table, Mitford leaped high, grabbed the rope, and began to climb hand over hand, as fast as he could go.

To Deborah, it felt like the van got rolling with agonizing slowness. Tony hunched over the wheel, his ravaged face almost touching the windshield as he tried to see between the bodies of clinging, writhing Loners.

Then she realized he wasn't turning the steering wheel at all. In gaps between Loner bodies, she saw the garage door filling the windshield. Suddenly realizing what was about to happen, she clutched Virgil even more tightly.

The swarming Loners abruptly vanished. Deborah cringed and braced herself.

The crash felt like an enormous punch in the gut as her harness locked, and she had to clutch Virgil desperately against the pull of momentum. The van rose off its rear wheels, then slammed back and shuddered in reverse for several feet. The engine died. A genie of steam hissed up from under the hood.

"Are you all right?" Tony asked, sitting back and shaking his head.

"Yes. But . . ." She pointed at the garage door.

He looked, winced. The only visible damage was a slight extension of the crack in the lowest panel.

"We'll never—" Deborah began, then screamed as a Loner's mouth slammed into the window by her head, its thick saliva smearing the glass. She jerked away instinctively and half-fell between the seats, her elbow crunching down onto something hard with bruising force.

"Are you all right?" Tony asked, helping her sit up, but all her attention was fixed on the object she had struck. A holstered gun. Suddenly, a conviction came to her with absolute clarity: She would use that weapon on Virgil and herself before she would allow a Loner to touch them again. Certainly before she would allow either of them to be pinned up on the wall like a butterfly on display . . .

". . . it again," Tony was saying.

"What?"

He restarted the engine. "I said I don't think the van can take an impact like that again. And even if we did break through, the radiator's smashed; we wouldn't get a hundred yards."

"Then what do you—"

Shifting the van into reverse, he pushed his foot to the floor again. "We'll try hitting it with something stronger," he said as they accelerated backward in a cloud of tire smoke.

"Stronger?"

Silently, he pulled a hand grenade off his belt and placed it on the dashboard.

Deborah's eyes widened. "You—"

"Hang on!" His foot slammed down on the brake pedal, and Deborah crashed back in her seat, Virgil's weight punching into her solar plexus and driving out her breath. From the edges of her scarlet vision, she saw clinging Loners hurtle off the van. Then the van stopped completely, and suddenly there was nothing between it and the garage door but open space.

Tony was already pulling the pin on the grenade and opening his door. He leaned out, drew his arm back, and started to pitch the grenade.

A Loner lunged in from behind him and sank its fangs into his shoulder.

Tony screamed, arm spasming, and the grenade flew wildly off into the darkness. Bracing its hands against the doorframe, the Loner jerked back hard, and suddenly Tony was halfway out of the van, still screaming, clinging to the wheel with only one hand.

Deborah didn't even think about it. Reaching between the seats, she drew the pistol from its holster, leaned across Tony, placed the barrel squarely against the side of the Loner's skull, and pulled the trigger.

Crack! Crack! Crack!

BAAAAARRRRRROOOOOOOOOOOOM!

The world outside the van suddenly turned a brilliant white, and the half of the Loner exposed beyond the van's door burst into flame. The van itself rocked violently and the Loner, much of its head gone, turned and began raking its talons at the flames consuming it, as if to kill them.

One of Tony's sleeves was blazing. Deborah screamed and hauled on his other arm with all her strength, and at last he slid back inside the van. Leaning over him, Deborah closed and locked his door, then slapped out the flames on his sleeve. He moaned, head lolling, eyes rolled back.

The rear corner of the garage was a sea of flame and smoke. Deborah realized what must have happened—the loose grenade had detonated under the fuel storage tank. Blazing gasoline had spewed all over the area, setting fire to everything.

Including the van.

Mitford clung ferociously to the rope as the explosion started him swinging and spinning. Jagged chunks of metal, some of them the size of manhole covers, whizzed around him, but he ignored that. He was too concerned about the broken glass that surrounded the rope above like a glinting ring of knives. He stopped the swinging as quickly as possible, then looked around.

He was dangling over a spreading swamp of fire—Christ, the fuel tank had obviously gone up. More than four hundred gallons of blazing gasoline were expanding across the floor like an octopus unleashing blazing tentacles. The garage door and most of the pegboard wall had vanished behind curtains of fire—ditto half the van. Mitford figured none of the fires would survive long with so little flammable material to devour—but while they burned, they would be savage. And there was no emergency sprinkler system in the garage. Well, so much for Garwood and Kosarek.

Then he noticed frantic movement in the heart of the fire, and realized that a half-dozen Loners had been drenched with blazing gasoline, too. Mitford grinned. Evidently, the Angels of Light had never taught the damned things what to do in such an emergency, because they dashed back and forth across the garage like Chinese dragons, shrieking, trailing fire behind them. But there were still plenty of unharmed Loners left, and as Mitford watched, they moved in to assault the van again. Single-minded suckers, you had to give them that.

Except for two of them. Mitford realized that a pair of Loners was sprinting toward *him*.

He recognized them instantly. One was a female named Tisiphone, and the other was—son of a bitch—*Chernobog*, with at least one 9mm slug in his skull.

Although Mitford figured he was at the upper limit of their leaping range, he intended to take no chances, and started climbing again. As he did so the rope jerked and turned under his weight, and he could feel it grinding against the frame of the skylight above. Hold on, hold on . . .

He glanced down again just as Tisiphone launched herself upward in a prodigious leap. Deliberately thrashing the rope below him around with his feet, he tried to give her nothing to catch. But she snagged the rope with one hand and her great weight pulled it taut, almost jerking it out of Mitford's grasp. Then the Loner, only a couple of body lengths away, began scrambling upward with the swift agility of an ape.

At the same moment, Chernobog reached the altar and did something Mitford hadn't expected—he used the table itself as a launching pad. Instantly, Mitford knew Chernobog was going to just reach him. Mitford stopped climbing, legs dangling limply.

Chernobog soared above Tisiphone and slashed his talons at Mitford's thighs.

At the last possible instant, Mitford pulled himself as high as the strength in his arms would allow, swinging his legs toward the ceiling. He felt the tip of one claw snip at the back of his thigh—and then the rope below him went limp. Chernobog's attack had severed it.

The Loners shrieked in frustration as they fell, dropping like safes. Tisiphone's bulk turned the altar into kindling. But both Loners rose to their feet again immediately, and screamed up at Mitford in fury.

"Assholes!" Mitford shouted as he spun around helplessly on the rope for several revolutions. Finally he got his feet twined around the shortened end and brought himself to a halt. "Assholes!" he cried again.

It was time to get back to work. Looking up again, he calculated he was about three-quarters of the way to the skylight. Good thing, too. Although he wasn't as weak as he'd been pretending to be all evening, neither was he as healthy as he'd prefer. In fact, his strength was fading noticeably.

And now there was another problem.

The air was getting unbreathable up here.

Tony shook his head. His ears hissed and his right shoulder throbbed with a fierceness he'd never experienced—and for some reason the left side of his face felt sunburned . . . then he realized that flames were lapping against the glass an inch away from his head. He jerked away, and shouted as a heavy dagger of pain sank into his shoulder.

"Tony." Deborah's voice, far away. He felt the touch of her soft hand on his forearm. "Tony. The van's on fire. We have to get moving. Tony, your foot's on the brake. *Tony* . . ."

We have to get moving. Well, that was what he'd been *trying* to do, wasn't it? Wasn't that why he'd come to this godforsaken place in the first place, to try to move her and her son out? Okay, so his plan hadn't gone perfectly. But he'd given it his best shot. God, why couldn't he seem to please anybody, no matter what he—

"Tony!" Her voice was frantic now. "Tony, please!"

He blinked, focused on her. She wasn't holding the gun anymore, but he distinctly remembered seeing it in her hand. He wondered where it had come from. Never mind. She had saved his life with it. Saved him from a Cannibal. What could he do in return? She was pushing against one of his legs with her palms. How come? He was so *tired*, and the pain in his shoulder was terrible, pulsing. Also, the Cannibals had returned again, scrambling over the windshield and Deborah's side of the van, jerking on her door handle, clawing at the windowframe. A small crack suddenly appeared on the glass. The Cannibals attacked it, and it grew longer . . .

"*Tony!* We have to *move!*"

The garage door had vanished behind an upside-down waterfall of flame and smoke. Move? Was she crazy? Driving the van into that inferno would be suicide.

So . . . are you going to give up now, Tony? Call it quits? Is that it?

"Okay," he said, and reached for the gearshift. It was already in drive. Who had done that? Deborah? He blinked, finally began to realize what was going on. The van was on *fire*. "Okay," he said, more strongly, and took his foot off the brake. "Okay, here we go."

The van began to roll and, using his good arm, Tony guided it away from the flames. As the vehicle built up speed, the fire licking at its side flickered and died. Cannibals instantly bounded in, hurling themselves at Tony's window. He heard their muffled screams: "*Crrrrrriminals! Blasphemerrs! Brrrrrrreederrrrs!*"

Fire or fang, he thought. *What a nifty choice.*

Then he looked across the room at the swinging doors that led back into the complex, and his hopes rose. "Hang on," he said. "I'm going to try something." Weaving around various pieces of machinery, he guided the van almost to one wall, then turned sharply and aimed it at a narrow gap between obstacles. At the far end were the double doors. Without pause, Tony shoved the pedal to the floor.

Clutching the dashboard as the van began its lumbering acceleration, Deborah said, "What are you doing?"

"Gonna crash those doors."

"This thing will never fit through!"

"I know."

Deborah gave him a wild look, then hunched forward over Virgil, assuming the position airlines recommend for plane crashes. Tony said nothing, concentrating on keeping the van on a straight course, hoping he had enough strength left in his one good arm to do what he had in mind.

One of the Cannibals clinging to the windshield glanced in the direction they were going, then turned and stared in at Tony for a moment. Suddenly it leaped off the front of the van and landed directly in the vehicle's path. Tony saw its teeth flash in a grimace of hate before it collapsed out of sight, and a moment later there was a distinct bump as the van's wheels passed over its body. Why the—?

There was a loud report, and the van lunged hard to the left, smashing a lathe off its mountings before Tony could regain control, roaring with agony as he pulled with his injured arm. But even through the pain, he realized what had happened: The Loner had slashed one of the tires, disabling the van.

But the vehicle was still moving ahead, although Tony had to haul hard on the steering wheel as the shredded tire flopped and the exposed rim tried to cut its own squealing track across the floor.

The double doors drew closer—closer—

Now!

In a way, the flat tire suddenly became an ally. All Tony had to do was let go of the steering wheel, and the van fishtailed into a sidelong slide.

Mitford had almost reached the skylight, but he had to stop and rest. There was almost no breathable air up here now; roasting blankets of smoke rushed through the hole above him, filling his lungs along the way. Coughing, he glanced down through streaming eyes. He could just glimpse Chernobog and Tisiphone still standing below, staring up at him and ignoring the flames that burned steadily closer to them.

So go ahead and wait, assholes, Mitford thought, and turned his attention back to the climb. As soon as he got out of here, he'd grab a case of C-4 and some incendiary devices from the ammo shed and toss them down on these assholes' heads. Fry the whole rats' nest once and for all. Teach them who was the top predator around here.

Overhead, jagged points of broken glass glinted in the moonlight. As he drew nearer, he could see that the rope was indeed fraying where it rubbed against the skylight frame. Even as he watched, a large strand snapped loose, unraveling all the way down to his clutching hands. He immediately stopped climbing, muscles locked as he waited for the rope to settle down again. Only then did he pull himself up again, slowly, carefully, a few inches at a time, holding his breath. Easy. Easy . . .

Finally the hole was at eye level and he could feel cool, fresh air on his face. He gulped it greedily, then reached slowly past the jags of glass, groping for a handhold out there in the real world. Wait . . . yes. Here was a solid chunk of rock.

His fingers had just closed around it when the rope broke.

Deborah's side of the van led the way in the slide. She closed her eyes against the sight of the wall rushing in at her.

The impact threw her into the door, and her breath burst out of her body. Her head smacked the window, shattering it, finishing the work the Loners had begun. Beside her, Tony shouted in pain. The engine stalled again.

When Deborah's vision cleared, she realized the van was sitting almost flat against the wall, and the passenger door was aligned with the double doors into Ginnunga Gap. Now she realized that Tony had used the van to both barricade the Loners inside the garage, and to provide her, Virgil and Tony with a way out.

She turned toward him. He was leaning forward, clutching his bloody shoulder with his burned hand and shivering. Beyond him, a Loner's talons clattered repeatedly against the window. Cracks had appeared around the edges. "Go," Tony said hoarsely. "Hurry."

She felt the need to say something, but there was no time. Cradling Virgil with one arm, she unlocked her door and shoved it open, slamming the inner doors open as well.

As she slid through the gap, she heard a buzzing snarl and glanced to her right. Not three feet away, a Loner was pinned between the van and the wall. Although its body was crushed and its head flattened so that one eye was almost on top of its head, Deborah thought it might be Kali. It reached toward her with a claw. "Crrrrrrriminalllll . . ." it growled. Deborah leaped out onto the ramp, staggered, ran clumsily to the bottom.

Behind her, Tony pushed through the doors as well. As his feet hit the ramp, there was movement beneath the van and Deborah shouted in alarm. He skipped away just as several sets of talons appeared, slashing at his legs. Pulling a big revolver from under his shirt, he pointed it under the van and pulled the trigger several times. There were shrieks, and the talons withdrew. Then Tony took a hand grenade off his belt. "Go!" he shouted over his shoulder as he pulled the pin. "I'll be right there!"

As he rolled the grenade under the van, Deborah bumped the second set of doors open with her hip and bolted down the corridor.

She had gone about ten yards when the doors burst open behind her and Tony's running footsteps caught up. Then an explosion popped her ears, and she glanced back to see bright orange lines of light outlining the doors. "That should seal them in," Tony gasped. "Or at least buy us some time. Do you know a good way out of here?"

"No."

He winced. "Okay. Follow me." Cradling one arm, blood streaming from his shoulder, he ran past her.

CHAPTER TWENTY-FIVE

MITFORD'S WEIGHT DANGLED from one hand, his body swinging freely as the rope dropped away beneath him. But that was no problem. He had a good, solid grip.

Then a burst of exquisite pain radiated out from his wrist, and he looked up to see a triangular piece of glass, still firmly lodged in the skylight frame, sinking slowly into his arm. Blood sluiced from the wound in an astonishing river. As he watched, the entire triangle of glass disappeared inside his arm, and the pain suddenly ended.

Mitford realized what was coming next, and quickly swung his free hand up to find a grip. But it was too late. With a sensation like small rubber bands breaking, the tendons in his wrist parted—and there was nothing he could do to keep his fingers from springing open.

His other hand, still reaching, grabbed only smoke.

The moon rushed away from him . . .

Mitford pivoted as he fell, instinctively trying to get his legs squarely beneath him, but the air surged past in an accelerating roar and he landed on his side among the fragments of the altar. In a white flash he felt bones shatter—pelvis, ribs, arm—and then his entire body was enveloped in a scalding cocoon.

But he did not pass out. He couldn't writhe in pain. He couldn't move at all.

Two great shapes loomed over him, the glow of the fire pulsing yellow on their faces. Chernobog bent down, grinning his broken grin. "None," he said, "escape the wrrrrrrrrath of Georrrrrrge."

"Amen," grunted Tisiphone. "Earrrrrth to earrrrrrrrth, ashes to ashes."

"Drop dead, shitheads," Mitford gasped. He wished something better had come to mind. But while he was thinking about it, great racks of teeth filled his vision, moving in.

The pain that followed was much, much worse than that of his broken bones. Worse than anything.

His screams were swallowed piece by piece.

Pendergast had gone to hell.

To his horror, it was just like it had always been portrayed in literature and art. First, there was the pain. Terrible, ripping agony, agony that wouldn't end, radiating up from his feet and out through his hands like a vast charge of electricity. And there was the regret, soul-deep. *Give me another chance! Give me another chance and I'll do better!* And there was the helplessness, because he knew that no forgiveness was forthcoming.

And there was the fire.

The last time he'd opened his eyes—a screaming millennium ago— he'd still been in Ginnunga Gap, down in the garage he'd had outfitted to Mitford's specifications. And below him, standing in an attentive crowd, had been a large group of Loners. Oh, the Loners . . . where had they gone wrong? Instead of being the solution to the world's problems, they seemed to be no better than human beings. Look what they had done to *him*. Look what—

Suddenly there had been a great blast, and everything below him had been swept out of sight by a roiling orange cloud. A minute later, harsh, stuttering sounds rose from it. What was *that*? What were the Loners doing *now*?

But curiosity does not thrive in the soil of pain, and the questions had died. Pendergast had closed his eyes and screamed hoarsely into the commotion.

But an eternity later there had been another, even fiercer roar, and agonizing heat bathed half his body. Pain atop pain! He opened his eyes . . .

That was when he knew he had died, and that the Bible was right, after all. Hell existed, and it was the realm of Bosch paintings and TV evangelists: leaping orange flames and rancid billowing smoke and unseen things that screamed madly. He coughed and gasped for air, the involuntary movements tearing at his body while the heat built up savagely around him. When a window opened briefly in the smoke, he saw the demons of hell below, some wearing suits of fire as they danced madly around blazing pools of oil. As he watched, two of them latched onto a human form with their mouths and lifted him off the floor. They pulled him back and forth between them for a while, then tore him in half.

Hell . . .

The smoke rose in garlands and braids, forming a huge inverted whirlpool overhead, utterly black in the center. Whirlpool. Void. Chaos. Ginnunga Gap. He had to turn his face away from its awful reality.

The wall beside him was on fire, and the flames were creeping toward him. Unable to flee, he could only stare at them as they grew larger and the heat intensified. Soon the new pain was even fiercer than the agony in his hands and feet. An eternity of this to face! Oh, an eternity!

He closed his eyes. "The first angel sounded," he whispered in a voice like sand, "and there followed hail and fire mingled with blood, and they were cast upon the earth . . . God help me."

And then there was no more air in his lungs, just terrible, empty heat. Hellfire—the kind that sinners must breathe forever.

Deborah hoped she'd never again see a human being as bloody as Tony was. Looking at him was like watching that old driver's ed film, *Signal 20*, which treated viewers to film of real car crashes and their victims. Tony even left red footprints behind him as he ran down the hall with a lurching, rolling gait.

"Tony—" she began, but could think of nothing more.

"How's Virgil?" he gasped. His face, in the few patches not cowled in blood, looked as white and shiny as pack ice.

"I'm not sure," she said, glancing down at her son again. "Not good."

He said no more. They hurried down the hallways in the lurid light. Every now and then Deborah glanced behind her, but the corridor remained empty. She realized she wasn't sure if she was expecting a Loner to appear, or Mitford.

At first she recognized the rooms they passed, then she didn't. In fact, she was beginning to wonder if Tony really knew where he was going when he pushed open a door into a large, well-stocked storeroom and pointed at a rectangular hole in the ceiling. "There," he panted. "I'm afraid it's a long climb."

"How far?"

"I'm not sure. But . . . I can't . . . I think you're going to have . . . to carry Virgil."

"No problem." But she eyed the hole uncertainly. "Maybe we should look for another way out. Or just hole up here and wait for help. Someone's bound to see all the smoke and—"

From the depths of the complex came a faint, eerie shrieking. Deborah and Tony both jumped.

"That could be steam escaping from burning wood," Deborah said hurriedly. "Brad once told me—"

"You want to take a chance on that?"

"No." She moved toward the hole in the ceiling.

Ten minutes later—or was it ten hours?—she was beginning to think she had made the wrong decision. Her shoulders were on fire, and there didn't seem to be enough air, and because she was determined not to let Virgil bump into the jagged rock walls of the shaft, she kept scraping her back viciously. Still, she kept on. She could hear Tony somewhere below her, gasping horribly. *Whimpering*, actually.

But they kept going.

It was only when her groping hand found no notch to grab that she realized she had reached the top of the shaft. Twisting awkwardly, she jammed herself in the opening, then slipped the sling over her head and lifted Virgil carefully over the edge of the metal box that crowned the tunnel. After clambering out herself, she immediately dropped onto a wooden crate, limbs shuddering madly.

"Help," she heard from inside the shaft—a weak, plaintive cry. "Deborah. Help me . . ."

With a gasp of self-disgust, she leaped to her feet and staggered back to the box. Inside, Tony's hands and the balding crown of his head were barely visible, and she heard him breathing in tearing gasps. Obviously, he didn't have the strength to pull himself up the last two feet. Squatting, Deborah got her hands under his armpits, which were slippery with blood. Although her own strength was negligible at this point, it seemed to be enough to get him moving again, and a moment later they were both sprawled on the floor of the shed, lungs heaving.

Then they looked at one another and burst into watery laughter.

Gradually the hysteria tapered off, and suddenly Deborah became aware of another sound—a crackling roar coming from somewhere outside. The little room around them was lit with a lurid orange glow, catching on the barrels of guns in grim little lines.

Rising creakily to her feet, she checked Virgil, then limped to the door and peered out. A thick braid of flame and smoke billowed up from behind a nearby pile of boulders, as if a volcano was being born there. "It's still burning," she said with joy. Let them fry. Let them all fry to death.

Tony appeared at her side, leaning against the doorframe. His face looked as pale as the moon above as he looked at the flames. "That's not good enough," he said.

"What do you mean?"

"See that old house across the clearing?"

She nodded.

"Take Virgil over there and get under cover."

"Under—what are you going to do?"

"Trash the whole complex. Make *sure* they're all dead."

"How?"

He pointed into the weapons shed. "There are explosives back there. I'm going to dump them down the shaft, then add a live grenade. That ought to do it."

Deborah stared at him. "How can I help?"

"Grab any of these ammo boxes and throw them down the hole."

They worked as quickly as they could, Tony holding the boxes against his hip with his good hand and then letting them drop, Deborah moving faster. After a couple of minutes, Tony bent over the shaft, listening, then turned toward her. "Better grab Virgil and go. I think I hear something moving down there."

Gasping, she gathered Virgil into her arms. He twitched and whimpered at the contact, and her heart lurched with sudden hope. Please, honey . . . please . . .

Tony was holding a grenade over the shaft, one finger through the pin.

"Are you sure you can run fast enough?" Deborah asked.

"Once I drop this thing, I'll *fly* out of here. Don't worry."

"Be careful," Deborah said, and hurried out of the shed and across the rough earth of the clearing. Next to the old house, she found a rock close to the crumbling stucco wall and knelt behind it, placing Virgil gently in a dusty hollow. A few feet away, the ground fell away into a yawning gorge. Virgil's eyes opened, closed again. Deborah clutched her hands together.

When she looked up again, Tony was in the clearing and running toward her with a lurching, heavy gait, his face contorted. "Get down!" he shouted. "Get—"

The ground flexed violently, as if a vast fist had slammed into it from below. Chunks of stucco from the house pattered down on top of Deborah, and in the clearing, Tony stumbled and sprawled on his face. Behind him, a slim spear of fire punched through the roof of the shed and soared upward like the exhaust of an inverted missile, briefly lighting the surrounding terrain as brightly as the sun.

Deborah ducked as a heavier, more brutal blast erased the shed and the surrounding twenty feet of terrain in a brief but spectacular fireworks show. There was a pause, and then the volcano behind the boulders spewed a huge jellyfish-shaped orange cloud into the sky. Bullets shrieked and cracked through the chaparral and chunks of blazing metal, rock and sagebrush hurtled high into the air, then fell again like blazing artillery shells. Deborah hunched over Virgil and covered her head with her arms. Echoes rocketed out to the Lagunas and rumbled back like return fire. Then there was silence.

Tony!

Deborah popped above the boulder again. Small fires burned all around the clearing, and the hole where the shed had been glowed dully; otherwise darkness had returned. Tony lay exactly as he had fallen, sprawled facedown in the dust with his arms outstretched. But even as Deborah started to get to her feet, Tony stirred and sat up. He stared for a moment at the nearby crater, then rose to his feet and staggered toward the house. He seemed to be barely capable of walking at all, but Deborah could see his grin from here.

Behind him, the bushes stirred and a Loner stepped out.

To Tony, everything seemed to have grown very far away. He knew he was walking, sort of, but his legs felt detached from his body; and his feet . . . were they even touching the ground? The endless chorus of aches and pains all over him felt as if they were shouting their messages down a long pipe. He knew he was going into shock. Didn't care.

When he heard a shrill screaming sound, he figured it must be more ammo firing off down in Hiber Nation, ricocheting around down there. A beautiful sound, really. It—

He felt a sharp tug on his clothing, then another, and a nagging weight fell away from him. A relief. But he stumbled over something, and stopped to blink at the ground. What was that? It looked familiar.

The scream came again, louder this time. But it wasn't a ricochet after all; ricochets don't sound like your name; they don't go: "Toneeeeeeeeeeeee!"

Finally he recognized the objects he'd tripped over: his Magnum in its holster, and Faust's automatic pistol. Scattered all around like ripe avocados were hand grenades. Hey. Who did that?

"*Toneeeeeeeeeeee!*"

A finger touched him gently on the shoulder, and he turned, expecting to see Deborah's face. Instead, staring at him was a *different* face. Familiar, though. Half-familiar. Tony recognized the one remaining eye, which reflected the firelight like a bloody red moon, and the grotesque upper jaw with its daggers of teeth—but below that, oh my, what a mess. The lower jaw was little more than a couple of hinges swinging around near the gullet, where strange shapes scissored and whirled; from the hole, a great tongue flopped out like a slimy necktie.

Below the neck was a long, lanky body clad in a blood-drenched smock.

"I know you," Tony whispered. To his amazement, he wasn't afraid at all. He was too fucking tired to be afraid. He'd been cut, bitten, blown up . . . how much was he expected to do, for Christ's sake? Why couldn't this business just be *over*? "Took you too long to get back here, though. You missed the party."

The Cannibal made an incomprehensible grinding noise and beckoned him with its good hand. Tony glanced down at his scattered weapons. No way he could reach them before the Cannibal sliced him to pieces. He looked up again. "You want to play some more?" he muttered. "Is that it?"

A scornful buzzing noise.

"Well, why not?" Tony took a step sideways, as if to circle around the Cannibal. It turned to follow. "Come on, let's do it. Come on."

Deborah, he realized, had been right about one thing: Soon, someone would be out here to investigate all the explosions. Tony wondered if he could keep the Loner busy that long before it got bored with him.

* * *

For a moment, Deborah's heart floated motionless in her chest like a boat without a motor. What could she do? Tony was out there with that thing, just the two of them—but did she dare leave Virgil alone to go and help? What if more Loners were wandering around, looking for her and Virgil?

Tony backed slowly across the clearing, the Loner walking after him. Suddenly, to her amazement, Tony swung a haymaker punch. The Loner leaned easily out of the way, but seemed surprised. Then it slapped Tony. He stumbled back several wobbly steps, the Loner following. Tony swung another punch, was evaded again. The Loner slapped him once more. Tony's knees buckled, but he didn't fall. He tried to tackle the Loner, but missed.

Suddenly Deborah realized the Loner wasn't trying to kill him—at least, not yet. It was not clawing or biting him. It was just *playing*. Still, Tony's struggles were obviously weakening; Deborah doubted he could have sparred a newborn human baby at this point, far less a Loner.

She looked down at Virgil. Maybe, she thought, there's more to ensuring a future for him than making sure we live through this single night.

That was ridiculous, of course. And yet, somehow, it was also perfectly true.

Across the clearing, the Loner and Tony moved out of sight behind the smoking boulders that surrounded the skylight. Tony was stumbling like a boxer on his second eight-count.

"Okay," Deborah said softly, and bent down to kiss her son gently on the cheek. He stirred, his face accepting her tears. "Enough."

Enough, Tony thought, and fell. It seemed to take a long time before he slammed onto his back among the boulders near the skylight, but no bed had ever been so comfortable. He stared up at a sky filled with smoke. It was beautiful smoke. It was *his* smoke; he'd made it, paid for it.

But it wasn't enough. Where were the helicopters? The firefighters? Where was the goddamned *cavalry*?

He sighed. *I did a good job. I really did.* At last, the thought came with no guilt attached. But there was still regret. Regret that a good job just hadn't been enough.

The Cannibal loomed over him, rattling and buzzing, talons flexing.

Tony smiled at it. "You're the last one left, you know," he said. "You're all alone in the world."

The Cannibal tilted its head, throat parts working, then reached down and grabbed Tony by what was left of his shirt. Hauling him bodily to his feet, it stared into his eyes, and Tony suddenly had the feeling that the *real* pain was about to begin.

"Come on," he croaked. "Get it over with, you asshole. Act like a man."

The Cannibal recoiled, snarling. Then it raised one hand, extended a pair of claws. Moved them slowly toward Tony's eyes . . .

"Hey," said a voice.

The Cannibal's head swung around abruptly. Tony looked over its shoulder and saw Deborah standing a few feet away, her hands clasped in front of her chest as if she were about to burst into romantic song. Then he realized that there was something *in* her hands. It looked so strange there, it took him a moment to realize that it was a grenade.

Her finger was through the pin.

"Let him go," she said in a voice as dry and raspy as an old canvas chair. Her face and arms gleamed with dirty sweat, her hair stuck up in twists; a combination of dried blood and mud had stained her clothes a uniform brown black color. She was radiant. "Let him go," she said again, and raised the grenade higher. "Or we all go together."

The Cannibal looked at her for a moment, then turned back to Tony. What was left of its lips curled up in a terrible smile, and without warning, it released him. He fell helplessly, as if he had no legs at all.

As he dropped, he saw the Cannibal whirl, a blur in the reddish darkness. Deborah cried out in shock as it grabbed her by her wrists, pinning them.

Tony crashed down among the boulders, his head striking one and filling with exploding galaxies. When they cleared, he saw Deborah struggling in the Cannibal's grip, kicking at its legs and wrenching backward with her upper body. But the Cannibal just stood there, unaffected. Then it yanked her closer and lifted her up by her hands, the grenade still trapped. From the creature's throat slid a bundle of twitching, scissoring organs. They reached toward her face.

Tony tried desperately to get to his feet, gasping with effort, but could not even manage to roll over. Deborah fought wildly, whimpering, her toes scraping the ground. The Cannibal drew her closer; its tongue rose like a snake and caressed her throat—

Then it halted.

The sound rising into the night was so unexpected, so alien, that for a moment Tony had no idea what it might be. It was high and loud, as clear as an icicle. A siren? Tony thought excitedly, but that was ridiculous, no one would use a siren clear out here. Then he realized what it actually was, and his breath caught in his throat.

A baby's terrified wail.

The Cannibal immediately dropped Deborah and whirled toward the sound, head held high and eager. Deborah collapsed onto her hands and knees with a grunt. The Cannibal headed straight toward Virgil's voice, clambering up the side of the nearest boulder, throat parts churning eagerly.

Suddenly Deborah was on her feet and bounding after the Cannibal. Quick as a mountain goat, she vaulted up the side of the boulder. A curtain of ash-filled smoke from Ginnunga Gap rose behind her as she grabbed the Cannibal's arm. The creature spun toward her with an angry jerk, one taloned hand sweeping around in a ferocious roundhouse blow. But Deborah was already throwing her own punch, and her fist slammed into the thing's gullet, pushing down so deep it seemed she intended to rip the thing a new rectum from the inside. Hacking loudly, the creature pulled loose and took a step back. For a moment Tony thought it might topple off the boulder into the rising flames, but its clawed feet held tightly to the stone.

Deborah was already fleeing, slip-sliding down the side of the boulder, slamming heavily onto her feet, hurling herself toward Tony. "Get down!" she shouted.

Tony thought, *As if I have a ch—*

Deborah thumped down on top of him, driving out his breath. An instant later, an ear-shattering explosion shivered off the boulders above. The Cannibal's head vanished in a brilliant flash of light, and shrapnel sang through the air. For a moment the Cannibal's body still stood there, clawed toes grasping the rock, hands outstretched. It took a wavering step, then pivoted slowly and toppled forward into the rising smoke.

"Is it gone?" Deborah whispered in Tony's ear. She was trembling all over, and one of her hands was sheathed in a glistening glove of blood and thick yellowish mucus. "Is that thing gone? Is it gone?"

"You stuffed a grenade down its throat, didn't you?" Tony asked.

"Y-yes."

"Well, it worked." And suddenly he had to laugh. It hurt like hell, but he did it anyway.

Who needed the cavalry, anyway?

Deborah lifted herself up. Tony was making a horrible panting sound, as if he couldn't breathe. Then she realized he was laughing.

Suddenly aware that her hand was burning as if it were swarming with fire ants, she looked down and saw that it had been cut in jagged zigzags by the Cannibal's throat parts. Yellowish mucus was raising blisters on the exposed flesh, and with a cry of disgusted horror, she wiped it on her pants.

Tony's laughter tapered off. His eyes were barely open now, and in the few spots where his face wasn't bloody, it was alabaster white. Was he passing out? Was he *dying*? "We have to get moving," Deborah said loudly. "More Loners might be out there."

"Loners?" Tony whispered.

"That's what Pendergast called them."

"Oh." His lips curled up slightly. "Well, you don't have to worry about it. The one you blew up just came here from . . ." He paused, smile fading. "From Del and Betty's house."

Pain swelled up inside Deborah as she realized what that must mean, but she pushed it away. Now was not the time for grief. "You really think we got them all, then?" she asked.

He nodded.

She sat up slowly, her clothing peeling stickily away from Tony's. "Are you all right?" she asked.

There was a pause. "No," he said softly. "I don't think so."

"I'm going to . . . Look!"

His eyes snapped wide open again. "What?"

Rising to her feet, she peered toward the west. Near the horizon, a small cluster of stars was moving. Her heart soared. "Something's coming this way—an airplane or helicopter."

"It's about time," Tony said in a barely audible voice.

"I'm going to go get Virgil. I'll be right back."

Oddly, she didn't feel tired at all as she ran back to the tumbledown house. Smoke was wafting out of it, too, she noticed. When she bent over Virgil, his screams stopped immediately, and he whimpered, "Mommy!" Sobbing, she swept him up. His face was crusted with dried blood and dirt, and somehow he reminded her of the moment he had been born, how beautiful and perfect he had been. Careful of his head, she hugged him against her shoulder. "I've got you, honey," she whispered, rocking him back and forth. "I've got you."

"Wan Woom, Mommy." A murmur now. When she looked at his face, he was asleep with one thumb socketed in his mouth. All he wanted was Brooke Worm. Would he remember anything about this night? Would he be afraid of the dark, see the bogeyman in every shadow?

By the time she got back to Tony, she could hear the oncoming *whock-whock-whock* of helicopter rotors.

She looked down, and for an instant was sure Tony had died. He was so still, eyes closed. But as she knelt next to him, his eyelids flew open and his eyes, wide and terrified, flicked around.

"It's okay," Deborah said. "It's okay. The helicopter's almost here."

She gasped in shock as Tony's hand whipped up and clutched her forearm. Although his grip had little strength, there was tremendous intensity in it.

"Don't tell them about the Loners," he said huskily. "If you tell them about the Loners, they'll take us straight to County Mental Health . . . and then some fool will try to go *down* there. Understand?"

"But—"

"Tell them nobody else was down there, we were the only ones—and tell them the place is radioactive or toxic or something. Anything to buy time until we can talk to the right people about this."

"Like who?"

"I don't know. But we have to convince someone to move carefully. Once those things' bodies are found, *then* we can tell about what *really* hap—"

"Bodies?" she said, voice rising sharply. "You think they'll find bodies down there?"

"Sure; fire never destroys everything. There's bound to be at least enough left to prove those things weren't human."

She turned and looked at the rising smoke. "One cell," she said.

"What?"

"That's all they need. The DNA from one cell."

He was eyeing her warily. "So?"

"Nothing," she said. But she was thinking about smallpox. Once a terrible plague disease, killing hundreds of thousands of people each year, it had finally been brought under control through vaccination in the early 1900s. By 1977, the World Health Organization had hunted the virus out of its last enclaves around the world, and smallpox vanished forever—except for a few samples kept in the then-Soviet Union and at the Center for Disease Control in Atlanta, Georgia.

Deborah had once asked Ted Scully why anyone would want to keep something like that around, and he'd shrugged. "They're supposed to destroy the last samples in late 1993," he said.

"Why wait?"

He grinned. "Because they might think of something to do with it in the meantime, of course. And if you think they're really going to destroy *all* of it, you're nuts."

Then she thought of something else. Viruses, essentially bundles of parasitic DNA, could be called living things only at the most basic level. But Loners were sophisticated, intelligent creatures, in their own way. Suddenly Deborah could picture a debate, argued on "Night Line" and in Congress and by ACLU lawyers across the country: "What is the legal status of a Loner? Is there enough *Homo sapiens* DNA in them for them to be considered human beings? Should they be accorded the same legal rights as any other sentient being? Freedom from unlawful restraint? The right to vote? Should they be allowed to pursue happiness?"

Deborah wondered if Pendergast had thought about these things. Probably. Probably he had been terribly amused by them.

"Deborah?" Tony said. "Are you all right?"

The thing was, just because someone sampled and tested Loner DNA, even if someone *kept* it, that didn't mean they'd do anything with it. Right? They wouldn't try to clone it, for example. Wouldn't try to grow it, implant it in a host uterus, nurture it, see what developed. Just because you owned a collection of guns, that didn't mean you had to shoot them, did it?

Did it?

Overhead, the helicopter crept into sight, its rotor ripping great garlands out of the rising smoke and curling them into giant mouse ears. A searchlight beam stabbed down on the crater where the munitions shed had been.

"Deborah?" Tony said again. "Are you all right?"

She looked down at her son, his face so peaceful, unafraid. "Sure," she said, and managed to smile. "Everything's fine."